# God of Summer

## by

## Kat Chant

**God of Summer**

Contact Information: info@thewildrosepress.com

Cover Art by *Kristian Norris*

The Wild Rose Press, Inc.
PO Box 708
Adams Basin, NY 14410-0708
Visit us at www.thewildrosepress.com

Publishing History
First Edition, 2022
Trade Paperback ISBN 978-1-5092-4402-7
Digital ISBN 978-1-5092-4403-4

Published in the United States of America

Fine then. She'd do the job for him. Get it over and done. While she had his power, she was going to wield it for a noble cause. Not just freedom for Angus. Freedom, too, for the people he owed. Once they were released, there would be no need for Manann and Breda to maintain their curse. Angus could get on with living, finally free of his past, and she could get on with her own life happy in the knowledge she'd repaid her debt.

Once she broke the seal, everyone got out of jail.

Dear Reader,

It thrills me to bits that you are holding this book in your hand. People across three countries deserve recognition for getting it there.

In Australia, my heartfelt thanks go to my early readers Sue, Lisa, Amanda, Sherryl, Loretta and Jon, and later beta readers, Cassie, Enisa and Sali. You encouraged me to keep on when I felt like giving up.

In Ireland, my boundless gratitude goes to Pam, Eileen, Ruth, and Helen. The first three held me to account on accuracy. Any errors are my own. A special thanks, though, to Helen, whose art and photographs inspire me to honor her spiritual home even if my take is rather more, um, earthier.

Finally, a massive shoutout to the team at The Wild Rose Press in the US, especially to Callie, my editor. I'm beyond delighted that you caught all my pagan references. Thanks also to Kristian and her tenacity over the cover design—you have captured the essence of my hero. A special nod to Rhonda—if only all publishers were so approachable and engaging!

This story began with me falling in love with both a man and his homeland. I started writing about the legends surrounding Newgrange several years after we both left Ireland. We were living in Australia, where I grew up, but I found myself homesick for green fields and stone walls. It's fitting that I write this note in Ireland, where we now live again.

Angus and Erin's story changed many times but, at root, it's always been about finding a connection to both a person and a place. My journey took me across the world to find mine.

Wherever your heart takes you, I wish you safe travels and a warm welcome.

Kat

## Dedication

For my darling Bryn,
Who won my heart when he gave me his place at the
winter solstice in Newgrange.

*[Angus] took Con by the hand, and in an instant they were standing in a lofty, cross-shaped cave, built roughly of huge stones.*

*"This was my palace. In days past many a one plucked here the purple flower of magic and the fruit of the tree of life."*

*"It is very dark," said the child disconsolately. He had expected something different.*

*"Nay, but look: you will see it is the palace of a god." And even as he spoke a light began to glow and to pervade the cave and to obliterate the stone walls and the antique hieroglyphs engraved thereon, and to melt the earthen floor into itself like a fiery sun suddenly uprisen within the world, and there was everywhere a wandering ecstasy of sound: light and sound were one; light had a voice, and the music hung glittering in the air.*

**A Dream of Angus Oge, Æ (George William Russell), 1897**

Chapter One

None but Me

Angus McCraggan led people into the dark, then showed them the light. He did it three times a day, but always to the wrong people and the light was never true.

Today, his failure gnawed, because, tonight, his past would demand a reckoning.

"Welcome to Newgrange." He jerked his head at one of humanity's oldest buildings: the earthen cairn fronted by a cliff of white quartz. Crowning a natural hill, the five-thousand-year-old monument rose high over green fields held tight by the curving river Boyne.

"In Irish legends, this place was called *Sí an Bhrú*. Loosely translated, this means an Otherworldly dwelling—specifically a *palace*." He swallowed a snort. "More accurately, Newgrange is an ancient solar observatory—pre-dating Stonehenge and the Pyramids of Giza. Treat it like a cathedral because it's been a sacred space since the Stone Age."

Caught out by his own advice, he paused to zip up his black leather jacket. A pretense that the lazy wind cut through him instead of shame.

"Does this mean Newgrange is a hollow hill? The kind fairies are supposed to live in?" In a gray jumper and jeans, with her brownish hair bound in a birds-nest of a bun, the young American lacked the colors and quirk

1

usually accompanying remarks about fairies.

The pallor to her cheeks and faint tremor in her voice churned his stomach. He should have kept to his usual script rather than unleash his angst on strangers.

The fault his, he softened his response. "It *is* a hollow hill—Ireland's most famous—but archaeologists prefer the term passage tomb." His lips twisted. "But when it comes to fairies and leprechauns, Good People and Courts of the Fae, the stories lie. Like snakes, they never lived on this island. The ancient Celts thought the *Tuatha Dé Danann,* Ireland's Bronze Age people, must be gods to survive within the earth. Over time, their status…," his throat squeezed, "diminished."

She jolted as if stung. "Gods, you say." Her gaze darted between him and the hilltop. "So which god lived here?"

Of course, she'd ask *that*. With false good humor he replied, "Newgrange is said to belong to *Óenghus Óg,* the Irish god of love."

Her mouth formed an 'O' before her forehead furrowed. "When you introduced yourself, didn't you say your name was *Óenghus*?"

A few people snickered.

In his seven years of tour-guiding, she was a first. Few tourists asked questions. Fewer asked about fairies because no one liked to look a fool. He wanted to dismiss her as his audience had, but her deep brown eyes stared at him with such an odd, unblinking intensity.

When he stared back, the warm gold of her cheeks tinged to copper. Despite blushing so beautifully, she continued to trap his gaze, compelling him to answer.

"I am Angus." Hope flared in the dark depths of her eyes like an ember smoldering under ash suddenly granted air. He stretched his lips. He'd let this run on too long. "Angus McCraggan not *Óenghus Óg*, because—as you might notice—this isn't the Bronze Age."

He turned to lead the group up the winding gravel path to the summit. Her glare burned between his shoulder blades. He tried to shake it off. Curiosity he could deal with. Suspicion must be snuffed. Yet his spine continued to prickle. *Too many questions, too close to the truth.*

He turned his back to a standing stone and waved his hand toward the great boulder. "Here we have the Entrance Stone." The diamond in the center of a ring of stones curbing the monument, it featured the famous trispiral: the symbol Angus wore not on a uniform but branded over his heart.

While his guests posed for photographs, the now familiar American voice said in his ear, "I was wondering about that list you gave of leprechauns and fairies and fae…" Her posture stiffened before she blurted, "Does it include banshees?"

Caustic as lye, her fear burst over him. It caught in his throat and cracked his voice as he demanded, "Who are you to care?"

"You can call me Liz." Her chin jutted. "Liz De Santos."

The defiant addition of her surname came as a relief. Not Irish. Not local. No one he knew. She had no reason to be so afraid.

As if fear heeded reason.

Relenting, he shook his head. "Add *púca* and ghosts to gods and banshees, and leave be."

"Is that the same list or a new one?"

"It's time to go in."

"Only if you tell me to my face that it's safe."

With a huff at her persistence, he climbed a few steps of the wooden staircase flanking the black limestone lining the threshold. Although the outside had changed beyond recognition, the inside hadn't changed enough. Not for someone who might truly believe.

Projecting his voice to the group, he gave the standard spiel warning those afraid of confined spaces or the dark or being buried alive to enter last so they could leave first.

Pitching to Liz alone, he added, "I wouldn't come in, if I were you."

Her face blanched to the color of beach sand before she jostled past the line of tourists in her haste to escape.

Marie, guarding the entrance, gave him a look.

"Keep her out," he demanded of his boss before ducking under the overhanging stone lintel to enter his earthen carapace.

Within the confines of the passage, his heart lurched into his throat as his chest cinched tight. No matter how many times he did this, it never got easier. There was always the skulking remembrance of what he'd suffered existing without a body and barely with a mind.

Nearly twenty meters into the mound, the low passage opened into the main chamber which branched, shamrock-style, into three recesses. Overhead, the ceiling defied the weight of rubble and soil it lay under, soaring into a vault shaped like the inside of an old-fashioned beehive.

While he waited for the tourists to file in, Angus filled his lungs with the stone-chilled air. It swirled through his chest the way the lavish designs swirled over the stones of the East Recess where he stood ready to

4

point out key features to his guests.

*No. Not guests. They paid to be here.*

*And they'll pay again before they leave.*

The Celts had worshipped him as a god. Perhaps because he'd sacrificed everything to save those he loved. And failed. During his imprisonment, his people had changed into something unrecognizable, while the woman he'd married had become a monster.

He, alone, lived again.

There was no restoring his people. Nothing he did brought their humanity back. As for his wife, the best he could manage was to keep her at bay.

*She must not take her revenge.*

*I must do this.*

After a few terse comments about the cairn's construction, he cut to the crux. "I'm about to switch off the lights to recreate what happens during the Winter Solstice and the shortest days of the year. To witness the natural event, you can enter an annual lottery. But I promise I'll do everything in my power to make this memorable."

The words had scarcely left his lips when Liz crept in, her face pinched and pale. Fecking Marie should've known better. The American did know better. She huddled by the West Recess, the smallest of the three alcoves, as though braced for a storm.

His jaw slackened then he shook his head. *She can't truly believe. Not if she's here.*

Squelching the niggle of foreboding, he flicked the light switch. Without the artificial light, it was darker than night. Rather than reassure, he stayed silent and let them linger. Just for a breath of time, not even enough to register on the scale of his own experience.

*How long did I wait for a light that never came in a darkness that never lessened?*

Someone coughed.

Someone muttered.

A young male—it was always a male—made a ghostly, "Oooooo!"

A few people tittered in response. The chamber grew quiet. A few seconds of waving hands in front of faces, with eyes failing to adjust, created a thrum of tension. Shoulders bowed and his pride in the packed dirt beneath his feet, Angus waited as the fear seeped into and sloshed around the chamber.

To endure tonight, he needed his strength.

Yet the means of gaining it rankled. He hated how fear was so easily drawn and so plentiful. An unexpected swerve of a car, speaking in public, trapped in the dark. Time locked in such moments, which was why many of his kin drew on fear for sustenance. In the realm of spirit, feeling was life.

Returned to flesh, he was no longer a creature of spirit. And yet, within this mound, he was more than a man. He was a god who accepted awe as his due.

The original builders had drawn time from the sun. Through his bond to this earth, Angus used the stonework to catch and concentrate emotions. The knack took instinct rather than skill and required absolute focus. He'd experienced the potential for harm first-hand. Within this chamber, the life had been drawn from *Óenghus Óg,* son of *Bóann.* Every particle of his being extracted until nothing remained save sentiment and sentience.

He had volunteered. His visitors had not. Therefore, he stole only what he created.

All it took was time and silence for the low thrum of nervousness within the chamber to peak. No one tittered or sniffed or even dared cough. They huddled together— young and old, foreigners and residents—grasping the hands of complete strangers.

All bar one.

From a single source, he caught the honeyed sweetness of pure belief. He licked his lips. Alas, it came laced with something bitter. Awareness.

Liz's consciousness imbued every drop he drew, forcing him to feel her soaring heartbeat, the growing numbness in her limbs, the dimming of her thoughts. She knew exactly what was happening and who to blame. The rest were afraid of the dark. She feared dying. Here. Now. Because of this. Because of him.

No!

He tried to jerk free, but she'd burrowed into the alcove and their connection snagged on the rocks. To counter the unexpected resistance, he yanked. A mistake. A hot, coppery gush of raw terror burned his senses. If communal anxiety had been warm beer, this was over-proof vodka.

He choked then spluttered. The flow didn't stop. A cold sweat broke over his skin. What if he scared the life out of her?

Jaw clenched, he clawed for the dial hidden beside him, swiping until the electric light installed farther along the passage glowed.

"As the sun rises on the shortest days of the year," his voice shook until habit and training restored it to coaxing, "it shines through the roof box of Newgrange, a special portal made only for the sun. And when dawn breaks, it looks something like this…"

A golden shaft of light appeared down the passage and slowly elongated toward them. His audience ahhed, childish fears thrust away once it was bright enough to see faces. The simulation was nothing like the real thing, but, after the dark, it was never less than miraculous.

Liz, alone, showed no appreciation of the change. Ensconced in the alcove, wedged into a corner behind a stone basin, her hands pressed against the enormous stones on either side as if she needed their support. Her eyes stared off into the distance, large and afraid. Her terror continued to roll off her and crash through him in waves.

"Even in the depths of midwinter, there is hope."

He meant to say light, not hope, and the artificial sunrise was supposed to get brighter, faster. Not today. Today, for her sake, he made it linger. Taking her fear, he used his link to the stones to feed the electric light.

On the fuel of her terror, the pale glow grew warm with life, transforming from gold to liquid amber. It filled him as it filled the chamber—for those with the Sight to see.

*If I can't be an ordinary man, I will be a god, not a monster.*

Awe rose like a phoenix from the ashes of their fear. It swelled far beyond what the appreciation of light after dark should be into a cloying nectar of reverence. It was for the beauty of the light, not him, but he took every drop until his blood buzzed with power.

With something that sounded suspiciously like a sob, Liz elbowed her way past everyone to flee down the passage to the outside.

To hell with the tour and protocols. He flicked the chamber light on full.

The tourists blinked, disoriented by the searing glare.

"My apologies for the sudden brightness, everyone." Too loud, his voice rang against the walls of the chamber. "I'm afraid we've run over time. If you could all make your way out…"

He hustled them back down the narrow passage to where Marie held her arm over the lintel to prevent those exiting from bashing their foreheads against the stone outcrop. As the tourists filed down the stairs outside in a happy daze, Angus faced his boss. "The woman who dashed out ahead of the rest. Where did she go?"

"You have the other half of your tour, Angus," Marie noted, as if he couldn't see the line behind her waiting their turn.

"You take it. This can't wait."

Before she could object, he vaulted over the wooden railing. The rest of the tourists would dismiss their experience by the time their minibus returned them to the Visitor Center. Liz would not. Liz *believed*. He couldn't let her go without speaking to her again; without ensuring he'd done her no lasting harm; without asking her how she knew who he was.

Chapter Two

Hunter and Prey

Maureen Erin Elizabeth O'Neill De Santos, currently answering to Liz but usually known as Erin, twined her fingers into the thin strands of grass where she crouched behind a cute stone igloo at the rear of Newgrange. Thousands of dollars of therapy told her the smart thing to do would be to join her tour group trickling down the hillside to wait for the return of their minibus, but she didn't move.

She couldn't move.

Instinct born of childhood nightmares had screamed to stay the hell outside the hill. Ridiculous, since she coped perfectly well with the subway back in New York. Besides, banshees and Bronze Age princes were myths. So what if her tour guide's smile reminded her of someone? She'd come here to face old fears, not resurrect daydreams.

*It's not him. It can't be. Those memories never happened. That boy wasn't real.*

That's what she'd told herself before entering.

Within, the usual muscle freeze, the scared-rabbit-thump heartbeat, the icy teeth on her skin had taken hold. Her mistake for entering a wolf's den with the wolf still inside.

Then Angus turned on the lights and all had become…glorious. Him, most of all.

Her shoulders shook with silent laughter. No blaming traumatic stress or oxygen depletion or brain injury this time. No one else had freaked out because no one else had seen what she'd seen.

Light did not seep into a man's skin and gild him in gold.

*I'm not nuts. I'm not.*

Better to run than throw herself at the guy's feet. No guy deserved that level of ego boost, especially one decked out in leather and denim, and with a mane of black hair; one who stood as still as lightning in a bottle and strode around like a roll of thunder.

*What if it is him?*

Her cheeks warmed, and she tightened her grip on the grass. If he was the stranger, she somehow knew, no wonder she needed to ground herself physically; the danger was in floating free and drifting down the valley.

"Liz?"

The soft call lifted the hairs on the back of her neck. A pinch of letters shouldn't possess any power. Unless quality counted with names, not quantity. Erin had chosen to add Elizabeth to her names when Confirmed into the Catholic faith. She'd lost that faith not long after; lost it along with her dad. And now, she'd also lost the bone deep terror that New York's finest shrinks had failed to exorcise.

"I need to talk to you."

His voice was richer than a chocolate fudge brownie, and she'd never seen a face more compelling. Not pretty or even handsome. His features were too strong for the first, too mobile for the latter. Rare for such

11

a masculine face to show emotions so easily. The hurt in those ocean-blue eyes when she'd demanded his word Newgrange was safe.

He'd make a fantastic actor.

He'd suck as a poker player.

Oh God, she *wanted* to go to him, like he was one of those fairy lovers she'd read about: the sort you craved even as they stole your life.

*Nuh-uh. Staying right here this time. I already maxed out my stupidity quota.*

He stalked past her hiding place on the wrong side. She held her breath anyway.

*I'm not here. Go away!*

Abruptly, he halted. His hand went to his throat, and he gagged. Erin rose a little higher to check he was alone. Yep. He'd missed his calling on the acting front. Or maybe this was mime?

Dark brows lowered; he scanned the fields below as if looking for someone. Most likely her. Ridiculous since the surrounding area contained sheep, and clipped hedgerows formed a tight wall enclosing the site.

Angus made another choking sound. Erin ignored him. She'd seen what he'd seen.

Behind a dilapidated garden shed near where she cowered, a fawn had stuck both a forelimb and its head through a gap in the rustic fence. Now trapped, the more it struggled, the more it sawed its throat raw on the wire binding the fence posts.

Angus and the fawn gurgled in harmony.

She blinked. Had he done that on purpose? She crawled closer. There was no doubt he'd forgotten his search for her because he made straight for the wounded deer, kneeling beside its frantically pawing right hoof.

Putting her feet under her in a sprinter's crouch, she tuned out her hammering heart.

Her stepdad would put it out of its misery and call it a mercy kill.

What would Angus do?

When he cupped a palm under its jaw and wrapped his fingers around the back of its skull, she had her answer. He was no better than Dan De Santos, ready to steal a life to prove how macho he was.

"Don't kill it!" she shrieked, running toward them with her hands flapping to shoo him away.

Man and fawn jumped together, the fawn's skull clunking the man neatly under the chin as it pulled free of his grasp. Angus' head flipped backward.

"Damn it! I'm trying to help the wretched creature," he snarled, even more vicious because his bottom lip was seeping blood. "It's scared shitless."

No kidding. The deer was making a horrible, screaming cry. Erin's insides chilled, and her brain locked down in a vain attempt to shut out the fawn's distress. She had to help it. But how?

Yanking off her sweatshirt, she pushed past Angus to drape the material over the fawn's head. The struggling animal immediately went limp, as if the sudden darkness equaled safety. Little did it know. With a humph of triumph, she put her hands to her hips and turned to its most likely source of danger.

He stood with his eyes closed, the dribble of blood down his chin congealing. Guts and gore didn't faze her, but that darkening red line sure popped her relief bubble. She clamped her arms around her waist, holding in a sudden nausea. Back off or go for broke? A no-brainer given she'd crossed the Atlantic for peace of mind.

"I didn't think you could bleed."

His lids snapped open, and he raised his wrist to his chin, spreading the mess further. "I wouldn't be if you'd left us alone."

"I thought—"

"I'd break its neck out of *empathy*?" His eyebrows lifted a second before he noticed the state of his cuff and screwed up his face. While leather had many fine qualities, absorbency wasn't one of them. His expression turned rueful. "I bleed because I'm as alive as you are."

"Says the man who glowed in the dark."

A curse under his breath confirmed what she'd witnessed. Not that he continued their conversation. Instead, he hunkered down beside the injured animal where his cursing turned to crooning.

*Oh, that voice!*

Entranced, she forgot to be wary. She kneeled beside him. "Let me help. I'm training to be a vet."

Or she would be, once fall semester started. It was the official reason for her coming back to Ireland: four years in at a Dublin university to get her postgrad qualification was a heck of a lot cheaper than an Ivy League college in the States.

"You're a tourist. Go snap a selfie or something."

He wedged his shoulder against the animal's neck then lifted the deer's chest off the lower wire of the fence, leaving a chunk of fur behind. The deer's struggles had scoured the flesh under its foreleg almost to the bone.

The steel wire contained iron, but Angus didn't hiss at the contact, although his breathing and the fawn's sounded in tandem. So much for the folklore about cold iron. Maybe she *had* imagined things inside the chamber.

"You'll need wire cutters to get it free."

He rolled his eyes, a lot like the deer had. "This is not your problem."

Then, pinching the thin metal, he slid his fingertips back and forth. With a musical 'ping', the wire snapped, creating enough room to ease the animal's foreleg back. Not that Angus did so.

"Be warned, this might look a little odd." Wriggling onto his back, he heaved the animal's chest up and put his mouth to the open wound, like some human-sized leech.

Fairytales never mentioned old gods feeding on blood. Bram Stoker had been Irish, mind you, so a vampire twist had a local element. Or maybe Angus needed the red stuff to sweeten the terror he'd sucked out a few minutes earlier.

"Gah, enough!" She reached to push him off. By the time her hand pressed against his chest, however, the deer's sore had puckered and closed.

Her hand stayed as her jaw fell.

"You…I can't believe…You fixed it." A laugh gurgled free before she swallowed it down. Faking calm, she leaned over him to examine the wound. "It looks like it's a couple days old already. That's awesome."

Beneath her palm, his body trembled. To heft the fawn's weight at that angle couldn't be easy. If he moved, he'd get kicked in the face—a face already covered in blood. Sometimes even a man who might be a god needed a helping hand.

"I'm going to grab its knee and hoof, okay? Now see if you can't wiggle backward."

He shimmied his shoulders a fraction in response.

In a smooth, swift motion, she rose and tore her

sweatshirt off the deer's head. The startled animal twitched back, involuntarily helping itself free. It stood on the other side of the fence on unsteady legs while Angus slumped flat, face to the sky. The animal linked to him somehow, because it darted forward to nudge his hair before bounding off.

Damn it, she should've used her phone and snapped a couple before and after photos, or even a video. Not to share. For her own sanity.

He'd healed the fawn. Cured her fear. Might he also have the other power the legends mentioned?

Should she ask? What she wanted was crazy.

He sat up then drew his hands through his hair.

Erin gave him a sidelong glance. Hair black as a raven's wing, skin white as snow, lips red as blood: he looked like an unhinged, male Snow White. "Feel better?"

"No, I feel like shite." He rubbed his chest with the heel of his hand, then spat a pinkish gob into the grass. "You don't have any water, do you?"

"Sorry." She retrieved her sweatshirt from where it had caught on the fence. "Wipe the blood with this. Can't have people thinking you're one of the living dead."

When he stared blankly, apparently mystified by her reference, she tapped her chin to mirror his. "You have leftovers from your meal."

He put the cloth to his face.

"You think I like my venison that rare?" The corner of his eyes crinkled as though he smiled beneath the material concealing him from nose to chin. "Blood-to-blood lets me give a touch of myself to a foolish young buck to mend it a little quicker."

It sounded reasonable—if she hadn't seen his link to

the animal before healing it. But what if he'd lured it over?

He scrubbed off his smile along with the blood. Then folded her sweatshirt and stopped. No guessing why, what with the slogan *One Crazy Bitch* emblazoned on the front.

She scowled. "I come with a warning."

Forehead furrowed, he traced his forefinger over the letters, his lips moving silently.

She snatched it from him. "No more spells on me or my clothing for today, thanks."

His scowl came back, fiercer than ever. "Not spelling. Reading."

Uh huh. Last she'd heard, the Bronze Age finished a couple thousand years back. More than enough time to learn one's letters. "How dumb do you think I am?"

With a slow shake of his head, he got to his feet. "Is it something specific or general that you have against me?"

"I don't have anything against you."

She balled her sweatshirt and held it against her chest. A pity putting it on would look gruesome. It was much warmer armor than attitude alone and the wind was cold.

"You don't like me on principle then, is that it?"

"Fine. I don't like you on principle, generally and specifically. Everything about you is false. Everything you say is a lie. You shouldn't exist, let alone be here pretending to be a normal human being."

"I. Don't. Lie." He ground each word out, cutting the air with a hand as if to end that line of conversation. Only to stop mid-wave and point his finger at her. "But you do lie, don't you, Liz? You're not here as a tourist.

You suspected who I might be from the start. Before I proved you were right to be mortally afraid."

Erin gaped, horrified how easily he'd seen through her. For the longest time her tough outer shell had been unbreachable. He scanned her from head to toe, his gaze mapping every inch her shapeless sweatshirt had hidden. Despite herself, her blood warmed at such a thorough appraisal.

"Planning to beg a favor, were you?" His lip curled as he took her silence for confirmation. "Let me guess, you loved a man, but he left and now you need my help to bring him back."

She shook her head violently. To hear her heart's desire spoken aloud hit her hard enough to make her eyes water. She never cried. Not for years. His fault for taking away the terrible, numbing powerlessness that crippled her whenever she revisited that awful day.

Her mouth worked in what would be another failed explanation. But he'd taken her fear. She owed him the effort. "Yes, someone I loved left me behind. Everyone said it was an accident, but it wasn't." Too much information, but her mouth motored on without brakes. "He wasn't my lover, if that's what you think. He was my dad, and he's been gone since I was fourteen, and I can't get closure because no one would ever believe—"

Her voice cracked on the last and broke the flow of admission. For the life of her, she couldn't add that she blamed a banshee for his death.

It should've been a sweet revenge to slap Angus with words. But she had too much guilt of her own to enjoy seeing someone else's. She turned her head.

The river purled along below. Would the water be as cold in spring as it had been that winter? She'd taken forever to get warm afterwards. Sometimes it seemed as though she'd never thawed. Inside was always cold. Cold and dead. Just like Da.

If only her father had died of natural causes. Then she'd have put it all behind her. But he hadn't.

*The wall, the screaming, the river...*

She grabbed at the memory, but it danced away like always.

A reassuring weight settled on her shoulder. Angus' hand.

She twisted around. His eyes were the blue of the ocean far from shore, the edges around his pupils tinted with gold. So human, those eyes. So sad and full of sympathy. As though he knew part of her had died along with her dad.

Impossible, since she'd never told a soul the truth. Grief and fear and guilt had made it impossible to talk. If not for a banshee, Da would still be here. Erin wouldn't have had to leave everything she knew and everyone she'd cared for to start again in America. She would have stayed plain Erin O'Neill. Her mom would never have married Action Man Dan and Erin would never have been relabeled a De Santos. She'd never have learned to doubt who she was or hide behind a false name.

Her chin trembled and still he held her gaze, far past what was polite. His blue eyes, gentle with understanding and soft with concern, poured into the cracks in her soul like a spring shower into parched soil.

The chill of the wind died as the rest of the world disappeared, leaving them behind. Not even her mother looked at her so long. One or two lovers might have held eye contact so intently, right before she dumped them.

The last person who'd seen her down to the depths of her soul was Da and his love for her had killed him.

Well, let Angus look. The chances of an ancient immortal falling for her were the same as him dying: zero.

Still, since he was feeling sorry for her, here was her chance to clear her conscience. She needed to know Da wasn't in purgatory, that he'd moved on to something better. If not heaven, then perhaps *Tír na nÓg,* the Land of Eternal Youth. If the God of Love and Youth was real, then maybe his Land existed, too.

She dipped her head to look at him through the wet clump of her lashes. "I do want a favor."

His hand fell away. When he spoke, he didn't look at her but gazed across the hills to where a cairn matching Newgrange rose in the distance. "What do you want?"

"Do you talk to the dead?"

Like everyone else, he laughed at her, but his laughter held a bitter edge—as though the joke was on him. "Don't we all?"

She eyed him carefully. Didn't lie, did he?

*Let's see you worm your way out of a direct question then.*

"When you talk to ghosts, Angus, do they answer?"

His gaze whipped back. His mouth tightened. For a long time, it seemed he wouldn't respond. Again. The man was a master of avoidance.

Then he blew out a sigh. "Some of them. Most people who die don't become ghosts and, even for those who do, the longer they've been dead, the more they lose who they were. I used to try pulling those lost to shadow back into the light. It never worked. If anything, it made them worse."

"I want to see my dad again. I want to hear his voice." *I need him to know I'm sorry.* "Can you bring him back?"

"Speaking as one resurrected," his mouth twisted, "returning is not worth the price."

"But can you do it?"

"I feel for your loss, but I don't dare upset the natural order." He ran a thumb down her cheek where a single tear had tracked. "Tell me how you know about me, Liz."

Her teeth clenched. She'd opened up to him more than anyone else, ever. If he wouldn't help her, she didn't need to share any further secrets. Sharing opened the door to trust, and trust was the seed from which friendship bloomed.

She didn't want to be his friend. It would never be enough.

"Why? You're a god, *Óenghus Óg.* Read my mind already."

The use of his real name was a mistake. For a second the glory returned, angular features lifting from their glower to a younger, brighter version of the same face. The face of the boy she'd never met, save in her dreams. Her lips parted as she fought the urge to caress from cheekbone to chin, to check if the change went skin deep.

He leaned in close enough to kiss her, only to bypass her mouth and go for her ear.

"You call me that, and you *believe in me* as no one has, yet you understand nothing. Two thousand and seven hundred years ago a Chieftain's son entered that mound, and a lesser man came out. I am no longer *Óenghus Óg.* I am Angus McCraggan. *Óg* means *young.* But I am not a boy. I'll never be a boy again."

She shuddered at his passion and twisted free from

his touch. She got it. When your past was too painful to deal with, it made sense to pretend it had happened to someone else. A new name for a new beginning. Mom hadn't been in New York a week before glamming up and hitting the dating scene under her maiden name. Angus had done the same by calling himself McCraggan.

"Whatever. You don't scare me, you know."

*Liar, liar, pants on fire.*

And yet. And yet… She wasn't afraid of him. Attracted, yes. The confidence of his loose-limbed walk was no less entrancing than those eyes. His voice whispered over her skin like raw silk. The curl of hair over his leather collar and his shadowed jawline promised a mix of textures her fingers itched to explore while those deft and gentle hands worked their magic on her body.

God, she was a sucker for a set of broad shoulders and a bad boy vibe.

"Mother of God, Angus," a voice called from behind them. "Haven't you seen to that girl, yet? The last bus is down there waiting for her!"

Angus twisted aside as an older woman dressed in a tour guide's weatherproof coat stormed around the mound, her face as grim as the weather until her gaze dropped to the scrunched material Erin clutched to her stomach.

Shock flared in the older woman's eyes. "Is that blood?"

She looked to Angus to answer, as if Erin wasn't someone to take seriously.

"It's not her blood, it's mine," he replied.

"There was a—" Erin bit off the rest. This was his problem. He'd told her so himself.

He waited for her to continue, wariness flickering across his face. She clamped her mouth closed. The other guide broke their silent standoff with an exasperated sigh.

"If she was injured or there was an accident, I'll need an Incident Report. Today."

A pinched line appeared between his brows. "You know I can't write one." He paused a beat. "It's Date Night for me, Marie, remember?"

He sounded like a schoolboy avoiding homework and his colleague—possibly boss by her authority—seemed somewhat abashed, if unrelenting. His reading claim might be true.

Also not her problem, except...*one good deed deserves another.*

To solve this for him would set them square. A thank-you for proving there was something rotten within the rolling green hills of Ireland, not just within the gray matter in her skull.

She pushed the wadded material into his hands. "Hope your split lip heals okay, McCraggan. You can keep this."

"I appreciate your quick thinking, Liz." He touched the cloth to his mouth in what seemed a gracious gesture of reinforcement, until her eyes traced the smooth line of his bottom lip. No swelling or cut in sight. There was still blood on the cloth. Thank goodness. "If there's anything else you want, you know where to find me."

Her heart quickening, she stared longer and more intently than she should into those too-familiar blue eyes. He met her gaze but held it with a frown. Oh. Right. Date Night, not a date, equaled one thing. *Married.*

Her spine stiff, she took a step back. "Thanks for the

offer, but I'm not planning on hanging around."

Not around Newgrange, anyway. If Angus was real, so was the banshee. And that meant Da hadn't been killed by faulty brakes. He'd been murdered.

Chapter Three

A Girl I Used to Know

Erin was prepping dinner when her grandfather came through the back door. Although in his late sixties, Jim O'Neill looked more like eighty, with wild gray tufts for eyebrows and a woolly head of white hair. The long estrangement from family and the death of his only son had aged him horribly.

Responsibility weighed on her. If she'd lied more when younger or been better at keeping secrets, he wouldn't have lost his family for so long. She was all he had now. A summer spent with him wouldn't make up for all those years apart, but it'd be a start.

"Ah, Maureen-girl," he said. "You needn't be doing that. You're my guest."

No one else ever called her the god-awful name listed on her birth certificate.

As a child she'd corrected him endlessly, unable to appreciate the sentimental value of being named for her grandmother. Since then, her identity changed like a kaleidoscope, twisting to refract her situation in false shards: Erin O'Neill in Ireland before her father's fatal 'accident', Erin De Santos in America with her mom and stepdad, Liz to guys she didn't intend to see again. Maureen was the dutiful young lady who made a lonely old man happy—even if she happened to be furious with him.

"I'm not a guest." She filled the teapot. "I'm family."

She grabbed a soda for herself then poured his tea, making it strong and sweet—exactly like his silent support in the days after she and Da had been fished from the river.

He sat with a sigh. It was probably the chair and not his bones that creaked. Hopefully.

"And what did you get up to today while I was checking on the cows?" he asked.

Out of habit, she opened her mouth to lie. But Granddad didn't share Mom's prejudices. He had his own. And Maureen, unlike Liz, was a truthful girl.

"I got used to driving on the wrong side of the road and around traffic circles. Then I played tourist and checked out the local sights."

"Were you after going to the Caves?" The censure in his voice was strong.

"Caves? What caves?"

"Newgrange, Knowth and Dowth. The hollow hills where Those People live."

"Yeah, I did. Just like all the other tourists. Newgrange was booked until late so, I hit Knowth first. It's nothing like when I was a kid." She pushed his cup of tea into his hands, as if pressing him to own how any insanity in their family began with him. When he sipped and said nothing, she risked looking as foolish in private as she had earlier in public. "Breda didn't show."

He grunted. "Our Lady rarely does these days."

Huh. Then Breda *had* showed in the past. Erin's memory of meeting her might be real.

"Then I hung out at the Visitor Center until the last

tour of the day to Newgrange. I was lucky to get a place. I think the staff took pity on me."

The draw to see the site had been as great as her trepidation. She hadn't understood why until seeing Angus. Her heart squeezed at the bone-deep sense she knew him—had known him.

Granddad regarded her from under lowered brows. "Who took your tour?"

"Some guy who called himself Angus." *Some guy who looks like a rock star and broods like a war veteran.* "He's *the* Angus, isn't he? I wasn't sure at first. When I asked him straight if he was *Óenghus Óg*, he said that wasn't his name now. He also said he didn't lie."

She rolled her eyes at the falsehood then grabbed a fork to mash the potato.

"Both are true enough. I made it a condition of him moving into my property: I'd house an honest man or none. He's not said a word of a lie since." Granddad scrunched his nose like he'd smelled something nasty. "Little did I know how Himself would turn that to his advantage. It's slyness and cunning on his part that everyone hears what they want to hear, whatever he actually says."

"Wait. You *house* him? Doesn't he live at Newgrange, the same as Breda lives at Knowth?"

"Angus is…unique…in being human again, the only one of his kind who lives and ages as we do. He couldn't stay at Newgrange. The best he can do is work there."

She stared into the creamy clouds of potato streaked with sun-bright butter, thinking of the beautiful boy from her dreams. *Human again. So that's why he bleeds. Why he's older.* With difficulty, she kept her voice level.

"You introduced me to his sister. Why not him?"

"His release from *Tír na nÓg* came after you left." Her head flicked up just in time to catch her grandfather's guilty expression. "He lives in your old home, Maureen-girl. I bought the place from your mother when she put it on the market. Means you'll still inherit it, when I'm gone. Until then, Angus rents the old house, while I work the farm."

She closed her eyes. In her confused recollections, young Angus and her old home had always stayed separate strands. Having them knotted in her absence hurt her head.

As for Mom, well, that part was old news. Ireland was as dead to her as her late first husband. Sometimes she acted as if her daughter had died here, too, when all Erin had lost was her innocence.

*My fault. I know that's my fault. But what did I DO?*

"I need to see my old home." *I need to check everything I remember.*

"Not with Himself living there, you don't."

"When you're due for an inspection, I could go then."

Granddad reached over to pat her hand like she was still a little girl. "There's no going back to the past. You've a grand life ahead, you should be looking forward."

She would've visited the place on her own today, had she found it. Unfortunately, rural Irish addresses were like Irish directions: useful only if you knew where you were. Without Granddad's house marked in her cell phone, she'd never have found her way back here this afternoon. Her own bearings were off, her memories all wrong.

Maybe she should ask Angus. She hadn't realized she'd said that aloud until her grandfather clenched her hand, his face stern and his voice sterner.

"Don't be going near him again, Maureen-girl. Whatever he's here to do, it'll be no good for the likes of us."

"You don't trust him." She slipped her hand out from under his to whip the potato into puree. "Yet you have him as your tenant—" She bit back *in my home* lest the hurt show. "Keep your friends close and your enemies closer, is that it?"

"I promised Our Lady I'd aid him. I've helped him get established and taught him some skills, and I keep an eye on him."

"You promised Breda…after the accident." She set aside the potato, now as smooth as whipped cream. Her fingers slid to a dent in her forehead near her right temple where Breda had left a permanent impression the day Granddad had taken her to Knowth, Newgrange's sister-site. Funny. She'd escaped unscathed from the crash that killed her father. Physically, anyway. Mentally, not so much. Freed from her old terror, a memory resurfaced…

\*\*\*\*

Enemies. Everywhere. Buzzing around her. *Not enemies. Family. Friends.*

They picked over the dead like crows.

"Did you hear what really happened?"

"Was he mad in the head?"

"Have you seen how she looks?"

She smacked her lips. Such a tasty mix of feelings. Disgust and pity laced with the syrup of sympathy. But too far away. No one came close enough for her to feed on the delicacies they offered others. *They don't know what to say to my face. I survived. Da didn't.*

How would she eat their feelings anyway? Her mouth felt foreign: lips too soft, tongue too thick, teeth like standing stones. *Because it's MY mouth. This body is MINE.*

The echo to her thoughts would fade as she ate the gnat's heart out. *No! I'll keep fighting you.*

The O'Neill pushed through the crowd, scowling aside the murmurs about his son. A delicious death. So juicy. *You killed my Da. I hate you.*

She hissed at him. It came out as a cough. Weak. Wet.

"Are you cold?" The old man guided her wing-tips—*fingers*—around a warm pottery vessel when she failed to hold it on her own. "Drink it up, there's a good girl."

The sickly foreign liquid scalded her throat. *Sweet milky tea. My favorite.* She spluttered and tossed it aside. "Don't want." *Granddad. Please help me.*

He looked at her then. Looked long and hard. His eyebrows crept together like caterpillars. "You're not yourself, are you, Maureen-girl?"

A grin split her face. Maureen. The gnat's name. She waited. The gnat stayed silent.

After everyone had gone, the O'Neill took her away, too.

The wheeled metal box sickened her. Enclosed. No air. The metal messed with her sense of direction. Only after the old man dragged her free did the power in the air burn through her, clean and caustic. Breda. Knowth. No.

*Why are we here?*

She dragged her feet until her shoes scuffed, her

palm sweating within his calloused grasp until he scooped her legs out from under her and stalked toward her reckoning. She shrank inwards. Let the gnat deal with the Lady.

"This the girl, Jim?" A red-haired woman wearing a tatty green cloak strode over.

"It is, Lady." Granddad bowed his head. "This is Maureen O'Neill, my granddaughter."

"Not Maureen." The gnat forced the words out her throat.

"Maureen is the name she was baptized with," the O'Neill insisted. "She hasn't been right since the accident. Barely eats. Won't talk. Could be the shock but I think it's something more. Something about her eyes…"

"Let's take a look at you, young lady." The Lady kneeled. Palms cupped her face without touching, though the hands lacked heat. Eyes, a clear pale green, examined her own. Deep and cool and calm, like a lough in the mountains. Deep enough to drown in. The gnat panicked. Her limbs thrashed just like she had in the Boyne. The tender heart fluttered too fast to bite.

They wrestled each other for control. Fool, mortal. The Lady would see.

The Lady's eyes narrowed thin enough to pierce flesh and skewer them both. "For us, it is different. We have a name to take. And a name to lose."

They stilled. Which would Breda take? Who would lose?

"I can free her," the Lady said to the enemy who paid her homage. "But you won't like the price."

"If it saves my granddaughter, I'll pay. Tell me what I owe."

"The sunlight shines once again into Newgrange. My brother's sleep grows restless. When he returns, he will need a friend. Someone to guide him in his new life."

"A friend. To one of you? I lost my son three days ago. This girl is the last of my line because of your banshee. Oh no, my Lady Breda, *you* owe *me*."

"Caer knows he is close to awakening because he's dreaming again. She loves him still, despite her madness. She doesn't understand that what she's done to survive has changed her forever. She doesn't realize that she's become a creature he can never love."

"Your banshee is your problem, not mine. I want my Maureen back."

"The two are related. Come away and I shall explain."

The pair drew aside.

While she waited, she gnawed on Maureen's young, tender heart.

The sun lowered. Shadows formed. Grandfather's lengthened into a long line. Though in the open, Breda cast none. Her own wavered as though viewed through water.

Her eyes lost focus the longer she stared. At the corners of her vision, between the nooks and crannies of earthworks and stairs, shapes writhed. The fresh, new part of her cringed. Poor shadows. Trapped in the dark. Scared of the light. Not like her. She'd gained a new lease on life. The older, darker half laughed, a wet hacking sound that brought the Lady and the O'Neill back.

"Loosen your hold, Caer Ibormeith," the Lady demanded. "This one is not for you."

Too late. The pair had bickered too long.

Caer stretched out her arms, ready to fight. "Mmmmaureen is mmmine." The remnant of the gnat whimpered, too weak to protest.

With a hard tug on the edge of her cloak, the Lady shifted the land. A ruthless move. It flung Caer sideways out of Maureen's body.

Both fell.

When Erin came to, her head ached. Granddad tutted and fussed, holding her too tightly and muttering about the lack of blood. Apparently, she'd struck her forehead on a rock. Her hand slid across a bump the size of an egg with a triangle chunk chipped out the middle. It throbbed but the rest of her lacked…feeling.

\*\*\*\*

Erin dropped her hand from her temple where the injury had left its scar. Back home, Mom had freaked. Big time. Within a week, they'd been on the plane and off to a new life in the New World. There, she'd almost forgotten how the banshee had owned her.

She hadn't wanted to remember until she'd grown sick of her own fear.

Now, when she was desperate to recall more, she had nothing. The last moments of Da's life—gone. All she had was the banshee's scream, the river, and a nightmare's face on endless repeat.

She banged the microwave door closed on a bowl of frozen peas.

Closure. What she wouldn't give for closure.

The timer over the broiler beeped—the sausages were about done. She cut one through its crispy grilled skin to check, then dished up the rest. The sole wounded sausage stayed behind. Bothering her.

Tonight, Angus wasn't alone because tonight was Date Night. She'd googled and, yep, he was taken Big Time by some stalker chick dream girl who'd literally haunted his dreams until he got up from his sick bed to rescue her. And yet...

She wet her chapped lips. "You said he's unique—the only one of his kind. But what happened to his wife? The one he found living on a lake as a swan. In the story I read online, it said he became a swan too and they fly back to Newgrange to live there happily ever after."

Her grandfather fetched out the cutlery and set the table with unduly slow diligence. "Since you're not leaving well enough alone, I'll tell you what I know. They didn't get a happy ending. He went into the hill, into *Tír na nÓg*, and she went mad with the loss. It's why I agreed to help him. With him back in the world, his wife calls on Himself now. Thanks be to Our Lady, she no longer calls on us."

The microwave pinged. A distraction to a logical flaw: Angus' wife had shared his dreams. Why hadn't they shared eternity?

She was about to ask when the '*us*' part registered. The bowl of peas narrowly escaped being spilled onto the table.

"Not *Her*. Not—"

Granddad made a loud, in-drawn breath of agreement. "The same. Our *bean sí*."

He used the Irish term. The word matched the English one, but he put the emphasis on the second syllable, not the first.

*Banshee.*

Erin gripped the back of a chair to keep her balance as the eerie screech echoed around inside her skull—as if the banshee wailed here and now, not eight years ago and five miles away. Every muscle in her body locked. *Don't panic, don't panic, don't panic.* The trick was not to fight. To relax. Eventually the effect would fade, and she'd regain control of herself. *Then* she'd head into her room and freak out properly.

But within a few heartbeats, she'd caught her breath. The shakes held off. The blackness, which always sneaked across her mind and stole her vision, never came.

How could that be? Was it because she'd found Angus was real, or was it something he'd done? There'd been that sensation, inside Newgrange, of poison draining…

*Angus…*

To her surprise, she found she could speak. "His *wife* is the O'Neill banshee?"

Granddad dished out his dinner, a clear signal he wanted to drop this. But if she waited, he'd answer. The relief of discussing a long-held secret was impossible to resist. Even Angus had succumbed to the need.

Now, thanks to him, she wasn't scared, but pissed. "What the f—," *careful*, "flipping heck—did *we* ever do to her?"

Granddad poured salt over his sausages before tossing a pinch over his left shoulder, then dusted his hands. "Our ancestors tricked them. The first Celts to arrive in Ireland, fresh from Spain, defeated the *Tuatha Dé Danann* in a great battle not twelve miles away. We demanded half the island. They agreed. 'Which half?' they asked then—too late." He waggled his finger. "Because the half our ancestors gave them was below the earth, while we took the land above. We forced them into their hollow hills to live in *Tír na nÓg* and they've never forgiven us for being cleverer."

With a wolfish grin, he stabbed his finger on the table. "The past happened here, Maureen-girl. Down the road, there is a fort on a hill. Beneath it is buried the great Celtic bard responsible for locking Those People away because of their unholy and forbidden powers."

"Like turning into swans? I don't see how that's dangerous."

Her grandfather pointed his butter knife square between her eyes. "With shape-shifters, any animal could be a spy in disguise."

Erin refrained from noting that if what she'd seen with Angus and the deer today was any indication, it was more some kind of kindred spirit thing than actual shape-changing. Because, hello, *shape-changing.*

Meanwhile, her grandfather applied himself to his meal.

Still jet-lagged from yesterday's flight, Erin struggled to eat. Besides, she was too hungry for knowledge.

"You said 'our ancestors.' How do you know we're related to the first Celts?"

Her grandfather's bushy brows wavered. "Tradition and evidence. Can you think of a better reason than why the banshee calls for the deaths of our family, hastening our end if she can? Thanks to Our Lady, yours will be the first generation to be free of Her."

Erin cut off a wild laugh before it became too crazy. *Free?*

That bitch had stolen her childhood. Just as dreams of an unattainable boy had tainted her teenage years. How many young men had she slept with trying to replace him? How many weeks had she lost to the cloudy world of anti-anxiety medication? How many therapists had she lied to again and again about her dad's death?

All because of one goddamned banshee.

Erin needed her out of her head and her life. For good.

*If there's anything else you want…*

If the God of Love couldn't remove her fake feelings for him, then she'd go direct to the source who'd downloaded them into her brain. Once she found her old house, she'd find both Angus and the banshee together, because tonight was Date Night.

First, however, she needed some direction.

"I thought I'd go visit Da's grave after we're done here. Mom never let me say a proper goodbye, and I really should've visited already."

*I didn't before because I was too afraid the banshee would be there.*

"A churchyard is no place to be after sunset." Her grandfather frowned. "Why not wait until tomorrow?"

"The sun won't go down for at least another hour, and I promise I won't stay long—I'm meeting someone after. You wanna join me?"

"Not this time. I usually go of a Sunday." His refusal was true to her memories. Granddad had his soap operas to watch after dinner and his routine ran like clockwork. "He likes fresh flowers, does our Liam. Take as many from the garden as you like."

"I will, but I need you to draw me a map to the churchyard. And to the pub. There's an old school buddy I caught up with online, and we plan to head out for drinks and dancing."

Technically, true. While she'd agreed to catch up

37

with her former best friend, she had yet to arrange when.

"If you're after drinking, don't be driving. It's no bother fetching my only granddaughter safely home."

"Thanks for the offer, Granddad, but don't wait up. I'll see if I can stay over at Annabel's—Annabel Hogan. She's the old school friend I used to have." She stood to kiss the top of his head. "Don't worry. I'll be perfectly safe."

\*\*\*\*

Erin was lost. Despite the map. Despite finding her father's graveyard.

She'd spoken to the Celtic cross of Da's headstone until the sky turn shades of lavender and apricot. She'd left while it was still light, only to spend the next half-hour looping between the three landmarks she recognized: the graveyard, a pub and a humpbacked bridge.

The lane leading to her old home should be somewhere in the middle.

It wasn't.

Driving as slowly as she could, past where she remembered and where Google Maps *showed* there was a lane, the thick hedgerow lining the main road didn't break.

*To hell with this.*

Someone inside the pub should be able to guide her.

Later, she'd arranged to meet Annabel here. An unmistakable landmark thanks to the wine barrel by the front door with a pair of scarecrow legs sticking out of it.

Liam O'Neill had dad-joked it took drowning one's sorrows too far.

The stick legs now wore rubber boots, otherwise

nothing had changed.

There were people here, although not many if the scant half-dozen cars and lone motorbike were any clue. She parked in their midst and took a moment to add another layer of lip gloss over the cracks in her lips. Proper balm would be better. She'd buy a stick tomorrow. Tossing it aside, she got out the car and blipped the key fob to lock it.

The twilight air grew hazy. Strange. Even the floodlight above the pub door struggled to break the gloom. A few steps later and the pub door blurred. She blinked. No difference. Rubbed her eyes. Shit. Now the barrel had vanished. What the hell?

The air thickened and chilled until tendrils curled around her: too heavy to be called mist, too thin to label a fog. Her chest tightened. Breathing became work. She licked sweat off her upper lip and slogged forward.

*Don't panic… It's a grand, soft day. Right?*

Halfway to the pub, the gossamer strands stopped her in her tracks then wrapped her in a cocoon up to her neck. A whimper escaped her throat.

A waif-slender girl fluttered toward her. Erin had once dreamed of meeting fairies. They ought to look like this: glimmering and lovely with cascading corn-silk hair and forget-me-not blue eyes.

"Do I know you?" Erin asked, feeling she somehow should.

The girl laughed—if such an awful noise could be called a laugh. Its keening edge skidded along her nerves. There was no mistaking the sound or the creature that made it.

The banshee.

Erin's heart pounded against her ribs so hard they'd

surely be bruised after. If there was an after. The floodlight buzzed and hummed, its light as far away and pale as the moon. The halo surrounding its feeble glow was almost a perfect circle, like a life preserver. She fought the urge to reach toward it, as if it might somehow save her. A childish urge.

*I'm fine, I'm fine, I'm fine. This is all a trick. Breda swore to protect me. I'm safe.*

Erin closed her eyes. She'd been standing directly in front of the pub. The doorway was below the light. No need to be anxious. She was a triathlete: she knew three different means of getting away fast. One of them was to run. Somewhere in the mist were her feet. They'd gone numb. No problem. Once she got going, she'd work through the inevitable pins and needles. She drew in a slow, steady breath through her nostrils, concentrated hard and willed her feet to *move*, goddamn it, *move*.

She might as well be rooted into the ground. Her limbs refused to budge.

*I'm trapped.*

Trapped and yet not terrified. Her calmness disbelief, not courage. Which meant she was not above calling for help. If she screamed, someone would hear. Breda would come.

*Then scream!*

The fog filled her mouth when she tried. Sputtering cleared it, while putting her nose high enabled her to breathe.

"Mmmiiine!" the girl cried in a harsh, nasal voice as her mouth stretched wide open, impossibly wide, her jaw unhinging like a snake's. There was no loveliness left as she warped into a disjointed specter.

Exactly how she'd looked when she'd called the

first time.

A stab of heat flared in Erin's chest. Not fair! Her father had died saving her life. In books, that kind of sacrifice protected boy wizards from the touch of their nemesis. *Why not me?* Adrenalin kicked through her veins, urging her to fight. With a mighty effort, she lifted her arms and got her hands halfway to her ears.

The banshee whirled around her head, turning the bubble of fog into a maelstrom for one. The force of it pulled at Erin from all sides. She wanted to sink down to the ground, as if facing a storm that might blow over. Bits of her would scatter to the four winds if she tried that. She was already falling apart, her composure disintegrating in tune with the high wavering wail.

The wailing eased for the banshee to draw breath for another blast. In the sudden silence, from somewhere far away, came a voice. It poured over Erin with the rich, sweet grace of molasses, warming her from the inside out. Maybe she'd died after all—died and gone to heaven.

Beneath her feet, the ground rippled with the sickening shudder of an earthquake and the spiderweb tufts binding her broke apart like cotton candy, returning to a pea-soup fog.

*I can move.*

The pub. The people. The man who sang with all his heart.

She staggered forward, stumbled over a step, and would have fallen had she not crashed into the door. Where was the handle? She had to get in.

Through the wood, the man's words rang with gospel truth. The singer was in love with some girl and, oh God, she wanted that girl to be her. She palmed the cracked paint in every direction, blind and frantic, her pulse knocking in her ears.

The banshee screeched and drew in the fog to reform around eyes now the pale blue of ice.

Shivering uncontrollably, Erin pressed into the doorframe, as if it might hide her from the death coming for her. The banshee would use her name to gut out her heart, the same as she'd done to Da. If only Erin was more collected, more centered, more *together* somehow, she might somehow hold on.

"Mmmaureeeen O'Neilllll," the creature called in cracked and wavering glee.

The name cut through Erin like shards of crystal. Or maybe that was her enemy, arms straight and fingers crooked, coming straight in for the kill. The banshee's claws hooked into her scalp and pulled, while she stood frozen, arms locked at the wrists as if chained. She fought her immobility, straining until it seemed her chest would burst. Her muscles refused to budge. Not even her lips moved enough to curse her own stupidity.

*Fine. Take Maureen. Take the trusting, dutiful granddaughter and her misplaced faith and hope. She's a fool. Just as Granddad was a fool. Just leave the rest of me alone...please!*

Oh, it *hurt* to be husked like an ear of corn, to have fingernails as sharp as knives ripping off layer by layer. The first time, all those years ago, had been a bullet wound—a short punch of agony. This was her soul being skinned.

*A name to lose and a name to keep...*

Without the power of Erin's true name, the banshee couldn't go deeper. Not in one go. Not yet. But the onslaught didn't stop. As the wailing kept her pinned to the door, those ghostly claws drove through her skull and into her brain again and again, ripping through her thoughts, shredding her secrets, and rending apart her dreams and memories and hope.

Her soundless screams flayed her throat and emptied her lungs, but she couldn't stop. Not even to breathe. Her chest burned as her oxygen died. Drowning. Surrounded by air. Asphyxiated by her own silent cries as the banshee carved her into pieces from the inside out.

*Somebody…please…help…*

*I'm dying.*

Chapter Four

When the Night Falls Silent

Thatched and quaint, and complete with a turf fire taking the chill off May, the pub was the sort of place tourists loved. It was a place where live music was both frequent and impromptu: patrons bringing a tin whistle or guitar or, often enough, singing *sean-nós*—in the old style—simply because the mood was on them.

Tonight, however, the only music was the wind howling outside like a lost soul.

Within, there was plenty of talk, but no new faces. With Angus present, the pub became one for locals only. Despite this—or perhaps because of it—he sat and drank alone, focusing on the beige cascade within his pint of porter to scry his fate.

*Ah, Date Night.*

The bubbles in his glass drifted downward in defiance of gravity. An impossible feat. Did it mean he needed to fall to be free? He could hardly stoop lower than stealing strength from strangers and their love of light.

Nor was glory an option. One bright moment and he'd been warned against knotting his own noose. He stroked his throat where the wire had...not...scoured his flesh.

A scarce-weaned deer did not leave its mother to try the short spring grass on a site so busily peopled as Newgrange without encouragement. No doubting the sender: while the few wild herds of red deer in the area roamed widely, the largest nearby came from the domain of Dowth. How like his Chief to remind Angus of old bonds by making the innocent suffer.

*I will never harm another, not even for my own salvation.*

A chill shivered down his spine. He took a long pull then set the glass down to regard the result. Now the bubbles told a likelier tale. After a temporary independence, they rose to the light only to be creamed from the top. Another sip and the head of froth vanished, leaving the stout black.

A bad sign. Dowth came from *Dubhadh,* the Irish for darkness. Without Angus, Manann and darkness would reign.

Angus circled the rim of his glass with his finger. Such a thin line, like the balance Breda brokered between Dowth and Newgrange, Manann and Angus, current chief and destined one.

And well he knew why she did… To become chief, his half-sister must bed him. And Breda had no more desire to do that than he did.

His glass keened a lonely cry as his finger returned to the beginning. But that was only half the problem. For a new chief to reign, the old one must die. He owed Manann his life. And his after-life. He didn't have it in him to kill his friend.

If only his wife had stayed strong. Then she would be Lady and his heart would be hers. Their people would be restored, and his oath fulfilled. Instead, she'd left him.

In their millennia apart, she'd become a screaming nightmare so awful he needed to drink to face her.

*Enough.*

With a grimace, Angus poured the long drink down his throat then wrapped his hand around his whiskey chaser. Here was the light, smooth and gold, just like he'd made it shine today for his American guest.

Liz, with that well of fear that had nearly drowned him inside the chamber. The first woman since his return to intrigue him...challenge him...tempt him. When she'd called him by his original name, he'd almost kissed her.

She'd wanted him to. The strength of her desire had flavored the air like mead.

A side-effect of their connection in the chamber. Had to be. Since she neither trusted nor liked him. Just like everyone he cared for.

With a laugh of despair, he sank his whiskey.

The door behind him banged open. Cold air gusted in along with the sharp manure scent of the fresh slurry recently spread onto the surrounding fields. Outside the wind increased its shrill moaning.

"Thought you'd be here." Marie closed the door and came up beside him. Tall, thin, and with overly long legs and a beaky nose, Newgrange's Head Guide always put him in mind of a heron—her short cap of gray-streaked hair making the resemblance stronger.

"Am I that predictable?" he asked his empty glass.

"A red lemonade, please, Neal," she ordered from the bartender instead of answering.

Her disapproval heated until it radiated off her like a peat fire. She didn't like young people drinking, especially to excess. Tonight, Angus didn't care.

"Another pint and a double for me." He put money on the table. "You should drink, Marie. If you're staying, it helps to be numb."

"Someone needs to stay sober to watch your back."

He almost smiled at her bravado. "I didn't think you'd come after this afternoon."

"It's not your fault there's always some girl who wants to arrange a private tour with you. Although, this is the first time I've seen you show an interest. Still, it's for the best she didn't take you up on your offer—given your one outside would tear strips off anyone coming near you." She shuddered. "And that's why I'm here, because you shouldn't have to go through this on your own."

"She wants me to break her heart. Every month. For nearly seven years. She begs it of me."

"I know why you can't. It would be the death of her."

She sipped her drink for a few minutes then began, in brighter tones, as if struck by a good idea. "Here now, there's an administration job going in the Visitor Center that might suit you. It's a higher pay grade—"

"No."

"It won't kill you to take some responsibility."

"It has before," he said without thinking.

Neal placed a glass of whiskey on the bar and began the lengthy process of pouring a fresh pint of stout. As Angus reached for the shot, Marie wrapped long fingers around his wrist in a gesture of comfort. She knew much and guessed more, having been the one to find him naked as a newborn one November morning, inside the tomb and behind the locked iron gate barring trespass into Newgrange. Since then, she'd mothered him with a vengeance: clothed him, taught him his letters, and garnered him his job as a guide.

He'd never thanked her. His gratitude was too boundless to articulate, the debt he owed her too great to diminish into words. And yet, too often, he took her for granted. He wasn't sure if that made him more or less of a son to her.

Neal placed a fresh pint before him, but Angus slid his hand out from Marie's to pick up his whiskey. She gave it a dirty look, then sighed. "I don't doubt your heart is in the right place, but I worry about your liver."

Angus didn't hear her. The pitch of the wind had changed. The sound soared up, higher and higher, underscoring the wind.

"What the feck is that noise?" Neal asked loudly, a light sheen of sweat glistening on the brown skin of his forehead. He hadn't worked a Date Night shift before. It was doubtful he would again.

With whiskey sloshing over his fingers, Angus set the glass down and flattened his trembling hands onto the bar. Caer. Here, again, to mock his weaknesses and shame his strengths. None better at such a task than a lover turned sour.

The pock and clicks of a snooker game in the adjoining room stopped. The warm hubbub of the lounge chilled into silence.

A flat bang rocked the door in its frame as if something—or someone—had slammed against it. His imagination. Caer wasn't real enough to shift more than sound and light. The strong wind had died but his warding would hold, as it had every month since they'd begun this duet.

Scorning his efforts, the banshee's keening wail

began again, stronger than she'd ever been, swamping through the walls and his protections as though they weren't there.

No one moved.

Terror did that to people: froze their nerves and shriveled muscles. They'd been good to him, his neighbors. Letting him pretend he was like them, they let him work and live among them as though he belonged. Such hospitality deserved something in return, and it wasn't this. Not a joyless room where the fire snuffed itself and the candles cast eerie shadows on the verge of turning nasty. If there had been any point, he would have cursed Caer out loud, but she was already damned—and to their Hell, too, by the people here who preferred their legends living in a distant past and not next door.

Angus struggled against the torpor. Helping the deer must have used too much of the power he'd gained earlier today from Newgrange. Fortunately, he'd drunk quite a lot in a short time and had plenty of firewater in his blood. Putting his feet to the floor, he swayed upright.

It might be his livelihood to speak in public, but he only sang to an audience when he must. In oral tradition, spoken words were law and weapons and tools, and when trained and talented, as he was, songs became spells. To work, however, there could be no hiding his feelings between the notes or the truth between his words. He couldn't fake indifference or pretend he was an ordinary Joe Soap with not a bother on him. The song needed to own him as much as his listeners and for that, he needed to suffer for his art.

Inhaling an almost steady breath, he let his voice into the room. Fueled with the black stuff and firewater he'd been drinking; it filled the icy space to warm the hearts of the living.

*"Of all the money that here I've spent, I've spent it in good company."*

The easy part done, he needed to bleed. He braced himself for the next lines: they had teeth and bit hard.

*"And all the harm that I ever did, alas was done to none but me.*

*And all I've done for want of wit, to memory now I can't recall.*

*So fill to me the Parting Glass. Goodnight and joy be with you all."*

The fire in the grate flickered back into life and his audience thawed. People blinked and shuffled as the blue tinge to their skin faded, staying silent out of appreciation, not paralysis. His next lines held a twist of irony he could have done without.

*"Oh, all the friends that I ever had, are sorry for my going away,*

*And all the sweethearts that I should have, would wish me one more day to stay."*

The door slammed again. A thud duller than before. Something wasn't right. That bang had mass. The door ceased its rattle though the wind still blew. Using the song as leverage, Angus threaded through the room toward it, leaning on tabletops as he went.

*"But since it falls unto my lot that I should rise while you should not,*

*I will gently rise and I'll softly call, "Goodnight and joy be with you all!"*

He put his hand on the latch, conscious of everyone's eyes on his back, aware they expected him to lock it and keep the devil at bay. He should stop singing, should end before the last verse, should leave as the song demanded. But on the other side of the door, he sensed the soapy, acrid tang of very human terror.

Not Caer. His once-beloved summoned only hatred and jealousy and despair. Time had taken her mind and marred her humanity. He couldn't love the vengeful scavenger she'd become.

Ah, but hope was treacherous. If she'd come back to him, his kin might too. He would finish the song.

*"Oh, if I had money enough to spend and leisure time to sit awhile…*

*There is a fair maid in this town that sorely has my heart beguiled."*

Except it wasn't Caer's face the words sketched. Instead, his mind's eye framed Liz with her quick wit, sharp tongue, and soft heart. How could she believe in him with such strength when she was a stranger?

His stomach sank as a terrible foreboding rose. For the enchantment to hold and the sake of those within, he had to finish the performance—regardless of who might be on the outside.

*"Her rosy cheeks and ruby lips, alone she has my heart in thrall.*

*So fill to me the Parting Glass. Goodnight and joy be with you all."*

He pulled the door open.

Something cold and soft slumped against his legs. A face reared up before him, wavering on a neck three times too long. Mummified skin stretched too tight across gaunt, angular features that were part human, part bird because Caer didn't know any more if she was a swan or a woman. A feminine body was feathered in dirty gray plumes, her elbows bent the wrong way, her hands elongated like a swan's pinions, but jointed like fingers. They curled in grasping greed toward him, while her black hole of a mouth began again to spew out a shrieking wall of noise.

Her breath, once fresh mint and apple was now stale cider and pondweed.

His mouth twisted at what time and loss had turned the girl he'd loved into. And he'd loved Caer so damned much. Loved her more than ambition and without compromise. For her, he'd given up his dreams.

In return, she'd betrayed his trust and forsworn his tribe to choose a false freedom that had ultimately turned her into this *creature*.

"Leave." The trispiral on his chest burned as he put enough heat into the demand to send her packing.

Caer stopped wailing long enough to laugh. Unlanded and unhoused, she had no source of her own to withstand him. Yet resist him, she did. So much stronger than she should be; stronger but no saner.

She reached down with those wicked fingers and grasped at the bundle by his feet. "Miiiiiiiiine!"

He heard as much as felt something tear inside her prey. Something deep that bled sun bright and marrow raw to his Second Sight. He'd known Caer as a carrion-eater of feelings for those grieving the sick or dead, pecking away from a distance. He hadn't realized she'd sunk to maiming first-hand.

He shoved her away, then kneeled to examine her victim. Fury, hot and acrid, whirled through him leaching away the last of his compassion for the banshee.

*It can't be.*

It was.

Guilt surged into his veins at the sight of Liz's blue face. His fault. Caer was like the rest of his people—

beyond saving. Wallowing over her ruin had not helped either of them.

"Get your claws off her!"

With all the gentleness in him, he lifted Liz's body to his chest, before turning his shoulder to block the banshee from rending her prey again.

"*Miiiiiiiine!*" Caer screeched and reached through him, because he'd never put barriers between them. Back when she'd been the girl who walked in his dreams, not this monster who hadn't died.

*This ends now.*

Outside of Newgrange, he couldn't drain her emotions. But his link to his ancient prison was something she hated, even feared. Having refused to be bound to the land they worshipped, Caer needed the freedom of sky and sunlight even knowing these had been cursed for their kind.

Time to banish her from his domain, cut their connection, and—by doing so—crush her heart.

Through the mark on his chest, he tugged on Newgrange, using its weight of time and belief and stone to shore up his strength. It hurt. Evidence, no doubt, he wasn't meant to use the trispiral scar like this.

"You no longer exist for me. I cast you off. And if you hurt another living soul, then so help me, Caer Ibormeith, I will sink you into the dirt and darkness myself."

The mark flared red-hot. Angus gasped as his heart burned. Scorching skin smothered the banshee's dank stench. The door to his soul, through which she had entered so often, shriveled, and closed.

Caer sobbed a horribly girlish cry. Then, gathering up her tattered wings, she vanished.

Angus didn't check she'd gone. Cradled in his arms, Liz seemed as thin and brittle as a dead leaf. Would she live? Her pulse fluttered through flesh cold as a corpse. The shredded strands of her soul wafted, fainter and fainter, tickling against his skin like tentacles. He tried shoving them back into her, but every time he almost had them, he found he held nothing.

She was dying.

*My fault. I told her she could find me.*

Wrapped about her as he was, she bathed within his own abundant aura. That gave him time. Surely he had time? There must be something he could do to save her. He had no tools save willpower and need, and the scar on his chest weeping fluid.

It ached with each beat of his heart.

It didn't hurt enough.

He had enough lives on his conscience. Long ago to the world, but fresh in his memory. This new life was his new start. Damned if he'd mar it with another needless loss.

Inhaling into his core, he focused on how his heart tugged against the brand on his chest. With every heartbeat, he drew power from Newgrange. Unlike his blast at the banshee, he let it seep into him, containing and building the energy like an oyster accreting a pearl. A mile away, he felt the trispiral within the inner chamber flare to match its twin on his chest.

*All I can give.*

The light illuminating Liz flickered one more time and died. Snuffed out.

"No, Liz, that's not the way," he told her in a broken whisper, playing his fingers along the length of her spine, trying to pluck up the life in her the same way he'd once plucked his harp. "Anyone can do that. The trick is to come back."

With reckless abandon, he focused on the greatest trispiral, the one on the Entrance Stone, and hauled. Lights popped inside his head and his heart strained with the burden. He kept going. Whatever she needed. Everything he and Caer had taken, he would return. Anything she needed, he would give. Anything and all of it.

*Everything I have.*

The pain grew so intense he dropped to his knees, buffering Liz by catching his fall on the doorframe. His breath rattled and his heart stuttered as if about to seize. He couldn't manage much longer, else he'd pass out himself. If he did, she'd never heal. This would have to do.

He clamped a hand around the base of her skull and put his lips over hers. Her mouth was tainted with salt. The weight in his chest lifted. As he exhaled, it passed between them. Everything he had, he gave. Unconditionally.

He hadn't known he had so much to give.

When he drew back to catch his breath, her shoulders shuddered in his arms and her spine arched. Tiny sparks fizzed blue-white over her body, bright and brief in the manner of flint striking iron. Deep in the center of her chest, an ember-red glow grew bigger and brighter, turning a rich gold as it expanded.

She was coming back to life.

When she gave an ear-cracking yawn, she sucked his power into her body.

Relief swollen, he kissed her eyelids, her forehead, her mouth.

She wriggled in his arms, then reached up to touch his face. "Were you kissing me, Angus McCraggan?"

Dizzily, he pulled away from the drugging tartness of bird-cherries. Unless it was cranberries from America. Whatever the fruit, it was not how Liz's aura had tasted earlier.

*What have I done?*

He forced a smile. "Messing with that banshee took a lot out of you. Are you well?"

She smiled up at him with her cheeks and lips chapped red, and her espresso-brown eyes brimful of belief and something much more than mere appreciation. His lungs ran empty. He needed to breathe. Drinking in the sight of her was not a replacement for air.

"Mm." Her fingertips traced from his temple to his jaw in a possessive gesture which lit a terrible, forbidden yearning inside him. "I'm about ten kinds of awesome and you avoided my question on the kissing."

"You needed a touch of mouth-to-mouth."

She giggled. "If I'd known CPR was so good, I'd pass out more often." Sliding her fingers from his jaw to his neck, she tugged his head close enough for the warmth of her breath to fan over his chin. "I'm feeling faint. Will you do it again?"

"Liz." His throat thickened with emotions he didn't want to identify. This wasn't love. She was merely high on life, a side-effect of his healing. Still, her happiness addled him more than the whiskey. "You're not yourself, *mo chroí*. You were as cold as the grave not two minutes ago."

Liz's smile turned crooked at the endearment, and she slowly wet her lips less than an inch from his own. "Then warm me."

This, he had not expected.

"Later…" Not a false promise, exactly. Blankets. Fire. Central heating. All approved methods of warming. Kissing was not on that list. Dying took a lot out of a person, not least their soul. Most likely she was as weak as a baby and newborns were fragile. The memory of what she'd been through would kick in. Anytime now.

So why wasn't he moving?

"I just thought of something," she murmured. "*McCraggan*. Wouldn't that mean something like the 'son of rocks'? And wouldn't that make you a rock god?" She broke into peals of laughter.

Angus found the resolve he'd been looking for. "Time to call it a night." Easing his arms from around her, he settled her into the doorframe then cupped her cheek as her eyes drifted closed. He was too weak to help Liz on his own. He needed Marie's aid. Heaving himself to his feet, he flung out an arm to the doorframe as the world spun. The bright interior light dazzled his eyes. Blinking cleared them but the sight before him made his stomach roil.

An audience. He'd forgotten. The pub was desperately quiet and still: his harsh breathing was the loudest sound. No one moved, but all eyes rested on him, and they were not kind. To suspect him was one thing. Quite another, to watch him face down a banshee and then breathe life into the banshee's kill.

Angus swayed, recovered, and found he needed the doorframe to balance. He should do something. Say something. But he couldn't remember ever being so weary. Without the doorframe, he wouldn't be standing.

"*Uisce beatha*, Neal," Marie ordered from beside the bar. Neal jerked like a puppet on strings, retrieving the shot poured earlier and pushing it toward her. She shook her head. "Fill it."

When Neal had done so, she carried the glass across the silent room and folded Angus' lax fingers around the base. "I'm told it helps. Drink."

*Uisce beatha* was not merely whiskey. In Irish, it literally became the Water of Life. He raised the glass to his lips, tilting it so the golden liquid trickled down his throat.

It revived him enough to splutter his gratitude in the language percolated through the land during his long sleep, *"Go raibh maith agat."*

She shook her head, as if no thanks were needed. "Goodnight," she told him pointedly. "And joy be with you."

He nodded. The song. Of course. He must finish what he started and complete the charm. But that meant leaving Liz who was yawning and stretching.

"I'll take care of her," Marie said, as his attention fixed once more on the woman he'd given everything to save. With a wrench, he dragged his gaze away.

Raising the glass, he toasted the room, "Goodnight and joy be with you all."

Returning the glass to Marie, he stepped off the stone threshold. The cold air struck him hard in the face as he left without looking back.

Chapter Five

A Dream of Hearth and Home

Erin De Santos woke and found herself sprawled in a doorway.

*How did I get here?*

She licked her lips and tasted the sweet burn of spirits. Had she been drinking? Must've been a lot if she couldn't remember doing so.

But she didn't feel drunk or hungover. More like the opposite. Like she'd woken from the best night's sleep of her life.

She scrambled to her feet and squinted into the light.

Huh. A pub. Inside were lots of people, all drinking fast. Except, she was on the outside. Why was that?

She cast her mind back.

There'd been a truck and a man driving it. A girl and a terrible accident. Erin had drowned.

No. That wasn't right. Her father had been the one to drown.

And yet, the memory of drowning was so vivid and fresh. The way every muscle cramped. How she couldn't see daylight, let alone swim toward it. The shocking chill robbing her body of heat while water stole the space in her lungs for oxygen. The world growing darker and darker, pressing in on her until she was…

Somewhere close to heaven with a scent curling

around her like peat smoke, an embrace as warm as sunlight, and a mouth burning hers with its heat.

Not somewhere. *Someone.*

Angus.

With a frown, she turned to where he walked unsteadily off into the night. *He* was the one drunk. She stifled her impulse to chase after him, her fingers finding her lips. He'd kissed her like she was too precious to lose. So why was he walking away? Had she imagined that kiss? She must have. Otherwise, he wouldn't kiss and go. Would he?

The best thing to do was go inside and get properly trashed and forget the yummy Irish god with a voice that made Elvis sound like a choir boy.

Twisting around to face the threshold she found the storky, older guide from Newgrange blocking the entrance.

"Is there some kind of new door policy to get into Irish pubs?" Erin laid on the sarcasm to conceal the hurt. "Because if you have to be a local, this used to be my dad's favorite pub and I'm doing a pilgrimage thing in his honor."

The guide's forehead wrinkled then cleared. "I knew something about you was familiar. You're Liam O'Neill's daughter, aren't you? God-Rest-His-Soul."

Erin did a double-take at being recognized. "Yes?"

"Good, then you know where Angus lives." Whatshername jerked her head toward the parking lot. "Apparently, he's bound me here for the evening, which is really quite distressing given what he's just done. I need you to get him safely home."

"Wait, what? Why me?"

"When does a banshee wail, Miss O'Neill?"

Erin opened her mouth to object that wasn't her name, then bit her lip.

A banshee wailed when someone died.

There it was. The missing piece. The something important she'd wanted to forget.

Everyone in the pub wore the same shell-shocked expression that had been the dress code for her father's funeral. No one, not a single person, met her eyes. Everyone somehow became extremely preoccupied with their drinks.

As if she was a ghost of herself.

"But I'm alive," she said in a small voice. "I'm alive because…" *Angus did to me what he did to the deer.*

"Because you were rescued by an Act of God." The older woman gave her a look that strongly implied she didn't know how lucky she was. "And now he needs you to help him home."

The guide pointed. Angus was attempting to get on a motorcycle, only he couldn't swing a leg over without losing his balance. Definitely not a fit state to drive. Well, then.

With a curt nod to the older woman, Erin headed to him. "You shouldn't get behind a wheel when you're wasted."

A half-laugh escaped him. "I'm only wrecked, not wasted."

"There's a difference?" She raised an eyebrow. "Look, leave that here. You'll fall off anyhow. I'll take you wherever you need to go."

She blipped the central locking on her shiny blue rental car and tugged him toward it.

Angus didn't resist until they reached the passenger door. "I don't like cars."

"Too bad. I'm supposed to take you home and you're too heavy to carry. Get in." She opened the door for him and, rather than reply, he collapsed on the seat and closed the door.

She started the engine. "Would taking you to Newgrange be better?"

His smile made a brief airing. Luckily brief because it took her breath away. "Only you would ask me that." His smile turned upside down. "Although, after tonight…"

"About that," Erin figured this was as good a time as any. "I just wanted to, you know, thank you for saving my life."

"But I didn't."

Erin did her best not to roll her eyes. Geez, Irish people did not take compliments well.

"Yeah, you did. Your boss said, and I remember your kiss—, I mean, giving me mouth-to-mouth."

"No, Liz. I didn't save you. You *died*." His voice cracked, and he looked away from her, the heel of his hand pressing against his chest as if stopping a hole. "The life was pouring out of you too fast. There was nothing I could do…I was too late."

"Riiiiight." She nodded. "So now I'm a zombie? As if."

"A fine sceptic you make!" He bucked up enough to give her an annoyed scowl. "Earlier today you asked me to bring your father back. Now you don't believe I breathed life into you."

"Exactly. You resuscitated me."

"I gave you a good deal more than air."

"How am I supposed to know what you did, given I was allegedly *dead?*" Not nice to piss off her own personal savior. She moderated her tone to be more reasonable. "Look, I'm trying to show a little gratitude here, so thank you for kissing me better or whatever the hell it was you did. Now where do you want to go?"

This time when Angus smiled it stayed, and Erin could not pull her gaze away from his face. Dimples lit up the high planes of his cheeks like miniature sunrises, while, without bitterness tightening them, his lips looked invitingly full and kissable. Not much chance of any repeat action, but a girl could hope.

Angus reached over and tenderly traced a line from the edge of her eyebrow out to her temple and along her cheek. Her eyelids fluttered closed, and she leaned into him.

"Your gratitude means a great deal, *mo chroí*," he whispered. "But I'll not take more than your thanks." He dropped his hand rather than draw her closer. She was excruciatingly aware of every creak of his leather jacket as he leaned away from her toward the door. "Turn right onto the main road here."

Erin snapped her eyes open and gripped the steering wheel hard enough to pop her knuckles.

"Got it," she said, meaning both directions and the rejection. On the road, she searched for a safer topic. "That song. Was it a spell?"

"Something like. It's an old song I heard once, but old songs have years and memories behind them. They can be used to a purpose if you know what you're about."

"Huh. You really only heard it once?"

"I can recall almost everything I've ever heard." He paused. "Always wanted to be a bard," he continued with a shy, sideways glance. "Almost finished the training for it, too. But, well, never mind."

"What happened?"

He shifted in the car seat. "My country was invaded, my people defeated and banished. Let's just say my death got in the way of my dreams."

"If you're immortal, you can't have died."

"I'm not immortal."

"Says the man who's nearly three thousand years old."

Hunching down further, he closed his eyes. "Right now I feel I could be, but I'd only seen something like eighteen summers when they sent me into the earth, and it's been less than seven years since I returned to the light."

*They sent me into the earth.*

Angus talked around topics like a lawyer.

"Why not just tell me you're twenty-five plus a couple thousand years in *Tír na nÓg*?"

He opened his eyes. "Slow down and take a sharp right here before crossing the bridge. Head down this lane a little farther and then bear right once more. My house is at the end."

Avoiding an answer. Again. What was really aggravating, however, was how she'd driven past this goddamned lane twelve times this evening and not seen it. Like it had been hidden. By magic.

"How many years have you lived, *exactly*, McCraggan?"

"Lived? I don't know…exactly. My birth certificate says I'll be twenty-six on October 31, but my people didn't chart dates like yours do. Plus, I spent the first year of my marriage as a swan and they age faster than humans. I might be a couple of years older; I could be a year younger. Shape-changing is fickle with time."

She laughed and he looked wounded. He was serious. Maybe she should work through his 'facts.'

"You have a birth certificate? A real one?"

"Marie," he pronounced it MARee, "was adamant I get the paperwork your culture seems to require. She put me in touch with the right people—priests, Guards, social workers—and I told them something of what had happened to me. They heard what they needed to hear. From what I gather, their version of events is a very sad story of me being orphaned and then imprisoned in a secret underground chamber by some cult until I escaped. An experience which has apparently left me psychologically scarred, not to mention uneducated and socially dysfunctional. It would have made the news, if Marie hadn't convinced them it would be too traumatic to publicize my situation."

"What about the time in-between? What was it like inside Newgrange for all those years?"

He stiffened. "It was a living death where I forgot what it was to be a man."

His voice was flat, all emotion compressed. She did the same when shrinks queried too closely into her father's death, as if mentioning the banshee could call it.

Biting her lip, she concentrated on the laneway, which was narrow, overgrown and winding. Misjudging him made her squiggle inside. If he was really twenty-six—or nearly—he was only a few years older than her and not some ancient immortal playing at being a youth. It was almost unbearable to think of how vulnerable he must feel, here, in an unfamiliar world and the only one of his kind.

"I'm sorry," she said. "I never guessed it would be so bad. I was told fairy hills led to *Tír na nÓg,* and I always thought that sounded pretty near heaven."

"Comes of having the victors tell my people's story. Banishing us to a life in the Land of Youth sounds a lot better than condemning us to be buried alive." His voice lost its deep smoothness and became rough and ragged. "Liz, I don't have the heart to be talking about this. Let it rest."

The forty questions spinning in her head over this version of events vanished as the headlights lit an old farmhouse painted buttercup-yellow with blue-trimmed windowsills and doorframe. The colors were wrong, but she knew the place. It was exactly the house she'd drawn as a child: three windows along the top, and a window on either side of a door down below. Her throat tightened until she could barely breathe.

"Here?"

She didn't need to ask, but it was more polite than, 'How's it feel to be living in *my* home?'

Angus didn't reply. Unless she counted the thunk of his head hitting the passenger window.

Panic bubbled through her stomach. "Shit, McCraggan. You had better not be dead."

There was a faint fog on the glass from his breath. He was alive, properly alive, not Undead or something in-between as she'd half-feared. She pushed on his right shoulder, and he slumped back.

The map light revealed an unhealthy pallor to his face.

"Angus?" She squeezed his arm, then, hesitantly touched his cheek. His stubble rasped under her palm. "Can you hear me? Are you all right?"

His eyelids flickered open. "Tonight took a lot out of me. More than I expected."

"Let me help you inside."

He shook his head, his eyes blinking fast and his jaw working. Not refusal, this was apparently an effort to wake himself up.

Without streetlights the night was coal dark, so she left the headlights on, came around to his side of the car and opened the door for him. He swung his legs out and levered himself upright using the car for support. She ducked to get under his arm, and he swayed and swore when her shoulder brushed against his chest.

Maneuvering as a unit proved tricky, but somehow, she led him down the garden path. It was uncanny. Every step closer to the house, another step further into her past. Memories thickened the air. Her vision wobbled, as though she was under water. Her feet seemed to sink into the ground until she was more wading than walking. The air in her lungs was cold and hot and moist and dry all at once.

Angus stayed solid beside her, his body warm and heavy against hers, the scent of peat smoke and whiskey an unexpected anchor.

But the house…dear God, the house wouldn't stay *still.* Its facade strobed through a stream of changes in a weird time-lapse—window shutters coming and going, garden plants flourishing only to vanish, day and night flickering by, and two very different color schemes vying against each other. The first had yellow walls and blue windowsills; the second was whitewashed with a black trim.

They reached a low metal gate.

Thumbing the latch, she lifted it slightly so that it swung freely instead of jamming on the thin strip of concrete pavement.

The tightness in her throat grew until she couldn't swallow. The house in front of her wavered until the white and black version stayed put. Black plant pots, wide-based and footed like witches' cauldrons, sat perched on the windowsills, filled with petunias. Blue painted the sky. The sun shone bright. A mild breeze stirred the air.

This version was her home.

She clung to the gate, unable to let go. Beside her, Angus panted, his eyes again closed. He looked ready to be sick.

The front door swung open, and a sandy-haired man came toward them. Shorter and balder than the screensaver on her cell phone but dressed in the navy blue uniform he'd worn for work—and for his last day on earth. The vision from the past pressed in from all sides, squeezing her throat until she couldn't breathe, let alone speak.

"Da?" she mouthed.

"Ah, home you are at last, Erin." Da's smile and eyes were warm although his tone turned chiding. "Are you not well and truly old enough now to know better than to swing on that gate? You'll warp the hang of it, and it'll never swing open properly."

Erin didn't care that he was a vision. Nearly eight years had passed since she'd last heard his voice or seen him face-to-face. She didn't care how such a miracle had happened. Only one thing mattered: he was here.

She reached for him, wanting to run and wrap her arms around him, but Angus didn't seem able to stand on his own. Holding onto him, she babbled to her father. Everything she'd wanted to say since she'd kicked out toward the air and light and left him behind.

"When she called, I was so scared and so selfish. I just left…" Tears threatened to blind her, and she blinked them away hard, hating to miss one second of seeing his face. "I should've helped instead of letting go, instead of leaving."

"You can't blame yourself for what happened." The voice was raspy and faint. Da's lips moved, but it didn't sound like him. "I knew she would come."

"Then why didn't you tell me? If I'd known, if I'd been prepared, I would've fought harder."

"It was not your fight."

"Why? Why would you do that? Why give up everything just so I could live?"

"It was my gift to give." This time the answer definitely came from Angus, but it was exactly the sort of thing Da had said to her mother, with the same sort of stiff pride after receiving another earful of why he shouldn't spend their savings.

Her father was fading. His hand lifted in benediction, and she lunged for him, letting go of the gate and Angus in her desperation to reach her dad.

"Please!" she cried, "Please don't leave me like this."

The black-and-white house vanished and took her dad with it.

Chapter Six

What's Yours is Mine

Frantically, Erin cast around for any sign of her home, only to scope unimportant, useless details in the minimal illumination provided by her car headlights: a new brass doorknocker, herb and vegetable beds where there'd once been flowers, peeling yellow paint beside the empty left-hand window sill.

The air turned cold and thin, the chill nipping her skin. White noise buzzed in her brain.

Granddad had told her there was no going back to the past, but she'd seen Da, spoken with him. It couldn't be a hallucination.

Angus said he talked to the dead. Had he done this? She spun around.

He was on his knees, upright only because he'd collapsed against the fence. He'd brought her dad back to her and what had she done? Dumped him without a second thought.

He startled when she put her hand to his arm, turning his head away from her like he couldn't bear the sight of her. No guesses why: she sucked as a human being.

"I'm sorry, it's just I…" What could she say? *I saw my dad now and I'm in shock on account of him being dead.* If Angus had done that, he'd understand. If he

70

hadn't, then she was losing the plot. Again. "I'm sorry I freaked. That was…" She pumped cheery into her voice. "You're amazing and I really, really appreciate…everything you've done for me tonight."

No response.

She bit her lip. "Let me help you up. You look half-dead."

Refusing her aid, he got to his feet using the fence. It seemed to take tremendous effort.

"I'll survive." He coughed the words out like they were going to be his last.

Since he didn't lie, she should believe him. But he'd passed out once already this evening and collapsed just now.

If healing a deer tired him, what did bringing someone back from the dead do?

"Seriously, McCraggan? Let me get a look at you."

She smoothed the flop of black hair from his forehead with her palm. Not feverish. A good sign, but he shivered at her touch and his eyes closed, the hollows under his eyes nearly as dark as his five o'clock shadow. Her hand stayed on his face, tracing and soothing around those wild, dark brows; along cheekbones so high it was a wonder they didn't have scaffolding; across a jaw stubborn enough to give pause to a heavyweight boxer. Such masculine features, yet he leaned into her palm as though craving her touch.

She sucked in her breath at the notion maybe he did. With her other hand, she stroked along his temple, into the silk of his hair. He sighed as though giving up an internal fight. Was he going to reject her again or did she have license to continue? Testing his resolve, she slid her hands deeper into his hair. It was incredibly thick, like sliding her hands into midnight. He swallowed hard enough to make his Adam's apple bob but didn't pull away. Her gaze rose from his throat to his mouth. His lips were fuller without the scowl and as sculpted as the rest of his face. When he'd kissed her awake, they'd been firm and warm.

The day she nearly drowned she must have swallowed half the Boyne and the water was still in her lungs, frozen over when Da died and Mom took her away. Erin had tried many things to ease the chill inside her chest. Alcohol, exercise, men. None worked for long. But as Angus wrapped an arm around her, tight enough to squeeze her ribs, the warmth from his body radiated through to her bones until she almost heard the ice crack as she thawed from the inside out.

She trembled with the need to kiss him, to connect deeper.

But getting him indoors was the goal, not getting smoochy.

"Do you have keys, McCraggan? Because that door isn't going to open itself."

His frame tensed, but he didn't let her go.

"Go home, Liz," he urged without conviction.

She stifled a sob by lifting her chin. "I am home."

If she belonged anywhere, it was here. In the house where she'd been raised, obviously, not the embrace of the man who had taken her terror, rescued her from the banshee, and granted her dearest wish. Despite that fact, the meltwater mix of relief and gratitude and hope swirled through her blood and swelled her heart fit to burst.

She didn't mean to kiss him, but it was better than crying. Angling her head, she rose to her toes, and touched her lips to his. Tucked into his side, her angle was awkward. Her lips didn't land flush to his but pressed against the side of his mouth. His stubble prickled.

No finesse, no flirting. Angus might as well have been her first for all the sophistication she was showing, so childishly desperate in her need to thank him, yet unable to speak.

If she said a word, Niagara Falls was going to have nothing on her.

Earlier, he'd skirted away from her touch. Now, the corner of his mouth lifted into a smile—a move which squared his mouth to hers because Erin hadn't budged.

She parted the seam of her lips, eager to give him access. He didn't oblige. Disappointment flashed through her when he traced the edges of her mouth and dropped a kiss in each corner. His breath smoked over her skin, his stubble hooking strands of her hair. He stroked along her face to free them, treating each strand as though it was priceless.

Where were hard and hot and horny when she needed them? She didn't want sweet and tender from a guy who looked like he sweated testosterone. Damn him. She couldn't cope with caring. She didn't cuddle and rarely hugged. She worked hard, most times, to be unlovable. And yet, her heart was close to overflowing. Her jaw dropped in indignation, ready to give him a piece of her mind, only to have him use the opportunity to slide along her lower lip in a series of dreamy caresses that sent lava running through her veins, melting her bones into goo, and burning down walls which had taken years to build.

She clutched the supple leather of his collar and

whimpered. A sound much like the fawn had made and for the same reason. She'd put herself here but didn't know how to escape.

Or if she wanted to.

Angus pulled back.

The gap between them, though scarcely an inch, felt like a mile. The loss was acute. Her eyelids failed to double as the Hoover Dam.

Leaking tears would have maintained a shred of her dignity so, of course, she bawled like an infant, crying as she never had before over the loss of her father and her childhood and her home.

Familiar with therapy jargon she'd heard of catharsis. Yeah, yeah. Of course, she'd grieved. She'd lied, again and again, to everyone but most of all to herself. She'd squeezed a few tears out at the funeral, a few more when they boarded the plane to New York, more bewildered than upset. Mom had been a mess, spurning the country her husband loved to return to her own, where articulated trucks didn't jack-knife over Fourteenth Century bridges. Erin had kept a grip, believing herself superior when really, she'd just been…heartless.

Now, she couldn't see for tears, she could barely breathe for sobbing, her ribs hurt like they'd been ripped open. Angus held her through the purge, pressing her into his side and stroking her hair but saying nothing, somehow understanding she was beyond the point of a rational response. Keeping her tucked under one arm, he stretched his other up to take a key from the top of a lintel.

*Great security. Not.*

Unlocking the door, he pushed it open and flicked

on a light, revealing the red-and-yellow clay tiles of the porch exactly as she remembered them. She cried harder.

He chivvied her inside and sat down on a sofa with her curled up on his lap.

Slowly, slowly, she pulled herself together, the flood waters easing until she was left sniveling into his collarbone, her arms still around his neck. His breathing was slow and regular, almost as if he was asleep.

Lifting her cheek off his shoulder, she pulled away.

"Stay," he said despite eyes half-closed.

It was appalling how she'd forgotten he was exhausted. He was too unassuming for a Celtic god, a Bronze Age prince, or even a fairy lord.

"Sorry, Angus, I don't normally cry buckets over someone I've just met."

"It did me no harm to be a sponge, *mo chroí.*"

She smiled weakly. His leather jacket was wet all down one side. Useless material.

"Ma cree," she repeated. Distant memories of Irish lessons in school glimmered but failed to enlighten.

Angus unwrapped her fingers from where she still clutched his collar, kissed them, then settled her palm over his sternum. "*Tá mo chroí istigh ionat.* My heart belongs to you."

*My heart.* Mo chroí *means my heart.*

"Do you always give your heart to a girl so soon after meeting her?"

"Only if she dies in my arms."

She shuddered, the memory of a mouth full of fizz and a fire in her chest surfacing then fading. "Tell me you're joking."

"Caer shredded your soul. After I banished her, the only way to help you was to give you my heart."

"You did WHAT?"

She straightened her arm to face him. Angus hissed at her sudden increase in pressure against his chest. Hissed in *pain.*

Erin, taking liberties, unzipped his jacket then and there. His white t-shirt was singed gray where it wasn't stained yellow. She sucked in her breath. Slightly off-center, right over his heart, a wound the width of her fist was burned into his flesh. Her stomach churned as she tilted him toward the light.

Although the wound was red, weeping, and puffy around the edges, the black charring of three interlinked spirals made for a very recognizable pattern. She'd seen such marks before on cattle—the same ghastly combination of charring and gouging.

Branded.

The placement over the thin skin of his sternum had to have hurt like hell. Had to *still* hurt like hell. She gave herself a mental shake and pushed her queasiness aside. The wound was fresh and needed treatment. A gauze covering, at the very least, if it wasn't to get infected.

"We should get you to hospital."

He swished a hand in dismissal. "And would the doctors believe this was self-inflicted?" He shook his head. "I've no wish to draw more attention to myself than I already have. I'm a little heart-sore, true, but it's a small price to pay for not repudiating Caer sooner. I held onto hope with her, and it nearly cost an innocent life."

Erin's fingernails dug into her palms. Caer. The banshee. His wife. A multi-generational killer. How did you say that to someone who'd taken third-degree burns on your behalf? There was bound to be an emotionally sensitive response if she could think of it.

"Your wife is an evil psychotic bitch who deserves to die. I hope you blasted her to bits."

*Excellent self-restraint, Erin.*

His expression clouded and cleared from anger to amusement, changing as fast as the Irish weather. It was those eyes of his that did it. That mix of deep blue and bright gold, like the sun here on a summer's day: fierce and gentle together. Those eyes, combined with a mouth that tightened and quirked with alarming suppleness.

"It was past time for a divorce, but I was reluctant to be the death of someone I once loved so deeply."

Her shoulders caved. She knew what it was like to cause the death of someone you loved. *I'm so sorry, Da.* But she kept her tone light and careless, as if Angus had made a joke, because maybe he had. Shock could hit some people like that.

"And divorcing her is going to kill her, how?"

His hand drifted across his chest then dropped. "Caer gave me her...vow...when she married me, that she would always be mine. If I died, she would, too."

"You know the whole 'death do us part' angle is a pledge, don't you, McCraggan? It means people intend to stay together for life, not that they have to die when they divorce."

"For your people, perhaps. Such vows are sacred to mine. Spurning her...gift...as I did tonight, will end her days because who can live with their heart crushed to dust? It would have been a mercy had I done it when she first left me, but I never suspected she would survive outside the earth after the banishment. It's my fault she became as she is."

A nasty notion wiggled inside her head that Angus might've slipped up there, weary as he was.

"You said before," she made air quotes to hang his claim on, "'you gave me your heart' and you have a freaking wound on your chest like this isn't some symbolic saying. How come you're still alive or can I expect you to go into cardiac arrest any second?"

Collecting her hand by her fingers, he rubbed his thumb across her skin as if she needed reassurance. As if. Still, she didn't pull away because she didn't want to upset him. That, and because she liked the rhythmic warmth of his fingers.

"I still have a pump in my chest that beats. This wound results from me mimicking a rite that only our highest priestess, the Lady of the Land, should conduct." He lifted her hand and kissed her palm, as he had before. Erin shivered as sparks skittered along her nerves and down her spine. "It married my life to yours."

She snatched back her hand. Her heart, his heart—whatever—was banging against her ribs so hard her eardrums were going to burst.

"*Married,* McCraggan? Are you insane? Like, hello, I don't recall giving my consent to this arrangement. If you loved her so much, why not give the banshee your heart?"

His brows tipped down and his lips pinched and thinned. When he spoke, his tone was tight, his temper clearly lit. "Do you think I didn't want to? Once I loved Caer so truly and so madly that I spent two years trying to find her in my dreams followed by a year of eating pondweed and snails. She gave me her heart, but I could not give her mine because I was forbidden thanks to my rank."

He snarled the last word, breathing hard enough that his wound began weeping as the blistered edges

78

stretched. He closed his eyes, his features drawn with pain.

"And tonight, I delivered her death sentence. Tonight, when none but my neighbors are welcome to join me when I drink, just as no one can visit me here without me granting them access. After you ruined my tour at Newgrange today, I never thought to see you again, let alone marry you, *mo chroí.*"

The endearment held no affection, only bitterness.

Erin bit back on interrogating him further. Whatever other side effects there were, she didn't want to know. She couldn't process this, and he couldn't stay untreated. Better for them both to have a Time Out.

"You have scissors, right? Because I'm going to need to cut off your shirt around where it's, um, melted, onto you."

He didn't bother opening his eyes. "Leave me be, Liz. You owe me nothing."

Like she'd buy his crap after that outburst. Idiot. She owed him everything. Only with his shoulders sinking back into the sofa and his head lolling after them, maybe this wasn't a good time to admit she hadn't trusted him. She'd tell him her true name later.

Meanwhile, the New and Improved Erin with Extra Heart was going to make sure he didn't get an infection. If he didn't have a First Aid kit, the one in her car should have what she needed. Plus, a washcloth and boiled water, because she was going to need to soak off the crusted mess of his shirt. A blanket would also be a good idea. It wasn't exactly warm in here and she didn't want him to go into physical shock on top of the emotional kind.

Gingerly she collected his jacket and draped it over

him backward like a straitjacket.

He didn't move.

She slipped away.

Outside, the lights on her car were a damning orange. Shit, her car battery was going. She turned on the engine to charge it, fetched her First Aid kit and checked her cell phone. Shit, shit. Three missed calls and two messages. She'd forgotten about meeting Annabel. Hastily she texted an excuse about coming down with a sudden bout of stomach 'flu.

She was removing Angus' key from the front door when her phone pinged in reply.

**At pub - heard u fainted & local legend took u home**

**Wish I could suffer same**

**Expect details**

Shit, shit, shit. Granddad was going to rocket through the roof when word got out. Nothing she could do about that now, save postpone the inevitable as best she could.

Funny. She hadn't much believed Marie or even Angus that she'd been the one to die, but right now she felt like a completely different person. Like she had a second—no, wait—a third chance at life.

The bathroom and kitchen looked nothing like she remembered.

Angus had to be the first bachelor on the planet not to have a microwave or a kettle, resulting in her boiling water and a washcloth in a pot on the stove. She found scissors in a drawer of clutter. She couldn't find a blanket anywhere.

Upstairs was…empty. Some dusty old furniture she didn't recognize was stacked in the room her parents had shared. Her old bedroom had a silverfish-eaten popstar poster on the floor of the built-in wardrobe. If Angus came up here, it wasn't often. His bed must be downstairs in what had been the spare room.

Jobs completed and radiators on, she returned to where he was draped out cold.

He didn't twitch a muscle when she snipped open his shirt to reveal a chest as sculpted as his face. Aside from the gruesome brand, a T-Bone spread of ebony hair tapered down to disappear under the button-fly of his jeans. The guys she'd dated waxed to show off their abs, but this…this was what a male in his prime was supposed to look like. The fine black hairs tickled against her fingers as she traced their path as far as his belly button, the intriguing texture causing a restless ache between her legs.

Grabbing the cloth, she cleaned and dressed the wound as best she could, then pressed her lips against the sterile bandage in the vain hope she could kiss him better.

## Chapter Seven

## Sunlight of the Heart

The light shining through the crack in the curtains was too bright and golden for moonlight. It had to be daylight, despite the fact Angus hadn't slept through a sunrise since his return.

Squinting, he discovered he was on the sofa tucked in with his usual blanket, his pillow propped under his head. The cushions by his side held the sort of dent someone snuggling into him might make, although he'd woken alone.

His chest ached, the space between his ribs oddly hollow as if something was missing.

With a jolt, his wedding night came back to him.

He pushed aside the blanket and found a neat white square of cloth taped over his wound. Liz had tended his injury. An unfamiliar warmth suffused his limbs. It had been a very long time since anyone had cared for him so intimately.

*Where is she? Did she stay?*

He levered himself up and bumbled through to the main living area of his house. Saving a life was worth feeling like death warmed up but, by the Lady, his muscles moaned and his bones creaked as if he was some ancient corpse drawn from a bog with his skin tough as hide and his flesh shriveled and dried like beef jerky.

"Liz?" he called, somewhat breathlessly.

No answer. No surprise, he discovered a moment later, since the bathroom door was closed, and the shower ran. He pushed the heel of his hand against the bandage over his breastbone, warmth filling the space between his lungs.

*She's still here.*

He headed outside to relieve himself, then halted. The back gates had been opened. Liz's car had been replaced by Jim's.

The gates would be because Jim was moving the cattle around to the pen at the rear of the house while he hosed out the barn. The second probably had to do with creating room for the first—Jim's car was well over to one side, whereas Liz's would have been right in the middle of the laneway through which the cattle would mill. Although where her car had gone remained a mystery.

Absently, he rubbed at his chest again, his gaze drifting to the eastern horizon. The hay sheds hid it from view, but behind them the misshapen hill of Dowth perched on the ridge beyond the fields of the farm.

Dowth: the Lord of the Dead's domain.

Liz had died, and Angus had drawn on Newgrange to stick her back together with bits of himself for glue. The power of the land was the Lady's prerogative. Restoring life was her Chief's. To commit both acts was unpardonable.

That was without his third crime: with his heart given to Liz, he would never become Breda's Chief. To lead, he must be Chief. To be Chief, he must marry the Lady. His impulsive rescue meant he'd broken his sacred vow.

Yet, he didn't regret his decision when it saved an innocent life. Besides, how could he regret being free of his burden and free of his past? It might be short-lived, but it put the responsibility of his people's fate into the hands of the Lady and her current Chief.

Where it should be.

There would be a reckoning soon, but he wouldn't be called to account while the sun remained high in the sky. When it dipped below the horizon, he'd worry.

He returned indoors. He had a guest, the most important he would ever have, and hospitality was due. The shower still running, he might as well fortify them both before he left for work. In the tiny kitchen that Jim always referred to as the 'scullery', possibly because it was mostly sink, Angus searched for the makings of a meal.

There wasn't much.

The last of his dark-speckled gull eggs and a slab of badger bacon were set aside in his bar fridge accompanied by a crockery jug of soured sheep's milk and a basket of mixed greens. It was the breakfast he'd planned for himself. He'd gladly give it to his guest, but he doubted Liz would accept. Marie had gagged when he'd told her about the badger, so freshly dead on the road the skald-crows had yet to find it. And gull eggs were much more strongly flavored than chicken eggs. Other than that, there was a hard round of goat's cheese on the kitchen counter and a small honeycomb. Nothing else.

He rubbed his chin, the bristles rasping loudly. Modern sensibilities were so difficult to work around. What would please an American other than the coffee?

Aha! Barley! He'd need to boil the arse out of the

grains to have them ready quickly, but they were wholesome and filling. He'd no sooner put them in the pot and turned the stove on high when a sharp yelp came from the bathroom, immediately followed by a series of plink-plink-plinks, a squeal of enamel, and a heavy thump.

"Owww!" Liz cried out faintly as an encore.

The muscle in his chest skipped a beat. Had the miracle of hot water gone awry and scalded her?

He dashed out of the kitchen. The door of the bathroom was locked. He opened it anyway. The shower water was still running. Steam hazed the room.

"A little privacy!" Liz yelped from a height just above his knees.

Her long legs were askew: one ankle hooked on the edge of the bathtub, the other tucked under her. The white shower curtain was wrapped around her torso, while one hand gripped the remaining strip of curtain still attached to the rail.

Angus struggled to make sense of the spectacle. "You fell out of the bath?"

"So clever of you to notice."

He assessed her for injury, bracing his knees and closing his mouth to act unaffected—difficult when she was the light of Newgrange forged into flesh. Wet hair poured down her shoulders in molten bronze, while the tawny gold of her skin glistened like honey. Her body was long and lean, fit as a warrior queen, with the muscles in her arm faintly defined as she clutched the curtain. The clinging fabric revealed more than it hid of pert breasts and a drum-tight stomach.

His gaze dropped lower. He groaned in dismay, the terrible weakness he had for a fine woman hitting an

85

unexpected snag. At the apex of her thighs, she was as bare as a girl. Women waxed. Sure, and they had in his day, too, but not there.

"You about done, McCraggan?"

His gaze snapped back to her face. Her cheeks were flushed, either with anger or the heat of her shower. He pushed how enthusiastically she kissed to the back of his mind. All the way back.

"Let me help you up." He reached forward.

She batted his hand away. "I can manage."

"Says the woman who fell out of the bath."

She glared at him.

A snuffle behind him gave him a start.

"What the—?" he spun around to confront a large Friesian languidly licking the window glass, its long tongue leaving a slimy trail of bubbles down the pane. "Ah, I think I see what happened."

Cattle were more curious than cats. He peered out the window and, sure enough, another two bullocks waited behind the first to see what was going on inside.

"That would be Jim letting the cattle into the pen behind the house. He probably won't come this far around himself."

"I thought there was some pervert staring into the window doing something dirty and it turns out to be a goddamned cow!" Liz grumbled behind him in a strange thin voice. When he turned, her face was pinched and pale. Delayed shock, perhaps? "You should have curtains!"

"I don't mind if cattle see me wash."

"It nearly gave me a coronary."

"Yes, I know. It wasn't as if I barged in here to check if you'd dissolved."

She raised her chin. "My towel, please. You're in front of it."

He grabbed the towel and passed it to her with one hand while switching the shower off with the other. Attempting to shrug free of the curtain, she turned as he reached. They ended up nose to nose, her waist against his arm, her skin warm and damp.

She smelled of his soap, the shared scent a claim to her body he hadn't known he needed to make. Her eyes were the same rich darkness as peat, and they bound him as surely as the earth he'd slept under. He couldn't look away, let alone leave.

"Are you just going to smolder at me, McCraggan, or do something about it?"

Such bravado and yet her gaze fell from his as she spoke. A reminder that giving his heart was a one-sided transaction, and she did not feel as he did. He forced a grin. "And here's me thinking a little smolder might dry you, *mo chroí,* since you don't seem to be planning on using that towel."

She flicked a length of hair at him, splashing his face. "You don't fool me, McCraggan. You like me wet."

"True." His lips twitched into a smile of honest delight, and she took a step back, her eyes wide and unfocused with the same stunned cast as someone poleaxed. "I'd also like you not to catch a chill."

Catching the edge of her towel, he started to wrap it around her, only to have her snatch it from his grasp and toss it to the floor. Leaning forward, she placed the palms of her hands on his bare chest. Her hands didn't shift, but her touch lit a trail down to his groin all the same.

She wanted him.

Such a desire was dangerous when she had no idea of the hunger it lit within him, no understanding of the responsibilities it created. If she was to stay, he would have to explain. But she was a tourist, and she would soon leave the country—as tourists did.

Kissing was safe.

He meant to sip and savor the soft, ripe sweetness of her mouth without the salt of tears. Yet, when her hand rose to lock around his neck and her tongue quested urgently for his, he deepened the kiss in an instant and instinctive response. Too long alone, abstinent and starved of affection, he appreciated her eagerness until it veered into impatience.

This should be a dance, not a fight to the finish. And she wanted to move faster and harder than he was ready for, tugging his bottom lip with her teeth and grinding her hips against him. Aroused from the moment he'd opened the door, he reached blindingly hard.

"Easy, *mo chroí*." He edged his lips away from her mouth to move against the thin tender skin of her throat. "You still need drying."

With her body slick, he used the blades of his hands to carve off the excess water from her arms, down the sides of her ribs, and over the round of her hips. She leaned against each stroke, like a horse being curried. Ah, she appreciated a firm hand. Or did she confuse rough with passion? A simple test to slake down the length of her spine over the curve of her buttocks, around to the tops of her thighs, then trail his fingers in long, lazy loops around her waist, the underside of her breasts and along her shoulders.

With a soft animal noise, she stopped resisting and started quivering. Last night he'd misread the sound as distress and pulled away. This morning he recognized it for surrender, a spur for more of what he was doing. As if he couldn't tell by how her arousal sweetened the steam or the lust-drunk heaviness to her eyes.

Via the slow route of her collarbone, he nuzzled upward to her mouth. She didn't wait for his arrival but met him halfway in a fierce, demanding kiss that sent his technique haywire and his tongue thrusting in a primal rhythm that left them both gasping.

Kissing was not safe. Not with Liz.

Her fingernails scored a blaze down his bare back as her frame molded to his, the hard beads of her nipples using his chest like a washboard. His cock strained against its denim constraints, his jeans the sole item of clothing between them. His chest heaved with the effort of reigning in his libido.

*She's not mine.*

Not of his people, she would never be his. He could be hers—if she accepted, he came at a price. If not, well then. Her pleasure did not have to mean his. From how she kissed, he already knew her other lovers had been selfish in their needs, taking instead of giving. He clamped his hands around her waist, ready to lift her onto the washing machine beside the bath, when she dug her fingers inside the back of his jeans. His buttocks clenched as she gripped them. No underwear. He'd never understood the point until this moment.

Her breath tickled against his throat as she giggled, then said, "Commando?"

He wasn't sure what soldiering had to do with the matter and didn't much care. Not when her hands slid around his waistband and captured his cock. He sucked air between locked teeth. Too long, he'd gone too long on his own.

"Wow, McCraggan, I get now why you were worshipped."

She thumbed the fluid around the head in a practiced gesture and Angus couldn't repress his low moan of desperation. If he spurted at her touch, he couldn't bear the shame. Any man might impress with size. Skill, sensitivity and stamina were a rarer combination. She wanted his body, he wanted her pleasure, and he couldn't unravel her if he was undone himself.

He pulled her hands free of his jeans then stepped out of her reach.

"Enough."

She blinked at him with dark eyes, her swollen lips parted in surprise. "Oh, right, of course. I've protection in my purse. If you pass it over, I'll fish it out."

It took him a second to work out her meaning.

"I'll admit I'm curious about wearing a rubber sock, but I'm not about to try it now with you."

Putting her hands on her hips, she tilted her head. "Then forget about going any further, McCraggan. I don't know how many women you've been with before and after they put you under the turf."

Behind her crude words came an acrid waft of something very like despair. He didn't know her well enough to understand the source. The best he could do was address her implied accusation she was one of many.

"One woman, Liz. My first love became my wife. Her, you've met." He sketched an avert with his right hand to ward off the bad luck of that connection. "Between her and here, I bedded down in the earth. I've been with no one else. I held true to my former wife, my love still fresh though hers has rotted along with her soul.

For years I wanted what I lost. No more. She is dead to me now. Should she return, I will destroy her for what she did to you."

Liz shuddered. She was getting cold. He picked up the towel, dusted it off and draped it around her.

"And here's me hoping you'd go again with the smolder." Her fake smile turned into a real frown as she lifted her nose. "Speaking of, can I smell smoke?"

"I was cooking you breakfast before you called—" Now that she mentioned it, there was a smoky taint to the air. "Bollocks! It's burning."

Chapter Eight

Harsh Truths and Bitter Greens

Angus bolted from the bathroom and took all the heat from the air with him. Closing the door after he'd gone, Erin grabbed her overnight bag and dug out her running clothes. She'd packed ahead, not just for credibility with Granddad, but in case she did overnight with Annabel.

Using the towel, she wiped the steam from the mirror and flinched at her red-chapped lips, too-flushed cheeks and stricken eyes. Proof she didn't have the first clue how to handle being spurned by a guy who kissed like he cared. She pressed her thighs together, the ache of being ready for a bump and grind on the spin cycle competing against the mortification of being handed her towel.

God, how was she going to get out of this?

If Granddad hadn't swung by the window while she showered, she wouldn't be in this predicament. A cow truly had startled her. But falling out of the bath came from playing duck and cover below the windowsill to avoid her grandfather copping an eyeful. Now she had to endure the excruciation of small talk because she was trapped here while Granddad saw to the cattle.

Letting down her guard last night was where she'd made her mistake. If you didn't care, you couldn't get hurt. Locking down her feelings and pretending they weren't there was a reflex action, the same as slathering on foundation and a nude lipstick to restore her to the semblance of cool, calm, and collected. But it wasn't enough. It was a mask that would crack the moment he pulled out that soul-deep gaze. Normally, she avoided eye make-up. Today, she needed it for self-defense. She applied a little. Considered the effect. Applied more.

Game face on, she swanned into the tiny kitchen.

"That oatmeal?" She buried her nose into Angus' shoulder, pretending to look while actually breathing in the musk of his skin as he scraped the non-burned bits out of the pot into two bowls.

"Something like." He drew her to one side to open the bar fridge and pulled out a basket of weeds. "There's fresh honey for yours." He pointed to an honest-to-God fresh comb on a cute wooden stand, angled for the honey to slide down into a saucer at the bottom. "And fermented sheep's milk, if you can bear to try it."

"I'll eat most anything, especially a meal made by a domestic god."

When he didn't respond to her attempted compliment, it spurred her to try harder. She peered into the basket of weeds.

"Are these nettles?" She prodded at the dark green stems with their telltale tiny white hairs then sucked her finger to ease the sting. Dumb question. Worth the pain, however, to have Angus fixate on her mouth. She hollowed her cheeks and let her eyelids droop.

After five full seconds of flat-out staring, he apparently discovered a pressing need to wash the porridge pot. This proved a complicated business which required him to keep his attention fixed firmly on the task at hand, even if it didn't happen to be much more than putting the pot in the sink to soak. Unfortunately, it put his back to her. The same broad-shouldered, shirtless back he'd presented in the bathroom with the faint blue-black bruise directly opposite the wound on his chest, sidelined by the marks from her nails.

Erin's stomach tumbled over. Again. What sort of person gave a stranger their heart?

"Those are nettle tips and charlock flowers," he told the skeevy dishwater, unaware of her discomfort. "The flowers taste a bit like mustard. I usually add a scraping of the cheese, over there, as well." He chin-tipped toward the counter next to the stove.

She pushed in beside him to unwrap the small bundle of greaseproof paper. "Woah. That's pungent!"

"Hence the scraping part."

She shrugged her lack of concern. It made sense that he preferred artisanal food; she couldn't imagine him snarfing down a bowl of mac and cheese if she tried.

"Can't be worse than tofu. Make mine the same as yours."

He flashed her another of those sudden smiles—thank God nothing like the devastating special he'd leveled her with earlier. This one was merely pleased. Heart-warming not heart-breaking. It still left her a little dopey.

She needed a jolt to recover. "I don't suppose you have any coffee."

"I have tea brewing."

Tea. Her grandfather drank gallons of the stuff. She'd long since lost the taste for it.

"Pass. And I can see there's zero chance of a cherry cola in this kitchen." She sighed. The man could cook and sing and kiss, but he couldn't magic up a soda. "I'm guessing sipping nectar or ambrosia or whatever is a myth since you also drink whiskey. What do you usually go for? Water?"

"Whiskey is more medicinal, but I do like it. My usual drinks haven't changed: peppermint tea, most mornings, chamomile of a spring afternoon, rose hip in winter."

The air thickened and charged as if listing herbal teas cast a spell. She couldn't look anywhere but his mouth. Despite the warmth of her top, goose bumps broke out across her skin and her nipples pinched.

His gaze dipped and held below her neckline, before his smile beamed on at a lower, troubled wattage. "Mead, fermented from honey, is my preferred drink for celebrating a special occasion."

A special occasion? This was breakfast.

"Just water is fine," she said, unable to summon any snark to save her life.

"The water here is pumped from a well, but it does come from a tap."

While she poured herself a glass, he took the bowl and sprinkled salt and splashed cider vinegar over the bitter greens, then mashed them down with a fork before adding them to the grainy stuff.

"I hope you're not too hungry, this mightn't be edible."

Erin was famished. Even post-scorching, it smelled of greeny goodness. Her appetite, unfortunately, wasn't limited to her stomach. Not this close to a shirtless man who still mostly smelled of peat smoke from the pub, unless you were close enough to inhale the wild, subtle musk from his skin.

"What if I'm ravenous?" she drawled, walking fingers up his bicep. Every muscle in his upper body tensed as he dredged on the sort of smile that usually came accompanied by the 'have a nice day' of a waiter on a twelve-hour shift in a crappy diner.

"Then you'd better eat." He thrust the bowl at her.

Whatever his body said, the man was not into her. Last night had been the drink talking.

Snatching her bowl, she went into the living room to sit at the kitchen table: the same one which had once been her family's. Did everything here have to sting?

He followed her, his expression growing bemused as he watched her wolf down her food. She ate fast because it was good. Really good. And because she had nothing to say.

"You like it?" His disbelief was adorable. Also, annoying because it was adorable. A man who could sing and cook and modest to boot. How was he still single? Oh. He wasn't.

"What's not to like?" she asked.

"I've been told the food I make tastes like feet."

"Feet are a delicacy in a lot of cultures. Pig trotters and chicken feet and frog legs. This, however, tastes like risotto."

He sat down at the foot of the table rather than next to her, but it was still too close. Even from halfway around the table, his raking gaze radiated her body. When he pushed a limp piece of nettle around from one side of his dish to the other, not taking a bite, it dawned on her that his mixed signals might stem from some deeper issue than her riling him in the kitchen.

Something was eating him.

He'd eroded her barriers with kindness and kisses.

Unfortunately, while she had one-thousand-and-one means of keeping men at bay, she was a one-trick pony when it came to drawing them near.

That left the small talk.

"You get many guests, McCraggan?"

He toyed with his spoon, tilting it over and back while staring at his warped reflection. "Only those invited can find this house. Marie stayed over a few years ago to mind me when I came down with a fever. The farmer I rent it from, Jim, checks in every few months. It used to be more often, but he doesn't need to teach me now. I can do most maintenance jobs on my own."

"Sounds lonely."

"I see people at work. From more places than I ever knew existed."

She ached for him. No friends in the habit of dropping around, a perpetual stream of strangers, and everything so different from his own time: language, landscape, culture and kin. Having experienced her mom moving them to the crazy-busy streets of the Bronx, she knew too well what that was like.

"There must be others like you."

Mentioning Breda would raise more questions than she was prepared to answer, but maybe Granddad had it wrong. Maybe Angus wasn't entirely alone. His eyes flicked to hers and he shook his head.

Small talk was a big mistake, but she tried again. "You were hurt. You should eat. You do eat, don't you?"

"When I have the hunger on me." His eyes heated. As if what he wanted to devour, was her. Then his gaze dropped to his food where his smile died. Swiping his bowl aside, he stood then started pacing. There plenty of room for his lunging strides since he wasn't big on furniture. Other than the Aga wood-fired stove—at least fifty years old—squatting against the back wall, there was only the table and a green storage cupboard.

He had her vote for Best Ass in Denim. As for inside the denim…what he packed in there left her mouth dry and her panties wet. It sucked that, other than those jeans, he now wore a Bad News Face. Those were never good.

The ambulance officer pulling the sheet over Da's body. *Your daddy didn't make it.*

Her mother, a week after the wake. *We're moving to New York.*

Angus last night, *I never thought to see you again, let alone marry you.*

Oh.

No wonder he'd made her breakfast and talked about a special occasion, because if he'd married her, then last night was his wedding night.

But, apparently, not hers.

Awkward.

Her own appetite gone, Erin pushed her bowl aside and set her fork down with deliberate care.

"It's this marriage business that's bothering you, isn't it? I mean, we only met yesterday and I'm not who you needed or wanted to marry on the rebound, so I completely understand you regret what happened with your wife. It should have been her."

He gave a bark of something that might be laughter if it wasn't so broken. "She is nothing to me but a monster who lives off grief and death. One who will soon expire. You did not deserve to die so she could live again, *mo chroí.*"

Erin chomped the inside of her cheek, hard enough to bleed. There had been a moment before being attacked when she'd seen the banshee as Angus must have known her: the spun sugar prettiness before the rot. If he hadn't interfered, would the banshee have been restored?

"How come you returned okay, and she didn't?"

"After our defeat by the Celts, my people were more than outcast. The judgment cast upon us was banishment into the land below, into the earth. It was necessary to become shadows of ourselves to survive being joined with the great goddess of the land, Anu. Shadows unable to live in the light. Caer was always afraid of the dark. She couldn't bear to be trapped. She refused the rites. Untethered from the sustaining power of the Goddess, she roamed above the earth as a lost soul."

"And the rest of you?"

"My mother, then the Lady of the Land and the voice of the Goddess, divined the solution to save us. My father, her Chief, undertook the Triple Death as atonement for letting our island be conquered, and I—as my mother's son—demonstrated my faith by being the first to be incorporated into my tomb."

Erin opened her mouth then closed it again. A straight answer and she barely understood a word.

"Does that make you Chief then, if your father was Chief?"

"Being Chief is not hereditary. It is the Lady, our high priestess, who Chooses the Chief who will serve her. My sister now serves as Lady." His mouth twisted as if he'd eaten something gross. "I'm forever grateful to you, *mo chroí,* for sparing me the burden of being her Chosen."

"Why would being her Chief be so bad?"

His eyes fixed on her without blinking. "A Chief serves his Lady with the whole of his heart. He pleases her out of love, not duty. Protects her without thought of the cost to himself. Loves her without condition. Dies for her, willingly and without question."

His intensity was too much. She sipped her water to drown the lump rising in her throat and tried to make light of such an archaically romantic setup.

"It sounds too idealistic to work. What prevents some Chief pretending he's head over heels?"

He ducked his head, his eyes sliding from hers. "A Lady may change her mind. If she Chooses another man, the life of her current Chief is forfeit."

"Wow, does that suck. What guy would ever want the job?"

His eyebrows flew to his hairline. "Men fought for the honor."

"But not you, because of your sister, right?"

"Not me, because I'm no longer fit to serve." He pressed his hand against the bandage. "I shouldn't be relieved to be free of my duty, but I am. If Caer could become a banshee, what might the rest become if I could return them to the light?"

"Maybe she's a bad example."

"My people and I are long past our due dates. Perhaps it's as well they are left as they are, unaware I have failed."

Despite his philosophical words, his torment was obvious in the hunch of his shoulders, the tightened ridges of his stomach and the pained lines around his mouth. Being the sole survivor gutted him.

"I saw you in Newgrange in all your shining glory. You're a god, McCraggan. What's stopping you bringing them back?"

"If I'm a god, I'm no more than a local one. To lead

them into the light, I must be greater. I must be Chief and that is no longer possible."

*"Why?"*

Angus spoke slowly, each word dropping from his lips like a jewel. "A Chief gives his heart to his Lady so he cannot help but love her, and I have given my heart to you."

That same heart rapped against ribs suddenly too tight. Or else his heart was too big. Whichever, it didn't fit, and her chest ached with the pressure. It had to go.

"It's not that I'm ungrateful, but it can't be good for you, McCraggan, me having your heart. I already give my stepdad angina. There must be some way I can re-gift or return it, or get a transplant, or whatever."

"I'm aware you had no choice in receiving my gift, but it was freely given." He put his back to her as he spoke. Between the defined lines of muscles, the fist-sized bruise glared. "When Caer attacked, my sole concern was to save you. It never occurred to me you would object."

He spun on his heel to face her. "Last night I rejected Caer in the full knowledge she still loves me, cannot help but love me, even after all this time. Do the same to me and we are done."

Erin's vision narrowed to lock onto the white bandage in the center of his chest while the jigsaw pieces of everything he'd told her resolved into an I-love-you-to-death nightmare. This wasn't some drunken Vegas married-by-Elvis scenario they could walk away from, both feeling a little foolish but made a lot wiser. Oh, no. He couldn't help but love her because he was *enchanted*.

Okay, so fine. It sure as hell wasn't because she deserved it. Impossible feelings she could deal with, irreversible feelings she could not.

"You said rejecting her would end her life."

"It will within weeks." Two strides and he was beside the table, clenching the back of the chair he'd abandoned with white-knuckled hands. "What is done, cannot be undone without paying a price. If you do not wish this, then I will pay it for you."

"Are you saying, McCraggan," her voice squeaked up an octave on his name, "that your life is in my hands? Because that's a crap load of emotional baggage to lay on a person."

"You're right, it is. Except for a Lady and her Chief, a one-sided match is rarely condoned. The tradition is for two people to exchange hearts because they cannot live without each other. It is the highest form of marriage my people have. My situation with Caer was allowed because she'd already taken refuge in my dreams. My situation with you is unheard of. It does not change the basics. I will love you for the rest of my life."

In a move she didn't see coming, he kneeled before her. "I am yours—as my heart is yours—always and entirely." His admission was low and raw and earnest. She tried to keep her shoulders from shaking while she stuffed her hands under the table and squeezed them between her knees.

"You can't love me." Her voice was faint. Airless. She couldn't breathe. "You don't know me."

"I assume you value yourself so lightly because no one has recognized your true worth." He reached out to rest his hands briefly on her shoulders before skating them up and down her arms, not quite chafing, not quite kneading. "My first impression of you was of a woman strong enough to risk making a fool of herself in front of others and courageous enough to face her fears despite being warned of the dangers."

She flinched under the rain of compliments. "All that proves is I'm an idiot for ignoring your advice."

"The same woman who sought to prevent the harm of an innocent creature and who later tended my wound and held a vigil by my side throughout the night." He used the same crooning tones he'd used for the deer and even though she *knew* he was, it didn't make a damn bit of difference. It worked the same. The tension leached from her body. "If those aren't enough qualities to love, there is one more: you accept who and what I am without question."

A nervous laugh spilled out of her mouth. When he learned she was a liar and a fake he wouldn't be so sweet. "You're making me into something I'm not. You can't trust me with your life."

"I already have."

*No, no, no.*

She wasn't aware of saying the words aloud until stormy eyes bore down on her.

"Tell me why I can't trust you, Liz."

There was no explaining what she couldn't recall—how she'd survived the banshee and Da had not. The best she could manage was a token gesture. A name for a heart.

"Erin," she croaked, her throat closing over in fear of how he'd take her deception. Liz was the name she gave a guy when she never intended to see him again and, for the first time, she wanted to be found. "My real name is Erin De Santos."

She shut her eyes rather than see his reaction. If her experience revealing lies was any gauge, this wouldn't go well.

Chapter Nine

In Memory Locked

"Air in," Angus said.

It was excellent advice so Erin took it, inhaling not any old air, but the smoke'n'sunlight scent she couldn't get enough of. Her eyelids snapped open to find Angus' firm, generous lips parted an inch from her own, close enough to kiss. His eyes were closed, the dark points of his lashes distinct against the white of his skin. Heat shifted from her arms to settle in the center of her chest and his expression turned pained.

"Ah, how you care, *mo chroí*, most especially when you pretend you don't."

She looked down. His hand pressed against her sternum while her heart bashed against her ribs as if seeking to return to its rightful owner and lodge in the palm of his hand. His fingers twitched and she looked up. A storm raging across his face, a tempest of desire, fear, and frustration.

"No! Don't take it!" Extracting her hands from her thighs, she shoved against his shoulders. She might as well have tried to shift Newgrange. "I need it."

Thundercloud brows twitched into a frown. "It's yours to keep, Erin."

*Air in.*

Not an instruction, but her name as she'd never

heard it before, like she was something he needed to live. Had she known it was a loose thread that could unravel her, she'd never have shared it.

"What are you doing, McCraggan?"

"Feeling what you're feeling."

For a second, *her* shock wrote itself across *his* face. Then his mouth pinched and his brow puckered. Her panic transmuted into a feverish heat. The heart he'd given her must be to blame, because her own had never felt like it was a furnace. The mix of the emotions churning inside her smelted into a single core of something new and precious and unfamiliar.

Erin almost sobbed with relief.

"There, now," he soothed. "Better?"

She nodded, afraid to speak.

"You had a lot to process, but a burden shared is a burden halved."

"Or you enchanted me and don't want to say."

"It would be easier if I could, but I'm afraid my talents don't extend so far. Within the chamber of Newgrange I can do more; outside it I'm limited to a little empathy and the ability to give something of myself."

He was too modest. Nor did she really believe he'd do anything underhanded, not since he was going to such lengths to confess the repercussions of his gift.

"Until you gave me your heart, I wasn't sure I had one." Trying to use the truth as a joke was a dumbass move, but she was out of smart ones. "When my dad died, it was like part of me died, too."

The memory sucked her under before she could muster any resistance.

\*\*\*\*

A freezing January day where had Da requested her company on a delivery run to Derry and back. Some company: earbuds in and music cranked, bored out her brain.

Until the truck jolted.

She opened her eyes. Huh. The Hill of Slane. Nearly home.

They steamed on down the hill. Too fast. Amber lights ahead at the crossroads, yet they didn't slow. And Da always so careful. Her heart lurched into her throat. Holy shit. They were going to run the red.

"Da?"

He didn't respond. Just sat there, casual as anything, one hand clenched on the steering wheel and the other hanging loose out of his open window. He didn't brake. Why wasn't he braking?

What on earth... He wasn't even looking at the road but past her shoulder, out the window.

"Da!"

He still didn't move. Not even a twitch. Just sat there, hair plastered in damp streaks across his forehead, nothing more than a sweating statue. His eyes darted from her window to the road to her. Frantic. She tracked his gaze. Her stomach shrank into a tiny, hard nugget.

God, no. Past the intersection, the road curved. Straight ahead. The castle wall.

She hunched her shoulders. Stupid. It didn't make the truck any smaller. They belted through the crossroads. Cars veered abruptly off to the sides, silent against the heavy bass of her favorite rock band. Too fast to stop.

Inside her, everything slowed.

She reached and wrenched the wheel to turn them aside from slamming into the stone. She yanked too hard. Didn't factor in their speed. The world slewed as the trailer whipped sideways then jack-knifed. The seatbelt carved into her hips and shoulder, knocking out an earbud.

The screech rang through the cab at a pitch sharp enough to peel skin. It snap-froze her muscles, including the ones in her throat trying to scream. A screech different to the grinding, squealing groan of the trailer scraping along the stone wall. The source slithering across the windscreen and in through Da's window.

A nightmare of a creature. Part-woman, part-bird.

Yellow hair, mouth gaping, frigid eyes fixed on Erin.

Not her father. *Her*.

\*\*\*\*

She blinked to find frozen blue eyes replaced by gentle, warm ones watching her with concern. Her lips were bone dry when she licked them. She could do this. This one time she'd get it out into the open.

"I was with my dad when he died. I remember flashes of the accident. Enough to know it wasn't his fault. But there's something terrible I've blocked. Something I did." She brought her fists to her temples. "It kills me that I don't know what." She dug her nails into her skull, wanting to claw the blockage from her brain. "Can't you help me?"

With his abilities, surely he could dissolve her amnesia.

Firm hands wrapped around hers and removed them from her face with exquisite gentleness. "I can't read minds, only hearts."

She sighed and tried to make the best of it.

"My head is pretty messed up. It took me over two years to kind of," she nibbled her bottom lip, unsure how to explain how very lost she'd been, "make myself over, I guess. Mom paid for a whack-load of therapy, but I never did commit to the process. I don't find opening myself up to be easy." *I don't want to let anyone else in.*

She gave him a wry smile, thinking of his past life in the Bronze Age. "I suppose you understand better than anyone."

"It would be fair to say I know exactly how you feel." He squeezed her hands while avoiding her gaze, unusually abashed for someone who'd been so forthright.

"I guess it can't be easy telling someone you're in love with them when there's no hope of them feeling the same."

He gave her a strange look and threaded his fingers through hers. The unfamiliar intimacy made her breath catch.

"Unless you're the God of Love," she amended, studying their entwined fingers to hide her reaction. Such elegant, musician's hands, which had played her body so effortlessly. "Because you wouldn't be scared about falling for someone, would you? You're kind of famous for it."

"I told you my feelings because I prefer to have a fighting chance—both at living and loving."

Suddenly, Erin couldn't pretend this was any old counseling session. Not when she sat on a hard, wooden chair as stiff as a throne and Angus was still kneeling before her, a knight before his lady. The fine hairs on her neck rose as if this was a bad omen.

"I'm not relationship material."

"You've never tried, Erin. You as good as admitted that to me earlier."

If she had, she didn't remember. Better switch to a safer subject. She spread her hand lightly across the bandage she'd taped to his chest. "How's your wound?"

"Tender."

"Can I see?" Her nails picked at the edge of where she'd taped the bandage down.

"You told me you were in training to be a vet. Why animals, when you could be a healer of people?"

"Veterinary Science is detective work, purely from symptoms and scans. No patients who can give me shit over drugs or treatments. Just me fixing animals who hurt. It's the fixing part I enjoy." Her usual spiel but not her full motivation. "And animals are helpless to help themselves, that's the real reason."

She frowned at her weird need to be more open with him. No doubt it was because he was so open with her but talking about herself wasn't usually this *easy.*

"Damn. This isn't coming off. How do you like your pain, McCraggan?"

"The opposite to my pleasure, Erin. Make it short and sharp."

She paused, diverted by the prospect of Angus taking her long and slow, stretching and filling her an inch at a time then lingering inside, making her wait for every withdrawal until she was frantic with desire. Anticipation streaked through her nerves. Until she reminded herself he'd taken casual sex off the table without an explanation. Maybe there was some cultural aspect he hadn't gone into, a ritual or a ceremony before consummation could take place. Or maybe there wouldn't be any consummation—just unrequited adoration on his part and endless frustration on hers.

"This might hurt," she warned, wincing for him.

He hissed at the pluck of chest hair. The wound was a pink-rimmed, yellow-scabbed mess.

"Why isn't it better?" She pressed the tape back instantly, an apology for her curiosity. "Your lip healed in seconds, the deer took the same."

"I'll heal faster once I'm at work."

Once he was back at Newgrange, where his strength came from, just like she'd suspected.

"Then why didn't we go there last night like I asked?"

"Because it was late and dark. I'm stronger in the light."

"What are you? Solar powered?"

"Something like."

He'd used the same understated phrase about his gourmet risotto, but without the attitude. Obviously, he'd reached his limit. No surprise since she'd been grilling him on everything from the moment they'd met.

"I'm sorry I've been pestering about your past, McCraggan. After discovering you're real, I can't help wanting to know everything about you."

"Something else we have in common." He dragged his hands through his hair. "As you've reminded me, however, I have work to go to."

"Can't you skip? It's Saturday."

"Saturdays are busy, and I'd prefer not to cause Marie any extra grief after last night."

"So it's because of her you have to go?"

"It's because it's Newgrange I can't stay away. If I wasn't working, I'd need to go there before sunset. I

111

can't be away longer than a day and a night." A shadow winged over his features. "If you leave Ireland to return to America, I cannot follow. What your departure means for me, I'm not sure. I'm hoping I'll be able to wait for your return; whenever that might be."

Her stomach twisted itself into knots. "Like the banshee waited for you?"

"Hopefully, you won't keep me waiting that long." He smiled ruefully. "I'm not immortal, remember?"

"Lucky for you I was, um, planning on spending the summer here until my postgraduate degree starts in the fall. Would you be around if I dropped in to see you every now and again?"

His face lit. "I'll take a summer if that's what you have to give me."

A tractor rumbled by the house: that would be her grandfather heading out to the fields. This was her window of opportunity to escape before he discovered she had broken his one and only rule for her. But some instinct deeper than reason told her if she left Angus now, she'd never have the courage to return.

Bravery came from practice. She'd taken up triathlons to force herself to swim in open water after nearly drowning. Chosen to return to Ireland where her world had fallen apart. Gone inside that chamber, despite it being a fairy hill. For his sake, she would try learning to love.

If only she had spit to speak, she'd tell him.

"Angus…" She stalled at the rise and dip of his Adam's apple as he swallowed hard at her use of his first name. Addictive holding that sort of power over a person. Addictive and terrifying. She wet her lips to buy her time and his eyes tracked her tongue, his pupils becoming black pools rimmed by the faintest line of blue.

"Angus, I'm better at running than staying. I won't be good at this." She grimaced, wishing she knew how to ask for his understanding. "No one's ever needed me before."

"Come here to me, Erin."

An order not a request. Leaning forward to close the space between them, she ran her hands from his shoulders to the tight, straining cords of his neck. His skin was smooth and cool, twitching under her touch. He lifted his head to stare at her through heavy lids, the movement making his thick, black hair drift across her knuckles. Then he put his hands to her waist and pulled her down into his embrace, until they kneeled knee-to-knee. He traced around her forehead with his fingertips to slide a line of her hair behind her ear, his touch sending hot darts along her nerves. His beard stubble scratched her cheek as he put his lips to her ear.

"Let me give you a reason to return to me, Erin, *mo chroí. Éirinn go brách.*"

*Erin, my heart. Erin, forever.*

Her eyes rolled back as his voice smoked through her. He kissed her neck and her pulse rocketed straight into the stratosphere while any muscle tone she might've had rendered into gloop. In case she somehow misinterpreted his offer, his hands scoped around her hips to rest possessively on her buttocks.

Her skin burned beneath his touch. "I got the impression you didn't want to get physical."

In reply, he lifted her onto his lap. His erection jutted within the denim of his jeans to rest in the juncture between her legs. Miniature lightning bolts crackled blue-white under her eyelids from the pressure.

"I needed to be sure, well, to be sure it's me you want, *mo chroí*, not just any man. And, to be sure what you want is what you need."

His hands were slowly, slowly gliding back and forth over the thin fabric of her running shorts with his thumbs angling inward to the apex of her thighs.

"How do you like to be pleasured?"

"Rough," she scraped out, her hips bucking against him with a will of their own.

He flashed the cheekiest grin she'd ever seen, and her stomach didn't so much flip as cartwheel. "Grand, then I'll shave *after* giving you a taste. Fortunately, I'm on the late shift."

Before her lust-hazed brain could form a snappy response, he crushed his lips against hers, his tongue— hard and hot—invading her mouth without preamble. Erin clung to his neck while her hips continued their restless, fruitless shifting to get him *in* her. Now. Never had she felt so primed, so ready to be filled, which made no sense given they'd been talking, not making out.

The world tilted and swayed as he rose to his feet, carrying her effortlessly over to the table to perch her on the edge. With a single swipe, he cleared away their breakfast bowls. When she tilted back in silent invitation, gripping the wooden edge of the table with both hands, Angus stripped her from the waist down with a clean jerk-and-lift.

Instead of undoing his jeans, he stood and stared at what he'd revealed with his forehead furrowed. He'd seemed so keen. Was he wigging out on her?

Erin levered herself up onto her elbows. "You got a problem, McCraggan?"

He ducked his head. "This is new to me: a woman bared."

Reaching out, he traced her folds with extreme delicacy until Erin was insanely wet.

More, she needed more. She moaned her need, and his gaze grew as greedy as it had been in the bathroom, while his breathing became labored.

With supreme slowness he withdrew his index finger before sucking it clean, his expression blissful. "I misled you, Erin. This is nectar I could live off daily."

Responding would have to wait until she'd recovered her power of speech, especially since he pulled up her chair and planted his face between her legs so tightly the bristles of his beard stubble rasped her inner thighs. His tongue plumbed and swirled, hot and slippery and too clever for words.

"Glad you like it," she managed between gasps, several minutes after he'd started. "No one's ever laid me out on the kitchen table and eaten me for breakfast before."

"I knew you'd taste better than anything I could cook. It's why I couldn't eat, earlier."

Then he put his head down again and changed up his technique.

Stiff, shallow and fast, his tongue probed the one spot repeatedly. Again and again. Never missing. Completely reliable. *Exactly* where she needed him. Her blood gushed through her veins while her inner muscles fluttered, Erin grabbed two handfuls of his hair to keep him right *there,* where every nerve in her body seemed to begin.

"Angus."

It was a plea to keep going, not her usual call that

she was ready, and could he stop with the teasing and get in her now, please? This wasn't teasing. An orgasm was inevitable. She was on the edge and tipping. Her hands slid from his hair to her breasts to add to her own torment. Pinching hard to send electricity down the nerves he was working so hard to send lightning up. When her spine arched, he held her tighter, his rhythm never faltering.

"Oh my god, oh Angus, my god, *Angus.*"

She came with the force of a star exploding, dimly aware of his rich, slow chuckle reverberating around her core, the vibration prolonging the sensations rolling through her. No one had ever laughed *inside* her before, let alone gone down on her with such success so soon after starting.

His was a mellow laugh, one of affection and amusement, as though she'd said something charming. Damned if she could remember what, else she'd say it again. He needed to laugh more.

And he was still down there, lapping gently around the edges and keeping the aftershocks rippling. If he kept on, she had a strong premonition she'd come again. Another first for foreplay—if that's what this was. She had an inkling Angus might consider this an end to itself.

As if she could leave him unsatisfied.

But rather than heave him aside, she weaved her fingers through the silk of his hair. "How'd you get so good with your tongue?"

He eased out from under her hands and between her thighs to cast her a cheeky smile. "Surely you know by now, *mo chroí,* I'm from an oral culture?"

She laughed as she sat up. "Ever hear the phrase what's good for the goose is good for the gander?"

Her legs wouldn't hold her when she tried to stand but since he was still in the chair, that wasn't a problem. Dropping to her knees, she stroked along his thighs, enjoying how his quadriceps tensed beneath her hands as she neared her destination.

"This is not a reference to my time as a swan, is it?" His face shuttered as the lightness dropped from his tone.

"It's an etiquette thing, same as taking turns to buy rounds in a bar." She reached for the defined length straining the seams of the denim. Good grief, he was massive. Her hands shook as she tried to unsnap the top button of his fly. "I've had my turn, now it's yours. Share and share alike."

"You don't owe me, Erin."

She rolled her eyes. "Yeah, I do."

"Not this and not today." Lightly, gently, he rested his hands on her wrists.

She shook him off. "Quit freaking, McCraggan. Anyone would think you'd never had a blowjob before."

"I haven't."

She gaped, unable to believe her ears. "What the actual fuck?"

"Those I've had, just not this millennia."

He sounded weary and with no better target, she went for his ex. "Are you telling me that bitch never went down on you?"

"It's not a common habit among birds."

A joke? Probably not. Her lips curved regardless. "Then I'll be your first. And who better? Since we're 'married' and all."

"No." He chipped out the word. "I'm married to you. You are not married to me."

She withdrew her hands to plant them on her hips.

"Most men in this situation—"

"I am not most men. When you can accept my love without condition, then and only then will I consummate *my* marriage."

Erin balled her fists. Here was the rub, and she had only herself to blame for her stupid comment he didn't know her. "I suppose because you're the one who reads hearts, you're going to be the one to decide when *I'm* ready. Is that how this is going to work, McCraggan?"

"You'll know when you're ready, *mo chroí,* because you won't be able to dream of anyone else but me."

It was the sheer arrogance of his claim that stiffened her spine, not the knowledge he already dominated her dreams.

"Your feelings should not be my problem," she railed. "I didn't ask for this."

"You're right. If you don't want to be with me, then I respect your choice. I won't seek you out. If you need a trade, let's stick to the essentials: I saved your life. You can return the favor by not taking mine."

His rugged jaw set hard, as though this was a matter of principle and not injured male pride. Much as she disliked the price he'd paid to save her, she was hardly going to spurn him if he was going to expire from unrequited love like some romantic poet. She might be a bitch, but she wasn't a murderer.

"Keeping you alive is a given, okay? It's just…this is weird for me. I was so cold and numb for so long. And since last night, I have these *feelings,* and it's all so super intense. And I'm grateful. Truly. But when it comes to expressing that gratitude, I'm a do-er not a talker, so I would really like to be the one to show you what you're missing."

She dragged on her panties and shorts to prevent herself rambling further.

His hand rubbed across his dark stubble. "If it eases your mind, I will swear to have none but you." His brows drew in. "My chief desire, however, is to protect you—even from myself. Should you wish to see me again, it should be somewhere with other people present."

Other people? Oh crap. Granddad. Getting him on-side was a must. Once she had some time to figure out how. That meant leaving here, pronto.

"Look, I need to, ah, clear a few obstacles before I can see you again. How about you give me your number, I'll give you mine, and we can sext each other in the meantime?"

He swung free of the chair, his mouth wry and his eyebrows raised.

"I have no use for a phone: Marie fields any calls. If you want to see me, this is where I live, and you know where I work. If you want me to come to you…" He captured her fingers and kissed them before placing her hand in the middle of her chest. "Use this and I will find you."

Chapter Ten

Remembrances of Yours

"I've never seen anyone work so hard doing so little," Marie said, her voice curt.

They were alone, the tours done for the day, but Angus kept his eyes closed and his booted feet on the desk while his hands rested against his chest. Marie was right. It was taking every ounce of effort to look lazy.

A day at Newgrange had restored his strength, but to say he'd been distracted was an understatement. Every tour had been a struggle, which was why he'd skipped one and swapped another. He hadn't eaten all day—he'd forgotten to bring lunch. But he hadn't been hungry, either.

*Love-sick.*

Yes, yes, he was. Several thousand years of accrued belief in his capacity to moon over a woman wasn't easy to shake off.

But the real problem was the yoke around his neck that made every swallow scour his throat like steel wool. The deer had been a warning; this was a summons. As the sun dropped in the sky, so too did his ability to resist.

"I'm not myself, Marie," he said by way of apology, not bothering to open his eyes. "I'll take an extra tour of yours tomorrow. Two if you like."

"Offering to foot a field of turf doesn't keep my

hearth warm if you never go to the bog," she snapped. "In case you've forgotten, I'm in the Visitor Center tomorrow, rostered on *your* shift."

Another of Marie's many favors for him. A shift within the Boyne Valley Visitor Center required staff to take phone messages, answer emails, and check website bookings—and a six-year-old was more competent at such tasks than Angus.

"Which is why I'm here now," she continued, "waiting to hear your version of last night's events and not giving you a bollocking for dumping me with that coach load of Australians today." She placed her hand on his shoulder. "Unfortunately, when our summer staff see you slacking off, or picking and choosing which tours suit you, I can't tell them you saved a girl from her family's banshee." His shoulder was given a squeeze. "You worked so hard to fit in and you've gone so long without any incidents, then *she* comes along and sucks the light out of you."

Frowning, he cracked open an eyelid. "Sucked the *light* out of me?"

Mouth compressed and the furrow between her eyebrows entrenched, Marie stood in her pose of perpetual disapproval, but for once he was not the target.

"You know I have the Sight. I can't say what everyone else saw, but—to me—you lit up like a sunrise, kissed the O'Neill girl, and she took the best part of you, leaving you a shadow of yourself."

He stared at her until his eyes dried from lack of blinking.

*The O'Neill girl.*

A local name for a local girl. That was how she'd reached the pub. And why she'd been Caer's target. He sank deeper into the swivel chair under the weight of Liz's—no, for feck's sake, there had never been a Liz—Erin's lie.

"How do you know she's an O'Neill?"

Marie dropped her hand and leaned against the desk, the better to watch him. "I didn't recognize her when she came here yesterday, but I knew her father. Liam died in a horrible accident off Slane Bridge. The truck he was driving smashed through the wall and went into the Boyne. His daughter was with him. It was a miracle she survived."

Angus rubbed his palms over his face. The waters of his mother's river, named for *Bóann*, were sacred to his people. A miracle she survived…

A cloak of foreboding draped over his shoulders.

"Can't say I blame his wife for returning to America and taking her daughter with her with Liam barely cold in the ground, but it created a lot of nasty gossip. Talk of a murder-suicide, even. Of course, Jim buying their house only added more fuel to the fire. That's why, when you showed nine months later, Jim O'Neill had it sitting there empty."

"Are you saying I'm living in *her* house?"

*Too many coincidences to discount as coincidences.*

"Well, you didn't fit in mine, not with how you can't sit still. Usually. Let alone what you like to eat." She mock-gagged. "And who better than Jim to accept my tall story of your unexpected appearance? Although I did wonder at him taking you with so few quibbles given their family history."

Jim and Marie were not close for reasons Angus had never pinned down. Angus replacing his granddaughter could be why.

"That solves the mystery of why she hid her car last night and left so late this morning," he mused. "She didn't want him to know she was with me."

The furrows in Marie's brow returned. "She stayed the night?"

He nodded.

She huffed out a sigh. "Rewind a little, I'm not getting this. Your song last night: it wasn't a final farewell to your beloved banshee?"

"It should have been, but Erin is the one who beguiled me. I forgot my singing enchants me as much as my audience, so when I followed through, I didn't consider the consequences."

"I'm aware of how you do nothing by halves. The publican locked the doors and the party carried on until three in the morning last night. I'm the only person who walked out sober, there was that much joy with us all." Face scrunched she mouthed the rest of the lyrics. "Heart in thrall? Oh dear. Tell me you didn't."

"Entirely hers. Your Sight was true in every respect save one: she didn't take, I gave. Now I am to her what Caer was to me: bound eternally."

*Unless she repudiates me.*

"Ah, Angus." She stood and paced around in a tight circle, arms not quite flapping, as though trying to contain her agitation. "As if it wasn't bad enough for you to pour your soul into your singing, you have to go pour your heart into a girl whose family already begrudge your existence."

"Erin. Her name is Erin."

"Yes, Erin, your fair sun who has slain your envious moon." She waved the detail aside. "You can't give of yourself like that and *not* have it do something to her."

Had he done something terribly wrong? Her heart had not been exchanged for his. And yet, when he'd sorted through her conflicted emotions this morning, he'd sensed she was halfway to feeling for him what he felt for her. That's why he'd demanded she must love him and think of no other before they lay together, why he could dream of her tart mouth whispering him endearments and those hard, clever eyes melting not merely with desire, but soft with affection.

Marie, however, was still fixated on consequences. "If she's like Caer was to you, will she be bound to Newgrange, as you are?"

"Newgrange? Why would she be bound to Newgrange?"

For outsiders to become of the *Tuatha Dé Danann*, rituals other than marriage were essential. Pledges to the Lady were required. A Blessing must be received. Then there was an initiation into adulthood—a rite where a child sacrificed their childhood in order to become an adult. Some chose a name, others a defining attribute. He'd given up his sense of mischief— particularly the joy of setting cattle to stampede—much to the relief of his mother's plowmen.

No fear of this being the case for Erin.

"She won't be bound. She's not of my p—" His throat ratcheted tight, cutting off his air and his ability to think with a summons he could no longer ignore. "I need to go."

\*\*\*\*

Angus parked his motorbike in the empty yard behind Knowth House. The building's rear facade, with its two mismatched windows and stitched scar drainpipe, glowered at his presence with the same level of disapproval his half-sister usually gave him. No surprise, this being her domain.

Crossing the road to the padlocked gate, Angus selected the right key and braced himself. The chill of Breda's aura was akin to being dropped into a springtime lake. It always gave his skin goose bumps.

In their time before, her company had been as warm as a hearth and as cheering.

Now she was another who'd chosen duty over love. Nor would Breda ever recover her warmth, since her womb of earth was blocked from receiving the light: the long shadow of Knowth House obstructed the morning light on the east, while the archaeological conservation efforts did the same to the west. His sister wasn't without other resources, but she stayed neutral in the dance between her brother and her Chief.

Or she had until Angus broke their stalemate by ceding his position.

Heaving a sigh, he strode past the Guides' Hut to Breda's hollow hill. Larger than Newgrange and about five hundred years younger, it was also an artificial hill on top of a natural one.

Knowth had been a powerhouse, aligned to the spring and fall equinoxes with two passageways to capture both sunrise and sunset. Two times a year, twice a day: four times more powerful than Newgrange and double the power of Dowth with its two midwinter-aligned passageways.

All three monuments were curbed with giant stones carved with mysterious curvilinear patterns that suggested moons and tides and sun rays, but the art here was richer, more numerous and more varied—even than Newgrange, reflecting Breda's love of knowledge.

"Come on, come on." He paced the tonsured top of Knowth's flattened dome in tight circles. "I'm here, so I am."

The wind whispered with the sigh of a million blades of tall grass, and he was no longer alone.

"How is my most recalcitrant subject?" a young male voice asked politely.

Angus stiffened, reluctant to turn around. Not that he needed to identify the speaker. There was no mistaking that arrogance.

Once upon a time, Manann had been a foreigner in need of a friend. Then a brother-in-arms, before becoming a brother-in-law. *Crom Cruach, Cenn Cruach, Crom Dubh*...Manann had many variations to his title, but Lord of the Hallowed Hills was his favored interpretation. Although, with his talents for scything both crops and men, *cruach* was an easy word to slur into bloodshed. Breda always gave it that inflection, thus making Manann the Lord of the Dead.

"I was expecting my sister," Angus said. "Why are you here in her domain?"

"Why should I not be on my Lady's land attending to the demands of our people? No matter how low and insignificant they might be, I am always at their service. Your need cried out across the miles between us—"

"Save the sermon. I was sent for."

"Indeed," the voice purred. "And you came as you were bid, did you not?"

Angus spoke through his teeth. "As I live and breathe and you do not, I owe you no true allegiance. I came as courtesy to my sister."

"Your sister and I released you from your tomb and restored you to flesh and blood. Such largesse does not come without expectations, and you are not meeting ours."

"I've had a bad day."

"Nor is it yet over."

The threat was so urbane, so understated, Angus turned to face his visitor.

Being spring, the Lord of the Dead was in his green and callow phase: a youth in his mid-teens with his body stretched and gangly, as if coming out of a recent growth spurt. He had a bad case of acne, and his hair was a curly blond mess, a haystack stuffed into his over-sized gray hoodic.

Manann hadn't been kept in the dark, out of sight and out of his mind. Reminding Angus of this was one of His Lordship's smaller pleasures. He might look young, but his eyes betrayed him. Old and hard, they shone gemstone bright: one emerald, one topaz.

Angus avoided staring into those eyes for too long. He stared instead across the valley to where Newgrange rose along the horizon, then over to where Dowth hunkered. The latter might not be open to the public, but one of its two passages still collected the light of the midwinter sunset. The rising sun against the setting—making him and Manann matched in power, if not in rank.

"You had one task, young Angus, and one task alone: use Newgrange to grant new life to the *Tuatha Dé Danann*."

"I vowed to lead our people, not grant them new life," Angus corrected. "What they have become cannot be led save in a hunt."

"Ah, but rather than call forth the hunt to avenge them, you called for your ex-wife to be culled.

Loneliness blighted her love, but the grief of our enemies kept her fed for the centuries she endured without you."

"Unlike Caer, I have no stomach for revenge long past its time to expire."

"So, you are turned traitor then."

A statement, not a question.

Angus stood straight-backed, eyes to the horizon, refusing to be bated. "My father forbade the destruction of our neighbor's livelihoods. I choose to uphold that law."

"You choose? A tool has no say how it is wielded, son of the *Dagda,* and make no mistake—you exist to be used."

"Do your own dirty work."

"That was not our arrangement, Oath Breaker." Manann leaned forward and tapped him on the chest at the very center of the trispiral brand. The insubstantial finger passed through cloth and flesh to pierce Angus' heart like a stiletto.

The world grayed.

Sucking in a ragged breath, Angus drew on Newgrange, and color returned to his vision as the pain in his chest faded.

"You begged for your wife to be saved and your sister spared," Manann continued—as though he hadn't made his point perfectly clear. "In exchange for this, I became your Chieftain and, as such, you will obey me, *Óenghus Óg.*"

"I no longer answer to that name."

"Do you not?" His Chief raised a crooked eyebrow. "Ah, yes. You call yourself by a new name. One written for others to read. And because it is written, you believe it has the power to change who you are—when it is merely a paper mask. I know you of old, and yesterday's exercise with my foolish young buck proved your nature has not changed—although you have it buried." His voiced deepened and became a command. "Remember, *Óenghus Óg, how you were when I put you into the earth.*"

Angus rolled from the balls of his feet to his heels to take the hit as the jagged shard of memory sliced through him and cut away the present.

****

The fields beyond *Óenghus* were green, but the soil beneath him was red. Red and damp and pungent with death. The smell surrounded him, seeping into his skin the way it soaked into the earth. He had slain the stag in its prime, his arrow catching its throat in the fullness of its glory.

*Óenghus* had spared the doe the stag had been servicing in the hope she would breed.

Once the beast was flayed, he draped the dripping hide over his shoulders. The stag's antlers were tied to his head. Henceforth, they would be as one. Its death serving his new life with stamina and fertility.

Around him, his kin stood in desperate stillness. They watched him, the remnants of his people. The rest had fled with the last of their elders to the four other provinces, taking their chances where they could in the many hollow hills scattered across the land.

Within the fifth province, the royal and sacred province of *Míde*, they left their hopes for the future under the fosterage of the royal house. Less than forty children, all below puberty, and unable to bond to the land on their own. Tears tracked down *Óenghus'* face as he gazed over rounded cheeks and chubby limbs. So few.

So young. So trusting.

Befuddled from the concoction of toxic plants steeped in honey-wine, he swayed, his balance wavering along with his vision. He should be numb after drinking such a volume. Yet his heart was so empty. How could he return the light to his people when his soul was so dark?

The silent crowd took on a watery transparency as Breda led him to the Womb's Entrance with its elaborate trispiral. Though one of his father's many children, he had been *Bóann's* only birth. Natural then, for him to be chosen to be the one born again from this, her earthen belly.

Goatskin drums beat a frenzied rhythm as the oldest woman of the tribe, the crone responsible for the rites of death and rebirth, enacted the charm to bind him forevermore to the animal of his spirit. She stroked and toyed until the stag's strength thundered through his veins and he thrust out his cock, thick and charged, straining to complete the beast's final act.

Manann stepped forward then, an ember glow reflected in his eyes from the brand he held aloft, ready to send *Óenghus* into the earth.

\*\*\*\*

The crackle and smoke of his own skin searing lingered in his nostrils as Angus returned to himself. Despite the fact he'd probably worn his modern clothes the whole time, they felt tight and strange. He touched his torc. The weight of the thick collar of gold around his neck never left him, though it was no longer visible. A legacy the same as the fertility ritual he'd undertaken—an invisible fact of his existence.

Twenty-seven hundred years ago, breeding their

way back from the brink of extinction had seemed a sensible approach. Times had changed. He could not.

Failure had a price, and he was here to pay.

Chapter Eleven

A Gaze Blank and Pitiless

"I see you recall at last." Manann smiled without a trace of humor. "Perhaps you also care, but you chose not to act. You chose to keep our children corralled, to deny our future their chance at freedom."

"You kept me imprisoned for nearly three thousand years through invasion, famine and war, while you roamed free," Angus returned. "The *Tuatha Dé Danann* faded centuries before my release if what our neighbors told me is true. The blame does not lie with me."

Manann spread his hands. "Shall I offer excuses? Our enemies' descendants feared us so greatly they left our sacred sites alone far longer than I anticipated. My Lady and I both tried, in separate attempts, to influence events. It was exhausting, even in spirit. But once Newgrange regained the light your time had come at long last. Even so, it took *decades* to find a woman desperate enough to beg my bride for a child—and to pay the price I demanded."

Each revelation was another stab to his heart. Angus clamped his jaw to resist asking how Marie had paid. It could only be Marie. And what a son she'd received, full grown and from another time. How disappointed she must be.

Meanwhile, Manann's air of boredom had been

replaced by a withering scorn.

"Now our savior has come, yet you refused to use your domain for our restoration. Hundreds of thousands of people attend Newgrange each year and you choose to transform their fear of the dark instead of scraping a few days from each of their lives—a little sacrifice they would not notice."

Manann recovered his poise. "Until last night, you refused to draw on your power. Your darling Caer keened for the loss of you as she eked out an existence, waiting for your return and taking her revenge on your enemies as a cat deposits mice on doorsteps. And look how you reward her loyalty—by choosing to love our enemy."

Angus would never forgive himself for letting Caer survive on the dregs of his regard, but he could do nothing more for her now. Not after giving Erin the kiss of life—and his heart. He locked down his expression. "The woman I loved in my other life was not a killer. She would have loathed what she has become—what you made her into."

"How am I to blame if you moved on from youthful follies and she did not? Swans mate for life. As you may now recall, however, that was never *your* true nature."

"Threaten me as you will, *Manannán*, son of Lir." While he remained bound to Newgrange, Angus could hold his own ground. To protect Erin, he must.

"Very well, since you ask it of me, I shall." His Chief looked sorrowful. "You try to be so terribly noble, which is why it pains me to tell you your conscience is no longer required."

Angus narrowed his eyes, guessing where this was going although it was not an angle he'd expected. "You mean to transform me into a beast as punishment."

He almost made it a question, because the logic of *why* escaped him. How could it serve Manann to add him to his herd? Without access to Newgrange, Angus would eventually become a beast. Ignoble, but the suffering would be minimal—and there was the rub.

"No, dear boy. My new task for you requires your own form to remain very much intact. It is time you used the gift you were granted. I require changelings. Two-score, in fact. You shall sire them for me. Set your nature free and become as your father, bedding the many women who desire you to do so."

Straightening his spine, Angus looked the other man into his old, cold eyes. "My nature, as you put it, is *mine*. You may have called it forth, but I remain in command of myself." With every word, he realized his spoken denial must be the plain truth. "If it were midwinter you *might* have the power. Inside summer's half of the year, my strength waxes as yours wanes."

Manann stood firm, his gaze pitiless. "A heart shared is a heart divided. I have the power and I swear you will be in rut from the Autumn Equinox until *Samhain*. Each babe you conceive will be replaced with one of our young. We have thirty-seven lost in limbo and I will not abandon a single one of them. Not again. They are your *kin, Óenghus Óg,* and you have betrayed their faith in you. You should thank me for forcing you to honor your vow."

Angus raised an eyebrow. Manann was bluffing. Best to leave now rather than engage in a pissing contest. He shoved his hands into his pockets and turned to walk off.

"No half-hearted measures, *Óenghus Óg.*

Remember, you have someone to lose."

The threat to Erin had Angus spinning on his heel, his temper flaring like a lit match. He thrust his hands out to grab that scrawny neck, intending to shake the fatuous young man like the puppy he was…only to have his thumbs pass through his Chief's windpipe. The other man had no physical form. He was a shade—having never died he was more alive than a ghost, but just as untouchable.

How foolish to forget.

"Ah *Óenghus Óg*, I pity you." Manann shook his head, as doleful as a hanging judge despite the laughter-tears. "So much passion and so little thought. I can squeeze the heart you gave her into dust at any time."

Almost idly, he centered his palm over the bandage Erin had taped. Angus couldn't touch *him*, but death touched everyone, and the Lord of the Dead's hand was heavy with time. It could suck in life and siphon strength, congeal blood, and stop its flow, draw flesh gossamer thin and brittle bones until nothing remained but dust and despair. Dark spots scudded across Angus' vision as the pressure on his chest increased.

This was how Manann had installed *Óenghus Óg* within Newgrange.

This was how he could reach Erin.

Angus didn't fear death for himself, but he would do anything, *anything* to protect his heart. It was the nature of his gift. It was why Manann had so eloquently discussed Caer.

"I will make *Liz* leave," Angus swore between gasps as he fought the growing darkness with light…and the very passion his lordship despised. "You cannot harm her if she leaves this land."

"Really, you two!" a female voice scolded. The bracing chill of Breda's presence was as unmistakable as her trademark tang of smelted bronze and cut rowan.

The force Manann exerted on his chest doubled as her arrival increased his strength.

Shaking with the effort of resisting, Angus sank to his knees.

"Enough, my *Crom Cruach*," she snapped. "Let him go."

The pressure on his chest eased and became a dull, fading ache. Soft laughter echoed around him as the Lord of the Dead departed.

Angus raised his eyes.

Beneath the green, patchwork cloak—the symbol of her rank, she wore a flowing ivory dress with a high frilly collar. In their time before, her hair had been a flame-bright orange, untamable mess of curls. No longer. Bound by a leather thong, it had become a true red—rich and dark as old blood—as it trailed down one shoulder, not a corkscrew to be seen. Creamy, flawless skin replaced her former splatter of freckles.

Once his younger sister, she could pass for five years his elder. After seven years, he should be used to her new age, but he could never reconcile how she'd changed from a teenager to a mature woman while he'd been sleeping. Trapped in spirit form, she should have remained the searingly intelligent girl whose outlandish ideas were as wild as her hair.

"Should I stay on my knees and beg for the vegetarian option you once proposed?" he asked her waist.

She looked down her long nose at him with pale green eyes, clear as fresh water. "Our kin are beyond

136

offerings of milk and honey and oat mash. You have withheld the light promised to them for too long."

"Don't let him do this to me. Stop him."

"I don't see why you baulk at the deed when every single woman will thank you for the pleasure. We freed you seven winters ago. You could have taken half a dozen women or more each year. Instead, you didn't act, you wallowed." She spread her hands. "A few a year or all in one batch. The result is the same in the end. I don't see why you complain: this is a duty you'll enjoy."

Duty. His duty to their father had broken him before. This would break him again.

"I would slit my throat before forcing a single woman—even if she *thought* she was willing." Angus fisted his hands, wishing he could shake some sense into his sister. "You can't romanticize a rapist into a fairy lover, Bree." She flinched, and he pressed home his advantage, his tone flat. "As for fathering changelings, what sort of people would our kin become if babes must die for them to live?"

"No child will die. Their souls can be reborn. Ours cannot. They have been lost too long to make such a journey."

Hard to believe she'd once been the soul of compassion, but she'd existed too long, untouchable and unfeeling, to remember genuine emotion. Just like her Chief.

"You're siding with him." Gorge rose in his throat. "Several millennia to plot and scheme and this is your solution?" He shook his head. "I've had seven years living in this world, reliant upon those Manann considers our enemies, and they do not deserve this."

"We cannot allow you to forsake your duty just

because you would prefer to forget your past."

"Forget?" Angus returned to his feet, the better to loom. "What happened feels like *yesterday* to me. And yet I can forgive those who played no part in our fate save to inherit what their ancestors took."

"And so, after drinking yourself senseless, you betray your kin and destroy our hopes by wedding the O'Neill girl in front of witnesses with the Sight?"

"Caer shredded her soul, Bree. On my watch in a territory I defended."

"Which justifies your decision?"

"I was no more going to restore a crazed killer with my heart than I'd offer it to you. I thought we had that long established, my sweet sister. If anything, I'd expect you to be grateful you're spared the trauma of me marrying you."

"It would be a trauma for you, too."

She turned from him to look toward Newgrange. The rear of his monument, lacking the white quartz façade, could have been an ordinary hill.

He shook his head though she couldn't see. "Not once you Chose me. You forget I held our father in my arms, covered in his blood. I know *exactly* how much he continued to love my mother even after she called for his death."

"You shared your weak and broken heart with a dead woman. How can I explain what you've done so you understand?"

Breda's voice licked at him with the low, intense heat of a furnace, each word a flame. As if he didn't know he'd restored Erin to life by usurping rights that were not his and abdicated his responsibility to his kin by giving his heart.

"Perhaps use small words when you tell me."

"Telling you teaches you nothing! I once thought as you did. To bridge our peoples, I saved a soul. The price I asked was so small: to be a friend to one in need. It proved too much to ask of an enemy. If you do not fulfill our Lord's task, then he will use my act of mercy to betray us both, you thick-headed, noble-hearted fool."

Her posture straightened and her expression grew distant, as it did when she drew on her authority as the Lady of the Land, the *Bantiarná na hÉireann.* "I grant you until summer's peak to guide your people into the light and restore them to flesh, *Óenghus Óg* who some call Angus McCraggan. Should you fail in the attempt, *or attempt to fail*, then my Chief's curse will fall on you in full."

In the driest possible manner, she added, "We cannot wait, brother-mine. Should you continue to do nothing, I will have to take over your heart and make you."

She didn't wait for his response. She vanished.

For a long while, Angus stayed frozen in place.

She'd shortened his deadline to midsummer, removed his ability to fudge his fate, and added the impossible: restore them to flesh. All because someone made a poor friend?

Roused by the lengthening shadows, he strode back to the first steel he'd ever worked—his motorbike. He ran a loving hand over the insectoid green-and-yellow of its chassis. A 1974 model Z1 Kawasaki, he'd rebuilt it to mint condition from near scrap under Jim's guidance.

Whether he could restore his people from their wreckage was another matter.

Again and again, he'd failed in his attempts to

reclaim his wife from the banshee she'd become—he'd tried talking, singing, begging. Nothing worked. The closest she'd ever come to words had been last night when he'd fought her off Erin. The Caer he'd known had dreamed of creating new life, not taking one.

The rest of the *Tuatha Dé Danann* within the bend in the Boyne were no better. They fought him at any opportunity with every tooth, claw, and beak they possessed. Which reminded him—night was falling, and he was weak.

His kin could wait. First, he must find Erin and warn her away.

Astride his bike, he gunned the engine, flicked on the lights—only to skid to a stop on the hard shoulder when within range of his own domain. Putting his hand on his heart, he tried to gain some sense of where she might be. He could hear an echo to his heartbeat, pounding regularly, but he had no sense of direction or distance.

He couldn't seek her.

For the first time he understood Caer's propensity to wail, because he wanted to bellow his frustration. Had he *her* heart, he could find her in an instant—exactly as he'd known Caer from a hundred swans on a faraway lake. But Erin held his. She could summon him; he could not summon her.

Thanks to Marie, he had a lead. Erin was an O'Neill. True, she hadn't admitted to the connection—indeed, she'd gone to some lengths to conceal it. He didn't care why. Her safety was paramount. He would do whatever it took to put her beyond Manann's reach.

Chapter Twelve

Innocence Drowned

"What on earth possessed you to come back here?"

Annabel's question jolted Erin's attention away from the stout wooden pub door. Facing it from the inside should have been a relief. No curling mists, no banshee clawing, no heated kisses on the threshold between this world and the next.

Focusing on her onetime bestie brought no relief from thinking of Angus. With big kohl-ringed eyes, big hoop earrings, and a big mop of black hair, Annabel looked ready to predict there was a tall, dark stranger in Erin's future.

Erin tried to smile. "It was your idea." Coming here so soon after last night's trauma was a mistake, but after her fight with Granddad she'd needed *out*. "You said it'd be dead quiet, since the *craic* last night was so mighty."

"It's a shame you missed it. The *craic* last night was beyond epic—we were dancing the Can-Can on these." Annabel slapped her palm down on the table. "But I wasn't asking about *here* here, I meant Ireland. Because, you know, New York. Why leave a place everyone else wants to go to?"

"A few reasons." Erin ticked them off on her fingers. "The veterinary course I'll be going to here has placements with the National Stud, my granddad isn't getting younger, and…" With an effort, she kept her eyes on her friend. "Closure stuff."

"It's hugely brave of you, after your Da…" Annabel looked away. "Anyway, so, the National Stud. Good to hear your passion for ponies survived the Big Apple."

Horses had been a shared obsession.

"You still competing?" Erin asked.

"A bad fall last winter left me a little delicate." Annabel supported this statement with a shoulder roll and a wince. "That, and Mam roping me into the family catering business. I'm supposed to be working on my Masters thesis, not pouring lattes, but Mam needs the help so…" She spread her hands in a 'what-can-you-do?' gesture. "It's a good thing you're here. Calcifer could use the exercise. He's supposed to be a hunter and he wouldn't clear a wall he's getting so fat. If you could take him out on a hack every now and then, I'd be hugely grateful. It'd be the same deal as before: just text me and go."

Her friendship had always come with a bonus.

Erin wriggled uncomfortably. This time around, she would give as much as she received. "I'd be glad to put him through his paces if it takes some pressure off your studies. Tell me about this thesis."

"It's on Post-purchase Cognitive Dissonance. I won't strain our friendship by boring you with the details. Basically, I'm exploring the nasty feeling you get when you buy something big before the joys of ownership kick in."

Erin resisted the urge to press her fist to her heart where she had her proof-of-purchase. "What makes it nasty?"

"Oh, there's a list. Everything from the opportunity

lost to spend your money on something else, to feeling tied down to repayments. Emotional stuff with long-term implications, like buying a house, tend to be the worst."

It parsed Erin's anxiety in a nutshell. Unless Angus wanted his death on her conscience, he was a lifelong commitment, not just a summer fling, and she simply couldn't deal with the implications.

"How do you get over the feeling?"

"Here's the funny thing. Ownership creates its own value. Once you accept something as yours, you find reasons why you made the right choice."

Not the answer she'd hoped for.

"It sounds like psychology. I thought you were studying Economics."

"Behavioral Economics," Annabel corrected with the false lightness of someone used to losing her audience, "is a mix of both. It should give me an edge when it comes to landing a job in the International Financial Services Center. That's my dream. What about you?"

Erin forced a grin. "To have you, with your multi-millions, employ me to take care of your stock of thoroughbreds, obviously."

"Cheers to that!" Her friend raised her glass in approval of the foregone conclusion she'd be a success, while Erin stared into her soda.

"Do you think we'd still have become friends if you hadn't had horses I could ride?"

Annabel gave an exasperated huff. "Of course! No one else but you was half as mad about horses as me. We'd have pined after a pony of our own together. We were thick as thieves right from Junior Infants until…" Her chatter slowed as the inevitable hurdle of Erin's dad and her subsequent departure overseas loomed. "Well, you know yourself what happened."

"Funny thing is, I don't. Know what happened, that is. The time around the accident is one big blur."

She tried to cast her mind back and hit the same old wall: the one she'd wrenched the steering wheel to miss. Sweet tea with Granddad and the incident with Breda was her other clear memory between hearing the banshee scream and waking up on a flight halfway across the Atlantic.

Annabel put a consoling hand on her wrist. "It's all in the past. Why not buy a stud ranch of your own? I thought your stepdad was loaded."

"Oh, he's loaded all right. Loaded, plastic and shallow. He's the complete opposite to my father, which is why we don't get along."

Cradling her pint, her friend sat back. "How's your mother?"

"I can't be sure, because there are muscles in her face that haven't moved in five years thanks to all the Botox, but I think Mom is happy. She was against me coming back here, but Dan talked her round and paid to get me out of his artificially thickened hair."

Mom had excised her first husband from her life with ruthless efficiency: changing countries, her name, and her values. As a child, Erin had been relabeled against her will. With the one constant left of her old life being Mom, it had made sense to land the blame on her stepfather. Poor Dan. There was no competing with a father who'd loved his daughter more than his own life.

*It was my gift to give.*

Some luck a second man offered the same—the kind of luck she could do without. She gave herself a mental shake. No, she had that wrong. It was the kind of luck, this time, she *could* do something about. Unlike her father, Angus was alive. If she learned to accept this, he could stay that way.

She looked over to where he'd first kissed her, her fingers drifting to her lips. She'd done nothing to deserve his heart except show up at the right place at the wrong time. That could change. She could change. For the better this time, not for worse.

Annabel propped her chin on her palm. "Expecting someone to join us?"

Erin dropped her hand, her cheeks burning. "I'm kind of hoping…not?" She didn't mean it to come out as a question, as though she was conflicted when she wasn't. She wanted to see Angus again, the banshee not so much. Wild creatures were at their most dangerous when wounded. Without any defenses of her own, she had to trust Angus was right and the banshee wouldn't return. "Anyhow, I'm here to see you, not him."

Annabel raised her pint glass and peered through the cider at her with a jaundiced eye. "I'm flattered, but not fooled. Your man has your head turned. Literally toward the door. Can't say I'm surprised you want to see him again, he's only gorgeous."

"He has the most adorable dimples when he remembers to smile." Gorgeous wasn't the half of it. Passionate and tender, honest and proud: he was the whole package. "Something I said made him laugh, and it was like Christmas came early."

Annabel plonked down her cider and leaned forward, eyes agleam. "I knew fainting was a genius move to get up close and personal."

"Collapsing into a guy's arms isn't usually my go-to introduction strategy."

Four years as a student in New York City taught a girl street smarts and self-reliance, not passing out in public bars.

"Vomiting isn't my preferred loyalty test either, but I'm led to believe a guy is into you if he stays and risks contamination rather than legging it when you're sick."

There was an implied question in Annabel's comment, and, with some guilt, Erin recalled her stomach flu text and how her friend's reply had reversed who rescued whom.

"He, uh, went to a lot of effort to make me," her voice caught, "breakfast."

Something must have shown in her expression because Annabel choked on a mouthful of cider. "Are you telling me you got the full Irish?"

The full Irish was a pan-fried breakfast traditionally served with sausages, bacon, and slices of both black and white pudding. Erin's brain jammed between the meat-heavy meal and the man.

"Uh." She stalled, unable to articulate what he'd cooked other than her ability to think. "Not exactly, but it was hot. I mean, the food was hot. Not that Angus isn't also incredibly hot, because he totally is, he's just got some old-fashioned ideals over commitment."

God, she was flustered, which was weird because talking about sex never usually bothered her. It had to be all these emotions. When she'd lived in fear, the world had seemed so black and white. It was strange having a full spectrum of feelings.

Annabel narrowed her eyes. "When you say commitment…"

"He's talking marriage." Erin stuck on a grin. "I

know, sudden, right?"

She grabbed her cola and sipped slowly to cool her head.

"How can you get to marriage in under twenty-four hours? Jesus, Erin, it's obvious what he wants from you is a green card." Erin nearly sprayed her drink over the table, but her friend wasn't done. "I wasn't going to say anything because there's never been a shred of evidence. The rumors are, though, that your man escaped from some messianic cult before Marie Maguire took him under her wing. How do you know you aren't being brainwashed?"

It was a valid point and nothing she hadn't said herself, yet it put her on the defensive.

"We have this connection…" There was no explaining how she possessed the heart of a god, not to someone who undoubtedly believed the *Tuatha Dé Danann* to be fairy stories. "It's complicated."

"I'll bet."

"It's not what you think." She picked up a paper beer coaster to toy with. Hopefully, Annabel had some clue how difficult this was for her, how much trust she was putting in a friendship abandoned eight years ago. "Did you go to my father's funeral?"

Annabel nodded her face puzzled but sympathetic.

Erin folded the coaster into halves, then halves again. "Was I there? Mom said I went, but she couldn't give any evidence to prove I did."

"It wasn't the sort of event where people took photos," her friend said in an odd tone.

"I can't remember any of it. Not the church or the service or the burial. Nothing."

"In fairness, you weren't yourself."

If she wasn't herself, it begged an important question. *Who was I?*

"What was I like?" she whispered, folding the coaster again and again until it began to split.

Annabel looked stricken, but she replied levelly enough. "I nearly didn't recognize you. You were so plastered with foundation. Mam told me it was to…hide the bruises, because of the rocks and because you'd…struggled to stop him, which was why your fingers were bandaged since you'd torn your nails."

*Scratched and torn…*

"What do you mean *him*?"

Her friend couldn't meet her eyes.

"What happened was an *accident*. The air-brakes went on the truck."

"Erin, half the village heard the brakes screech the whole way down the hill."

"You weren't there." Her mouth operated on its own. "Nobody knows what happened except me. I was frightened out of my mind. When Da tried to save me by pushing me out of the window, I panicked and lashed out. Getting free of the truck is what ruined my fingers."

The lies tripped out with conviction—she'd do anything to clear her father's name—but her folding of the beer coaster stalled. She looked down. The layered paper was ready to fall to pieces, barely held together by the printed green sheets on the front and back. From far away, she heard the words she'd just spoken.

*I was frightened out of my mind.*

Brainwashed. But not by Angus. By his wife.

With a trembling finger, she dug a nail into the frayed corner of the coaster and peeled it back. The edges of old memories came unstuck like the beer coaster in

148

her hands.

Time to face what had happened after.

*After the hill. Before the water.*

\*\*\*\*

The truck careened down the final stretch of road before the ancient bridge.

Erin wanted to be sick. Her skin went cold and clammy. Her hands numbed. Air trickled from her lungs. Da didn't move. He couldn't. Nor could she. Together, they stared at their doom. The O'Neill banshee. Real. Here. Wailing for them both. Or was she?

The banshee's icy eyes stayed locked on Erin. Her head tilted then her beaked mouth spread into an unholy grin. That proved her sole warning. Lightning fast, she dove into the cab and ripped into Erin's skull.

Darkness flooded her vision. She clawed at her face to gouge out the intruder. But the sting of her nails didn't go deep enough. Her brain crackled with memories not her own: murders in a string like fairy lights. Countless, indistinguishable years like lengths of tinsel. And one bright star shining in its singular sanity: reuniting with the beautiful boy she'd lost.

*Óenghus.*

Draped across his harp, shoulders rocking as he laughed over something she'd said. His arms around her, his embrace strong and safe, while they slid the tips of their noses together. The heat in his gaze when he watched her as she spread her legs and circled the wet heat between her thighs with her fingers. If he reached for her, she left his dreams. Or had, before he'd rescued her. Once she'd given him her heart, she'd grown braver.

Brave enough to kill for him.

*Not me. This is not me.*

Erin's consciousness stretched thinner than spider thread, leaving her aware but helpless.

"Take me," Da begged, leaning across the cab to grab her shoulders. "Spare her and take me."

"Liammmm O'Neill," the banshee screamed with Erin's voice. She raked his throat with her blood-strained nails. His eyes bulged. Mm, yes. She'd feast well tonight. *No. I won't.*

The truck punched through the low stones wall of the bridge like it was made of peanut brittle. Metal crunched. The world shook. White exploded across the dash. Erin slammed into the air bags face first. She coughed powder as the truck teetered then slithered off the bridge to fall like a slain beast into the river.

She awoke to the click of her seatbelt releasing. Hard hands around her wrists. A wrench as Da dragged her across his warmth. Water gushed in through his open window. He pushed her against the flow. Beyond the cab, everything was dark and cold. Far above, light glimmered.

Hope surged. *We can make it.*

The banshee wove her fingers into Da's shirt. For a fleeting moment, his hand covered hers. She drew in, found his mouth, and sucked the last bubbles of his air along with his soul. *Stop. Don't. You're killing him. Da, I'm sorry. This isn't me. I swear it isn't me.*

\*\*\*\*

The bubbles were still there, rising inside her throat.

"Excuse me." Erin pushed free of her chair. "I've gotta go to the bathroom…"

She staggered around the tables to pinball her way to the Ladies room. She reached the sink just in time retch a thin brown liquid into the basin. It looked alarmingly like river water.

Using cold water from the faucet, she splashed her sweating face.

*It wasn't me. I didn't kill him. He knew it wasn't me.*

Da had forgiven her. He'd called his sacrifice a gift. The tightness in her shoulders eased.

*Can I forgive myself?*

To heal, she had to face the truth. All of it.

She'd been possessed. No denying it. But she'd done so for years. Blamed herself at some deep level for causing Da's death. Doubted who she was and what memories were hers for years after leaving Ireland.

Everything she'd made herself into came from the uncertainty of knowing where she'd ended and the banshee began. The detachment, the lying, the personas, everything including her need to help the voiceless was the direct result of being possessed. She'd craved connection and feared it, forgetting the details of why, just as she'd used physical pleasure to replace the fragmented memories of a thousand kisses and a million caresses from a boy she'd never met.

She'd justified her need to return because Da was buried here, because Mom had whipped her out the country so fast her head had never stopped spinning, because she'd needed to see with the calm, rational eyes of an adult that her teenage self hadn't invented a banshee to blame.

At some level she'd known the real reason.

*You won't be able to dream of any man but me.*

She'd gone straight to Newgrange to find him. Had known him the moment he smiled. Older. Sadder. But still the boy of her tormented, teenaged dreams.

The boy she'd fallen in love with.

*I need to tell him everything.*

He trusted her with his life, it was only fair to trust him with her past. To explain how, in a sick sort of karma, the banshee had taken one man from her and given her another. The same act had sowed the seeds of Erin's revenge. All she had to do was let Angus love her. Let him woo her. Learn to let him in.

She reached up to her reflection. *Tell me I'm not crazy to think we stand a chance.*

In the mirror, the notched scar on her temple she'd gained the day she met Breda caught the light like a flame. Erin's breath fluttered.

A mark, certainly, but of premeditation not protection.

*His wife has become a creature he can never love…*

Caught between forms, Caer wasn't human. Or physically real. That was why she'd tried to take over a new body. One the right age. The right gender.

*This one is not for you.*

Breda had cast Caer out and let Erin live. For the time being. But she played a long game. One where she'd set up Granddad to mind Angus and tagged Erin for future reference. A vessel ready to be hollowed and refilled, like a living Trojan horse: outwardly one person, inwardly another. Thanks to the banshee, Breda had a way around her brother's issues with becoming Chief while also keeping her promise to Erin's grandfather.

Erin was never meant to have Angus while in her right mind. Clawing her fingers, she scraped down the face in the mirror.

*What if I'm a trap?*

She shuddered an exhale. All the more reason to tell him the truth.

"I refuse to be afraid of my feelings," she told her likeness.

"Those feelings aren't yours," her reflection returned.

"I know." She rested her forehead on the cool, hardness of the glass. "But since they belong to me, maybe I can own them."

Chapter Thirteen

Rue with a Difference

When Angus went to Marie's for their monthly Sunday dinner, she insisted he enter her house by the back door. The front door was for strangers or special guests, she'd explained. He was neither to Jim, but he pressed the bell for the front door all the same, because he'd never been invited inside his landlord's home. Nothing personal. Jim was simply not the most sociable of men.

Nevertheless, Angus dragged a hand through his hair and wished he'd brought a peace offering to counter the upset he was about to create.

Footsteps echoed down the hallway as a blurred figure neared the dappled glass of the door. "Ah, Maureen-girl, you've seen sense! I have your key, right here, for—" The door opened. "*You.*"

"Jim." Angus dipped his head to the man who, in days gone by, would be the clan chief to this branch of the O'Neill's. The older man's eyes were wild and his color high. He seemed distraught. "Isn't Maureen the name of your late wife?"

"It is, and it's on her grave, I'll be cursing you."

"Curse me?" Surprise rolling through him, Angus set his weight onto his heels. "Why would you curse me?"

"For enchanting my granddaughter."

"Enchanting? If you mean saving her from the banshee—"

"I have your sister's pledge my granddaughter is safe from your *wife*."

"My sister pledged you safe-keeping for Erin?" Angus furrowed his brows. "My *ex*-wife will threaten your family no more. Last night I spurned her. There is no hope for her now, I belong to another. Should she have the strength to return from wherever it is she goes, it will be to die."

"You don't fool me, young Angus, making yourself out to be the hero. My granddaughter was never at risk. Your Lady promised me years ago, and she keeps her word. She, I trust. You, I do not. Never have. And wise I was not to do so, when you repay the years I spent in helping you fit in, teaching you skills, and providing you a home by betraying me with my own flesh and blood."

Every word his landlord uttered was a hailstone that ricocheted through Angus' chest, leaving icy trails within his lungs. Where had this come from? Someone from the pub must have misinterpreted what they'd seen, much as Marie had, and misinformed the old man.

Angus opened his mouth to object he was no threat to Erin and couldn't say the words, because he *was* a threat to his beloved. Manann could reach her through him. Precisely why he needed Jim to be his ally in protecting Erin, not his enemy.

Recovering, he tried to explain. "Caer attacked Erin last night. Breda made no intervention. I did. For the sake of your granddaughter, I have betrayed my kin. My Chief has demanded I make reparation. My Lady supports him. And so, I have come to you."

"You've come for me?"

Jim's eyes widened wide enough for white to rim his irises as he stepped back to take refuge deeper within his doorway. A home was a sacred space, and one did not cross the threshold unless invited. Cars were much the same. Angus couldn't get in one belonging to another person unless expressly invited. Jim knew this because he'd been with Angus those frightening early days when nothing made sense, and everything moved too fast.

To have him seek such protection could only mean his landlord was afraid. Of him. Did Jim see more than the beast within? The best of hunters thought like their prey, and Angus had hunted both men and meat.

Unclenching his fists, he eased his stance and tried to make himself less threatening. But Manann had ruled he couldn't hide his nature and now it showed.

"You must know I'd not harm you, Jim. And I'd sooner die than harm Erin."

"Sooner die?" The old man scoffed from his haven. "Sooner seduce, you mean."

"I can't deny I want her." He kept his voice low and his temper leashed. "That is why I need her to leave. To keep her safe. From me. Before this summer ends, my Lord and Lady will make me a beast with the face of a man."

Manann's game plan unfurled in his mind. Forty women, minimum. Only a God of Love could woo so many and yet keep them close enough for Breda, as a patron of midwifery, to ensure they delivered their changelings safely.

Erin would be his first and the rest would follow.

Jim looked unimpressed. "All men who become monsters blame someone else. I know what you are and why you need her to live."

"You do?"

"A parasite needs its host to survive. When your wife couldn't take the last of my line, my only son's only child, your revenge is to make my granddaughter yours."

"A parasite? Like a tick or a flea or a leech? I have no taste for blood, Jim."

"Not blood. Life. A fairy lover who steals the soul from those he lures into sin."

"Ah." Angus nodded. "You mean a *leanán sí.*"

It was almost funny because he could have become such a creature. Had his situation with Caer been reversed—her in the earth, him stranded yet forever bound because she held his heart. In that scenario, false love and the joy of sex would have been his meal tickets to eke out an existence.

"I always knew you were biding your time," Jim continued. "But why now? Why her?"

This must be the real reason why Marie and Jim clashed—and her frequent anxiety over the women who wanted a private tour. Marie believed his heart was in the right place, Jim did not. Well, then. Not a friend, but still an ally when it came to Erin.

The truth was a weapon he could wield with his landlord. He would use it to cut the ties between them. Anything to shield his beloved.

"Why Erin? Because she is the last of the O'Neills, and she came within Caer's reach. As for me, I told you I want her. Only her. I would accept her heart in an instant and treasure it forever. But I am required to sire my people's future. You could have saved your breath in wishing me cursed. I already am. I will love only her, yet I am expected to impregnate every woman who lets me."

He closed his eyes as the full magnitude of what Manann and Breda proposed sleeted through him. To consciously and carefully select and support every woman who wanted him, breaking his heart piece by piece over the summer months by betraying Erin and himself in a drip feed.

Or being cursed in full.

As a beast with the face and guile of a man, he'd be indiscriminate. Any woman able to breed would be fair game. Stags gave up everything, even food, to mate. Prior to the rut, they rounded up their harem, enticing the does to stay close, and fighting all challengers.

Soul-bound to Newgrange, he had daily access to hundreds of women and the means to make them crave him. A cult would form around his parody of a love god. Those who tried to take his women, he would fight—and he was a warrior, trained to kill.

No wonder Caer had lost her mind. He'd be no saner.

As his guts churned and his gorge rose, he stared blindly at the other man.

"And I will do it, Jim," he choked through bile, hating himself already. "I'll take them all, because I'll do whatever my Chief demands if it keeps Erin free of him. So, if you love her, you must either make her hate me enough to break my heart or make her leave."

Dizzily, he retreated to his bike. The cool metal centered him enough to face his mentor. The man he'd considered his modern father figure. The man who'd always seen the monster hidden inside.

"Consider this warning to you as reparation for your many kindnesses to me." His mouth twisted. "And revenge for making me unable to lie, even to myself."

He left. The rush of cold air through his open helmet cleared his nausea. He didn't travel far. Rather than return home, he went to where he belonged.

The summit of Newgrange was barred to the public. Barred to the guides, too. The maintenance crew were the only ones allowed to climb the mound and only when they needed to cut the grass. With a grunt of effort, Angus pulled himself over the projecting concrete ledge up onto the mound. After scaling the slippery grassed slope, he edged toward the front, where the wall of white quartz met the grass. Hanging a leg over, he set his heel on one of the dark nubs of granite protruding from the wall like iron bosses on an old oak door. In such a manner, he made the whole of Newgrange his throne, to rule over his misery like a king.

Below him, invisible in the moon-dark night, the rushing waters of the Boyne sang him a lullaby. It was childish to hope his mother might watch over her son from within the river's waters and fruitless to think she might have any advice to offer. Yet, here he was, praying for divine inspiration because he couldn't bear to live cursed, but he had problems with dying.

The *how* of it escaped him.

Burning seemed best. Although he mustn't discount Breda's affinity for fire or her ability to heal. Perhaps casting himself into the ocean would do. But Manann came from the sea and held the powers of resurrection.

Dead, he'd cause no harm to the living. But dying, alas, was not the easy way out. It might take another thousand years, but eventually the Lord of the Dead would pull Angus' soul back from the brink and stuff it into whatever form he deemed fit to breed.

Angus threw himself backward onto the cool grass

and closed his eyes to the indifferent stars. If only he could somehow melt his flesh back into the earth beneath him, drain into the sand like water, and meld again with the stone of his prison. Limbs and organs would become dirt and rubble as his consciousness spread thin until he was aware, but not alive. He remembered it too well. Lost in a nightmare he could not wake from—a permanent hysteria rising through his phantom chest to lodge in his absent throat, unable to escape from lips that no longer existed, forever unable to scream.

Better to be trapped inside his own personal hell than harm another living soul.

Unfortunately, also not an option. The Lord of the Dead's power had pushed him into the stone as Manann and Breda's power had pulled him out. Along with whatever payment they'd extracted from Marie.

By the Goddess, Marie. Another heart broken.

If only he'd never been reborn into a time of so little faith. This was the age of smartphones, not miracles. Yet, removing his bond and forsaking his power was no solution—even if he knew how. Without Newgrange, he would become as Caer—caught in the ancient Celtic curse, unable to protect his love, too weak to counter his Chief.

If only he could fulfill his vow.

These past years, he'd chosen to see his kin as the creatures they'd become, creatures who had survived long past their due. His focus on Caer had blinded him to the fact that here, within the bend in the Boyne, his responsibility lay with children—innocents interred by the will of adults who wanted them to have a future, in the hope they would *have* a future.

A future he denied them, rather than pay at the

expense of the living.

Guilt was a rancid slime thick enough to choke on. Somehow, he must try to free his kin. Then he might save them all. If not…

*Six weeks before I destroy everything and everyone I love.*

\*\*\*\*

The summons from Erin came a few hours after midnight—the tug insistent, not urgent. The call drew him as relentlessly as the moon pulled the tides and had him winding through the medieval streets of Drogheda in tightening spirals inward to a single point. A nightclub. After parking the motorbike, he walked back to the venue, careful to stay within the patchy glow of the street lighting.

A bouncer blocked his entrance. Angus stared him down then added with the authority of a Chief's son, "I'm expected."

The bouncer stood aside.

Inside, the décor was modern with a nod to a layered past: glass and stainless steel, with walls stripped back to bare bricks. Angus stalked a circuit, scouting exits, hazards and behavior.

This place was terribly alien. The throbbing synthetic music was loud enough to lift the ceiling and the dance floor heaved with a mélange of movement of varying rhythms. The hot purple glow of artificial lights made his head ache, and the dancers look demonic as their teeth flared and eyeballs glowed.

Then again, the fast and steady bass beat stirred elements inside his soul he'd long kept locked. His body tensed and his blood buzzed with battle-ready intensity. Within Newgrange, he was always the most dangerous person in the room. Here, he relished rather than quashed the knowledge there was no one present who could hope to harm him: save the woman he sought.

She, alone, threatened both his sanity and his soul.

He circled her with a hunter's stealth, keeping his distance and ensuring he never broached an open space. Not that she was prey. He simply assessed the situation to determine the best approach.

She danced as he understood the term: her body a long fluid line led by her hips, her arms an elegant counterpoint, her silhouette perfectly proportioned. There was a sheen to her skin, and an absorbed, almost entranced, expression on her face.

He'd thought her lovely before. He'd been wrong. She was beautiful, shining with an inner light no one else possessed.

Another woman, whose curly black hair and ready smile seemed vaguely familiar, danced companionably close. The pair were surrounded by a crowd of youths eyeing them with more interest than he liked, but without any obvious intent.

Erin must have called him here for no better purpose than she wanted him.

Before she caught sight of him, he slipped away and headed to the bar. Providing a drink to quench her thirst would almost make his interruption natural. More to the point, it would put the coltish lads crowding her in their place.

But what to order?

"Something with cranberry," he told the bartender. "Keep it refreshing, not syrupy."

She gave him a slow once-over and raised a pierced eyebrow. "You don't seem the type."

"It's not for me." Belatedly, he recalled the friend. "And something fruity, but not fussy." When she gave him another long, scrutinizing study, he added, "Also not for me."

She prepared something pink in a tall glass, poured a pint of something golden from a tap, then asked, "What *is* for you?"

"You tell me."

Her tongue toyed with a stud under her bottom lip as she pondered. "Something strong and traditional. A whiskey on the rocks?"

"My favorite." This was true of modern drinks and yet he hadn't meant to sound quite so...approving. Enough to make the bartender dip her head in pleased embarrassment.

Conscious of his error, he paid cash.

A nod, a swirl to clink the ice, then he drained his glass to avoid an overloaded juggle. The alcohol blunted the edge off his tension, the smooth burn down his throat sharpening his physical awareness. Collecting his token gestures, he approached the dance floor from behind Erin. Leaning in, he said into her ear, "I had a feeling you'd be here."

She jumped, covering her heart with both hands. "It worked!"

Unceremoniously, he passed the yellow drink to her stunned friend then touched the ice-cold glass of the pink drink to Erin's outer hand, so the beaded water slid between her fingers. She gasped at the contact, her eyes widening as she looked up at him. Taking her hand, he raised it to his mouth and gently sucked her knuckles dry, watching her intently despite the dim light. Her fingers spasmed within his, the shiver chasing along her body.

Her reaction gave him ideas completely unsuitable to a public venue.

"Thirsty?"

She wet her lips. "Parched."

Her fingers shook as she accepted the glass. Unlike in his kitchen, there was no teasing to her gaze when she hollowed her cheeks to drain the glass through a straw in one long, extended swallow. She really was thirsty.

It aroused him regardless; he hadn't been able to shake the image of her *wanting* to go down on him ever since she'd tossed the comment over her shoulder this morning.

The instant she finished the last drop, he took the glass from her. "Let me taste."

Ignoring the empty glass, he took her chin lightly between his thumb and forefinger to tilt her face to an angle that suited, then lowered his head to claim her mouth. The blend of cranberries and lime was fresh and feisty, the spike of vodka adding a concealed kick. The perfect drink for Erin…*O'Neill.*

The dark-haired companion elbowed in the moment Angus withdrew. "How'd you know we were here?"

"She called me."

Erin took a half-step toward her friend, her loyalties clearly torn. "Introductions," she shouted over the music. "Angus McCraggan meet Annabel Hogan."

With easy possessiveness, he drew Erin against him and looked over her head, tipping his chin at the friend. The scent from her hair was intoxicating. His own shampoo and yet it seemed so much lighter and more feminine. He dropped his nose to nuzzle around the edges of her ear.

"We've met," said Annabel with antagonistic

164

shortness.

'Met' was an over-statement. He'd seen her in the cafe at the Visitor Center the few times he'd been forced to make an appearance for some team meeting or other. She been in the pub on other Date Nights.

"You're a local." Locals remembered more than they should and liked him the less because of it. They'd always suspected he'd underplayed what he could do. Earning their goodwill was one of the reasons why he'd shielded them from the banshee.

"How is it you know Erin then, Annabel?"

"We went to school together."

"Here in Ireland," he confirmed with a frown, noting her accent. Erin, too, was a local.

Within his grasp, Erin fidgeted. He held her tighter. She twisted around in his arms. "McCraggan, I can explain."

"No need, Miss *O'Neill*."

He ground out her surname rougher than he intended. It would be simple to blame his curse behind his aggression, but his ignorance chafed, and his pride had yet to bow to the yoke of being at her beck and call. Then, too, this place, with the noise and the darkness and the sex in the air, raised the hackles on the antlered animal lurking within.

For a brace of heartbeats she wilted, and he could have cursed himself twice over for shutting down her attempt to be open, especially when he caught that whiff of old despair.

Then she pulled his head down level to hers. Not to kiss, but to slide the tip of her nose alongside his, first down one cheek then the other in a gesture of affection between paired swans. An intimate and long abandoned gesture he'd once shared with Caer in their most private of moments.

A gesture he'd never shared.

His heart stalled. Last night, the banshee had ripped into Erin, leaving her soul in strands. There had been nothing to keep her together. Until he'd donated his heart, inside her there'd been a void. When she claimed a part of her had died along with her father, she'd spoken the truth. As a result, it was horribly, morbidly possible his ex-wife had somehow clothed herself in Erin's flesh.

He stood transfixed, his head in her hands, mining those dark eyes for a trace of the ancient soul he'd rejected. There was none. Nor was there a giddy sense of relief, only a dawning realization there was something wrong, something rotten between them, whether from his gift or her past he couldn't tell.

"How?" he begged, unable to formulate the full question. *How could you know?*

Her hands slid to his shoulders, and she leaned in closer to speak to him alone. "I drowned for you, years before I died in your arms."

A riddle. One he couldn't solve here. Nor could she explain. A proper conversation over the racket here was impossible. What he latched onto, therefore, was not her words but the emotion behind them. A new lightness. A purity of intent. An acceptance of herself. Demonstrating the same raw courage she'd shown within the chamber at Newgrange, she'd drawn in the toxic smog of despair cloaking her and vanquished it.

As if he needed more proof, she lifted her chin and said, "I'm ready for you to love me, Angus."

With those words, she claimed him. He became hers, utterly and always.

His insides glowed, strong and warm, in the light of her acknowledgement. To be hers was a joy, to serve her a delight, to love her the most precious honor. He wanted to make *them* happen despite the knowledge he was doomed to fail. He wanted her as he'd never wanted another woman. He wanted Erin not for a lifetime, but forever.

Strong and fast and true. His mother had warned him love would be like this once he gave his heart, but she hadn't explained how acceptance sealed the exchange.

The techno beat banged a frantic rhythm of want-want, take-take. Other couples tongued and spooned, making out heedless of observers. Five minutes ago, he hadn't minded being part of a crowd.

Then Erin had spoken. She wanted him to love her.

For the first time in his life, words failed him.

Instead of attempting to speak, he cupped his hands around her face the way one did with a rare and delicate flower, making no effort to conceal his adoration. She needed to be shown he cherished her above all others. He would make this moment shine for her as much as it did for him by refusing to succumb to the fever in his blood.

He touched the tiny scar on her forehead with his lips, withdrawing a fraction to catch his breath in wonder at the elegant curve to her eyelashes as her lids fluttered. With a feather-light touch of his mouth, he pressed her lids fully closed then drifted his nose along the petal-soft skin of her cheek until her face tipped blindly toward his, as if he was her sun.

While the stroke of his thumb along the line of her jaw keeping her mesmerized, he unhooked one of her hands to twine their fingers together in a silent promise of companionship to anchor his every caress. When her mouth curved, he couldn't resist brushing his own back and forth across the bow with slow and tender devotion. When her lips parted, he breathed the warmth of her air into his lungs, reveling in the exquisite torture of withstanding the release of a true kiss.

When she leaned forward and rose a fraction higher to close the distance, he slid aside to anoint the throbbing pulse on her neck and lick the salt from the hollow girded by her collarbone.

Denying them both was deliberate; a signal this was something different, something special. It began pure of motive, but it became a game. A chase of kisses across her brow, the catch and release of his earlobe, a skirmish of noses.

He was losing and losing fast. He couldn't withstand her body's trembling, her jagged gasps. Sucking the sensitive skin of her lower lip became a drag of his teeth. Sly teasing dips into her mouth with the tip of his tongue became urgent and deep stabs, rapidly pulled. His need to kiss her became urgent and unrelenting. But if he kissed her, he wouldn't stop. Their chemistry was too potent, his control too fractured.

"We need to leave," he said.

Chapter Fourteen

Still Better and Worse

"Good call." Erin's voice was breathless, her eyes bright. Then her face fell. "Because we need to talk."

Not the response he'd expected, but his priority remained the same.

"I brought Annabel here," she added. "She needs to come with me."

Her poor choice of words forced him to consider the friend.

Annabel stood with her arms folded and her gaze fixed on the floor, her lower hand pinching the rims of not one, but two glasses. When had she taken Erin's? He couldn't remember. As if aware of his attention, she raised her head to look at him. There was no doubt her earlier antagonism had slanted into something new, but there were too many people, too close, for him to discern what hers had become.

Not desire, thank goodness.

*Not yet.*

The afterthought sickened him because he knew, deep in his core, it would be local women like Annabel he would seek first. Women he knew. Women who lived nearby. Women from among the neighbors he'd always sought to protect.

"She's not coming with me."

Erin took one look at his face and went to shout earnestly into her friend's ear, her expression dismayed until Annabel shouted something back. The pair hugged, Annabel said something else and there was more hugging, until, at last, Erin slipped her hand into his and gave a nod.

They were off the dance floor, the exit within sight, when she tugged him to a halt. "Cranberries might be super-good for the kidneys, but they come with a catch."

Angus had no idea what she was talking about.

"I gotta pee," she muttered with exasperation. She glanced over to where a group of women waited outside a closed door. "And there's always a line for the Ladies."

The door nearby with men emerging had no such issue. "Go in there," he pointed. "I don't want to hang around."

"McCraggan! I can't—"

But he was already striding toward the Gents and dragging her with him.

"Wait here," he ordered before heading in and glaring at the last man standing to get out. When the guy was done, he opened the door for Erin and swept in a hand.

"All yours. No one else will join us without being invited."

She entered with a wrinkled nose. "What is it about male bathrooms that makes them smell so bad?" Distaste aside, she didn't hesitate to make for a cubicle.

With no need to guard the door, Angus let it swing closed then went to investigate the vending machine attached to the wall. The mechanism seemed to require the use of coins, a minimum weight in exchange for release. He had some money, but not enough. Hmm.

Breda was the metal worker in the family but needs must. He thumbed the larger of his bimetallic coin, shifting its composition toward heavier components, then inserted it into the slot and put his ear to the machine.

While he tapped and jangled the contraption, Erin came out and washed her hands.

"Anytime you want to explain what you're doing, McCraggan, feel free."

"This is one of those condom machines, isn't it?"

"I told you I have some…" She ducked her head and looked aside. "Admittedly not *on* me. Then again, coming here was a spur-of-the-moment decision. The plan, *if* you arrived, was to talk."

"To talk," he repeated vaguely, still toying with the mechanism. At last, his manipulations caught the right sequence and a rush of thin boxes tipped out.

She lunged to catch them. "You seemed adamant this morning we needed to get to know each other." Clutching her haul to her chest, she cocked her head. "Did something change?"

Between his curse and her acceptance of his offer to love her?

"Everything."

To make her hate him, he must first make her love him. He captured her in his arms, and nibbled on her earlobe, all the better to whisper. "Talk to me now and we can go somewhere else to continue our…conversation with the aid of those."

When she sorted through the packets, he figured they had a deal.

Until she gave a gurgle of amusement.

"Three packets to a box and three boxes. You sure are ambitious for someone who has to be at work in the morning."

He wasn't rostered on-site tomorrow. Better she didn't know. "How many times can each one be used?"

She pulled a face. "Ew, gross. That would be *once*, McCraggan."

"Where can we go now? Where are you staying?" He knew, but it wasn't a lie to ask.

Erin's body tensed against his, her breath catching. *Tempted, definitely tempted.*

"I'm staying at my grandfather's house." Her tone was defiant, almost daring him to comment on her earlier deception. "Not the place for gentleman callers, given he's pretty old-school in his beliefs. He's partly why I needed somewhere…neutral…to meet you. Not to mention that my options got pretty limited once the pubs closed."

"I understand."

His house was problematic while her grandfather worked the farm, while Newgrange would be difficult for her after her experience in the chamber. It didn't leave them much in the way of alternatives, especially not past one in the morning. Staying in the men's room much longer was also out of the question, what with the muted shouts of annoyance and door-banging going on.

"We should move before we start a riot." He relieved Erin of her load. "What about a hotel?"

"We won't talk in a hotel." She planted a kiss on his jaw, swiftly and lightly, before ducking free of his embrace. "I guess my car will have to do." She groaned as she watched him tuck the boxes into his inner jacket pocket. "Except, you don't like those, do you?"

He was touched she remembered. "Trapped in a metal box full of stale air is not to my taste, it's true. If you don't mind dark, damp and dirty, there's somewhere not far from here where I can guarantee we won't be disturbed. While we talk."

"You're really not selling it to me, but it can't be worse than urinals."

When she pulled the door open, he sent a quelling scowl in the direction of the irate men forced to wait, before tucking her into the safety of his embrace to hustle her through the gauntlet of their speculation.

****

"Where are we headed?" she asked when they were outside.

"It's a ruin I have a certain sympathy for." The gatehouse was a relic of the old city walls. Once it had guarded those within from those without, but the town had grown beyond its boundaries leaving it lost in the city center. "It's closed to the public, but I can get us in."

After indicating the direction, he automatically fell into step a pace behind her and slightly to her right, keeping between her and the road as they walked.

She twisted to catch his hand. "What are you, my boyfriend or my bodyguard?"

"Both," he said, pleased she already considered him the former. The latter went without saying.

"Ease up, McCraggan. No one's going to pull out a gun and take me hostage."

"It would be the worse for them if they did."

"Because you'll use your powers to stop bullets or something?"

"Or something." He scanned the sky. Hours yet before the dawn, and the moon scarcely a sliver. On such a night his kin liked to roam. With his left hand in hers, his right remained free—and empty. He hadn't held a blade since his return, but for the first time his palm itched to grasp *Moralltach*, the sword Manann had gifted him as a sign of their friendship. Little use though it would be since he wouldn't wield it against his kin, and it wouldn't touch them if he did. Apart from the fact he'd tossed it into a bog more years ago than he could count.

Erin stopped walking. "What's that supposed to mean? 'Or something?'"

"It means any bullets that might come your way will not hit you."

"Isn't that what I said?" A little pinch formed between her brows. "No, it's not, *exactly*, what I said, is it?" She glared at him. "Tell me, precisely, why they won't hit me."

"Precisely?" He frowned and dragged his attention entirely to her. "I'm not familiar with guns and how they work to prevent one firing. Besides, it takes time to work any metal, even one as soft as lead. This makes the most likely scenario being me taking the hit." When she recoiled, he raised her hand to kiss her knuckles. "While I'm with you, Erin, you will never be harmed."

The irony that he would soon be her single greatest threat didn't escape him, but he was reluctant to broach the subject of his curse out in the open.

Blinking rapidly, she glanced away. "It's a good thing this is hypothetical, because I have a real problem with you dying to save me."

"Do you?" He considered it the perfect outcome. It would, in fact, solve a great many of his problems and permanently, too. "I'm not afraid to die for a worthy cause."

"I appreciate you've got a seriously over-developed protective streak..." she began. "Actually, that's bullshit. I *don't* appreciate you've got a seriously over-developed protective streak. This isn't New York. You don't need to be paranoid. No one's going to mug us here."

"I'm not worried about being mugged, *mo chroí.* I'm worried about being haunted."

"The banshee?" The hand holding his tightened its grip.

"No, but nor can I rule out the possibility. I was in the habit of summoning her once in a new moon, but I can't find where she goes between times. The others of my kin, however, I have no command over and they have no fondness for me. It would be best not to meet them while I'm at my weakest."

"Because you get stronger with sunlight. I remember."

They walked on and there was no thickening to the shadows, but there was a bite to the air. Erin's short skirt and thin top were not enough to keep her warm outside the close atmosphere of the club. It would be cooler still within the stone walls of the medieval building. With the double turrets of the gatehouse within sight, he paused to fish out his keys and slide off his jacket. After propping the leather around her shoulders, he used the lamplight to sort through his selection. The padlock on the rusted metal door within the arch almost matched one used at Newgrange. With a tiny flex of power, he made it fit here, too.

"Mm, I could get high on how you smell, McCraggan." Erin buried her nose within the collar of his jacket and inhaled audibly. "Woah, that's potent." She swayed against him her eyes dopey with desire. "You'll catch me if I swoon, won't you? I've never done

175

it before so I can't be certain I will, but it seems likely."

"How about I hold you? Just in case."

He drew her into his arms then jiggled the key in the lock. She relaxed into his embrace as though she belonged there, and he almost kissed her. Doing so, however, would prevent any talking for the foreseeable future and since she'd called him for that purpose, he intended to listen.

Inside, the gatehouse was much as he suspected: dismal. The space was cramped and the light almost non-existent, save for the rim around the door's edge and the high grated window. Most of the room was taken by the stairs leading to the tower. Decaying birds-nests and a raft of cobwebs were the key fixtures.

This was not one of his most romantic suggestions.

"Sure is dark in here," she murmured, freeing herself from his hold. "Can't you cast a witch-light or something? You lit up like the Fourth of July inside Newgrange."

"Newgrange is designed to capture sunlight, and I had the energy of twenty people contributing to my glory. Not to mention," he added, with considerable self-annoyance, "an electricity supply."

"Lucky for us then I brought some modern technology." From the tiny bag slung across her shoulder, she pulled out her phone and tapped it a few times before placing it on one of the steps. The screen cast just enough light for him to see her face. She shone it his way. "Ta-dah!"

"Your car would have been a better option," he grumbled, circumnavigating the edge of the room.

"Yeah but keeping still would drive you nuts." Gingerly she found a perch on one of the wider steps and watched him roam.

"Already you know me so well." Time to correct the imbalance. "Why are you no longer an O'Neill, Erin?" She flinched as he spoke the surname. "I ask out of curiosity, not to accuse. You had a right to be wary of giving me your true name."

"To be fair, you're taking the whole 'I'm not as foreign as I sound' thing amazingly well, McCraggan. Most guys would be pissed." She waited for a response, but he saw no point in reminding her he was not most men. "Anyway, it's simple enough. When Mom remarried, I wanted to keep my surname in honor of my dad, but she flipped out and threatened to burn my Irish passport and…oh God, how come I never…" She went silent for a moment. "Sorry, something Annabel told me just clicked. If it's okay with you, I'll come back to this after. Right now, I can't deal with saying it out loud."

She scrubbed her face with her palms and sighed.

"There's a bunch of stuff I need to talk to you about." Her gaze traveled across his face as if gauging his reaction. "It's not going to be easy to say, and it might be hard to listen to."

"I'm here for you, *mo chroí*." His own troubles could wait.

"Yeah, you are. You found me, exactly like you said you would." A smile flickered then faded into the shadows. "All right, I'm going to pretend this is a counseling session and just get everything out from the beginning. So," she heaved a heavy sigh. "The beginning. That starts for me in America, where my parents met. Dad was on a J1 Work Visa as a construction laborer and Mom was the site office intern. They fell in love over an office block build and got married in the US. Then my grandma here in Ireland died unexpectedly from a heart attack, and my parents came for the funeral and never left. There was the family farm, you see, and Da had gotten traveling out of his system. My mom…resented his lack of ambition. They had me, I think, almost to give her something to do."

She looked uncertainly up at him through her lashes. "Here's your first revelation."

"That you were born here?"

"No, that my legal first name was Maureen, after my grandma. I hated it. Too old-fashioned and so not cool. The deal I made with Mom was that I changed everything, not just my surname. And that's the official version of how Maureen O'Neill became Erin De Santos."

Erin was a variation of a name given to one of his people's most celebrated leaders, making it far older than Maureen, but he couldn't question her taste.

"I love the name Erin."

"How you say *Air-in* melts my brain."

Conveniently, his pacing brought him to her feet to test this up close. Reaching out, he stroked the line of her cheek. "Is that so, *Erin*?"

As her jaw slackened and her head tilted back, he noted the effect for future reference. Would she be so receptive when he told her he also loved her? His gut told him it was too soon for a straight-out declaration. She was ready to be shown, not told, but it was her turn to speak. He edged out of her space, away from her soft skin and rapid breathing, to review what she'd shared.

"A childhood name is no easy label to cast off…" His throat tightened, although this time it was not from a summons. A name carried so much of a person's identity, to alter it could alter a person entirely.

"Pretty much everyone already knew me as Erin so dropping Maureen wasn't so bad. Losing the O'Neill though was tough. It was like losing my dad all over."

A sacrifice, indeed. He mustn't show his unease in case she misinterpreted his foreboding.

"Then where did Liz come from?"

"Liz you'll have to wait for. If I skip ahead, I'll never get through the rest."

Worryingly, she then remained silent for a long time, her shoulders bowed and her focus internal. His hands itched to soothe her tension, but that might snap the line of her concentration. When she finally raised her head to look straight at him, her gaze was so fixed, he knew she didn't see him at all.

"This is where it gets tough for me, Angus, because I've never spoken of this to a single soul." She twiddled the zipper of his jacket. "I have to go at it from an angle and hope I can get round to the core."

Her use of his name had him aching to hold her again, but she'd drawn her knees to her chin and clutched them tight. She'd closed herself off so completely, he couldn't use his gift to share her burden. He dragged a hand through his hair then forced himself to stillness.

"When I was fourteen, before I left Ireland, I was," she rocked and her voice dropped to a whisper, "not so much 'abused' as 'assaulted' by someone I'd been told not to fear. There is a...history...in my family from this particular individual, but both my parents denied the possibility."

So much for stillness. Hidden from view, Angus clenched his fists until his knuckles cracked. His ribs pulped his lungs as he concentrated on keeping his

179

breathing slow and quiet. The urge to tuck her into his embrace warred with his need to break something, preferably made of bone.

Neither would do.

From Caer, he knew being held might not be a welcome response. Not yet. Until he heard the full details, until Erin gave him some cue of how she preferred to be comforted, his job was to be a trustworthy set of ears.

"Were you badly hurt?" he rasped.

"Not so much on the outside. The damage was more…internal. And by internal, I mean emotionally and mentally. It happened so fast. So fast, that by the time my dad realized what was happening it was too late. He tried to intervene, but the timing was all wrong, and he died when I needed him most."

She cut short a gallows laugh.

"God, that sounds so selfish, but I was fourteen and I lost my father and my childhood, my friends and my home, in one fell swoop. There didn't seem to be anything to cling to, except for my mother, and she was a mess. I didn't realize then, but I've just learned she worried Da's death was a suicide. And thought he meant to take me, too."

The tension dropped from her frame.

"And there you have the second revelation, the one I never saw coming. The real reason I'm no longer an O'Neill is because Mom thought Da hated her. And the part that sucks most is I can never tell her he didn't. I can't tell her how I know and—even if I could—she's moved on so far she wouldn't care."

Whether she held his heart or not, he would have admired her. She took the world head on, fronting up to her fears like they were enemies she could defeat single-handedly. Caer had been flighty in form and thought. After rescuing her, he'd tried to shield her from the world. Both of which had stoked his ego. The world, however, was bigger than he could ever be. Too big to shelter her from its harshness. Erin didn't need a protector. She needed a partner. Someone who would stand by her and refuse to let her deal with this alone.

"Is there room on that step for two?" he asked to gauge how she might receive his company.

"I'd prefer to stand. This stone is *freezing*. My ass is half-way to becoming an ice block."

He helped her to her feet and wrapped his arms around her as a human blanket.

She snuggled in and made herself at home. "Unfortunately, I'm not done."

"I hear bad news comes in threes."

"Yeah, but this next bit is where it gets personal." She switched off the light on her phone. "I can't tell you this while I'm looking at you."

Chapter Fifteen

Its Hour Come Round

Since her back was to him, Angus didn't understand what difference it made, but he was glad to have the reassurance of her weight against him in the dark. Inside a building, he had no concern about his people slipping out from the shadows, but he disliked being alone.

"About the same time as everything else, I…happened across this boy," Erin said. Unlike before, her tone was reverent. "Such a beautiful boy, never short of a smile and with a laugh as warm as summer. God, I thought he was perfect. He was a few years older than me, but incredibly mature for his age and hugely talented. Anyway, I crushed on him so bad, you wouldn't believe."

He did believe. Breathless and giggly, she hadn't lost her girlish infatuation.

"Until him, I used to pin pop star posters up on my wall. After him, I…" She cleared her throat and shifted against him. Nervously, he assumed, until she writhed her chilly butt into his crotch. "I would touch myself and pretend he was the one doing the touching…"

Her arousal leached into him and inflamed his own.

It took a few seconds to identify the venom snaking through his blood alongside the heat. Jealousy was an unfamiliar poison, a sourness he wasn't sure how to combat. This was how he wanted her to think of *him*. Exclusively. And yet this boy was from her past—it made no sense to be jealous. It made sense to help her out, his groin begged as she rubbed. His heart was not convinced this was the sort of comfort she needed. His hands compromised by twining his fingers through hers, letting her lead. Except she fisted their doubled-over hands over her stomach and stilled to speak.

"But he loved someone else and never even knew I existed. Plus, he was here, in Ireland, and totally unattainable. The more time went by, the more he seemed too good to be true, especially when I began seeing boys my own age. They were just…gross. Sloppy kisses and clumsy petting."

She made a gagging noise.

"Older boys had more experience, but they also expected to go further, faster. Unfortunately, the sex mostly wasn't worth the effort of sneaking out to get it. But I was so empty inside, so cold and numb. Physical intimacy made my blood hot and gave me some sense of feeling *filled*."

There was a roaring in his ears. Possibly from the rush of his own blood downward.

"So, I created a new me for hook-ups. One more confident, able to demand what she wanted or take it anyways. I used the name Liz, from Elizabeth, the name I chose at my Confirmation—not after the saint, but because I admired the kick-ass Queen of England who ruled a world of men."

This time when she laughed, she sounded genuinely amused.

"Then, in my senior year, I dated this one guy. A college boy. He wanted me to move in with him. When

I refused, he told me I had 'daddy issues.' After I dumped him, I realized he was right. Because of my dad's sacrifice, my standard of what true love means is excessive."

His chest froze with the strangest kind of dread.

Erin did not relieve his fears.

"Here's your third and final revelation. It's a doozy but I need to get it out. I've spent *years* repressing facts and feelings because they were impossible. In my world, that is. In your world not even death is the ending it's supposed to be."

"There are worse things than dying, *mo chroí*," he began. "There's—"

"There's being alive and yet dead at the same time," she finished for him.

Yesterday he'd thought that was the worse. Today he knew better.

"Or wishing you were dead and being unable to die." He capped her comment lightly, hoping she'd consider it a general situation not a specific example.

"See, I can tell you because you'll get it. You mightn't like it, but you'll get it. And I need you to get it, so you get *me*."

She took a deep breath, and he held his own. When she said 'get me,' exactly how did she mean? Because if she was in a giving mood, he'd take the lot. Body, heart, and soul.

"So here it is," she said in a rush. "My Dream Boy is you. Was you. It took me a bit to realize because, you know, you're not seventeen. You're older. You hardly ever smile, and I've only heard you laugh once. But it's you I used to dream of. The same voice, the same heart, the same guy."

She sounded smitten, but the breathless, giddy quality was absent. It had to be a peculiar madness to envy his past self, famed for his first love and now the object of obsession to the love of his life. She wanted what he'd been, not what he'd become.

He stifled a snort. "Not the same." He wasn't the man he'd been this morning let alone his past self. "We've only just met. How can it be me you dreamed of?"

"Because last night wasn't the first time the banshee assaulted me. The first time, when we went over the bridge at Slane, cost me my dad when she…possessed me. The second time, last night, she knew to gut me from the outside first, not from within like before. That bitch has been living off my childhood and surviving on my father's death trying to get back to you, because she loves you beyond reason."

If Caer was a knife in his gut, then Erin's every word twisted the blade until his intestines were wound so tight and hard, he wanted to double over. Possessed. No wonder she'd identified him at Newgrange with such certainty, why she'd been drawn to the pub at the same time as the banshee, why she trusted him when she should not. Her unwavering belief in him hollowed his stomach until he fought the instinct to retch. What had been done to her could never be undone. Father slain. Childhood stolen. Soul scarred. How many crimes had the banshee committed in his name?

He bowed his head. "Forgive me."

"What for?"

"I'm responsible for what that monster did to you. Had I been truly merciful, I would have cut my bond to her in one, clean blow before I was imprisoned within the earth. But I couldn't let her go. I hoped, in vain, that if I kept her heart, she would return to me in my dreams. It never occurred to me I would be gone so long. She lingered, hanging on a thread of hope through the ages, all because I couldn't bear to sleep alone."

"Oh, Angus, you're not the one to blame. You weren't even resurrected when it happened, so there's nothing to forgive."

She was wrong.

Roaming unattached to the earth, Caer should have died. She'd survived because he'd taken her heart with him into Newgrange. Forever linked, forever apart. Her suffering had driven her mad, and in her madness, she'd murdered and maimed. For him. Had he known the extent of the banshee's depravity, he would have refuted her immediately.

As for Erin, she was too free with her forgiveness. At Newgrange, she'd accused him of pretending to be a normal human being. He'd deflected her charge and played her false. Now, her courage shone a light on his own cowardice.

"You are very brave, *mo chroí*, to share this with me."

"If I'm fearless, *Óenghus Óg*," she said, a smile in her voice. "It's only because you took my fear."

Her lightness didn't lift him. It weighed on him. A guilty conscience was a curse of his own making—one he could lift the moment he confessed.

"*Óenghus Óg* is a part of me, but I'm not him, *mo chroí*."

"You sound the same." She squeezed their interlocked fingers. "Holding hands with you feels the same as...I...remember. That's a crazy thing to claim, isn't it? But I paid for these memories." Her voice turned ardent. "They're *mine*, Angus. And you gave me your heart. That makes you truly mine, doesn't it?"

"Yes."

"So why won't you kiss me, Angus?"

"Kiss you?"

"Yeah, you know…" The falter was new as she twisted to breathe in his ear, "What you haven't been doing all evening." Her shift meant their hands were no longer docked parallel against her hips but askew—one below her ribs and the other down her thigh.

His livelihood came from giving speeches, yet his tongue was thick in his mouth and his focus lost to the friction of her arse on his lap. "Because I've been…celibate…a long time and you're very responsive. When we kiss, it makes me want to…bed you."

"*Bed* me? I'll bet that's totally what you're thinking: *I want to bed Erin so bad.*" Her laugh was a delight, free and happy. "Annabel said it was like watching a first dance at a wedding where the groom can't wait to bang his wife but is trying to stay respectable."

"She's right," he managed, his focus entirely on the slow circle her hips were making. Indeed, her perceptive friend was right on both counts and the analogy used was unfortunate. In his culture and hers, once formally matched, the tradition was to mate. His heart squeezed in counterpoint to the throb of his cock, his brain losing the battle to insert a sober thought in edgewise.

"This is not the place for love-making," he hedged. Gatehouses were places in-between and any place in-between belonged to his sister.

"We could make a start."

He wanted so much to be the man Erin believed him

187

to be, but the choices he'd made in the past meant there was no future for them. This morning he'd hoped for as much as a summer together. For her sake, for tonight only, he would be her beautiful boy.

Dipping a fraction, he drifted across the line of her collarbone with his tongue. She'd sweated as she danced and tasted of salt. He swirled the salt into a spiral to mix it into the musk of her skin until the chord in her neck stretched tight then he clamped his teeth down lightly on the line and sucked hard.

Her moan was the sweetest music. He needed to capture the sound. He reached for her mouth and her lips were softer than butter, melting open and meeting his own with a sizzle he swore he heard. He didn't kiss her so much as consume her. Mixing tenderness with need, love with passion, he told her in complete silence how he adored her smart mouth and her secrets, her insecurities and her strength.

She sobbed as she kissed him back, writhing desperately against his erection. He took the higher of their combined hands from her ribs to tug and tweak her breast, while taking the lower to the cleft between her legs. His hand there still covered hers, but his fingers were longer, and they were agile, pushing aside the damp material of her panties to spiral inwards from rim to core until she whimpered.

"Is this what you want, Erin? Is this how the boy you fell for would touch you?"

"Yes!" Her throat bobbed against his cheek as her back arched. "Angus, please…"

As she gasped his name with her accent as modern as his name, he forgot his good intentions. He was named for one passion. And there was only one thing on his mind and one thing only. *Her.* He wanted her bucking against his cock, lost with pleasure and wild with abandon. He wanted her coming so hard she almost blacked out.

He wanted her for himself, as he was now—changed and cursed and broken—not for who he'd been. He rubbed his stubbled jaw against the soft skin of her throat while he dipped to the depth of his first knuckle. "Tell me what you want."

"More."

His teeth rimmed her earlobe, almost in punishment before he pushed in a little deeper, then withdrew.

"Tell me again...*Erin,*" he caressed her name and her sex.

Her hips jerked as she groaned, low and guttural.

"I want you, Angus." She clutched at his wrist. "Please. You bought enough protection to do me six ways to Sunday. And today's Sunday. Officially."

*Protection.*

The single word echoed inside his empty skull like the clangor from a bell. Greater than his need to please, was his need to protect. Erin was not Caer, whose childhood had left her too damaged to bear a babe. If he took her, she would conceive—a daughter with her mother's brown eyes, or perhaps a son—that was the price of loving him and he could not imagine her wanting to be a mother. Resting his forehead against the back of her skull, his breath puffed her hair as he laughed rather than cried.

"Angus? Are you okay?"

No. He'd lost the run of himself in the need to be lost in her. His curse would be like this, when it came on him in full. This time he laughed, loudly and wholly demented, because a man free of prison should never forget he was on parole.

"What's wrong?"

Children were the greatest legacy a man could leave. And any children he fathered would belong to his enemy. How foolish he'd been to forget. Breda was right. Explaining would not do. He passed Erin's cell phone to her.

"Stand up, *mo chroí,* and I'll show you."

Methodically, he toed off his shoes then undid his belt. Better he pull on his past than Manann. If Erin hated him after this, it was for the best. If he was dead, he could do no harm to the living.

Chapter Sixteen

A Slave to Circumstance

"Shine your light on me, *mo chroí*. See me as I am, not who I was."

Erin swiped the screen on her cell phone. His eyes flashed like a mirror as she swept the torch beam down his body rather than blind him. His shirt was off. His pants already below his knees as he stepped out of his jeans. He rose to stand.

He was magnificent. From the breadth of his shoulders to the shape of his calves and, most especially, everything in between. The cell phone slipped a little as her palms sweated.

"You, ah, you're mighty..." *Hard* wouldn't go past her lips. It wasn't enough. "Impressive."

"You told me I shouldn't be here, pretending to be a normal human being. And you were right—I was pretending. Since my release, I've lived like a monk, and fooled no one but myself. I can't pretend any longer. And, after what you've shared tonight, you have to see me as I am."

"What...what are you saying, Angus?"

"I want to fuck you, Erin."

Her mouth dried. She couldn't speak. The best she could manage was a nod. It wasn't enough. He didn't move, just watched her with wild, stormy eyes that never left her face. His bad boy vibe strummed every nerve until her body hummed with need.

She cleared her throat to choke out, "I'm game."

He gave her a look. Not one of his torn *I-want-to-but-I-shouldn't* looks, but one that said *Yes, you are.* The fine hairs on her nape lifted as her skin tightened and heated. This was new, this flinty resolve hardening his features.

"Use the light, *mo chroí.*"

When she dialed up the brightness, gold at his throat gleamed—an inch-thick bar wrapped about his neck, open-ended like a shirt collar, each end embossed. On his head, he wore a strange brownish-gray crown shaped like antlers. But there was no circlet, and she couldn't see any straps.

"Um, how are those staying on?"

He tossed his head enough to show the twin branching pairs were as fixed as his ears though they sprouted somewhat closer to his temples.

"*Antlers,* Angus?"

She glanced down at her screen. No antlers. No gold. Just skin. Lots of bare, beautiful skin. She looked up and the new additions were undeniably there. What the hell?

He bared his teeth in what might be a smile then stalked toward her. Her hands trembled. God, how he moved. Really, she should video this. Slow and deliberate, each step closer a study in masculine grace, form and power. It mesmerized. He took close to a minute to circle her and the entire time she didn't shift a muscle, not to press record, not even to blink. She didn't want to miss an inch. Or a second. Whatever.

He took her phone from her nerveless fingers and

placed it where she'd been sitting.

She'd thought the heated leather of his jacket smelled good, but the musk of his skin smoked around her like incense and destroyed her mind. To steady herself, she put her hands on either side of the trispiral brand. He'd removed the bandage. The wound had healed—although the scar was still raised and shiny-pink like a fresh blister. Hesitantly, she pressed a featherlight kiss to the scar's center, over his heart. Then another on the ridge of his collarbone where the gold collar rested. The metal was warm against her cheek.

*It's real.*

"What are you doing, Erin?"

*Building up my courage.*

She stretched a hand to his face, climbed her fingers from his cheek bone, past the edge of his eye socket to his temple and…oh, that was seriously weird. *Warm* bone, sort of waxy and furry together.

"They're part of you!"

"Yes."

"But they're new. They're not something I remember…"

"Before going into the earth, I accepted a stag's tenacity and stamina. So that, upon my return, I could perform—however heartbroken I might be and regardless of who I was with, to increase our numbers."

He sounded like a soldier reeling off an order. All emotion masked. A man of duty, not the sensitive lover of her dreams with a smile on his lips and his heart on his sleeve.

"Perform?" She gnawed her lip. Thinking was so difficult up this close with him smelling so good. "You mean like a stud animal?"

Whatever about a deer. She'd have chosen a stallion. An Arabian, spirited and intelligent, with an occasional high-necked arrogance.

"Something like. Your ancestors worshipped me, and a god needs faith. Your belief brings out elements in me I thought I had under control. This is me as the god I was meant to be."

Huh. Funny how she'd forgotten he was a deity. His anguish was so human.

"A sex god isn't so different to a god of love, right?"

Her fingers somehow found purchase in the rope of muscles lining his shoulders. She dug in her nails and buried her nose in his neck. A convenient means to press her stomach against his pelvis. Wow. So this was virile. Her ovaries ached like they might actually explode. She'd always thought that was a meme, not a symptom.

His hands went to her hips to hold her in place as he dipped his knees and rocked his pelvis against her pubic bone. "Is this what you want? Me inside you?"

"See, you *can* read my mind."

His soft chuckle seemed to thicken the air. "Then fetch out those rubber socks."

"Oh, thank God." If she was any more ready, she'd deliquesce.

Plunging her hands into the pockets of his jacket, she grabbed a box. Getting a single foil packet out the box, however, took all her concentration. Her fine motor skills were entirely shot. When she jerked the foil open, the condom came flying out to land on the floor with an accusing patter. Shit.

"Leave it. Try another." He stroked his cock while he waited, thickening it still further.

Entranced, Erin used her teeth on the second packet,

only to spit out latex. Urgh.

"Third time lucky, right?" God, it was embarrassing to sound so desperate. Taking it super careful because of her shaking hands, she got the condom out in one piece and managed to hold on to it. "Here, now, let me put this on you."

She rolled the condom down his length, her technique perfect despite him twitching under her grasp. Was it too tight or just unfamiliar? Something about the tilt to his head, the edge to his stance, put her in mind of a horse unaccustomed to wearing a bridle.

His brow furrowed, his lips pursed, and the condom split like a banana peel from tip to base. Who knew they even did that? Erin almost screamed as she hauled it from him with a roughness that had him baring his teeth again in something a long way from a smile.

"Careful, *mo chroí*."

Every inch of her skin goose bumped at the warning. His voice had lost its smoothness and gained a ragged edge, but it still commanded.

"Sorry, I don't know what's gotten into me. It's just I want you so bad…"

"Fetch another box."

With a nod, she did as she was told. Why hadn't she thought of that? Probably a faulty batch. Except not one of the next three were any good, either. The seal was broken on one, another split, and the third wouldn't unroll at all.

She stamped her foot. "What the hell kind of bad luck is this?"

He laughed, but it didn't sound as if he thought the situation funny. It was far too harsh. She was reaching for the final box, when he came up behind her and took the jacket from her shoulders, casting it who knew where. The heat from his body enveloped her as he drew her against him by cupping his hands to her breasts.

"I can't hide what I am any more. Should I try, I'll be cursed." He nuzzled against her throat as he spoke. She hadn't known she was sensitive just below her ear. It made her head loll and her knees soft.

"C-c-cursed?" Her brain cranked as it tried to function. Angus didn't do allegory. If he was cursed, he meant in a Biblical sense, like handing over a first born or being an addictive lover one couldn't live without. She had a bad feeling it was that last one.

"Remember the fawn yesterday? When it's full grown to a stag, it'll go into rut. My Lord and Lady wish to have me suffer the same affliction."

"English, Angus."

"Later this summer, I'll be required to have sex. Constantly. Relentlessly."

So he was a little anxious about going from famine to feast. Understandable. Still…

"Doesn't sound so bad," she managed, almost passing out from the weight of understatement. "But it's only May. Let's worry about that later. You know," she mumbled, rubbing her palms down the taut muscles of his thighs because she'd forgotten he'd removed his jeans. "I've never gone bareback. You'd be my first."

His teeth nipped the edges of her ear before he whispered, "I'm not a horse, Erin."

Maybe not, but he was hung like one. Oh God, she didn't want him anymore. She *needed*. The ache was vicious. She'd never known anything like it.

"Bareback is without a condom. I'm on the pill, I won't get pregnant."

To her shock, he hiked up her skirt and wrenched down her panties.

"Like this? Here?" His scorching cock thrust between her legs—not in, but near.

"Yes." She squeezed her thighs together to trap him in place. Standing made sense since she didn't relish her spine being pushed against a rough stone wall. There might be spiders. Given the cobwebs.

With a nudge and a slide, he started to ease into her then halted until his mouth claimed hers, kissing her as he sank in deep, then deeper still. She almost sobbed at how well they fit together, how wonderfully he filled her. There was no pounding, no pumping. He simply kept pushing inwards, his lips faint with whiskey, his presence as reassuring as sunshine on her back, the heat of him supercharging every cell in her body until she could power Manhattan.

Then he stopped.

Other than the soft huff of his breathing, he stayed silent, his whole body taut.

Erin clenched so hard she nearly came but his hands locked her hips in place, preventing her getting that tiny extra bit of friction she needed. She'd known everything would be different with him. She hadn't counted on it being this intense. Oh, she'd *dreamed*, but those were second hand and shabby. Her fantasies had grown more vivid as her experience had grown, but she'd never factored in how complete she felt in his embrace.

Except for the whole *not moving* part. He was killing her holding steady. She was going to implode from the pressure. He knew that, didn't he?

"You stopped. Why did you stop? Please, Angus, it's sooooo gooooood…"

"Shall I continue then and make you a mother? Because I promise you, Erin, I'm very, very fertile and you are very, very ready."

He sounded the way she felt: stoned. Only this was turning into a really bad trip.

"I'm on the pill. I *can't* get pregnant," she insisted. To a man with antlers who made her ovaries ache. Oh God, the condoms. He'd wanted her to see for herself. She cringed. A mistake since tightening her abdominals nearly undid her. She wasn't ready for motherhood. She was barely ready for a relationship.

And yet, when he withdrew, she couldn't stop her traitorous pelvic floor undertaking Kegel gymnastics to make the super-hot baby daddy finish what he'd started.

*Want. Him.* Her body screamed.

"Maybe I could just get morning-after pills," she suggested. "As a backup."

"You'll want to keep any child I father," he said in the same matter-of-fact manner he might've said, 'It's raining out', as if arguing otherwise was ludicrous.

"Wait, wait, wait…." But he didn't. He pulled back with terrible, gentle slowness. It was exquisite and excruciating and if he just rammed right back in, she would've loved it.

"But…" She spun around to face him.

"Erin. Enough," he panted, his entire frame shaking. His eyes were black holes with barely a trace of blue. The antlers were longer, more branched. The tips of his ears were pointed. Not like an elf, like an animal. "The more I fight, the closer to a beast I become."

"This morning…" she breathed. "That's why you didn't want me."

"Oh, I wanted you." His fists clenched while the

chords in his neck strained. "But sex and fertility are linked for me. To have you bear a child I fathered..." Tenderness bled into his voice, and she heard his yearning before he lashed his head from side to side. "It was too soon. It *is* too soon."

He stepped back into the shadows, his breathing harsh and heavy.

"I will *always* want you, *mo chroí*. Unfortunately, I won't want you alone. I'm told over three-dozen women this summer will be *thanking me* for the pleasure of impregnating them."

Her synapses must've misfired or her hearing had been damaged in the club. "Did you say three dozen?"

"Their babes will have their souls changed for the children I failed to set free."

And there was another button of hers pushed: the helpless being hurt. "When did this happen?"

"Sunset."

"Today?" she pressed in the hope he might mean some other sunset several years ago.

"Yes."

"It's because of me, isn't it? Because you gave me your heart."

Angus said nothing, which was answer enough.

*I knew it.*

Cursed because of her.

Everything she loved, she ruined.

"Thanks for giving me the lowdown so intimately, Angus."

She straightened her skirt and grabbed her phone.

"And if I'd said nothing?" He sounded so incredibly weary, her ribs ached for him.

If he'd said nothing, she would've let him screw her

sideways. Assuming he was as potent as he claimed and his curse nullified her pill, she'd be pregnant by midsummer.

"It's *how* you told me." He'd known the emotional and physical shock would be a double whammy. "It was a dick move after what I shared with you tonight, after you sharing my feelings yesterday, when you know I'm in love with you…."

She put her hand over her mouth.

For a second, he glowed, bright as he had within Newgrange. Then the glory of the god faded to the tour guide with a trispiral-scar on his chest and torment in his eyes. The man wore the guise well, but his heart wasn't in it.

"No. You are in lust with me as I am and in love with the man I used to be."

It was just as well she was in the dark: her face flamed so hot it made her blood boil. Every breath she snorted came out as steam. How dare he call her out. She'd *trusted* him with her most secret self. So, what if that part of her originally belonged to someone else? It wasn't her fault. How dare he make her feel *less* because he was so much more.

She hated him for being passionate and tender, trustworthy and proud.

Hated him more for being right about her not being ready.

And hated him most for speaking *her* truth, that it was the boy she loved, not the man.

To have him know was unbearable.

Her jaw tightened until her teeth hurt. "I knew you were too good to be true, McCraggan. You told me giving me your heart meant I was the only woman you could love. And now you're telling me I'm just the first of your thirty-six-seater harem."

"Thirty-seven," he corrected. "Including you."

"Whatever." She didn't want to share him with anyone. He was hers. He'd said so and she'd believed him. She'd been sold a dream yet bought a nightmare. Strapping on her customary callousness to hide the hurt, she gathered her panties and the strewn condoms into a bundle. "This just shows the legends were right. You really are a cheat, *Óenghus Óg*."

Without waiting for his reply, she shouldered the door open and walked out, leaving him alone in the darkness.

"*Mo chroí*, wait!" he shouted from within the stone. Wasn't it too bad that he had to get himself dressed and—if he was as conscientious as she recalled—lock the place up?

She walked quickly, ducking down a backstreet toward the river rather than returning down the wide, open main street where he'd spot her instantly. Of course, if he could find her in the middle of a nightclub, he'd find her soon enough. For now, she needed to cool off and cry a little. Once she shunted aside the pounding, slavering, savage need for him riding through her.

For a major urbanized town, it was seriously dark. And quiet. Most nightclubs closed at three a.m. Her phone told her it was nearly four. Spotting a bin, she stepped up the pace and tried to ignore the mix of friction and fluid from going commando. Damn Angus and his paranoia, too. She couldn't shake the feeling of being watched.

After disposing of a rotten business and dusting her hands, she fetched her keys from her purse and threaded them through her fingers to form a knuckle-duster.

From the corner of her eye, the shadows moved, and she almost heard something. Yet when she faced the dark corners straight on, there was no lurker within. It had to be a trick of the light, making the shadows seem thick. The Boyne cut through downtown and maybe it was the river that gave the air an iridescent sheen. Not exactly mist, thank God. She didn't need the banshee taking an encore.

*Keep moving.*

Gritting her teeth, she walked away, fighting the urge to glance over her shoulder.

"You must be Liz," a light male voice said from the shadows.

Shadows which had been empty.

Chapter Seventeen

Share and Share Alike

Adrenalin spiked Erin's heart, sending it into a frantic flutter. A dark street, alone in a short skirt and heels...

Until this moment, she'd never considered herself too stupid to live, but there'd been *no one* in the shadows. Gripping her make-shift weapon tight, she kept it low and to her side, ready to strike and run. She spun and slashed before his use of her name registered, her hand and keys passing right through a thuggish young man without him so much as flinching.

Shit.

He had to be one of the *Tuatha Dé Danann,* a ghost like Breda or the banshee, which meant she could be cursed or killed, but she wasn't likely to be raped.

Small comfort.

To hide her fear, she gave him a long, slow survey.

The blond youth dressed like a try-hard gangster, with a t-shirt several sizes too small, and baggy camo pants several sizes too big. The ultra-thick gold collar around his neck though, that was real bling. He kept his arms folded, all the better to show off the tattoos on the backs of his hands. As if a sheaf of wheat and the hand-tool that cut them—what was that thing called? A sickle?—could be menacing. Strange eyes, as hard and glassy as marbles, raked her from head to toe and everywhere in between with clear calculation and possibly x-ray vision if his too-knowing smile could be believed.

The first flush of panic over, Erin's brain played catch up. "How'd'you know who I am?"

"A mutual friend," he said with a dryness that shriveled the air.

Friend? Unlikely. *Liz* did not do friendship, she had hook-ups. On the other side of the Atlantic. Angus was the one person in Ireland whom she'd told about Liz. If he was the mutual 'friend,' then this guy was someone Angus didn't trust.

*An enemy.*

"Are you going to introduce yourself any time soon?" She folded her arms. "Because if you're going to make me guess, I'm running with Rumpelstiltskin."

"I go by many names and more titles, but that is not one of them. *Manannán Mac Lir* is my full name," he drawled with an amused air, completely at odds with the fading pimples and wispy attempt at a Van Dyke beard. "You, however, as my newest subject, may call me 'my lord.'"

Lord. Not Chief. Phew.

"Sorry, Man, not going to happen. Last I heard, this country was a republic and if you're hoping for something more personal, I'm taken."

"*Óenghus Óg* cannot be spared his destiny, Liz of the O'Neills," the young man said, confirming her intuition he was not a human threat.

"I don't know what you're talking about."

"Our lost soul was so persistent in hunting down your line, and so clever in her madness. By her rites, you should be doomed to a life in the shadows."

"I'm no changeling." Erin backed away, preparing to run. If he was a ghost, she could go through him the same as her keys.

He crooked his finger.

Her hips hitched and her legs swung. Panic and loathing had her attempting to stem the betrayal, trying to hold herself taut with her knees braced and feet stiff, but when he beckoned, her body obeyed. She stopped when she was nose to chin with him. Too close. Way too close. It wasn't much consolation that her foe looked almost uncomfortable.

"Correct. You are an abomination. I would kill you now would it not also end our reluctant savior." He thrust his hand, the one with the sickle, into her chest. "As you must live, I place you under the same conditions as your heart." Somehow, his fingers wrapped around her heart in icy bands.

Despite the night's chill, she found herself flushed and sweating, her heart burning like she'd eaten a jar of pickled habaneros. Keeping her balance became a challenge, running an impossibility. She couldn't catch her breath, her ribs throbbed with each gasp.

The heel of her hand found her breastbone, layered over his non-touch. About now would be a good time for Angus to show. Beneath her palm came the familiar and welcome flare of heat.

Her assailant let go with alacrity. "What are you?"

"A bitch."

His laugh was oddly pleasant. It was the easy and relaxed laugh of a man in command.

Nothing like the crazy-loon effort Angus had made after she'd asked if he was okay. Her insides folded, collapsing on old lines as if she was a pre-creased sheet of paper. Compressing, smaller and smaller, as complicated and precise as origami, until they closed with a mouse-trap snap. How could she have missed it? Shackled to Newgrange, branded like he was a possession, cursed to act like an animal, and perpetually miserable as sin.

*God damn you, Breda and your asshole Chief.*

Angus wasn't okay.

He was a slave.

It wasn't modesty that kept his abilities tame and his attitude downbeat. The pride was there. When goaded, he had a king's share of it. What kept him mired was the sticky combination of old guilt and fresh shame. Someone else claimed or controlled every part of him. His work life tied to Newgrange, his social life haunted by his ex-wife, his body cursed by his kin, his tongue forced into honesty by her grandfather, until all he had to call his own was his heart. So what had he done? Given it to her. The last person he should entrust it to. A survivor who wouldn't hesitate to end his life if it saved her own. Her father was the evidence when it came to the crunch, she fought for herself.

"I'm afraid you lack the traits of a female dog," said His Asshole Lordship, echoing her thoughts. "You could be trainable but are not capable of the necessary loyalty."

He leaned in, his top lip lifted in disgust. No surprise since she probably smelled like sex and Angus. Except Mac Lir didn't draw away, he made a grunting huff and smelled her *again,* the top lip thing happening big time. A bunch of animals used the Flehman response to pheromones, but humans weren't among them, so this couldn't be that—no matter how it looked.

"An intoxicating perfume. Dare I say it? You appear to be a touch…frisky."

"I don't expect it to last." Despite her hot face, she kept her voice cool.

"How curious our mutual friend would leave you unsatisfied." Her attacker frowned. "Usually, the selflessness of the son of the Dagda is as wearisome as it is reliable."

His frown deepened. "Let me see…"

He raised his other hand as fist—the one with the sheaf—and a faint scent cut through the night air: fresh hay with a hopped edge. Lighter than how Angus smelled, but no less intoxicating. A strange drunkenness flooded through her veins, as if she'd been knocking back beers at an Oktoberfest. She inhaled with almost sinful indulgence until she saw how her deep lungfuls made those glassy eyes glitter.

"Smell something you like?" he asked.

Mouth breathing, she shook her head. God help her, she couldn't be *attracted.* For Chrissake, if he wasn't a freakoid teenager, he was still someone she'd swipe left on a dating app to delete.

*Pheromones. This is nothing more than pheromones.*

"You share his heart and so you shall share his nature." He smiled indulgently. "You are now in heat, my fine brood mare, but earlier than I can make use of."

"What. The. Fuck." It wasn't a question; it was a strangled wheeze of outrage.

"Usually, I would accept. Alas, not yet." The hand with the sickle dove into her stomach. "Until then, let me ease your burden."

Within the brackets of her hipbones, a cold and

grasping pain pinched and tugged at her insides like he was picking off grapes one by one. Like the hand that had gripped her heart, it had the finesse and delicacy of a nail gun. A sinking feeling below her navel ached worse than period pains, like her uterus was lead-lined and tearing her insides apart.

She screamed.

What the hell was he doing?

Where was Angus when she needed him? Angus who'd promised to save her and sworn she'd never again be harmed. Relying on him had been a mistake. How could he rescue her when he couldn't save himself?

The pain ended as soon as Manann withdrew his ghostly grasp from inside her body. With a tender expression, he held out his hand, palm forward and fingers spread. A small droplet pooled on his fingertip, rounding into greenish-white globe like an etched transparent pearl.

He pinched it delicately with the fingers of his left hand, the one with the sheaf, then held it up to admire. "A small harvest but quite perfect. One berry of mistletoe is all I need to claim a kiss."

*Mistletoe?* "Tell me you didn't get that from me."

He eyed her. "Time to find out how much of his power he gave you, Liz O'Neill."

She knew about kissing under the mistletoe. Everyone did. That's why you either avoided the damn branch at Christmas or hovered under it—depending on the proportion of hot guys to creepy ones. Manann was totally the latter. But when he held the single white berry over her head, she couldn't back away. Her neck strained as she resisted yet still her chin tilted up, her lips parted… She tried to push against him, but her hands passed through his chest as his mouth pressed against hers to form a perfect seal.

Erin flailed. A panicked mental flail as well as one with her arms all over, but it made no difference. She couldn't break free.

His mouth was a void. There was no breath from him, in or out, just a numbing emptiness. More alarming was how she didn't seem to be breathing, either. When she'd drowned, there had been an anxious pressure, a constant strain on her lungs. Instead, a warm swirl softened her insides.

The swirl quickened. The warmth rose like sunlight, spiraling out to her limbs and toasting her toes. Nicer than mulled wine in winter, cozier than hot chocolate at bedtime, it made her thoughts muzzy around the edges. A little drunk, a little high, and real mellow. Yeah. Mellow. It was soooo gooood. This was the warmth she'd craved ever since the banshee had hollowed her out, a big ol' dose of love'n'kindness delivered in the signature style she associated with Angus McCraggan. She'd always taken for granted she would keep her wits about her come what may, but she didn't want this to stop. Nothing this nice could be bad. If Angus was the source, it was harmless.

You couldn't get too much love. Right?

Besides, this flow of power from Angus wasn't something she could refuse, even if she knew how. She was only the channel between him and Manann. She was full to overflowing with a seemingly endless supply of love and sunshine, yet it kept on coming. None of it left. It stayed inside her, unable to escape. Which meant whatever Manannaaan…Mahna-Mahna…His Assholeship was doing wasn't working right. He was getting nothing. Zilch. Nada. Bupkis.

Yet the flow didn't stop.

Dear God, did Angus have to be such a giver? Too much sun. Every part of her felt cooked. Then there was the spinning. What was with that? Up and down and left and right. Different parts of her body were riding all the rollercoasters on Coney Island. Simultaneously. Urgh.

She felt like a water balloon ready to burst.

Would there be bits of her on the pavement afterwards or would her skin just hang loose? Because right now it was super-tight and itchy and hot. This was the trouble with being hard on the outside and soft within: if she was Erin all the way through, she'd expand until she dissipated; if she was Liz alone, she'd be solid like a superconductor and Angus would be gone in a snap. Neither was a good option, not least because they were currently a two-for-one deal.

*Any second now, I'm gonna hurl...*

It was the spinning. The energy swirling around faster than a Catherine wheel. If she never saw a spiral again, it would be too soon. There had to be some means of finding relief. The outside spun faster than the center, so she pulled her awareness inwards, tightening and narrowing until she was a speck in the middle. Going within, there was a way out.

She took it and went elsewhere...

\*\*\*\*

She was in a canyon, caught between two steep-walled cliffs: one side cool and flawlessly sheer, impossible to climb. The other side pulsing and glowing with molten intensity. The place between, where she wandered, was a thin fault line that neither widened nor closed.

She followed its route, there being no other option. It was like half of a maze of mirrors, made of…rock? Glass? Ice? Whatever it might be, rather than reflecting her, the images were of other people. Children, mostly, dressed in muted plaids and soft furs; the clothes of a very different era. The amount of gold gleaming around throats or in hair or on wrists was excessive. Some of the bigger kids, both boys and girls, carried adult-grade weapons with the ease of familiarity: swords, spears, and bows. In contrast to the snub noses and chubby cheeks, their eyes were wary, their mouths tight. Child soldiers forced into war.

If she was more than a prick of consciousness, Erin would have shivered.

Above the children, looming on the upper cliff fronts, carved out like Mount Rushmore, were two faces. A man and a woman. The woman had the same uncompromising features as Angus but cast in a feminine mold. The man had more of a bluff, friendly look to him, not unlike a rugged Santa Claus.

"What is this place?" she asked aloud.

"This is the fissure within my brother's heart," a woman replied. "The break that doesn't heal."

From the bright and shining side, a flaming-headed figure stepped out. It cooled to become someone she recognized.

*Breda.*

"I'm definitely having a mental breakdown," Erin said.

"It does require a certain flexibility of perspective. Our philosophy is less binary than yours, less black and white. We see a spectrum between life and death, a spectrum which allows for many more layers of reality

211

than you're used to."

"Does that mean I'm dead?"

"Not this time. Not yet. You're in an altered state of consciousness, going within rather than without."

"So, I'm dreaming." No big deal. "Except I'm not asleep." In other words, a mental breakdown. Fine, she'd survived those before. A pity she wasn't channeling the Dalai Lama or even Da, rather than Breda. "If I wasn't so Zen right now, I'd be really pissed. You promised my grandfather I'd be safe from the banshee."

"My promise was conditional—and I did save you when I made it."

"Uh huh, yeah. In a manner of speaking." If Erin had a head, she'd shake it. It was obvious the bar for normal was forever going to be beyond her reach and Breda was to blame. Safer to change the subject than argue with the only spiritual guide she was going to find in here. "Who're those two up on high?"

"Our father, the Dagda, and Angus' mother, Bóann. Angus is not alone in revering them, but they failed him, as parents so often do, by being human. He can't forgive them for that any more than he can forgive himself."

"Nothing to do with you and your asshole Chief keeping him penned like an animal in a zoo and cursing him to get busy with a breeding program?"

"No, sister-in-law, it was not me, but his parents who set him on this path by handing him—and me—the problem they could not solve themselves." She studied the pair with dispassion. "My brother longs to put his past behind him. To pretend it doesn't exist and start afresh—as you were made to do."

"I'd be the first to tell him it wasn't any fun. The whole reason I came back to Ireland was to get my head in order. Clearly, not a strategy that worked." Erin looked again at the cliffs within her lover's heart. "How come you're here?"

"He keeps us here, frozen in memory, so we cannot disappoint him, and he cannot disappoint us." Breda indicated an image on the dark and cold side of a much younger version of herself and, weirdly, a much older, buffer version of Manann. "Angus may have a godlike aspect, but he is, at heart, only a man. He would forget us altogether, if we let him, but he is our light and we cannot let him go or we shall never be free."

Erin noted an absence. "Where's that bitch, Caer? Is she burning in the fire on that side?"

"He excised her from his heart for you."

"Is that what caused this chasm?" Because—no pressure—it was a *lot* of space to fill.

"This fissure is between his past and his present. He cannot bridge it alone, and Caer proved…unsound."

"No kidding." Bridging. A shame she wasn't one for building connections. Breaking them, now that was something she excelled at. Speaking of… "Angus said Caer left him way back when. That's the part I don't get, given she was supposed to love him endlessly and unconditionally, yada yada."

"Caer didn't trust that Manann and I had her beloved's best interests as our priority. By remaining free, she sought to safeguard his future return. She survived because Angus took her heart with him into the earth, but it was through binding herself to your bloodline, that she gained her strength."

"Was I supposed to be her new home?"

"I believe so."

"Great. That's just great." And now Erin was

rooming with Breda. The hell no to this being permanent. "How do I get out of here?"

"This furnace is you. What is left within Angus is stone dead."

"He told me he'd die if I spurned him. But you can survive without a heart, Breda. I should know, I went eight years without one."

"The best part of him—the part that makes him Angus—would die. But he is more than a man. He can exist as a god, but a god without a heart is not a loving god or a forgiving one." Breda gave a small, sad smile. "That is why he cannot live without you. You are his heart now. You are our hope."

"So you're telling me to stay, not run. Right?"

"No, Erin. I'm telling you to play or be played."

Chapter Eighteen

A Glimmering Girl

Angus found Erin and Manann locked together, mouth-to-mouth, in a parody of passion. Her eyes were wide open and frighteningly absent, the rest of her a molten haze so bright Angus had to squint to look at her. Every single cell within her body glowed—as if she'd swallowed the sun.

The trispiral on his chest had flamed to match, burning from his sternum through to his spine as Erin continued to draw on Newgrange through him. The heartburn was so bad he could barely breathe. He used the pain as a spur, pushing him to reach her faster.

*All I can give. Everything I have.* So he'd sworn and so he'd give. Unconditionally. Everything he possessed, he'd shared: his life, his strength, his heart. She was no longer who she had been or else she'd already be crisped to a cinder.

Marie's words rang in his ears. *You can't give of yourself like that and not have it do something to her.* Unintentionally, he'd also made her one of his people, subject to the rules of his existence, and therefore subject to his Chief. A fact Manann was using to his advantage.

*Once she has all my power, he'll kill her to take it for himself.*

The realization hit Angus like a bull's kick to the crotch. Erin had no defenses of her own save those of her blood—to walk in daylight and be clothed in flesh. Under normal circumstances this would be protection enough. But she'd also died and passing through death gave Manann dominion over her soul. She had no means of resisting the Lord of the Dead.

Nor could Angus block her from taking his own power.

But there had to be something he could do. His Chief might be untouchable, but he was distracted—his focus on Erin. To strike him was impossible, but what if he countered his claim?

Breathing in what might be his last lungful of air, he stepped into the semblance of the other man. Standing in the shade of death was cold, colder than a tomb although a strange burning circled his throat, as though he could feel his father's torc around his own neck. He put his warm mouth to Erin's chilled one, hoping his love would be stronger than the kiss of death.

The moment he touched her, a thunderbolt shot through him from gullet to groin, the crack boomed down the street with a force that shook the walls. Her body fell limp into his arms, but her aura stayed blast-furnace bright.

This was the opposite to when she'd died: too much power and too contained.

Ungrounded.

As the Lady of the Land, it was Breda's job to teach a novice how to earth power. But if she ignored this, then he had an alternative. Inside the chamber at Newgrange he could extract Erin's excess energy to restore her to a safe level. The difficulty would be getting her there.

As he shifted his hold to scoop her into his arms, her limbs dangled, and something metallic fell to the ground with a jingle. It was the least of his problems. Riding a motorbike with an unconscious passenger wasn't a viable option and Erin wouldn't wake. Her skin was feverish and dry, her gaze vacant.

*This is my fault. I made her run.*

"*Mo chroí*," he whispered from a mouth dry as ashes. "Erin?"

Manann laughed softly behind him.

Curses rushed to Angus' lips. What had possessed him to speak her true name? Setting her against the wall like an over-sized doll, he turned to her assailant. The man he'd failed to protect her from.

His Chief leaned against the stone wall keeping his face partly in shadow. The side in the light seemed calmly speculative, as if Angus had passed some sort of test a little earlier than expected. The darker side was far more judgmental. The glint to that eye suggested its owner knew full well Angus had everything to lose. And nothing to bargain with.

Angus clenched his teeth until his jaw cracked then forced his speech out in stages. He did it in the old tongue; a language not spoken since his people had been interred.

"I, *Óenghus*, son of the *Dagda*, beseech you, my—" He choked down the word master. Not yet, but soon. "My *lord*, the *Crom Cruach*, the reaper of souls, to grant me a boon."

"Do you indeed?" Manann tilted his head and tapped his finger to his chin. "My curiosity is roused."

A strong start but a false one. Manann was the master of death, and his dominion was fear. His Chief

217

would make him beg.

"It was my decision to gift her with my heart. You bound and cursed me as punishment for this treason. *Me*, not her. She had no say in being saved, no choice in being changed. Send her back over the sea, if you must, but let her live."

Eyes narrowing, Manann's mouth spread in a tight and mocking smile. The very smile he'd worn when pressing the trispiral brand into Angus' breastbone. It did not bode well.

"She is nothing but a vessel. A flawed repository for your power. Through her, I can conquer you. Why would I give up such a delicious advantage?"

The question threw Angus back to a simpler time when the man before him had pushed him to think, not goaded him to react. He almost smiled as he replied, "Because a good farmer waits until his crops are ripe before he harvests. Our Lady gave me until midsummer to find another way to make amends. If you take me down then, at the peak of my strength, your gain will be greater and your victory sweeter."

It needled his pride, but for Erin's sake he let his shoulders slump with a penitential weight. "She is my heart. You need her to leave before your curse takes effect—else she will spurn me and your breeding plan will fail. Swear by Our Lady to let Erin live. Swear, and if I cannot guide our kin to freedom, I will give myself over to them of my own free will."

"Well played, son of the Dagda." Manann delivered an ironic, soundless golf clap. There was something stuck to his palm. A pearl. It flexed then burst, revealing itself as a shell. A thick stem squirmed out, sickly green as pea soup, twisting and lifting like a worm as it grew outwards and sprouted fat, tongue-shaped leaves. Mistletoe. Not a native plant, but then Manann was not a native. "I will let her live. And if she wishes to leave this land, I will not stop her. So, I swear by Our Lady."

Without further ado, he vanished. An effective means of gaining the last word.

Prepared to do battle, his opponent's unprecedented agreement left Angus shaken. It had cost him nothing. Somewhere, somehow, he had missed something important. Determining what, however, would have to wait.

There, lurking in the darkest places, were dark shadows. Shadows that moved when nothing else did. In the bright light cast by Erin, he could make out something he'd never been able to see distinctly before: Beasts and birds with oversized heads and long coiled bodies like snakes but free of scales or fur or feathers; great footed with perfect, pointed talons and wickedly sharp beaks or gaping fang-lined jaws. Dead-eyed monsters trained to hunt as a pack and rend their prey into pieces.

"Great Dagda."

The feral, starving remnants of his people were here, and, since he had nothing to give them, they weren't about to rally to his side. Unlike Caer, nothing human remained. They'd lost all traces of speech and sense. All that remained was hunger. All they wanted was to feed.

He was in serious trouble. *Erin* was in serious trouble. Of them both, she was currently the tastier morsel. They needed to get inside, somewhere with doors. A car would do. Her car, if she'd driven and if it was near. He found her tiny bag, slung from right shoulder to left hip. Her phone inside, plastic cards, cash.

No coins.

What had jingled? Her keys?

Stretching his fingers he tried to extend his senses for any nearby metal. Nothing. He'd have better luck using Erin as a torch. Looking around her, however, was difficult. She was far too dazzling.

Shadows seethed out from the stones. With no streetlights nearby, the darkness was thick and it heaved. The air had a warp to it, sinuous and sleek as satin, it made the distant streetlights shimmer and gleam as if through water. The normal night sounds were absent, replaced by the chitinous natter of fangs and claws.

Panic streaked through him.

They respected strength and his was halved, while Erin had none.

Preoccupied with trying to hoist her onto his shoulder, he ignored the change in air pressure until it popped his ears. As he shook his head, something very like the Aurora Borealis cloaked Erin's shoulders. The shadows cringed and retreated.

"You always were a fool for love, weren't you, Angus?" a voice that was not Erin's said with her mouth.

Those holier-than-thou tones were unmistakable.

"You shouldn't be in there, Bree. You weren't invited and she wouldn't like it. You're supposed to be the moral one, remember?"

"You have this situation under control, do you, brother? Then I shall leave you to our kin's tender mercies."

"And lose us both?" Without Breda's presence to awe the shadows, Erin would be torn apart, and he would follow.

"You, I have already lost."

"Then save her and leave me."

"You further my point."

Biting his tongue to keep from bickering away the opportunity Breda had granted, he released Erin completely to scavenge more rapidly around her with both hands. At long last, the cold bite of metal twitched under his fingers.

"Can you ground her so she can show me where her car is?"

"She must have her own earth if she is to withstand my *Crom Cruach's* lust for light."

"In the name of our father," Angus muttered. "The car then. Can *you* find it?"

Erin's arm flopped out with the finesse of a puppet. "Give me the keys."

He handed them over. The faster he got her to safety, the less chance his sister had to make herself at home.

"Help me rise," Breda ordered.

Together, they staggered down the road to the carpark like a pair of drunks. The shadows trailed behind them with a rising raucousness, baying as a pack of hounds do before a hunt. Fortunately, they were not far from Erin's car.

"Blip it open," he suggested when Breda's coordination didn't stretch as far as inserting the key into the door.

"The energy Erin absorbed shorted the circuits."

"Lucky for us it's the old-fashioned kind." He wrapped his hand around hers to unlock the door manually. Not trusting her any further than he could throw her, he wedged himself into the open door first and clambered across to the driver's seat. His knees were halfway to his ears and the steering wheel was denting his thigh bones but adjustments could wait.

No sooner was his sister inside the vehicle than the darkness deepened.

Leaning over her, he yanked the door closed and flicked on the central locking. Not a moment too soon. Metal groaned and screeched as the shadows tried to get in. If it wasn't for the fact that most people treated their car like a hard bubble of personal space, he'd be dinner. His sister's presence might save Erin, but all that was saving him was the convention of needing to be invited in, an ancient rule of hospitality his people still adhered to.

Putting the key in the ignition with one hand, he found the lever for his seat with the other. Pushing it all the way back, he was able to ram his legs into the footwell and gunned the accelerator.

"Don't count on staying, Bree." He released the handbrake and slammed the automatic into drive. They shot forward. Frantically, he corrected his over-steering as they did so. Fecking cars. Give him a horse any day. "After tonight, I wouldn't be surprised if Erin takes the first plane out of here."

Breda merely smiled. He knew that look. It was the one she kept just for him. The smugness of a younger sibling outsmarting her big brother. Her complacency making him anxious for Erin's sake, he clenched the steering wheel one-handed, his other arm slung across her body because he hadn't waited for seatbelts, and drove like he was the one possessed.

By fleeing, he had triggered a Hunt. Perhaps that was why Breda was smug.

Pelting down the road to Newgrange, they came to a treacherous section of road—sheltered by woods on one side, with the road tracing the arc of the Boyne River on the other. A dangerous place, liable to ice over in winter and collect rotting leaves in fall, it was also close to a battlefield. Too many lives lost here, with too much suffering. It would be a tempting place for an ambush.

Anticipation made his nerves sing shrilly.

Of its own accord, the radio switched on and shrieked around the dial. Fog swept in, rapid and thick, to slow their pace. Caer's doing. The glare reflecting from the headlights was bright enough to blind. On the one hand, it kept the shadows at bay. On the other, Angus couldn't maintain his high speed. He sat poker straight, the hairs on his arms rising with unreleased static, his heart aching as its beat quickened. Sweat slid down his spine as he slalomed through the whiteness.

The banshee's wail, however, never came. Her fading strength, a small mercy.

The fog thinned and departed when they crossed the narrow Mattock river over its humpbacked bridge. Without it, the shadows grew brave, pawing at the windows and fawning over the windscreen. They were too dark. Too twisted. Too lethal. How could he bring such creatures into the light? They were not children, they were animals. No, less than animals. Time and neglect had whittled them down to hunger and revenge.

There had to be an alternative. A sidestep to both avoid his curse and fulfill his vow or escape both together. If there was, he couldn't see it. Not that he could take it anyway, thanks to Breda.

The attack grew fiercer. One final effort as they neared Newgrange. The driver's window cracked under the pressure, spinning a spiderweb into the glass. One of the headlights blew with a pop. The engine strained in harmony to the radio.

"They want what you can give them, brother. They see what you gave a stranger and want it for themselves. How can you deny them?"

His jaw tight with tension, Angus couldn't reply. His grip on the wheel remained white-knuckled as he skidded to a halt directly in front of an iron-barred gate set into the hedgerows. It took him a few seconds to absorb they had arrived in one piece and to pry his fingers from the wheel and kill the engine.

This was *his* earth and proximity to his dominion was power.

That said, gathering himself took twice as long as it should. Breda-in-Erin was out the car and by the gate by the time he was ready. As Angus clambered out the car, the shadows kited close enough to ruffle his hair and run long, triple-jointed fingers over his face and throat. He caught glimpses of them in the heaving mass of darkness. Filmy wings ripped and torn. Hanging tails and hollowed ribs. Dead eyes and open mouths. Hungry mouths. Mouths with sharp, over-sized teeth. Sweat leaked from his pores.

They were in famine, and he was meat. They would pick his bones clean.

They could smell his fear. He saw it in the drips of saliva, the tensing of their bone-thin limbs. More real than he had ever seen them, they made true sounds: crystallized wings clinked, and mummified hides grated, talons clicked and teeth gnashed. Worse than a plague of rats, more fetid than a nest of cockroaches, the *púca* slid and clambered over each other as they swarmed in banks on either side of him—champing against the wall of his will.

Shaken, he pointed Erin's car keys like a gun at them, using the metal as a focal point to blast the swarm. They fled—but only to the edge of his field of vision. Exerting himself to his limit, he strengthened what was left of his wards, keeping the shadows back down the hill in front of them and into the bordering hedgerows.

Once through the lower gate, he slammed it closed out of habit. It made no real difference since this was an open-aired site. He barred access by force here, not protocol.

Which reminded him there *was* a guaranteed means of getting rid of his sister from her possession of Erin's body.

"Farewell, Bree."

Scooping an arm around Erin's waist, he leaned down and touched his lips to hers. Then, in case his sister doubted his intentions, he softly pulled at his lover's lower lip with the tip of his teeth, making the gesture not merely intimate, but carnal.

Breda left with a gurgle, whipping away the cloak of her command with a colorful light-show, the metallic astringency of her aura instantly replaced by Erin's tart sweetness. She tasted glorious. His power gave her essence a liqueur potency that left him light-headed. He could only imagine what it was doing to her.

Erin signaled her return to consciousness by turning her face aside.

"Angus?" she asked, her tone uncertain, her gaze unfocused. "Is that you?"

"It is, *mo chroí.*"

"How do I know it's you, not that Womb Raider Asshole Chief of yours?"

*Womb Raider? What did Manann do?*

For a second Angus hesitated, stalled by a fresh concern Manann might have attempted to steal more than power. Unsure of how to prove himself other than kissing her, he replicated the nose-to-nose slide Erin had used on him in the nightclub. It was the right move. The tension immediately dropped from her shoulders.

"Why's it so bright?" She put her hand to visor her eyes as though this might shade them. "Everything's all shiny and silvery."

She looked around blindly. "I'm seeing things." She rubbed her eyes. "There's something seething over there. Seething Things."

"We're not safe here, Erin. I can't keep the *púca* away much longer." The shadows swooped their prey in a first, exploratory strike. He yanked her around to face the Entrance Stone. "Can you see it? Can you see the door into my hill?"

"Oh yes!" She sounded reverent.

"You can run, can't you, Erin? I'll race you there."

She kicked off her high heels. "Ready?"

"Go!"

After giving her a head start, he pounded up the hillside.

Chapter Nineteen

Their Perfume Lost

Night vision was a bonus Erin could get used to, but it wasn't green like they showed in the movies. A silvery, iridescent membrane spread over the landscape, stretched tight in every direction she looked save the entrance into Newgrange. Something, no, wait, a bunch of somethings, seethed underneath.

Against the world glittering in grays, Angus stood apart. Not as a man, but a guttering orange-hued flame, his form and features obscured. It was only when she looked closely she could see the trispiral embedded deep within his light. The lines spiraled endlessly, tricking her eyes and sickening her stomach.

A strand came from where each spiral dove inwards, the three twining into a pulsing rope which led to the earthen mound: an umbilical cord tying him to Newgrange.

*No! Nothing so romantic.*

*He's a slave. It's not a bond. It's a chain.*

Digging her toes into the soft sod carpeting the hillside, she set off at a run—her destination the light on the hill. In bodyguard mode again, Angus kept back to let her win. She lengthened her stride to prove there was no need. She was fit and fast and running was her bliss.

As she neared the Entrance Stone the etchings across its surface flared. The light beckoned, rather than deterred. Distracted, she didn't see the wooden fence blocking her from reaching the stone until she ran into it. Air whooshed from her lungs. Something, possibly a rib, cracked.

*Ow.*

The pain went almost the moment it registered.

In front of her, the giant stone hummed softly, a vibration below the threshold of hearing, calling to her. Feeling for the wooden beams, she clambered between them. With outstretched arms and a zombie-shuffle she drew closer to the illuminated grooves forming the largest and most famous trispiral. She touched her fingers, feather-light, to the stone.

Angus made a noise somewhere between surprise and pain.

She snatched her fingers back. "Does it hurt?"

"Leave it be, Erin. Please. You need to get inside." He sounded strained.

The metallic creak of another gate drew her attention to the chamber entrance where the flame of Angus stood, his light growing steadier and stronger. In the daytime, the doorway had been cave-dark. Tonight, with her crazy-ass vision, it glowed faintly orange, like firelight from a hearth.

"Get inside, *mo chroí.*" No please this time, but a terse and anxious order.

She glanced behind her. Dozens of creatures climbed the fence she couldn't see. Fantastical coiled and curvy animals in every shade of shining gray from pewter to platinum. Too stretched and thin to be real, they wound in and out of themselves and each other like something daydreamed by a talented scribe and scribbled in the margins of a sacred text. Every single one of them wriggled and struggled to push through the silvery membrane which shrink-wrapped the land and kept them trapped in another dimension. These must be the shadows she'd seen as a child.

"The *púca* cannot follow within. Get inside Newgrange and you'll be safe."

Safe? Inside? She eyed the mound more closely. It sat like a bubble within the sheen on the land. How could going inside the bubble be safe?

Noise pressed on her eardrums. More pressure than sound at first, it built into whispers and mutters, a rustling and a slithering as if a multitude of animals and humans were squeezed together, frantic and frightened.

They needed help.

"Why are you so afraid of them, Angus?"

"Because they're deadly."

"Deadly?" She cocked her head. She'd used *deadly* as a kid all the time. This band is deadly. That outfit is deadly. It didn't mean lethal, it meant amazing. Her childhood term fitted the seething *púca*. They were weirdly fascinating and oddly beautiful. And desperate, so desperate.

"Erin, they'll tear us both apart." He came up beside her. "Please, *mo chroí*. I've already failed to protect you once this evening. My people are attracted to your light. They want it for themselves."

"Wow, everyone in your realm sure wants a piece of me. Wait, what? *These* are your *people*?"

"They are not what they once were."

She winced, hearing again what he'd said before. Neither was he. He wasn't the boy she'd dreamed of and

229

yet she did have feelings for the man, she just wasn't sure what they were.

She entered the passageway to conceal her confusion. The tunnel was tight and narrow, warm after the night air, and not dark as it should have been, but rosy with the light bleeding from her pores. A second trispiral was carved several yards in on one of the massive upright stones. She didn't need to touch it to see it was also connected to Angus. It throbbed with a heart's beat.

A trispiral on the outside, then this one within. Newgrange wasn't a bubble, it was an airlock. With a third trispiral on his chest, Angus was the key. She frowned. A key on a chain. He might be free of the silvery binding keeping his people within the earth, but the cord linking him to the trispirals kept him permanently tethered.

The chamber within seemed much larger without a crowd. The walls and crude domed ceiling roared in her mind's eye with the cherry-red of a furnace. A rounded belly of earth, a tunnel for a shaft of light to penetrate…

*This is a womb.*

From it, Angus had been reborn.

Granddad had told her Angus had been released from *Tir na nÓg* for a reason and he was right. Angus had vowed to lead the *Tuatha Dé Danann* to freedom. When his people had sent him into the earth, they'd sealed him into Newgrange—the most prominent and renowned of all the hollow hills in Ireland. He'd gone in first and come out first, making it across the divide on a one-way ticket. If she had it right, Breda and His Assholeship could come and go both ways, but only in spirit. Nobody else got a pass. Well, maybe on Halloween, if tradition held true, but it wasn't a permanent visa to stay.

Yet Angus claimed he couldn't lead without being Chief and he couldn't be Chief because he'd given her his heart. Excuses. He didn't want to lead what his people had become. He saw them as a threat. It was telling that his prison should also be his sanctuary.

Angus had the strength, but no will to fight.

Erin could fight, but hadn't the strength to win.

Until now.

*If I'm this juiced, he has to be drained.*

Fine then. She'd do the job for him. Get it over and done. While she had his power, she was going to wield it for a noble cause. Not just freedom for Angus. Freedom, too, for the people he owed. Once released, there would be no need for Manann and Breda to enforce their curse. Angus could get on with living, free of his past, and she could get on with her own life, happy in the knowledge she'd repaid her debt.

Once she broke the seal, everyone got out of jail.

"Aren't you coming in?" she called to the flame hovering at the threshold to the chamber.

"I'm not sure grounding yourself through me would be wise."

"It does sound kind of kinky."

He laughed. A genuine laugh of good humor. She could've sworn it sent sunbeams bouncing around the walls.

"Grounding is when we connect to the land to regain balance with the Goddess. The idea is you're supposed to connect with the Goddess through a sacred earth—something you don't have. My mother used to teach that it's possible to connect with the Goddess anywhere, because all land is a part of her, but novices find it easier to connect with a place they have chosen themselves, somewhere they feel safe and comfortable.

"When we were banished, it was necessary to take that a step further, to find a shelter within the land. Your people and mine respect where the dead are laid to rest, so the barrows and tombs of the ancients became our, well, *residences* for want of a better term. Or, to be more exact, our spiritual homes since our bodies returned to dust."

He fell silent and the wild-eyed faces of all those children loomed in Erin's mind, before he spoke again in a falsely cheery tone that mocked everything he'd suffered. "Newgrange is my earth, bonded to me, and me alone. You have my heart, however, so you should be able to ground here."

"Or you could just suck the difference out of me with a kiss like your master, right?" Her mouth never knew when to shut up.

"He is not—" Angus cut himself off.

"You can't say it, can you?" she asked, much more softly. "Because it's true."

When he stayed silent, Erin wished she could slide in between the giant stones lining the chamber. Or maybe banging her head against one would do. Angus had his pride. Nor should she get all judgy given how a crook of Manann's finger had made her body his puppet. She wiped her arm over her mouth as if that might scrub off the memory.

"Have you had words with your sister about her choice of men?"

"She had no choice. The only other uninjured adult capable and available was me."

"Ah. Um, so what's our Man god of, anyhow?"

"For a time, he was of the sea, but he changed and became the Lord of Death and Darkness, Slaughter and Survival."

"Oh." She put her hand to her abdomen where the Lord of Death had scythed through her. Bile edged up her throat and she swallowed, hard. "We're screwed, aren't we?"

"There is no 'we,' Erin. I can't protect you from him. I can't even save you from *me*. After tonight, you must understand why it's best for you to leave."

She couldn't argue with his logic. Love could save someone a time or two, but death always won in the end. No wonder he was a defeatist. But she wasn't ready to give up hope she could repay her life with his freedom.

"A clean break." *Of your chains, not of us.*

"You've burned for me long enough. You should be able to ground here by working directly through the stones. Normally I ask visitors not to touch them, but you'll need to. Give it a go."

"What are you going to do?"

"I'll stay here. I'd prefer not to take anything you don't freely give."

Such a different man to his Chief. Angus reassured and explained, reluctant to act unless pressed. The flipside to this gentle heart was a distrust of its opposite: he judged theft and dishonesty and murder with smelting harshness.

She touched her forehead where meeting Breda had left its mark. The corner the banshee had used to peel her apart. The last time she'd been in here, she'd feared Angus would do as the banshee had done and consume her from within. There was the nook she'd cowered in, terror leaking from her until the chamber was awash. She ran her hand along the crisscrossed lines and zigzags lining the stones. Nothing special about it. Nothing but cool stone, ridges and dents. How could she connect to stone? If it was Angus, now, the ridges and dents of his ribs, the heat of his torso, then this would make sense. A tiny burst of sensation, like when she summoned him, flickered and faded.

Behind her, he gasped. "Don't!"

"Don't what?"

"Don't call me in there with you. I can't refuse a plea from the heart, Erin."

"Is that what I'm doing?" She'd done it at the trispiral, too. "Would you being in here be so bad?"

"This is my earth. Everything you give, I take. Give too much and you will wind up inside Newgrange, as I was, and I don't know how to bring you out."

"Lucky for you I'm not a giver." She pressed her hand to her heart. "I'm one of life's take—"

The rest of her warning was lost as he entered the chamber.

The place lit up with a *whoosh* as his presence filled the space and he became an amber man-shape within a glittering, golden-walled room. The floor thrummed, sending tiny pieces of gravel and grit tickling over her bare feet. The artwork carved on the upright stones danced in rainbow hues and there was a distant sound, like a far-off choir, which seemed to bypass her ears and go straight into her brain. The air thickened with his smoky scent, and she inhaled until she was dizzy.

"You haven't heeded a single warning I've given you," he groused. "If you'd stayed outside the day we met, you wouldn't be here now."

"Because I'd be dead. If you hadn't taken my fear

that day, I wouldn't have been able to withstand the banshee for a moment and you'd have an Erin-shaped homicidal nutjob to explain to my grandfather."

That shut him down.

"Very well then my brave, bold lady, hold out your hand."

She extended her hand, ready to shake. His soft chuckle washed over her and ended too soon. It was, if possible, better than his singing.

"We're not striking a deal, *mo chroí.*"

Large, strong fingers wrapped around her hand and rotated her wrist. His touch sent a jolt down her arm. Tiny bolts of lightning flickered from her fingers to his. Her hand tingled, not unpleasantly, as a familiar languor seeped into her limbs. His hand spasmed and he made a sound similar to when she'd traced the trispiral outside.

Instantly, she let go. "Angus?"

"I'm grand. Your feelings have more strength behind them than I expected."

"That was grounding?"

"Something like," he said thickly. He cleared his throat. "Let's give it another go; except this time, I'm going to put your hand on my heart."

His heart was directly under the trispiral. Perfect for her plan to steal the key from his chest and break the seal between Newgrange and the land. If he could give her his heart yet keep a muscle beating in his chest, then she could snatch the magic from inside the brand.

Probably.

She chewed the inside of her cheek. *Maybe this isn't such a great idea.* "Should we try somewhere else first?"

"I am strongest here. That makes this the safest place in Ireland for you."

"I don't want to hurt you."

"Do not tempt me to draw this out, Erin."

"Tempted? I thought you liked your pain short and sharp."

"Being your channel as you ground is extremely, ah, gratifying from my perspective. Just balance us both, as quick as you can, and, by the Goddess, Erin De Santos, *listen* to me on this if you want to walk out of here."

She nodded and trained her gaze to the trispiral on his chest. There was her target.

The banshee's desire to maim and murder had never been hers, but from Caer she knew how to tear out a man's heart. The same principle surely applied to tearing out an enchantment. When she clawed into his chest, she must be careful. Like a tattoo, the brand—awful as it was—didn't go more than skin deep. The goal was to save him, not kill him. But worst-case scenario, she held more than enough power to kiss him better.

Without warning or waiting for further invitation, she placed her hand flat on his chest, palm square on the intersection of the three spirals.

Angus groaned, his spine arching. The flow between them was super-fast and crazy powerful. The grit beneath her feet might have been beach sand getting washed out from under her by the wave of longing sweeping through her with the force of a tsunami. She scrunched her toes and crooked her fingers. As he fell to his knees in ecstasy, the brand slithered and slid under her grasp like a freshly landed trout. While he was lost to the pleasure she was giving him, she stabbed in her nails to lock it down and pulled.

He cried out, and she wasn't sure if it was from pleasure or pain. The damn trispiral was caught on something underneath his skin. Trying not to think too hard, she slid her other hand into his chest and found it tethered to something a little smaller than a golf ball. Something smooth and solid, sheared down one side and cold as the stone surrounding her.

Breda had shown her the two halves of his poor broken heart.

*Oh God, I have the rest of his HEART in my HAND.*

Panic tussled with growing lassitude.

She had to free him from slavery and his curse. Ripping it right on out though—that was something the banshee would do. *Not me.*

*Please let him be okay, please let this work.*

If she hurt him, she'd never forgive herself.

Holding his heart with one hand, she twisted at the trispiral as if she was twisting off a cap from a bottle of beer. It came away with a jerk. The spirals unwound in her palm into strands, one long and one short. They slithered like snakes, the short one wriggling through her fingers to worm into the stony heart still held in her hand, the longer whipping through her arm to whisk her blood into a froth.

The light died. The darkness was absolute.

She and Angus panted in unison.

He was still breathing. She was still standing. It was all good. Probably.

"Angus? That...what I did...that didn't hurt you or anything, did it?"

"Hurt me? Ah, Erin. Such bliss only hurts when it ends. But what of you? Are you well, *mo chroí*?"

"I'd be better if it wasn't so dark, and I could see you to know you're really okay."

A rustle was followed by the distinct click of a

switch. The dim electric light made a poor substitute for the splendor he'd created. She scanned him from head to toe, hoping he wasn't injured or angry or damaged.

He wore his jacket without a shirt and his jeans hung low at the waist because he hadn't fully buttoned his fly. With his black mane of hair, he could have been some early Nineties rock god fresh from a sell-out stadium gig. His chest was unbranded, as unmarred as the rest of him. Her heart tripped like a groupie's on speed.

*I did it!*

Atlantic-blue eyes met hers, and she couldn't look away. When he smiled and sent his dimples dancing, she had the strangest sensation of weightlessness. He was free. Because of her. She floated on a sense of achievement, ridiculously happy because the slate between them was wiped clean.

No other reason.

Okay, there was the minor fact she could stay here for the summer now, safe in the knowledge his Chief held no more power over him and therefore no power over her. An entire summer with Angus. Starting with today. Her cheeks ached from grinning.

"I thought nothing could be more beautiful than my first sunrise. Until now. Seeing you happy…" His Adam's apple bobbed as he swallowed hard. "I love you, Erin De Santos."

She couldn't hold his gaze after that. It was enough to glory in his words without her usual knee-jerk need to deny she was worthy of affection. Her heart had been like the Grinch's and now it was swelling so big the chamber felt oddly confining. If this kept up, she might, maybe, be able to tell him she felt the same. One day.

His hand cupped her cheek and tilted her chin.

"Come watch the dawn with me."

It sounded wonderfully romantic. She risked a glance through her lashes. "I have the feeling today is going to be a new start for us both."

Chapter Twenty

The Center Cannot Hold

Angus shared Erin's good mood if not her optimism as they stood together in the space between the doorway into Newgrange and its Entrance Stone, waiting for the sun.

It was not darkest before the dawn. Whoever had coined that phrase must have been a late sleeper. Pre-dawn light was weak and monochrome and uncertain, but it was always bright enough to see. It was, however, coldest before the dawn. The chill seeped under his jacket, and he held Erin tighter against him, luxuriating in the simplicity of having the woman he loved in his arms with no immediate task other than keeping her warm.

She fit against him comfortably and well, tall enough for her hair to tickle against his nose as he breathed, her frame slight enough for him to enfold her. While shielding her body with his satisfied at a primal level, it also merged their auras. Together, they could withstand any danger.

Not that they were under threat. Not for now.

While his own strength and willpower rose with the sun, his people were in retreat. Their place was within the earth, yet he was conscious of their proximity, aware of their presence with an acuteness he hadn't had for years. Unease prickled the hairs on his nape.

Something had changed.

Exactly what, he couldn't define. Erin's grounding still clouded his thinking, the intimacy of her life-force channeling through him still fired through his bones.

There had been that single moment, the stab of fear, when she'd panicked. During an exaltation close to ecstasy, there had been the unwelcome sense of being undone. He couldn't explain it. Everything he could give her, he had. It must have been her emotions he'd felt, some relic of the banshee's brutal act which had sparked her reaction.

He couldn't be prouder of how his marvelous, courageous lady had gathered herself and pulled through.

He watched color flush across her face from the pinking sky as the sun launched a new day, enjoying how the light caressed her features. Sliding from her high forehead with its notched scar in the top corner, along those level brows and into those espresso-dark eyes. She glanced up at him through thick, long lashes, her eyes tender.

He dipped his head as she lifted her chin and their mouths met in the middle. Sweet and easy, soft and natural, kissing her had become second nature. Closed kisses opened as affection heated, teeth and tongue turned simple sharing into a complicated dance of give and take. When she shifted to face him, he adjusted his hold and hands became involved. Hers possessively planed back and forth over his chest; his split between breast and buttock to gain the best of both worlds. For a while he massaged both—one soft, one firm—appreciating the contrast. She whimpered and squirmed against him, her hands curving over his shoulders while she twined a foot around his calf, welding her body to his.

Even as his blood simmered with need, his heart rejoiced at how they moved together in such harmony. But he wanted her to forget her worries, especially those concerning him. Now she was fine, so was he. And he intended to prove it. He trailed his hand over her hip and hitched up the stiff fabric of her skirt, distracting her with tiny nips along her collarbone. She was bare underneath and slickly ready for him. He grazed his knuckles across her sensitive flesh, and she clamped his hand between her thighs.

"Don't tease me," she begged. "I'm so close…"

"Then give me a free hand and I'll get you there."

The tension immediately seeped from her body. Her legs parted. He rewarded her trust by delving a finger between her folds. She moaned something wordless into his shoulder. One finger became two, playing her like he'd played his harp, with rising fervor and increasing friction, until she stiffened in his arms and sang his name.

When she sagged against him after, unable to hold her own weight, he lifted her and carried her over the stairs.

"Where are we going?" she asked through bee-stung lips.

He struggled to form a sentence. "I need to give you more."

"More is good."

The grass grew longest at the rear of the site, ironically near the gardener's shed; grass heavy with dew and scattered with old dandelions and young nettles. He set her on her feet and took off his jacket, laid it over the grass. She licked her lips a trifle nervously then gave a wiggle and twist to shed her top. She wore a bra underneath, a garment as odd to him as underwear.

"It looks tight." He sat beside her, traced the lower ridge where the material met her skin. "Does it hurt, to be so bound?"

"You've never seen a bra?" She arched an eyebrow then shook her head. "Of course, you've never seen a bra. To answer your question, it's a godsend when running and a nuisance when it's been on too long. You unhook it at the back."

He shifted so that she sat between his knees, her back to him. It was easy enough to figure out how it worked, but it was more fun to use his ignorance as a reason to explore, to slide his fingers in and out and around the constraints, dip in and out of the cups, put his mouth to where his fingers had touched, and undo her instead. The marks where her shoulder straps had rested were a particularly sensitive area, he discovered when massaging the damage with his tongue. It made her spine soften and her head loll. Scooping aside her hair, he lipped along the chords of her throat and nibbled the edge of her ear until she hummed with pleasure. Only then did he remove the garment, replacing the fabric covering her breasts with his palms. Her hands found his thighs, anchoring herself with her nails as she arched then twisted, seeking his mouth with hers.

This time, when they kissed, gorging on her mouth wasn't enough. Her breasts, high, round and bared to the morning light made the most delicious feast and still he wasn't satisfied. From between her legs, he drank his morning nectar, as he'd promised. It was sweet and salty, and he drank deep and long, until restlessness replaced

243

her languor, and she made his name a curse.

He raised his head. "Would you like me to stop?"

"Yes, no, I don't, I can't." She had the grass gripped, a handful on either side. Her eyelids hung heavy, eyes dilated despite the daylight. There was a tiny line between her brows of frustration as she worked through her demands. "I need more."

"More." He ducked his head only to have it wrenched up by his hair.

"Not like that," she almost yelled, and he laughed at her mock outrage.

"It's not funny," she complained. "You know I mean more of you." Her gaze slipped from his face downward and her hands followed. His fly was half undone, his cock protruding—eager to enter the conversation. Eager to enter, at any rate.

She had wonderful hands. Soft and skilled. His breath hissed out between his teeth.

"You're so warm," she murmured. "And I'm so tired of being cold."

"Cold," he repeated, shifting forward as she freed him from his jeans.

"I mean inside me," she said. A sad smile lifting into mischief as she added, "Although it is kind of chilly out."

"You do have goose bumps." He dropped a kiss to her stomach. Her nipples stood puckered and tight like tiny blackberries. He rolled his tongue around each one before planting his hands on either side of her shoulders into the turf. "Is this better?"

"Mm, you being a rug does help." Her fingers came up to burrow into the hairs on his chest. Beneath him her hips shifted in a silent request. Something shimmered in her eyes before she squeezed them tight. Alarm ripped through him.

"What is it, *mo chroí?*"

She bit her lip and shook her head. The poison of despair teased his nostrils.

"Tell me what's wrong, Erin."

She stared into his eyes for the longest time before she broke. "I want you to be mine. For real, not just in my dreams."

He didn't hide his confusion. "You must know I love you as truly and fully as any man can. You are my heart, and I am yours, Erin, for always." Her body tensed beneath his, as if to hold on to his words, and yet he sensed what he'd said wasn't enough. "You don't believe me. I speak the truth. I love you."

"You know your feelings aren't real," she said. "They're just an enchantment."

*Ah.*

"Erin, my love for you isn't going to fade. It may twist in madness, as you have seen with my former wife, but I will *always* love you."

He dropped his hips, to graze his cock along the inside her of thighs. She pressed her legs together, imprisoning him briefly, preventing him going further. Driving him mad.

"You're going to leave me," she whispered. "You get this close and then you'll pull away."

He did. No, he *had*. Why was that? Why was he hurting what he loved? Need laced his veins, urgent and unrelenting. Grasping his cock, he guided himself into her heat. He eased into her slowly, slowly, slowly, torturing them both, until he was so deep, he almost couldn't tell where he ended and she began.

Erin whimpered, her breathing shallow and fast, her

nails delving into his shoulders. He withdrew a fraction, and her face grew fierce, her legs wrapping around his waist and her ankles locking to hold him in place. "Don't leave me!"

"I'm not leaving you, *mo chroí*. Not this time."

When he dropped to his elbows, something crumpled within his jacket. A box? Boxes?

"Tell me again you love me," she whispered, ending his distraction.

"I love you, Erin."

"Oh Angus," she moaned, her hips lifting to take him in deeper, her mouth finding his.

When they kissed, he lost his head completely, need to fulfill her trampling everything in its path. There was no control, only delay. As he waxed thick and full, she made a crooning noise deep in the pit of her throat. Their movements grew increasingly enthusiastic, the percussive slaps of their bodies meeting coming faster and faster. She met him stroke for stroke until she tensed suddenly beneath him, taut as a bow-string ready to let loose.

He couldn't hold, he was going to…

"Erin!"

Her name was a warning, a plea, a benediction.

Her eyes rolled back, and she made a low, keening cry as his own spine tightened and his balls lifted. With a bellow, he flew with her. Together they soared, their bodies united, and their souls entwined. This was what it was to be alive. This was how it felt to be whole-hearted. Returning to earth embedded within her wasn't a fall. After thousands of years lost, he was found.

As he lingered inside her, she clung to his neck and sobbed. Heart-to-heart and skin-to-skin, he didn't doubt they were happy tears, but he liked to be sure.

He thumbed one aside gently. "Will you tell me what caused these?"

"I've never done that before."

"Cried after making love?"

"Both of those."

The dew catching the morning light was lovely but Erin weeping for joy was far lovelier. He wanted to compose something in her honor, to sing something new, because she'd dredged poetry from the depths of his soul along with his seed. Absorbed in the wonder of watching her, he almost missed the whistle of wings and the flurry of white leaving from the top of Newgrange. He stilled, clenching his jaw to keep from turning his head.

They had been watched.

She shivered beneath him, and, in case it wasn't from the cold, he kissed her again for reassurance. What started nobly, grew quickly inflamed. As they rolled to change positions, Erin gave a small cry.

"What is it?" he asked.

"A damn nettle stung the inside of my knee."

Short of dock plants nearby, he plucked some plantain and crushed its leaves against the lumps on her leg. What stung him, however, was a glance at the sun's position.

"We'd better move. One of the guides will be along to open the site here soon."

She shifted to her knees to straighten her skirt and put on her bra and top, then screwed up her face. "Oh, gross."

"What?"

"No panties, and my purse is in my car. I think I might have a couple tissues in there."

He should have guessed a woman who liked to be as clean as she did might find the aftermath of lovemaking outdoors unpleasant.

"There's a bathroom in the Guide Hut below."

"A shower?" she asked in almost comical hopefulness.

"Toilet and sink." He collected his jacket, retrieved a handkerchief from inside a pocket. And the condoms. They both stared at the crushed box in his palm until she closed his fingers over them and held his hand between hers.

"What I am never once crossed my mind. You'll conceive from this. How could I have forgotten?"

"It'll be okay. I told you, there are options. But I think," she worried her upper lip between her teeth. "I think Manann already did his reaping on me. Here." She grabbed his hand and placed it below her navel. "He made me so cold, Angus. It hurt like I was dying inside, but you burned the sensation away."

Fury crashed through him, and it must have shown on his face because she looked alarmed but didn't shy away. She stroked his cheek and traced the line of his jaw. "Did you feel...different, to how you did before?"

If she was asking what he thought she might be asking, he wasn't sure how to answer. If Caer was air, Erin was earth. One was ephemeral, one was forever. He located his jeans, damp now from the knees down, and pulled them on.

"After an eternity alone, you are my heaven."

Erin blinked hard and swallowed visibly. "You sure know how to drop compliments on a girl. What I meant, though, was your chest. Without the scar. How does it feel to be free?"

With a start, he looked down. No weeping wound. No scar tissue. There was no hair, either, where the spiral had been, but she'd mussed the rest enough to obscure the lack.

Dread iced his veins as he tried to pull on Newgrange…and got nothing.

Couldn't be.

With Erin trailing behind, he strode around the monument to feel the Entrance Stone directly. Not so much as a tingle. The resonance of his earth remained inside but there was no spark he could grab.

The dread sank into his bones.

"I'm free?" He struggled to understand her logic. How was being powerless, free?

"You can leave. You're not stuck here. Your Asshole Chief can't command you anymore."

She was so earnest, so very pleased with herself. She hadn't the faintest inkling she'd sealed his doom and possibly her own. There hadn't been enough time for him to explain, or else he'd done it badly. Her betrayal was kindly meant and crueler for it. Head to toe, it stripped the joy from him faster than sleet rain.

"I am Manann's to command because he is my Chief, a claim I could contest without acting on, because my power was equal to his while Breda stayed neutral. That balance shifted when I saved you." He dragged a hand through his hair. "If I'm anyone's slave, I'm yours."

She flinched and took a step back. "Don't say that. I don't own you. If I could give you back your heart, I would. I know I don't deserve you." Her lips trembled then twisted up on one side in a failed attempt at a smile. "All I want for you is to be free. And, for that to happen, your people have to be free, too. That's what they want more than anything."

"My people?" He cast around wildly, as if they might suddenly appear despite the daylight.

"They were locked under this filmy stuff, like the silver skin you get on cuts of meat. Elastin, I think it's called. Anyway, it was connected to Newgrange and to you, and with those bindings broken, there's no need for your curse."

Disbelief kept him outwardly calm, while his gut burbled. No protection. No power. To hide his face, he made a meal of bolting and locking the iron gate into the passageway. It took every bardic technique he knew to keep the horror and panic out of his voice. "Those were *my* bindings. I put them there."

"*Your* bindings? *You* did that to them?"

His jaw cracked with tension as he faced her. "Yes. Now ask why."

"Because they haunt you. I get why now. Breda showed me how they're dead to you."

"*Breda*." He spat the name. Breda was a healer. She knew exactly how to slip in and out of another's body, but she'd never overstayed her welcome before. Never taken control like she had Erin. Necessary to save her, of course, but still a step too far.

"I told you my grandfather appealed to a higher power. He did a deal with Breda after the banshee attacked me the first time. She saved my life, but she didn't come help the second time, even though she promised him I'd be safe. If he befriended you. And he did. Yet she didn't come. He trusts *her* because he thinks she's a saint. Shows you what he knows."

It didn't show Angus what Jim knew, it showed him

this was conniving, not coincidence. A soul saved. In return for friendship with the unfriendable.

He turned aside as his eyes blurred. Erin gripped his arm, but he couldn't look at her. He couldn't look anywhere. The day was bright with sunshine, but all he could see was darkness. Always in the dark. It came of living under rocks for a couple of millennia.

"But he wasn't a friend to you, was he, Angus? He thinks you're the devil." He recoiled at being labeled evil. "Sorry," she amended quickly. "I don't mean *the* devil; I should've said *a* devil. Could be the antlers, although they're nothing like horns." She touched his scalp where the antlers had sprouted, almost as if she missed them.

She'd lost her father. She wouldn't lose her grandfather, too.

"Not his fault," he squeezed the words through the mangling mess of his throat. Jim had failed Erin not through any fault of his own, but because Breda had chosen the one man who could never befriend an enemy. And so he'd broken his word, leaving his half-sister free to escape her obligation.

"I think you're too forgiving." Her voice was as soft as her touch. "You're so lonely, all the time. How could he not see that? How could he know you and not care?"

Rather than answer, he started down the hill to the Guide Hut. Space, he needed space, but he couldn't escape his thoughts. Within the turgid tumble of his innards, a horrible suspicion arose about the deeper game Breda and Manann might be playing.

Although initiated and claimed by messy and dangerous means, Erin could legitimately be considered one of his people. Instead of being trained, however, she'd been uprooted. She had no earth to call her own. She had no defenses. She had nothing to stop the banshee or Breda taking possession, or Manann or himself taking advantage.

Tools, as Manann had reminded him, were there to be used. Through her, the Lord of the Dead could have taken every last drop of Angus' power had Manann known Erin's true name. That much Erin's removal of the trispiral had prevented, but she was still leverage against Angus and a potential vessel for his sister.

*A vessel for Breda…no, by the Goddess, no!*

His gut lurched and bile climbed his throat. He stopped to choke it down, gave up and spat it out.

"What's wrong?" she demanded, her voice edged with worry, catching up and clutching his shoulder. "Is it my grandfather? Because I already told him I want to be with you. I couldn't tell him why, not until I'd told you first."

She cared for him. Truly cared. It was close enough to love to do what he needed. He could bear no more burdens. He was too close to breaking.

"Bathroom for you," he croaked. "Kitchen for me."

He unlocked the door to the wooden Guide Hut and while she was busy, he rinsed the sourness from his mouth, drank some water, and gave himself a cursory wash with the aid of the kitchen sink and paper towels. Then he raided the cupboards and fridge for food to share. Sweet biscuits and stale bread. Not much of a meal.

There being no shower, she wasn't long.

"This isn't my usual style," she said, her hand touching her hair and her smile uncertain. "I hate feeling like I'm a complete mess."

"You look loved," he corrected, picking off a strand of grass she'd missed. "My house is your house," he said as if he wasn't aware it always had been. "And you know I have a fully equipped bathroom."

"Granddad will be there." Her gaze bounced below his waist then back to his face. She covered her transgression with a plaintive, "Besides, you don't have coffee."

"Then drop me into town to collect my motorcycle and you can go back to his place."

He hustled her out to her car.

Her hands went to her head. "Omigod! What the hell happened?"

"My kin wanted to get in." He opened the driver's door for her then gave her the keys.

"This is a rental," she moaned. "I'm never going to get insured in this country again!"

It was the least of her problems, but he wasn't sure how to break the news there were greater. Piecemeal would be easier to swallow, but where to start?

He nodded at the crack in her windscreen. "It's as well for us, we weren't on my bike."

"They wouldn't really attack you, would they? Not when they need you to save them."

Angus stared out his window. Was that a wisp of white? For once the weather was cloudless, but it was cool enough for a natural fog to creep over low land, out from the river.

"They are children mad with hunger who have been told I will feed them. Therefore, they believe me to be food. You filled with my light. That's why they saw you as they'd see me."

"I must have been out of it," she said as they set off

with a clunk. "Because I have nothing after Manann did his suck-face trick."

Angus dug his fingers into the vinyl at the reminder of his negligence. Never again. But her admission gave him the opening he needed. "You don't remember Breda moving in?"

Erin flicked him a surprised glance. "You know I was with Breda?"

"It's more accurate to say Breda was with you. She…managed…your body after Manann drained me through you."

"You mean he tried. He got nothing from me. Now you're free, he won't try that again."

Angus sighed and pinched the bridge of his nose. "Thanks to me, he knows now you are Erin not Liz, or he could have taken all I could give. As his subjects, he can make us do as he pleases, Erin. Both of us."

"But I freed you and that frees me." Behind the stridency, doubt and fear were hawking their wares. "I thought you'd be a heap happier about that than you seem to be."

"You freed me from Newgrange," he confirmed, letting her believe them safe a little longer. "As I no longer have an earth of my own, it's likely you have also relieved me of my geas to return here daily." That part was pure luck, but it was no advantage. Fewer restrictions gave him greater scope to operate under his curse.

"Does that mean you could stay with me in Dublin?" Excitement colored her face and brightened her voice.

"I'm not able to leave *Míde*—my father's old *tuath* or territory, what you might know as the Fifth Province of Ireland—until I fulfill my vow."

"Hello, there are four provinces. One for north, south, east and west."

"And one to rule them all."

"That's supposed to be a ring. Didn't you read the book?"

"Hardly, given I'm illiterate."

"Really?" Her mild surprise turned to chagrin. "I figured you might be, but I keep forgetting since you speak better than I do."

"People visited Newgrange for centuries before I was fully awake. Their chatter filled my dreams. And, as I told you, I have a good memory for what I hear."

His chatter now avoided a harsh reality, which was why he gave her directions to where he'd left his motorbike rather than discuss letters that wouldn't stay still. But how to frame the words?

When she pulled in beside his bike, he was still undecided and so he sat in silence while her engine idled. Erin fidgeted while she waited. When she spoke, however, it was with her usual confidence. A clever trick to conceal the anxiety he sensed underneath.

"If you need to rest, I can take a rain check on today. I can't understand why I'm not yawning my face off after practically no sleep for two days. I must still be jet lagged or something."

"It's not jet lag, *mo chroí*, it's power." A fine mist painted the length of the river. Natural, not isolated, yet its presence convinced him to speak now rather than delay. "You needed the dark to share your past. I need the light to discuss our future."

Chapter Twenty-One

This Mortal Coil

Angus twined the key to his bike through his fingers, unwilling to get out of Erin's car and unsure how to ruin her hopes with a light hand. "You won't like what I have to say."

"Just hit me with the bad news, okay. I saw you were nearly sick at Newgrange, and I hoped it was from relief. Guess I should've known better."

He cleared his throat. "I vowed, of my own free will, to serve my people and accept the stag's mantle after I *volunteered* to be interred. I am a god of love made a god of fertility by *choice*. I cannot escape what I chose to be made into. I cannot change *what I am*."

The little crease reappeared between her brows. "You want to be cursed, is that what you're saying?"

Was that what he was saying? He hadn't intended it to be. He scrubbed his face as if this might scour his thinking clean. "It would be easier on me, but not on those I love." There, blunt enough. "If I could die, rather than become as Caer is, I would."

Erin raised her palms to make twin stop signs. "Woah, woah, woah. Back up there. Free, remember? You're no longer a slave. Nobody has to die."

He took both her hands and layered them over his

256

unblemished chest. "The brand was not to enslave me. It was to honor me. To grant to me, alone, the strength of Newgrange when I was once again made flesh. Being free of my earth does not free me from my responsibilities."

"But it wasn't like that fancy gold collar or a tattoo, it was a *brand* and brands show ownership. I saw for myself how it chained you to Newgrange."

"We had no time and few resources. Since I needed something fast and permanent, Breda took a mold of the inner trispiral to cast as a brand for Manann to wield while she wove the cord of my rebirth."

The hand on his chest spasmed and he tasted the acid burn of her shame.

"You couldn't have known," he said, gently.

"I could have asked."

"Not as you were, pumped overfull on youth and light and love." He squeezed her hand. "You make altogether too fine a vessel, *mo chroí*."

"I nearly wasn't. I was halfway between being hard-boiled and evaporating before I found myself chatting to Breda." The little crease deepened. "Maybe she's how I survived drowning. I don't remember anything between going under and being found."

"You told me the banshee came at you, the first time, from within. Would it not have been Caer?"

"Y-e-s-s-s, but her taking over, I remember. At least, now I do. With Breda I go someplace else."

Her free hand went to the scar on her forehead. "I got this the same day my grandfather pledged me into her care. She knocked Caer out of me by banging me against a stone at Knowth." She gave him a wry if worried smile. "Quick and permanent, huh?"

He couldn't resist touching the tiny scar for himself then sliding his fingers around to cup her face as the map of their future unrolled before his mind's eye. "I think you have the right of it with Caer. She is a creature of instinct, not planning. Whereas Breda—"

"Saw an opportunity to get around your psycho Lordship," she finished for him. "I'm feeling a little sick myself. Let me see if I have this straight. In your people's nutty system of government, the high priestess chooses the Chief, and if you'd saved me with Caer at the controls, your whacko former wife would totally choose you as her main man."

Despite himself, his lips twitched. "I see you do listen, and your logic is sound. With her heart mine, Caer could Choose none but me. There is one problem with your theory: Caer could not become the Lady. She fears the earth and has no stability of mind. The Lady must be mentally tough and morally strong, else she could not bear the burden."

"Burden?" Erin's lids dipped and her lips parted as he traced along her brow.

Angus struggled against the urge to kiss her again, their topic swaying him toward sense. "If a Chief is maimed or proves unworthy, the Lady *must* replace him. It is a duty she can postpone, but not avoid, else everyone suffers."

"Suffers how? War, famine, plague, and all that jazz."

"Yes."

"Oh."

"I know how heavy it is to bear the Lady's burden. To kill someone you love is the hardest of duties."

"You killed someone?" She clutched his wrist, her

eyes rounding as wide as an owl's in dismay and disbelief. The same look as when she'd thought he'd kill the fawn. "Of course, when you broke Caer's heart."

Ah, then. Here was leverage to send her away as knowledge of his obligations had not.

"Caer will die of grief, but she is not yet dead. I've killed many people, Erin. I was a man at fourteen, a husband at sixteen, and a blooded warrior at eighteen." He was done with dealing death, but it didn't change his past deeds.

She mulled this over. "But you said someone you love."

Such a clever mind. He sighed. "My mother decreed my father must die three times to atone for our defeat." He let his arm fall with the weight of his conscience, but she didn't let go. Her faith in him was false. It was time to tell her what had torn him in two. "My father wanted someone he trusted to complete the ritual." Angus forced a smile. "Who better than his son to kill with kindness?"

Erin snatched her hand from his. "How could you kill your own father?"

"How could I not? I was his nominated heir, and a new chief must slay the old to demonstrate his loyalty."

"No. You're playing with words again. I won't believe you. Not until I hear you say you actually killed him. As in you cold-bloodedly took his life with your own hands."

*Cold blood. Such a false phrase when the flow is so warm.*

He flexed the fingers of his right hand before balling it to match its mate. "His heart was crushed, his soul dispersed, but his body...I slit my father's throat with this hand and stopped his breath with the other. He died because I killed him."

The color drained from her face, and she shook her head, again and again and again.

Her horror swept over him like a blizzard. Good. It would freeze any tenderness and cool any ardor. He let it coat his soul and ice his empathic gift so he wouldn't feel her disgust, so he would be numb when she broke his heart. The silence between them stretched and still she didn't refute him. Just closed her eyes and draw in a series of long, calming breaths before plastering on a pale imitation of her usual mask.

"That can't have been easy for you to tell me." She spoke slowly, as if choosing each word. "I'm sorry I pushed."

Air escaped his lungs in a slow exhale. Not a sigh of relief. Not exactly. This was one secret he regretted the need to share. Never again would she look at him with the light of love in her eyes. The shadow of what he'd done would always be between them.

He bowed his head. "You know now why I can never be the boy of your dreams."

"Yes, I can see how that would be impossible. I think it's fair to say there's a bunch of things clear to me now, that weren't before."

Again, her words were careful and measured. As if she was afraid to rile him. They sat so close beside one another, enclosed from the outside within the bubble of the car, and yet between them lay nearly three thousand years. It was too great a difference. His culture and hers had too little in common.

"I can't harm you without hurting myself," he reminded her.

She gave a start. "I know."

She licked her lips and, again, took a moment before she spoke. "It's just…you've turned everything I thought I believed upside-down, and you're not done, are you? We've been talking about your past, and you said we would discuss our future."

Something tight inside him eased. She wasn't going to storm off in righteous anger. He had a chance to explain his fear. He raised his eyes to hers. "My past is our future."

"I don't see the connection."

"It's a theory, like your own, but I can't find the flaw."

"I'm listening."

"Breda reigns as Lady, but only in spirit. She needs a vessel, and you have my heart. Should she take you over and Choose me I would become her new Chief without taint of incest. Nor would there be threat of harm to his Lordship—Manann does not live, therefore he cannot die."

Erin tilted her head, considering his words in much the same manner she'd considered the problem of the fawn in the fence. Her ability to lock her emotions down was a useful mechanism for coping, although when her feelings burst out later, they did so in a torrent.

"You'd know it wasn't me," she said. "You'd know it was her *wearing* me."

"Factor in my curse. I have no power now to resist. All Manann need do is lay it on me, and I won't care and nor will she." He spread his hands in a helpless gesture. "I think the last is why Breda tipped the balance against me, since the initial consummation between Lady and Chief cannot be avoided. But after that first time…" He looked past Erin's shoulder to where the river flowed in an arc and out of sight. "After, she would be my Lady and, I, her Chief. It would mean I can fulfill my vow to my people and restore them to flesh."

Erin leaned in. "Won't that break your curse? You'd come to your senses."

"Yes, but Manann will be restored along with the rest."

"Well, that'll be awkward for Breda. She doesn't strike me as the type who'd go for a threesome." Her hand clapped over her mouth then spoke through her fingers. "Except it'll already be a threesome, won't it? Because where am I in all this?"

He wanted to reassure her. To claim she would be fine. But he didn't believe that to be true. "You'll be trapped."

She blinked above a trembling hand then nodded. "Unless I could find my way back to you. Since you gave me your heart and all."

"I won't be there, *mo chroí*. Once my task is done, Breda need only order *my* death for Manann to rule by her side as a living man. With me gone, you'll have no anchor and no earth to escape to. You'll be a voice inside Breda's head if you're strong enough, otherwise you'll fade away while she remains Erin-shaped for the rest of her mortal days."

"She is *not* getting my body." Her voice thrummed, low and fierce. "I've worked way too hard to make it *mine*."

"Then save yourself and leave."

"I already did that once."

"Then you know how to do it again."

She laughed, but it was without humor. "You gave me your heart. I owe you."

262

"Then honor my gift by saving yourself, *mo chroí*."

"And what about you?"

"You'll always have a part of me with you."

"Don't be so melodramatic. I mean, it's not like you're dying—" She cut herself off and looked away. "Oh, Angus, that's the one way you can truly be free, isn't it?"

"I can't ask it of you." Erin treasured life, so she refused to take it. "I *won't* ask it of you." *I need you to choose it yourself.*

"Good, because I won't go there." She lifted her chin. "I can't have your death on my conscience. Not after my dad. There has to be alternative."

She reached out to touch his arm. A wave of something unexpected flowed through him. Best to call it compassion or caring, but it was damn close to being something more. Something unbearably like pity.

"The alternative is I die anyway at Manann or Breda's hand and you are left lost and alone." Saying it out loud caused a terrible ache beneath his breastbone, as though his ribs were caving in. "I can't fight now, Erin. I have nothing left to fight with."

He raised a finger to stall the guilt writing itself across her face. "And it's not because I don't have Newgrange. Last night, Manann learned he can access the power vested in my earth through you—something you have now, so brilliantly, prevented."

His chest heaved with the effort of ripping his confession out. "I can't fight, Erin, because the moment I gave you my heart, I gave Manann the power to control me. He doesn't need to curse me—in fact, I will suffer more if he doesn't—because I will do whatever he wants to keep him from…harming you."

He gave Erin a defiant stare, but she merely nodded. Then again, she didn't know how he'd failed her. Again. Manann had sworn not to kill. Nothing more. That was why he'd agreed so promptly then left to gloat.

Angus dropped his eyes. "Breda tried to tell me I was a fool for giving so freely. But I know why I did it. I don't want to bring back my kin, and I don't want to be their chief."

"I guessed as much, but I want you to tell me why. It'll help. I promise."

Yesterday, last week, seven years ago, he couldn't have explained. He'd known he lacked. He'd thought it was because he was not Chief. That was a technicality. The truth was much more humbling, which was why he'd hidden from it so long.

"They aren't the people I suffered for, just as I'm not the man who pledged to save them. They have been in the shadows for thousands of years. They have stayed children all that time. They were always wild and daring, now they are capricious and cruel, and I don't have it in me to give any more to bring them into the light of reason and kindness."

He laughed at the irony, a laugh frayed at the edges. "I used to have such a light inside me, Erin, but I used the last of it to protect your world from mine."

For a moment her mask wavered. "The light you gave to me."

"Yes."

She sat back. "Breda knows how you feel. She knows they're dead to you. But they're not dead. You've seen them. I've seen them. While they're alive, they have hope. While you're alive, you have hope."

"No." He tried to smile, for her sake. "I don't. If you

stay, then Manann will curse me. Breda will possess you. To have hope, I need you safe. If you won't break my heart, then you must leave, because I will fail you as I failed you this morning—when making love to you was as easy as breathing. I didn't resist, because I couldn't. And nor did you."

"And you think that has to be because of a curse, not because we both wanted it."

"You fear my feelings aren't real because of an enchantment. I fear yours *are* real for the same reason. The only proof that you are with me of your own free will is for you leave and never return."

"But—"

"Tell me I'm wrong. Find the flaw, Erin. I'm a killer soon to be cursed and you are still here with me when I've just told you your fate is to live a nightmare."

He was almost frantic with the need to make her see sense, to have her make the one choice he could live with. If she left, Breda's clever plan fell apart. If she left, he would still be required to breed, but Erin would never see what he'd become. She could remember him at his best, as he'd once remembered Caer.

"But that doesn't get you off His Assholeship's hook."

"No, it doesn't." *Do you see, Erin? There is no hope for me.* He was already doomed. Once night fell, Manann could curse him. If not tonight, any night thereafter. But it made no difference. His fate was sealed.

"What if I can't leave?" she whispered. "What if your Chief and Lady stop me going?"

"Then you know what to do. I can't square the circle from inside. It's up to you." He sat as still as he could while she deliberated, his usual restlessness gone inwards to blitz his guts and fry his brain.

"It's your life or your sanity, isn't it?

At last she understood. "Almost. It's *your* life or my sanity."

His death was a given. She could make it quick and honorable, or she could give the task to Breda after he'd gone mad with lust.

"Crisis decision-making sucks," Erin complained. "We need sleep and time and perspective."

He tensed, his fists kneading the vinyl of his seat.

She looked at him, her dark eyes assessing. "You don't need another burden to bear, Angus, so I'll go. On one condition."

"Anything."

"Don't do anything stupid, okay? We have *six weeks*. That's a lot of time to think. There'll be a way out. There must be. I don't want to hear that you're mortally wounded or something, okay? Because I will *never* forgive you clocking off early. I don't care how justified you believe it might be. You can't fix anything when you're dead."

"So, this is goodbye then, Liz O'Neill?" He couldn't keep hope from lifting his voice.

"I see what you did there, hoisting me by my own petard."

"A petard? What's a petard?"

"No idea. I always figured it was some kind of rope." She pulled out her phone. "Can't check either. My phone is fritzed." She gnawed her bottom lip. "I guess I won't see you round, Angus."

"It's for the best."

"Yeah." She stared at the crack in the glass rather than looked at him. "Don't kiss me goodbye. I know how you get."

**\*\*\*\***

Although his home lay back along the route they'd come, Angus took a different path. He didn't want to return to the home that had never really been his, so he took the longer route, scouting along the road Erin would take to her grandfather's.

Caer had almost managed to form here last night. She was trying to return to him.

One last time.

Being early enough on a Sunday morning, the traffic was almost non-existent. He opened the throttle to full as he followed the back roads lining the Boyne's southern bank. The sensation of outrunning the wind was always one he'd enjoyed. Today it felt close to flying.

Erin was leaving.

A bittersweet victory, but he'd never known any other kind. Bittersweet he could live with. She was his heart and his hope. Nothing was more important than her safety. And this morning they'd made love out of joy not destiny. This morning was a memory he could cherish, because this morning hadn't been due to a curse.

Without a home to go to, he could lie, a little.

Behind his helmet, his eyes burned. He blamed the wind.

Given his circumstances, he couldn't be happier.

Out from Donore and past the Boyne Valley Visitor Center, his shoulder blades prickled. Possibly it was Erin coming along behind him, although when he'd roared off, she'd stayed safe in her car with the engine idling. He didn't look behind. He looked ahead to where the road curved, close to the river and following the Boyne's line. The hedgerows blocked the view, but the morning mist had dissipated.

Disappointment dipped his mood until an odd whistle sounded over the noise of his engine. Angus cut his speed to make sure the sound was mechanical.

The air hissed.

Fog clouded around him, sudden thick, smothering. What? How? He stiffened; eyes wide and mouth open. The hairs on his arms and the back of his neck rose. This was no illusion.

The banshee was here. In full daylight. Without a wail of warning.

With him open and exposed, Caer needed no invitation to overcome ancient protocols. If she could form from the mist.

*She should be too weak.*

He focused, narrowed his will and dove into the central core of his power.

It wasn't there.

*No!*

As always, he'd spoken true. He had nothing left to give. The sunburst of energy he intended to release was barely more than a warm breeze which ebbed through him and faded away. The banshee hovered—for the barest of moments—but whatever caution or deference she had for him was no match for the feed he promised to be.

Adrenalin surged through him. His vision narrowed to the road ahead of him, to the clear space that would exist beyond the cloud where the day would, once again, be bright. His heart rapped a staccato, his breathing shallowed. He clenched in on himself, tight and low; made himself more streamlined. A sharp twist of his wrist on the accelerator gave the bike a burst of speed as white enveloped him like a mantle.

She was little more than heartbreak and hunger, yet she was strong. Her teeth—cold as frostbite—ate through the leather shoulder of his jacket thanks to her over-sized unhinged jaw. A crack sounded in his ear as something tugged on his helmet. A wing darted its way across the thin plastic visor reaching for his eyes beneath.

Instinctively, he shook his head like a dog mad with fleas. The bike jiggled and shook, mimicking his struggle. She held on to swipe across his chin strap, a blow that sliced down his throat and sent hot blood crawling under his collar. An arm, spiked with feathers, wrapped around his neck in a winged embrace. Clawed and webbed feet dug into his right hand. Choking, his grip unpicked, he couldn't hold on as the front wheel bucked.

*Fuck.*

When falling at speed, rolling was the trick to surviving. He twisted, but his right leg was trapped in something heavy, something that refused to give. Pulling hard, he tried to force it, only to find it stuck fast. Then his left arm hit the ground. The bone snapped with a whip crack. The impact jack-knifed his knees into his chest, the sudden jerk pulling his right leg free of his bike and shattering his ankle as it did so.

It never occurred to him to scream.

The landscape blurred as he slid off the road and down into the ditch. The loose gray gravel which had accumulated along the verge proved more effective than sandpaper at stripping back the denim of his jeans. It even wore thin the thick black leather of his jacket in the hours it seemed to take him to come to a halt.

He lay there for an eternity, shackled by the prickly

branches of a hawthorn hedge, watching the explosive burst of white blossoms pinwheel over him like snow.

He seemed uninjured. Unhurt. How could that be? Then he remembered another time, long ago, when he had fought beside his father and Manann and never felt a single wound until after the battle was over.

*The pain will come.*

He'd no sooner thought that when his bike, ever faithful, came scuttling along the road like an exotic green beetle and slammed into his side.

Chapter Twenty-Two

At the End of Every Dream

Erin watched Angus leave.

Letting him go was the right thing to do. The only thing she could do, given what he'd told her. The man was a killer. He'd admitted that fact straight out, his face absent of the usual riff of emotions, used the same deadpan delivery to add he'd cut his father's throat. Blunt words for a brutal act. For *murder*.

So why had she wanted to reach out and hold him?

What the hell was wrong with her? He was dangerous.

She'd judged him safe because he'd rescued a deer and saved her life. She'd thought him sweet because he liked to sing and cook and couldn't read. She found him sexy as hell because of how he moved and smelled and kissed. She'd ignored the signs he was damaged. Instead, she'd screened out his talk of invasion and conquest and banishment because those had all happened thousands of years ago. Those were folklore and legend.

To her. Not to him.

When Action Man Dan bragged about the animals he brought down hunting, he spoke louder than usual and stood wide with his chest out, like taking innocent lives somehow made him more of a man. If Angus had done the same, she'd have run and kept on running, right onto the nearest airplane off the island. But, no. His admission had been terse and closed and come only after she'd pressed, because he wasn't proud of his deed, he was devastated. To Angus, the memories were clearly too fresh and too painful to talk about.

Her first impression of him had been accurate. He was a war veteran. A boy who'd wanted to be a bard and become a soldier. A son who'd taken his father's life on his mother's command. A man who'd fallen for the woman his ex-wife wanted to kill.

*And I thought I had issues.*

She'd been right in believing he didn't want to lead, that his misery came from being a slave. She'd been wrong to assume his shame came from being branded. He hated who he'd been and what his past was making him now.

As if nearly three thousand years in solitary confinement wasn't punishment enough.

No wonder he thought his death was the best solution. He couldn't live with his past and his past needed him to live. The pressure on him was insane. It was amazing he hadn't totally cracked. But he was close. He'd pushed her away because he was close. He might love her, but that didn't make her less of a burden. It made her another weight he had to bear.

*He's already cursed because of me, and I went and took away the one thing he was proud of: the trispiral. Keeping his heart safe is all he has left.*

Leaving was smart. Staying was stupid. If she got in any deeper, she'd never get out.

She put her hands on the steering wheel. There. She'd leave. Like she said. If she could, because there had been that little chat with Manann about a heart condition. With Angus already wigging out over whether his curse had fallen, mentioning that would've done more harm than good.

Dear God, everything about his world was seriously messed up.

His world was messing her up.

Getting emotionally involved with a guy was so not how Liz O'Neill did things. Liz did not come when a man said her name, no matter how cute the accent. Liz stayed in control and extracted herself early. That way, there were never consequences.

She touched her stomach below her navel then, with deliberate effort, put the car in gear. Time to shift her ass. She needed a shower and she needed to pack. Once Granddad bumped into Angus, her lover would be honest, and she would be homeless. When she was in Dublin, she'd get a morning-after pill and go back to being Liz. This was why she needed her alter-ego. Erin couldn't be trusted not to hurt those she loved.

****

About half a mile past the Visitor Center, something bright and green shimmered in the sunshine. She slowed. That was metal. Those were wheels. She slammed on the brakes. Ahead, by the side of the road, lay a shiny greeny-yellow motorcycle. With its distinctive coloring and retro styling, there was no mistaking it.

*Angus.*

Her heart gave a funny sideways lurch.

She strained forward, leaning on the steering wheel. Beyond the bike, half in the ditch…her gaze tracked the rest of the distance to alight on the crumpled, bleeding mess wearing jeans and a black leather jacket.

*No, no, no.*

She put her fist to her sternum and closed her eyes. There. A waning patch of heat.

*Waning?*

Yes, his light was fading. Still there but dimming fast.

She grabbed her phone then remembered it was fried. Her First Aid kit was in the trunk and fat lot of good it would do. Getting out of the car, she quickly surveyed the road. Her shoes she'd left at Newgrange.

Shit.

Barefoot, she navigated a litter of smashed plastic lights and fragments of wing mirror and a discarded helmet, refusing to accept what that implied. He hadn't been in a good head space, but this? Couldn't be. He'd promised.

Yet the evidence seemed clear. No helmet. No skid marks. No other vehicle in sight. The one section of road around here on the straight and narrow. He'd wanted this.

She could walk away, and no one would ever know she was responsible.

She swallowed down a sob.

*I would know.*

This was on her. She'd let him go fully aware he was at breaking point. She'd let him go *because* he was at breaking point. Wrong call.

*So own it.*

Locking down her fears, she raised her head. Her eyes absorbed everything in stages, her brain struggling to stitch it together into one coherent image. His bike, resting on one leg. The arm on the same side at a weird angle, the leather of the jacket shredded away to reveal a jagged cream shard jutting from his skin. His elbow in a pool of blood. So much blood. Rich, dark, venous blood. His other arm reached for her, as though pleading for aid.

Her heart cramped. For a split-second it shut tight, refusing to let her own blood flow.

His face, far too pale despite the vivid parallel gashes across his cheek. His eyes, closed in false peace. His head, free of his helmet, rested in the lap of a white-winged angel. An angel, almost invisible in the sunlight, who stroked his temple with an affecting tenderness.

No. Not an angel. Blonde and feathery-winged and female, yes. But her beak-mouth was stained red and so were her claws.

The banshee.

Angus hadn't attempted to kill himself. He'd been attacked.

Erin half-folded, knees weak and heart surging with a rush of adrenalin as she slid shaking fingers along the side of her face to the tiny notch at her temple. She could call Breda and maybe the goddess would come or maybe she wouldn't. She hadn't before, but then Erin hadn't known she'd been marked on purpose.

Screw Breda.

And screw the banshee, too. Erin was not going to let her childhood nightmare screw up her adulthood.

*I'm never being a victim again.*

"Time to move on, bitch," she ordered, edging closer.

Wing tips rustled as the creature twisted to face her rival. Cornflower-blue eyes blinked solemnly as the banshee rasped, "Poor *Óenghus* kept in the dark. Poor sweet boy in the dark, dark ground."

"Where you left him," Erin snapped, because

arguing while Angus lay dying in the banshee's arms was a great strategy.

Not.

Still, Caer was speaking actual words, not wailing. That was a plus. And she was less wretched, less transparent. Her skin had gained a waxy fullness, her features and form no longer wraith-like but plump with flesh. Had taking Maureen caused the change or had she taken something from Angus, too?

"You got your revenge so go and die already."

"Can't," the banshee cried. "Can't die. Always homeless. Always hungry. Always bound to my heart." She ended on a keening note.

*Oh.*

Breda was right. Angus had held on to Caer's heart and so the banshee had lived, unable to die. Did that mean, since Erin held Angus' heart, Angus wouldn't die, either?

Somehow the knowledge wasn't as reassuring as it should be.

"He gave his heart to me. He's mine."

"To have, but not to hold." The banshee grinned. Or maybe her mouth did that always. Then she dipped her head to lap the blood from the road.

Stomach churning, Erin took her chance to take another step closer, wary of the wings with their clawed fingers. She stopped outside what she gauged to be striking distance when Caer lifted her head and licked her thin, rigid lips with a pointed tongue as if tasting something delicious.

"Such a feast!" The banshee's breathing was an awful rattle, her voice cracked and warbling. Batshit crazy, but almost making sense.

"Hello, since when do you *eat* someone you love?"

"Sunlight and sorrow. A rare dish."

Erin stopped. Wavered. She replayed her own words, remembered something Angus had said about hungry children needing a feed, and him pressing his mouth to the fawn's wound to—

What had he said? Give something of himself?

*Oh. My. God.*

Even for a giver like Angus, being lunch to bring his kin back was the limit.

Not that he'd have that problem if he bled out.

"I need to help him," Erin explained using the soothing tone she'd tried on Angus when it'd seemed he was going to freak out. "Please, or else he's going to die."

"Kiss kiss, bye bye." Caer sounded…sad.

"No! I can't let him go. He saved me." She stared the banshee in the eye. "He saved me from you, and he saved me from myself."

"Bright heart."

"The biggest and brightest," she agreed. "But it's fading. He's losing too much blood."

If Caer took Angus's heart from Erin, all three of them would die. A neat end to the banshee's revenge. And yet the banshee wasn't making any sudden moves. Nor had she landed a killing blow to her ancient lover. It all came down to how she felt about Erin.

"Please," Erin begged. "Please let me save him. He deserves a second chance."

She was within reach of both Angus and the banshee. She took the final step.

The banshee shied and raised her arms in mimicry of the moment she'd taken Maureen. Almost. With her elbows bent backward the pose was almost aggressive. She moaned, too, but it wasn't the ear-splitting wail, but a weak and animalistic sound of pain.

The banshee had been more fog than physical. Now the opposite was true and being half-swan, half-human, was all wrong.

Pity was the last emotion Erin had expected to feel for her old enemy and current rival, but there it was. Damn Angus and his stupid, caring heart.

"I'll look at him, then I'll help you. I promise." Taking the risk, she sank down slowly to kneel, the asphalt of the road warm beneath her shins.

The banshee scuttled sideways so fast Erin had to lean in quickly to scoop under Angus' neck to take the weight of his head before it banged onto the road. Hopefully, his neck wasn't broken. Leaning over his face, she felt his breath on her cheek then ran her hands from his neck to his shoulders.

She'd studied biology. Done dissections on animals. Where, fact was, you couldn't go much wrong on something already dead.

Gritting her teeth, she held his arm on either side of the break jutting from his bicep and did her best to rotate it from the shoulder so the injury rested higher than his head. It would be enough to slow the bleeding, but she wanted to examine it properly, suspecting a pressure bandage might be needed to slow the flow further.

His chest rose and fell but it was barely discernible. She patted down his free leg. It seemed fine. When she shifted his bike, however, the state of his boot and the remaining strings of denim told an unpleasant story.

She propped the damaged leg onto the motorcycle wheel to elevate that, too.

Then, putting her fist to her heart, she closed her eyes in the hope this could help see the light inside. A dim flicker and a whiff of peat smoke.

She was losing him.

Her ribs went tight, like they were caving in and compressing her heart. *His* heart.

Overhead bees buzzed among the mayflower blooming as thick and white as popcorn. The sun was shining on fields of lush green grass. It was too beautiful a day for him to die.

"Not today you don't," she whispered.

Manann had pulled power from Angus through her heart, and it'd gotten stuck inside her until Angus used *himself* as a conduit to send it into Newgrange. No, into the *earth*. He'd been specific; had said any earth would do, although one's own was easier.

Well, if you could put something in, you could take it out, and taking was something she could do.

Slapping her palms flat against the road she pressed against the tiny stones, not to push into the road but to *pull* the tickling feeling she'd felt from the Entrance Stone out and into her. Anything to feed that dying flame. The tickle was frustratingly close, yet behind a barrier. Something that blocked her from pulling it through to her heart.

What was it? Was it her or did it come from outside?

Dammit, her father had died to save her. No damn way would she lose another man to save her sorry ass because she was too afraid to give. The blockage had to be her. Time to let go of her last defense.

*This is goodbye, Liz O'Neill.*

She threw his words at herself, and the barrier splintered but didn't fall.

She needed help. She needed…

Dear sweet lord, she needed the banshee.

"Caer, I could use a little help. I need you to strip away Liz O'Neill from me. You got that? Liz O'Neill. I don't need her anymore. She's my name to give away, so take her already."

"*O'Neill,*" the banshee spat.

"Yeah, the last one you'll ever need according to Breda."

"Noooo!" It was almost a scream as Caer's too long neck stretched and swayed with a series of clicks and creaks. "Can't take, won't die."

Her refusal was both unexpected and unfortunate.

"I took Newgrange from him and he's going to die, and I don't know what to do to keep him alive."

"Kiss kiss, bye bye," repeated Caer, sanguinely.

Since the banshee had totally lost it by becoming a pacifist, Erin slid her fingers to her temple once more. How had she come across Breda the last time? It'd been a sort of going inwards and centering and…wait. Doing that, she'd wound up *inside* Angus' heart and he was dying, so that wasn't going to be any use. Same thing when she'd grounded in Newgrange, it'd been *through* Angus, so again, not useful. Except. Hadn't he warned her that everything she gave, he would take? And if any old earth would do…

*So give it to him already.*

Liz O'Neill had always been a construct. A hollow and hard suit of armor to keep Erin insulated from the losing someone she loved. Was it any surprise she'd never gotten warm when she'd shielded a vacuum?

But what she was prepared to let the banshee take, seemed a stinting gift to give the man she loved. Her stomach did a weird dropping bounce like it was hooked to a bungee cord. A delicate, fragile cord braided as much of yearning and desire as it was of something finer and rarer and purer.

"I love him," she said, so surprised she said it out loud.

Angus had always been her yardstick to measure other guys against and none of them came close. To be fair, how could they when he was a god of love? And a sex god. And something more, something she hadn't expected beneath the passion and the tenderness of the lover she lusted for, and the honest and proud boy she'd dreamed of. He was a man who was decent and kind and smart.

It had never occurred to her that she should want such qualities in a man. Now, she couldn't imagine wanting a man without them. A man she was about to lose if she didn't act now.

She lay a palm on his sternum, hoping her hand wouldn't slip through as it had inside the chamber at Newgrange. Then, drawing in a deep breath, she scouted for that inner fire. It was no longer a furnace. It was barely a spark, but a spark was all she needed. A spark she could fan.

She pressed her lips to his.

*I need you to live. I need you to love me because I love you.*

A fuzzy feeling enveloped her hand, and a build-up of static sucked the draping material of her top in close to her skin. It was working! Hope flaring, she rubbed her lips against his inert mouth as she exhaled slowly and willed him to take what she was giving.

*Be my earth, Angus.*

Teeny starbursts skittered over her skin and shot down her veins to her feet. The flicker grew to a spark. A creeping warmth suffused her as the spark caught and surged. The lovely ooziness overtook her muscles. This time, instead of fighting the flow, Erin let go of Liz and went with it. Only she couldn't stop. She was dissolving, disintegrating, disappearing through Angus, then spreading out through his blood across the ground and sinking into the earth.

*Oh shit, oh shit, oh shit.*

This was not the plan. She'd done it wrong. Again. And this time there was no one to save her and no going back.

Chapter Twenty-Three

Moonlight of the Mind

As she sank into the land, Erin expanded. Her perceptions muddled and jiggled until, somehow, she could smell birdsong in the woods, taste the gritty coolness of the stones that formed the passage tombs, see the orange stench of cowpats in the fields beyond. With no anchor, she drifted through a place that was nowhere and yet everywhere.

*Tír na nÓg.*

She'd been here before. After she'd drowned. The experience then had been no less terrifying than it was now. Alone. Lost. Everything and everyone she knew gone. The multiple personalities she'd created to shield herself from herself—those were gone, too.

She had herself, nothing more.

It was enough.

*Here you are, me: here I am and I'm also…all this.*

If she could hug herself, she would have. It was like finally coming into an inheritance that she'd been unknowingly preparing for, or self-gifting a surprise. She was okay with this state of non-permanence. She could deal.

After all, she'd escaped from *Tír na nÓg* once before so she could get out again. Although *Tír na nÓg* was not exactly a place. More a place between places. A time apart. Or, perhaps, all times together since there was the Boyne—a torrent of energy flowing alongside her, widening and retracting, adding a canal and removing it, but always flowing.

Once she'd identified one location; the rest followed.

The road she'd been kneeling on was like her old house after Angus had gifted his heart: strobing in and out of existence, from asphalt to dirt to meadow. The sky flickered when she put her attention to it, but otherwise it settled somewhere between night and day. Not quite dawn, not quite dusk. A green smudge of energy stretched from the ground into the sky. Those must be trees.

Right then. Where was Angus? She'd gone through him so he had to be close, yet she couldn't see him. Maybe the better question was *when* was Angus?

The problem was her perspective had grown too broad. She sifted through time searching for him, each sift more anxious than the last. Living creatures winked in and out of existence like fireflies. How was she supposed to tell one from the other? She could locate the benighted realm of the Lord of the Dead, glooming over in Dowth. Newgrange and Knowth were, strangely, less present. Emptier, somehow. She couldn't locate Breda any more than she could Angus. The only other strong presence was that of the banshee. Caer was a consistent moan across the ages.

*Where is he?*

He'd been beside her and Caer. Caer, rootless and homeless, neither here nor there, and now bound to Erin's bloodline. Caer, the bridge between *Tír na nÓg* and the real world. So then—

Concentrating as hard as she could to focus on her former foe, Erin reached out and caught the banshee on the cusp between changes. Pain exploded through her from organs distorted and misshaped bones. The agony was unreal. The pity Erin had felt before blossomed into compassion. This had to stop. No one deserved to live like this.

The banshee's thoughts invaded her brain.

*Save him, save him, save him.*

Given Erin wasn't sure if she currently had a mouth, she 'spoke' her thoughts to the banshee.

*Show me* when *he is hurt.*

Images of Angus flickered in front of her.

A youthful Angus with a thick collar of gold, his hands red with blood, sobbing uncontrollably over the gray limbs of a corpse he cradled in his arms. The same Angus cleaned and stripped of all clothing save for a deerskin, his face blank and his eyes dead, as a hot brand scorched his skin and pushed him into a decorated stone. Then something weird—or weirder still—happened and there was a long, long *absence* of Angus of any kind. Of course, he'd been in Newgrange for practically forever.

And there he was, her Angus, Angus McCraggan, back and shouting from a pub door, breaking the heart of the girl who'd waited an eternity for him.

Then…this wasn't right.

The older Angus, her Angus, but with the best part of a beard growing and his mane of shaggy hair down to his shoulders. As coal-black as his hair, the beard made the blue of his eyes fiercer and more magnetic. His boyish charm might have been disarmed by the way the new growth hid his dimples, but their lack made him seem wiser and steadier. His cheeks were thinner, their hollows highlighting the underlying firmness of his features. There were lines between his brows that hadn't been there before, lines of determination and suffering. This….this was the man he could be, but wasn't yet.

Erin saw him and every last doubt evaporated. This was the man for her, for always.

Before she could reach for him, he was gone and, there, for a flash, was the mangled mess she'd left. Erin slammed a mental 'pause' on the moment. This was the *time* she wanted, and she made it stick with everything she had in her, just like when she'd put her hand on the gate at home and the strobing stopped.

*Got him.*

Okay, right place, right time.

No telling for sure, but if that other Angus was a future Angus, he'd live. Whether she'd ever get to him was the million-dollar question, but he'd be worth the struggle.

*Okay, now how can I help?*

Caer dumped more memories on her.

She shared the exhilaration of flying above the clouds, wings spread and long neck straight, as a swan. Of flying upstream but in a different element, as a fish not as a swan. Of being flicked out of the water, her ribs flexing and squeezing to suck in a substance too thin to breathe. Drowning in air until, on her last gasp, she'd drawn in on herself, pulled the heat into a focal point bright as a star, then burst into her natural form as a girl-child.

Wait. That one was *her*, Erin, as a teenager, with the bad hair and acne.

She'd changed shape. She'd been a freaking *fish*.

How the hell had she done that? Oh, hold on, wasn't Caer the goddess of dreams? This was a trick. Had to be. Right? Then again, with a neither-here-nor-there living example in front of her, Erin allowed the possibility shape-changing might be real.

*Me, me, me.*

*Help, help, help.*

*Promised.*

Caer's thoughts battered at Erin, weak and desperate.

Ah crap, she'd promised to help Caer, hadn't she? And her question just now hadn't been specific about helping Angus. The more fool, her. Now Caer was dying, in incredible pain, stuck between forms in this eternal nowhere, since the banshee didn't seem to be able to change shape on her own anymore, and Erin was going to be stuck with her, since she had no clue how to get out any more than she knew how to put the banshee out of her misery.

Unless…

*What do you want to be, Caer?*

Erin crossed mental fingers and hoped the answer wasn't a girl. She wasn't sure her forgiveness could stretch that far.

*Free,* came the reply.

*I need you to be a little more specific. Girl or swan?*

The joy of flying came through solid and singular, on condition. *Free to forget.*

That part Erin wasn't sure she could manage, but maybe it came as part of the package. There wasn't a lot of brain in a swan compared to a human.

*I think I know what to do.*

Relying on the second-hand experience of a

madwoman was questionable, but if the subject was willing…

Anxious not to lose Angus by letting the time-lapse kick off again, Erin tried to see if she could swipe at the banshee like she was flicking through apps. Just as when she'd tried to get the tickle to rise, she had the sense of *almost* being able, only to have something block her.

*Not backward, less.*

The banshee's thought? Her own? Whichever, it couldn't be good. There was only one technique Erin knew to make the banshee less, and that was to do to Caer what Caer had done to her. Twice.

Erin grappled with her conscience. If an animal was in pain and couldn't be cured, you didn't let it suffer. That was mercy. Caer wasn't an animal, she wanted to *be* an animal. So, if it was what she wanted and she was in pain and this was the only cure Erin could provide…then, wasn't that also mercy?

When Angus had passed judgement on his ex-wife, he'd called her by her full name. The banshee had called Maureen's name and her father's before stripping away her old identity and taking both their hearts.

Before the courage of her convictions failed her, Erin stood on her own two feet.

*Oh, so that's how you do it. You just decide they're there.*

"Caer Ibormeith, I'm going to take you from yourself." Erin stretched out a trembling hand to the banshee. Caer came forward and bowed her head. Erin licked dry lips as she crooked her fingers. "Be free." She slashed her hand down across the strange feathery hair. It was easier than she expected. Not so much husking a fresh ear of corn as one dried and brittle. Caer was barely there, more a memory of a girl attached to a cause the banshee no longer had the heart for. Within moments and without a whimper, she'd dwindled into an old, frail swan.

As the last wisp of who she'd been faded into the gloaming, the swan brushed a wing tip against Erin's cheek.

*Bless you, Bright Heart.*

Then, released from her torment, the swan threw back her head and honked a trumpet of farewell, before beating her wings hard and launching herself into the air.

Afterwards, with the remnants of the banshee motes of dust around her, Erin wondered if any of what she'd taken could've gone to Angus. He hadn't healed. He remained the same as before she'd dealt with her former foe, locked in that false fairy-tale sleep, as if no time had passed.

Maybe it didn't for him here. Maybe it did just for her, since she was the one who'd locked him in stasis. She was back to herself now, legs, arms and all.

*If he stays as he is, I have all the time in the world to figure out how to get out.*

*I can get help.*

She kissed him again and stroked his forehead. "Hold on there, McCraggan."

Her grandfather's home was a couple miles down the road, but only a few hundred yards away she'd driven past the Boyne Valley Visitor Center.

Setting off was tough. This was why Caer had struggled to get airborne. The land warped and shifted around Erin as she walked. As at her home, she found it more like wading, not least because her feet kept slipping *into* the asphalt. It made for slow going and a lot of stopping. She had this idea in her head from her recent visit to Knowth, where the tour guide had stood on top of a hillock and said each step down was going back one hundred years because time added layers. If digging went deeper into the past, Erin didn't dare go down even half an inch lest she lose the *when* she wanted.

*So tired.*

By the time she was through the parking lot, she was breathing through a stitch. She dragged each foot along the last distance along the pavement to the main entrance, seeing through the smudge of green of an avenue of native trees to the building ahead. It was peculiar. Designed to imitate the tumuli it served, it wasn't so much a building as part of the hill, with a thick, visible layer of concrete supporting a roof of grass-covered turf.

If she was going to stay on time, she had to figure out how to leave *Tír na nÓg* before going in.

She eyed the glass door with the metal handle speculatively, absently rubbing at the scar on her temple. Opening the garden gate hadn't done the job: she'd gone back to the old version of her house where her father waited. It'd taken letting go of Angus to return to the right time. Since he wasn't here now, there went that hope.

"What if it was me all along?" she asked herself. "Would just deciding hard enough do the job?"

"I'm afraid not. You cannot leave until I let you."

The cool tones came from behind her. Erin whirled to face Breda then took a step back.

*Woah.*

The other woman was decked out in a period dress of pale colors and fine linen, a forty-shades-of-green patch-worked cloak, and a stupendous amount of gold. There were loops around her nose, bells in her hair, discs in her ears, and a wide flattened collar rather than the torc Angus and Manann had worn.

Erin had the strangest urge to curtsy then stiffened her spine and stayed strong. Breda was far more of a danger than the banshee had ever been, whether as an ally or an enemy.

"I was wondering if you'd show. Angus needs help. I tried grounding him only to wind up here."

"Without an earth of his own, he cannot ground."

"But he said any earth would do!"

"When you have an earth of your own, that is true. Without an earth, if you are lucky, you find your way into *Tír na nÓg*."

Breda didn't need to say Erin had taken his earth from him. That much was obvious. She could wallow over her mistake later. Right now, she had one priority.

"Since you're here, can you heal him?"

"As I am, no. The little power I have left in this state went into saving you. The rest will be to curse Angus, should he live, so he won't know what he does."

Did she think she deserved kudos for that attitude? Erin rolled her eyes. "Do you even know your own brother? You've *broken* him, Breda. He can't live with what you're making him into. He can't live with who he was. Put those together and where does that leave him?"

"Finding an alternate means of fulfilling his vow."

"Which he can totally do when he's dead," Erin snapped. "So, tell me how to help him already, unless you're planning on having me wait here forever, in which case none of us gets a do-over."

"Caer once thought as you do. That she could

survive here, in this time beyond lived time. You saw how she got stuck in a moment. This is a place to visit rarely and briefly. It enables reflection when there is no time to reflect, but it is unwise to linger."

*No kidding, if staying sends you crazy.*

Damn, her options were narrowing fast.

"So where does that leave us, Breda? We both want to save Angus, but you can't, and I don't know how. Caer showed me Angus as he was…and, I think, as he could be. Doesn't that mean there's a way out of this where he pulls through?"

"Sometimes one catches a glimpse of potential, but never the decisions needed to achieve it." Breda sounded close to tears, a big shift from her earlier attitude. Was she regretting giving her brother a bum deal?

Erin pushed her advantage. "Is this where you make the big announcement of how we can 'join forces' and fix him together? Because I'm not keen on being a puppet. I want to be a player."

A pleased expression spread across Breda's face.

"Once before I inhabited another—on her request— and together we accomplished many great and noble deeds. Times, however, are not what they were, and I am no longer the best candidate to deal with these times." Her sigh was almost soft enough to miss. "You have proven yourself worthy of becoming greater in your own right, Erin of the O'Neills."

Breda went still and, when she spoke, the tone of her voice took on an uncanny echo. "Therefore, I offer the mantle of the Land to you, as you are. Will you accept and take this responsibility freely, to become the agent not only of your own destiny but of our people, the *Tuatha Dé Danann*?"

"Wait. What? Say that again, because I thought you just made me an offer for me to become the Lady of the Land."

"I did."

"I get your candidate pool is real low right now, but are you really going to make *me*, a descendent of your ancient enemy, your high priestess?"

"Can you suggest a better approach to peace?"

This was a rhetorical question because there were no other candidates, least so far as Erin knew. This opportunity she had *not* expected. Nor, it seemed, had Angus. He, at least, had done his best to take her through the small-print, something Breda was conspicuously omitting given the old chief needed to die when a new one was chosen. It might not be first-degree murder, but that still made her ultimately responsible, didn't it? And what would killing another man do to Angus?

"Let's say I accepted. As Lady, do I get to Choose a new Chief?"

"Choosing a Chief is both the privilege and the burden of the Lady."

"Does the old chief fight the new one?"

"The tradition is for the old chief to be slain by the new chief, either before or after his Choosing, as the Lady wills. It is a kindness to Choose first, but it may be necessary to have a candidate show his strength to the tribe and loyalty to his lady before he is Chosen, or to strengthen a current Chief's standing by eliminating his rival."

"Yeah, well, unless this gives me the power to cure him, Angus isn't about to win a battle to the death."

"You cannot choose a maimed man, so you cannot choose Angus as he is."

Erin wanted to scream in frustration. What was even the point then? If Angus survived, he still had to recover and who knew how long that was going to take, especially if he didn't want to live because…

"Manann's conditions. Can I control Manann?"

"The terms under which we live derive from the current Chief. They cannot be changed unless our *Crom Cruach* changes them, or a new Chief creates new terms."

Erin's head spun, but the gist seemed to be 'do this and you'll buy not just time, but hope.' She drew herself up, acutely aware she could not look less like a Lady if she tried.

"I'll do it. I accept. And I swear on my father's grave I'll do my best."

"Kneel then, Erin, to receive my mantle." Breda undid her shabby, patchwork cloak using a penannular broach, not unlike the Tara Brooch housed in the National Museum. The fabric draped over Erin's shoulders weighed nothing. Surely such a responsibility should be heavy? "And rise as the *Bantíarna na hÉireann*, the Lady of Erin."

*But Erin is my name…*

No, she had it wrong. Erin was Ireland. The Lady of Ireland was what Breda meant.

"That's it? That's the whole ceremony?"

"The ceremony is brief. The preparation is long and uncertain, for few can draw on the love of a people for their land and fewer still have the courage to wield such power. A Gathering, on the other hand, is required to swear fealty to a new Chief."

"Sexist much?"

"Those drawn to high deeds of valor and acclaim

have more often been male, but not always. Showcasing the Chief protects the true source of power."

Erin clutched at invisible edges, her fingertips registering grass and concrete, pine needles and potatoes, sea foam and lake water among the threads.

*I'm wearing the land as a cloak. I'm wearing* Breda's cloak.

The same cloak which had spread and spread to cover the land Saint Brigid required from an unwary king for her monastery. The monastery she'd used to become Ireland's other patron saint. Again, not the public face like Patrick, but the protector of home and hearth and heartlands.

"You can bend time to enter *Tír na nÓg*. This gives you the ability to bend space to travel across your domain."

"So, I *can* leave and go to Dublin."

Breda smiled sadly. "You can go, but not stay. The Lord of the Dead reigns until his defeat. Therefore, you must have an earth of your own as all the *Tuatha Dé Danann* do."

"But Angus already gave me his heart—"

"Thus entitling my *Crom Cruach* to take his life should Angus come near you—now you are Our Lady and his rival for chieftain. Wait, Erin. Wait and then decide whether to Choose the man or what has been made of him."

On that ambiguous note, Breda put her hand to the door handle. "To leave, you create an anchor in the earth and haul yourself out. If you trust me, I can share your mind and show you how."

Nuh-uh. Give Breda a couple square yards and she took a couple square miles.

"Thanks, but no thanks. I prefer to go this alone. You must think I can, else why mention the technique?" Putting her hand below Breda's, Erin focused on the cool smoothness of the metal and *pulled.*

Sure enough, the world flipped inside out, and she was standing in a patch of sunshine. The glass of the door reflected a blood-stained, bare-footed and bushy-haired woman. It didn't show her invisible cloak nor her invisible goddess mentor, which stood to reason. Appearances were deceptive; everyone said. Besides, if she didn't save Angus, she'd gone to hell and back for nothing.

Stifling the urge to giggle and prove she was looney tunes, Erin went into the foyer.

She might be entering a building built unto a hill, but unlike the dark and narrow stone interiors of Newgrange and Knowth, the far side of the Visitor Center was almost entirely glass. This lent the cascade of floor levels within panoramic views of the valley, while also capturing sunlight and warmth.

Instead of an Entrance Stone, an enormous stone circle formed a desk for staff to take bookings and greet visitors. When Erin strode in, none other than a very surprised and worried-looking Marie met her.

"Is that blood?"

Marie's question gave Erin a terrible dose of déjà vu. Despite herself a nervous laugh burbled up and out. Fingering the mad textures of her cloak, she got a grip on herself.

"Yes, and it's not mine. It's from Angus. He crashed his bike near here and he's bleeding out. I need you to call an ambulance for him. Now."

Wherever that note of authority came from, it

worked. Marie nodded to a colleague who got on the phone right away.

Erin swayed with relief. Standing was taking an unreal amount of effort. The room was dipping and tilting while she seemed to be both rising and falling. She stumbled back until her shoulder blades bumped into something prickly. This turned out to be the render of the wall behind her.

Her entire body went super-sized. Her spine somehow stretched and straightened until it rose three stories high, a match for the column housing the elevator.

*What's happening to me?*

"It's Erin, isn't it?" Marie was asking from somewhere *inside* her. "Are you hurt? Do you need to sit down?"

She did, but there were no seats near big enough unless she counted the whole mezzanine level. It seemed she'd grown too big for the house. Only she wasn't sticking arms and legs out windows and doors because she no longer seemed to have any limbs. The line between what was her and what was the building blurred then vanished. The sunshine outside falling on the grass-covered sod of the roof was as warm as if it fell onto her scalp. The people inside breathed as regularly as if they were her own lungs, the internal walls were her bones.

*Did the Visitor Center just become my earth?*

Erin whimpered. This was too much. *She* was too much. She couldn't cope with being a building.

Grounding sucked.

"It'll be okay, Erin." Marie wasn't just talking, she was rubbing something tiny and weak and soft. *My arm.* "Angus will pull through. He heals fast."

Chapter Twenty-Four

A Fire in My Head

Angus drifted into awareness with his vision fogged, his tongue fat and dry, and his body stiff. The world was no longer still and stable but flowed and ebbed in and out with his breath. Despite this, he could find no waves through the slats of his eyelids, only a great deal of white.

*What am I doing in a cloud?*

It wasn't as if he'd shifted shape. With everything so fixed and certain in this era, he wasn't sure if he still could.

Did clouds beep though? This one seemed to. A very annoying, rhythmical sort of beep. He wanted to swoop away from it. Swooping and wheeling like the starlings he watched from Newgrange would be fun. He tried to swoosh his arms and legs, like a swimmer in the sky.

They didn't move.

The beeping tripled and his woolly cloud world disappeared.

Instead, twinkling strings of agony along his leg culminated in a screeching bag of angry cats clawing into his ankle. Starbursts of shrapnel grated in his chest every time he inhaled and his bones ached as if their marrow was being leached out. His head had bloated to ten times its normal size. It was crushing his neck, which was already on fire. Presumably he still had fingers on his left hand, but he couldn't feel them. The rest of that arm was as numb as if he had plunged it into the Boyne at midwinter.

He groaned.

"Ah, you're awake," a cultured male voice noted.

Panic had Angus opening his eyes, but it wasn't the Lord of the Dead. It was a dark-haired man wearing green pajamas and a pair of tiny square glasses.

*Great Dagda, there really are leprechauns!*

Then he realized the man was a normal height and that he, himself, was not on the ground but lying on some sort of metallic bed. This sort of setup struck a chord somewhere. He'd seen it on television.

*A hospital.*

That would make the man in green a doctor in scrubs. A physician, not a leprechaun. Under the circumstances, Angus wasn't sure which was more useful. He could do with a few wishes.

"I hurt," he croaked.

"I should say you do," agreed the doctor. "Young man, you are very lucky to still be with us. We nearly lost you several times."

Angus made a grunt of dissatisfaction. Life would be far less painful if he were dead.

Caer had meant to kill him—to do what Erin could not—and save him from the fate that had befallen her. And now he was here. In bits. How had that happened?

Lightning flashed in his skull. He panted.

"Mm, we may have to increase your medication." The doctor motioned to someone else nearby.

As the pain ebbed, Angus drifted away with it into a jumbled sea of giant halogen lights, chilled x-ray tables and a cascading array of masked faces.

\*\*\*\*

The days slipped and blurred together.

The glaring fluorescent lights never fully dimmed into the darkness of night, water-stains in a paneled ceiling took the place of scudding clouds across an open sky, the twitter of nurses and doctors replaced the chatter of finches and wrens.

But Angus preferred the welter of unfamiliar sounds and scents and sensations to those other times. The times when the room danced then the walls faded, and he slid into a world without sound or color or sensation. A gray place of phantoms and fen mists seeking to lure him astray.

Visiting time provided the most diversion. Marie appeared most often, but they seemed to repeat the same conversation, again and again and again.

"Mother of God, Angus!" she would say in a violent whisper. "Why aren't you healing?"

"You always told me I needed a break."

"I didn't mean *bones*, Angus. I meant a vacation, like going to the Costa del Sol. I suppose it was the better class of drugs that swayed you."

She knew he couldn't travel, so he suspected this was meant to be humor, but it was just as likely Marie was a product of his medication because she never listened.

"This is for the best," he'd insist.

"If only I could get you to Newgrange."

"It won't help, Marie."

Newgrange wasn't his powerhouse anymore. He should feel more strongly over losing his domain. He should feel more strongly about a lot of things. It wasn't as if he meant to be indifferent. He tried to focus, but his bones were cold, and his blood was hot, and his heart was heavy. His growing weakness should have made letting go of life easier.

Why it was taking so long for him to die?

"What day is it?" he would ask Marie, to show he cared, when he'd never understood what made a weekend special or a Monday awful or why modern people painted time in repetitive stripes instead of paying attention to where the moon was or what flowers bloomed, or which days were longest.

"Today is Wednesday. You've been in Intensive Care for three days."

"Today is Friday. The doctors say you have a blood infection. Why aren't you healing?"

"Today is Tuesday. They need to operate again to reset your ankle."

Marie's answer would change, but whatever the time period, her distress would roll over him like a thunderstorm, and he'd fade away with ozone stinging his nostrils.

Once, he thought he saw Jim sitting in the chair by his bed watching him the way a hillside shepherd might watch a distant lone wolf. Not a welcome sight, but not yet a threat. If his landlord really was there, he didn't talk. His presence felt stale and contracted, and Angus couldn't shake the sense he was under probation; one he was close to failing.

Erin never came.

*Good.* She'd listened to him at last and put her own life first. That meant there was no chance he'd beg her, like Caer had once begged him, to put him out of his misery.

301

\*\*\*\*

When Marie next visited, she sat and twisted a bedraggled bunch of wildflowers into pot-pourri. No updates. No questions. Just incessant fidgeting. Odd.

*Maybe this isn't a dream.*

He raised his head off the pillow. "What is it?"

"Everything's gone pear-shaped since I last saw you, but I kept on hoping…" Her voice trailed off as if she couldn't bear to finish her sentence.

Their conversation had changed. Angus perked up a little more. "Hoping what?"

"Hoping I was wrong about your Erin."

Jagged arcs of pain shot through him as he sat bolt upright. "Erin? How is she?"

"The opposite to you. Thriving. She has a glow on her an angel would envy." Marie didn't sound pleased. She sounded pissed. "It's not Herself so much. It's the company she's attracting to the Visitor Center."

"The Visitor Center?"

"I told you there would be repercussions for her, Angus." Marie gave him a stern look although her scolding was gentle. "She has the same need to be at the Visitor Center that you had with Newgrange, so she's working in the cafeteria as a barista. She took over from a friend of hers when she discovered she can't leave longer than a day and night."

It sounded like Erin had figured out how to transform the Boyne Valley Visitor Center into her earth. Set into a hill and roofed with turf…it was perfect. How like Erin to find herself a modern creation with a link to the past. But if Erin could earth, was she still herself?

"I need to see her."

"She said you'd say that. I'm supposed to tell you

you're to wait until you're whole and that her staying away proves you're not cursed."

"She told you about that?"

"It came out during a discussion about her failure to visit you."

"That must have been some 'discussion.'"

"It was a fierce heated one, to be sure." The happy glint in Marie's eye dimmed as she scanned Angus from head to foot. "I'm to add she's holding her own, but I've the Sight to see for myself and she isn't on her own. Those you held in their hollow hills are gathering. There's more arriving every day as the light in your Erin grows brighter."

*Gathering?*

The choice of wording had to be a coincidence, because there was only a Gathering when the Lady was ready to Choose her Chief. All potential candidates felt the draw, a yearning to be where the Lady dwelled. Yet he felt nothing.

"Who's arriving? Where?"

"Your kin. To the Visitor Center."

"Not Knowth?"

"If that's you asking after your sister, Stephen says he hasn't seen hide nor hair of Breda since your accident."

As the Head Guide at Knowth, Stephen was Marie's equivalent in more ways than one—he kept the secret of his hollow hill for its true owner. Angus stared at the stark fluorescent light in the ceiling until his own eyes burned around the edges. Possession, like shape-shifting, was a game of mind over matter. If Erin was under Breda's sway and he was *not* cursed, then he should be able to free his heart as he had before. With a kiss.

"I have to get to her, Marie."

Marie took a step back at the stridency of his demand. "Sorry Angus. It doesn't work that way. You have to be discharged and they don't consider you well enough." In a painfully patient tone, she added, "It's a bureaucracy. There's paperwork."

"Erin won't come to me, so I need to get to Erin." He reached out and grabbed Marie's hand. "I can come back for the paperwork."

"It's not that simple. In case you haven't noticed, you have a shattered ankle, broken ribs, and a compound fracture all on the same side. Half the blood in your body isn't yours you had that many transfusions. Four weeks at the earliest, the doctors told me, before you can walk and that's assuming you don't need more operations to re-pin your ankle."

*Four weeks?*

"You're saying it'll be a *month* before I can leave?"

"At the earliest," Marie repeated, like he was hard of hearing. "You were in the ICU for over a week, Angus, and you've been delirious nearly as long again."

"How long have I been here, Marie?"

For the first time she looked truly worried. "Angus, it's been over two weeks since your accident."

"Two weeks? Impossible."

What had seemed romantic as a teenager, now struck him as weak and ignoble.

He dropped back into his pillow then rubbed a hand over his face as if this might wipe away the indignity of her claim…and found he had a beard. He'd always stayed clean-shaven and such a length of facial hair seemed to belong to someone else.

Four weeks until he walked?

*Feck that.*

Later, after Marie had gone, he made a break for freedom.

A cast encased his left leg from knee to purple-sausage-toes. His left arm was in a cast held in a sling. His ribs were taped but if he breathed too deeply, they became blades slicing into his lungs. His right hand alternated between being tingling or numb but at least he could use it. Gripping the bed rail, Angus kicked his blankets back with his right leg.

It took unexpected effort to hoist his torso off his pile of pillows before swinging both legs off the bed. Gritting his teeth, he eased his weight onto his good leg and used his right arm for balance.

He tried some weight on his left leg. "Feck, feck, feckitty, feck-feck-feck!"

Sweating, he increased the load his left leg was bearing while easing off on his right hand. Someone sawing through his ankle with a bread-knife would hurt less.

For a heartbeat, he stood unaided. Then his left leg buckled. He toppled and grabbed the mattress as he fell. This wrenched his right shoulder nicely and flicked out the needle lodged in his vein like a dart. It also made him fall onto his arse, rather than onto his knees.

*Bollocks and shite.*

He sat with his legs splayed like a child's doll as his ribs became a corset of barbed wire. Every breath he took made him dry-retch with pain. In the battle between his lungs and his stomach, the compromise seemed to be hyperventilating.

A slow seep of blood colored the dressings on his thighs where the road had stripped away his skin. He'd overstretched himself. He couldn't stand, let alone leave.

Yet his kin Gathered.

A man must be whole to be Chosen as Chief.

If Erin required him, Angus would make himself whole. The question was: how?

Caer, gifted with the power of entering dreams, had used her ability to become a nightmare. To her, this hospital would be a banquet: the weak and dying plated in rows, ready to be served. Her wailing serenade would have been the last thing they heard as she fed on mortal fear dressed with the heart's despair of those who grieved. From there she'd eventually moved on to the meatier meal of murder.

Angus had never been able to stomach the darker emotions. He'd needed Newgrange to transmute tourists' fear of the dark into wonder and hope. Now he had no earth. His abilities without his anchor were limited. What use was empathy and the ability to give something of himself in here? None.

He must trust that Erin knew what she was doing. She hadn't called on his heart, so she wasn't in immediate danger. And if she'd bonded to the Visitor Center and updated Marie on his curse, then it was unlikely Breda had moved in. He had time to heal. If he was patient.

He'd never been patient. Nor had he ever been this weak, while in human form: unable to help himself, let alone rescue the woman he loved. From between his teeth came a thin, stream of sound as his pride deflated. Beneath it, however, was the bedrock of determination.

*I must recover faster. Whatever it takes to get to her, I will do.*

Somewhere there was a control unit. There it was,

dangling off the side of the bed with its big red button. With intense deliberation, he tightened his diaphragm and filled his lungs with as much air as they would take. His broken ribs screamed in defiance of every millimeter they moved as he stretched to grab it and pressed for help.

A nurse came in, took one look at him, and said in a strong Jamaican accent, "Don't move!"

He raised an eyebrow in defiance of this order, unable to do much more, but she'd already left.

When she came back with two orderlies, he wanted to make light of his fall from grace, but the words wouldn't come. It took both men to scoop him up, one behind him leveraging under his armpits, the other lifting from his thighs.

After awkwardly dumping him on the bed— admittedly dumping with a great deal of care—the orderlies left, and the nurse gave him a once over from head to toe to make sure he hadn't injured himself further. She reinserted his drip and muttered something about his ruining the catheter line with backfill.

"That can stay out," he told her, too sharply. He moderated his tone. "Please."

She made a scribble on his medical notes, slapped the binder back into the holder at the end of his bed. "If you promise to call for assistance, I'll make a case to your doctor."

"You have my word." He frowned at the jumble of letters on her nametag. "I'm sorry, I can't make out your name."

She eyed him, her expression dubious. "Vera."

"You have my word, Vera."

Her gaze softened, but she was no less business-like

as she checked her watch and gave him another dose of meds. "The trouble with you young ones is you think you're immortal."

Angus shook his head. "A god maybe, but not immortal."

"A god but not immortal?" She chuckled as if he'd made a joke. "Have you seen yourself lately?" She patted him on his cast as she headed out. "It'll do you no harm to remember you're only human."

Chapter Twenty-Five

A Foul and Pestilent Congregation

Angus stared at his injured leg. *Only human.* He'd tried to be.

For the past seven years, he'd done his best to be an ordinary man. He'd boxed everything he didn't want to be and packed it into Newgrange. In the fullness of his strength, he'd declared that darker, more primal self a monster. He'd done the same to his kin. To Caer.

How self-righteous he'd been to judge her fall from his secure and lofty height. How arrogant to use Newgrange to keep his kin and Caer out of sight and claim it was solely to protect his neighbors, when a very large part had been about hiding them from his conscience.

*Was it any wonder I saw them as shadows if I stood in front of their light?*

Now he was alone, as they'd been alone.

Now he knew how much they hungered to be free.

He was supposed to be a guide, yet he'd made no attempt to live by example. He'd let fear rule him, not love.

*No longer.*

Erin's instincts had been right. Released from his bond to his domain, she'd freed him from his own delusions. But between the trauma of losing Newgrange and the battle for his life, he hadn't faced the facts let alone accepted them.

Less than a decade was a pittance of time compared to the nigh on three-thousand years that had gone into making him a god. A Chief's son trained as a bard, a warrior and a hunter, a god of love and fertility: *Óenghus Óg* was part of Angus. And *Óenghus Óg* was a god. A local one, maybe, but one with local people who believed in him.

That was why Jim watched him so warily and Marie waited so impatiently. They knew he was more than a man.

So, too, did Erin.

His kin were Gathering. There would be a Choosing. She'd asked him to come to her when he was whole. Asked, not called—to let him decide when he was ready. She believed in him. She always had.

What he needed to do was believe in himself.

The bed squeaked as he settled back into the thin hospital mattress. Such a stark modern setting gave pulling on his cast-off parts an air of unreality. Yet, oddly, it helped. He didn't fit in to a world of fluorescent lights and the smell of disinfectant. He never had. Out-dated and old-fashioned, the rite that had bonded him to a stag truly came from another era. Humans these days wanted to believe they were above animals. So, he'd rejected that part hardest, stashed it deepest, because it gave him away as nothing else did; thus, giving Breda and Manann the greatest possible leverage when twisting it against him.

But the bond they'd brought to the fore granted him more than an animal's nature. It gifted him with tenacity and strength. If he wanted to save Erin, he could no longer hide what he was. Not even from himself.

He was a man and a god and a parasite.

After all, a god of love and fertility thrived on hope. A hospital held as much of that as it did of despair. Newgrange could contain and concentrate feelings—as it did for sunlight—but it took a god to make the change. He could convert darkness into light. Belief was the catalyst and he had enough to make this work.

The cost would be his humanity. He would get to Erin whole in body but perhaps not in mind. She would judge him a monster. As she had judged Caer. As *he* had judged Caer.

But if he saved her from Manann and restored his people, he'd pay that price.

Closing his eyes, he let his body relax and allowed his mind to fade into the gray world of heartache and desperation. The first tasted sharply acidic, like vinegar or tainted wine. The second was thick and heavy, petroleum-scented like tar. Absorbing them was unpleasant. He took them in sips, trying not to gag. In return, he breathed out the sweet vanilla of hope.

Tiny amounts but every day Angus grew stronger, faster. He refused to shave or be shaved. As the wildness inside him grew, it seemed fair to have some outward sign as a warning. But each day, it took more and more effort to eat real food and to keep his appetite for emotions small. The more he consumed of them, the greater his hunger.

When Jim returned a few days later, Angus saw the difference reflected in his landlord's face.

Jim had dressed as if he'd come straight from the farm in trousers with both pockets torn loose and a mud-smeared shirt. But under the cut grass and a faint trace of cow manure, Angus tasted the acrid lye of fear smeared with the now too-familiar tar of despair. He almost absorbed it before he remembered he could talk.

"How is she, your granddaughter?" Angus asked.

"She's all the family I have left. I can't lose her."

So few words to say so much. "She has the best part of me, too."

"I can see that." Jim ran a heavy hand across his face as if he couldn't believe his eyes. "Safe and sound is all I asked for—and my girl is neither safe in body nor sound of mind. She's cursed, Young Angus."

"Cursed?" Angus choked on the word, praying it was coincidence.

"She tried to hide it from me. How she's tied to the Visitor Center; how the *púca* act like pets around her. She's not the girl I thought she was."

"Marie told me something was going on. She also said Breda is missing. Is that why you've come to me?"

"She asked me to mind you." Jim's worn and wrinkled face took on a strange, hesitant cast as if broaching a forbidden subject. "And I swore I would foster ye as my own, but I never did, Angus. Not in spirit."

"Are we talking about Breda or Marie?"

Jim stared at his hands. "Your sister. It was an arrangement we were after making. She couldn't help you herself, she said, and you would need help coming into your own once you were out of The Caves. If I minded ye, she would mind Maureen when it came to that plague of a banshee. But I've the neighbors telling me 'twas you who did the saving."

"Maureen?" The name tinkled at the back of his mind, but his bardic memory told him Maureen had been

Jim's wife.

"Maureen is the name my granddaughter was Christened with despite the way she took it into her head to be called Erin."

Of course. Maureen was Erin except when she was Liz. *Or Breda by another body.*

Angus' ribs tightened. "Yes, it was me. Breda was…busy."

"Ah, now. Don't spare me. We both know I broke my word to the Lady and so Mau—Erin would have paid the price if not for you. I misjudged you, Angus. You were never a bother in all the years I've known you, and it's taken my own flesh-and-blood to show me the trouble you could have been."

"What kind of trouble?"

"There's a man stalking her. I think he's one of yours. She's afraid of him, Angus, but she can't keep away."

Angus went cold. "She has a right to be afraid. The darkness in Dowth was never locked away, Jim. Not as I was." Unclawing his fingers, he pretended to be calm. "I need to get to her before it's too late."

"Marie said you'd take no convincing. She's after having some notion you've fallen for my girl."

"I would die for her."

Jim made an audible inhale. "You love her that much?"

"With all my heart."

The old man's expression firmed. "What do you need me to do?"

"Believe in me."

\*\*\*\*

Focused on healing as fast as possible, Angus

ignored the mundane. He had to be whole. He didn't have to be healthy. After a few days, he was off most of the painkillers. After a week and an x-ray, the solid ankle cast was changed to a removable boot to aid with physiotherapy. Comments were made on his remarkable progress—and his lack of appetite.

As he improved, the draw of the Gathering began to pull at him. Beckoning. The urge growing stronger the more his bones knitted. One more week and he would be ready to attend—altogether, he'd be healed in less than half of the four weeks Marie had told him he'd need.

Two days later, during breakfast, Erin Called.

Angus pressed the button for a nurse.

Vera was on duty.

"I have to leave," he said.

She looked at him sideways and pursed her lips. "You should eat your porridge. You're wasting away."

He suspected she had the Sight since her doubts about him coated his tongue with an unpleasant thickness that had nothing to do with the oatmeal. It didn't matter. Nothing mattered except reaching Erin.

He put down his spoon. "I'm much better."

"You see the size of me here?" Vera pointed a thumb at herself. "Do I look like I was born yesterday?"

"Let me put it another way. I'm leaving. Apparently, there's paperwork."

"You need a doctor to agree you should be discharged."

A bard was taught how to use his voice to coax. A chieftain's son learned how to command. A god, however, could compel. "Then you need to get me a doctor." The man left in him added, "Please."

"I expect that porridge to be gone by the time I'm

back."

He inclined his head: acknowledgement, not agreement.

While Vera went in search of a doctor, Angus used the hospital landline to call the one number he could dial.

"Something's happened to Erin," he told Marie. "Let Jim know—he's promised to help."

****

The doctor was stubborn. It took a minor miracle, but Angus convinced him.

Marie didn't take long to arrive. Seeing Angus, her eyebrows furrowed. "Are those your clothes?"

He glanced down at his buttoned-down shirt and dress trousers, the nicest clothes he owned, although rather loose. "What's wrong with them?"

"Nothing." Her mouth stretched into a false smile. "It's just a bit chilly out. Do you have a jacket?"

"They had to cut mine apart to get it off my arm."

"Ah. Well, then. You'll be grand, I'm sure." She held out a walking stick. "I brought this for you. Borrowed it from my father."

With one arm still in a sling, walking proved a challenge, but Angus had the knack by the time they left his room and reached the nursing desk.

"And what is this?" Vera folded her arms, her eyes narrowed in disapproval.

"I told you I'm leaving."

"Not that like you're not. Hospital policy requires you leave in a wheelchair. I'll order one. In the meantime…" She handed over a sheaf of paper.

Angus gave the documents to Marie to read.

"This is the hospital's way of saying 'On your head be it and don't come crying to us if you hurt yourself.'"

Marie pointed to a blank line. "Sign there."

"Grand, so." Angus scribbled his name on the bottom.

Vera rolled her eyes.

An orderly brought around a wheelchair.

Angus looked to Vera. "You've got to be kidding. I can walk."

"I never did have the joy of pushing my son in a buggy," Marie intervened. "You could give me that."

For her sake, he sat. In fairness, it was a faster mode of travel than he could manage on his own as she whisked him down the corridor at a near run.

Outside, the cold clasp of fresh air as the double doors parted was as welcome a reunion as meeting an old friend.

Climbing into Jim's SUV with an arm in a sling and a walking boot wasn't easy but Angus managed it without aid.

"Drop me at Newgrange on the way to the Center," Marie said after she returned the empty wheelchair to the hospital foyer and checked her phone. "There's something weird going on."

Drogheda was quiet as they passed through the town, it being too early for the shops to be open. Out past the town, Angus stared at the rolling green fields. He hadn't realized how much he missed being outside. As they drew near the monument, however, they came across an unexpected complication.

Jim gazed at the crowd of disgruntled tourists. "What are all these people doing standing around?"

Angus, tasting the crowd's annoyance, withdrew into the car like a snail poked with a stick.

Marie picked up her official jacket, put on a face of

professional concern, and strode into the throng. After a few minutes of intense conversation, she returned.

"No one can get through to the Visitor Center," she said grimly. "They're not taking any calls, not even on mobile phones. That's between us, by the way. The official line is there's a road blockage stopping the buses."

Her dread wafted in through the window. Angus swished it back out. "This must be why Erin needs me. Don't worry, I'll fix it."

"Then I'll hold the fort here while you do," Marie replied, her confidence in him rock solid.

Angus directed Jim to drive to the Visitor Center's bus depot. To limit traffic congestion and control visitor numbers, mini shuttle buses were used to transport visitors to and from Newgrange or Knowth.

Most of the Center's shuttle buses were there, parked and empty.

The semi-circular shelter, where there was always a waiting group of tourists ready to head out, was unattended. It was a damp day, but poor weather did not excuse the lack of people. Poor weather reduced numbers; it never stopped them all together.

*This is very wrong.*

"Park anywhere, Jim," Angus said. "I don't think it matters."

Jim pulled in and turned off the engine. "Can you walk?"

"Thanks to Marie I have a cane, but I'll be faster if leaning on your arm."

Together, they zigzagged down the path to the river where a suspension footbridge crossed the Boyne, connecting the bus depot to the body of the Visitor

Center on the southern bank.

Running water dissipated the static energy of the land around it, but a fast, fresh river like the Boyne carried its own power. Angus could sense nothing on the other side, but he didn't need extrasensory abilities to see something was amiss.

On the river side, the Visitor Center was entirely fronted with glass panels. On a normal day, the café would be visibly bustling with people sipping cappuccinos and munching on cake in climate-controlled warmth. Today, however, nothing was visible through any of the windows—their full lengths a crystalline gold, as if frosted with sunlight.

"You should stay this side of the river," he told Jim.

"Not with my girl in there."

Jim strode forward without him.

Angus followed at a hobble, using his cane to keep his balance. As he crossed the river, he dedicated a silent prayer to his mother.

After throwing open the entrance door, Jim gasped something similar of his own, "Jesus, Mary and Joseph! They're dead, Angus. They're all dead!" He put his hand to his chest as he held the door wide enough for Angus to see inside.

Sure enough, the café and ground floor were stone silent for all they were full of people. No one stood. Not one single person was upright. They were slumped, sprawled, propped against walls or each other, everyone knocked over like so many skittles. Fallen in the midst of whatever they had been doing without a moment's warning to crouch, curl up or cower. Not a soul moved so much as a finger.

His skin turned icy and clammy all at once. He had

no sense of any emotions coming from inside. As if they were dead to him, too.

"They can't be," he said aloud to reassure himself as much as his landlord.

A strange tickling sensation enveloped him as he entered the building—like passing through a burst of bubbles flavored like summer wine.

By the door, he noted bus drivers in a great pile of uniforms. A red-haired woman and her matching miniature held hands, collapsed halfway up the nearer of the double spiral staircases. A bearded hipster in the café had his cheek planted into the side of his granola, yogurt pillowing his face. In the tourist shop, a member of staff drooped over an open cash drawer, her black corkscrew curls spilling across bundles of notes.

*Why am I not affected?*

Morbid curiosity tousled with self-preservation and wrestled it down.

Were they alive or dead? He had to know. Even if touching them meant joining them. Light-headed, he reached out an unsteady hand to wrap his fingertips around the woman's thin wrist to feel for a pulse. Her skin was warm to the touch, but if there was a pulse, he couldn't catch it. He lowered his mental guards to prod, gently, at her aura. It pushed back, whole and undamaged. Ahh…

Breda and his mother had both cast this kind of sleep for desperate surgeries.

*Asleep and alive. All of them.*

His tension released in one long, slow breath.

"Jim!" he called. "They're not dead. They're bespelled."

No response.

He wheeled around to find the old man crouched down just outside the door. He sped back. "They're alive. They're grand. Only sleeping."

"Sleeping grass," Jim murmured, his face contorting and his breathing labored as he gripped his left arm. "Like the stories. They trod on sleeping grass."

Angus was about to point out that there wasn't a blade of greenery to step on—not the stone slabs outside, not the polished concrete floor within—when a hideous, evil hunger clawed his gut.

Life leaked from Jim's body the way it had from those within the hospital.

The old man's heart had given way.

Angus licked his lips, salivating at the promise of such a bountiful feed. "I can take your pain." Asking changed everything. When someone offered freely, it wasn't stealing, it was receiving a gift. "Would it kill you to trust me?"

Jim raised his right hand. As a blessing or to ward him away? "No…"

No, he couldn't trust Angus, or no, he refused his help? The blond bubbles lining the glass blurred his expression, just as his pain blocked Angus' ability to read any of his landlord's more subtle feelings.

*If he would just take that final step over the threshold…*

A threshold. An enchanted sleep.

With his good hand, Angus grabbed the sleeve of Jim's heavy coat and jerked the man indoors. Jim passed out the moment he passed through the golden haze.

The emptiness in Angus' belly didn't ease, but his desperate hunger to fill it did. After taking a moment to gather the remnants of his strength, he dragged the old man inwards.

The door swung shut.

Further inside, something clattered.

His heart jolted, not at the noise, at the sudden tug of a summons. Erin. She was in here. In trouble. Damn morals. If he'd taken the boost from Jim, he'd be whole.

"Erin?" he called.

Movement caught the corner of his eye. Slithering down walls, sliding from under bodies and tables, they gathered beyond the edge of his vision. His heart sped and his flesh chilled. He was so weak he couldn't see them, let alone fight.

"Hold, my little ones." Manann's casual command filled the enormous space along with the sweet scent of hay. "We welcome our long-awaited guest before we go hunting."

"How are you here?" Angus scanned the room for his enemy. The Lord of the Dead was not a morning person. His strength came from day's end and night's fall.

"We are within my new Lady's domain and am I not the Lord of the Hallowed Hills?"

The acerbic tones came from the cafeteria.

Angus risked edging closer. They each stood on either side of the food counter—his enemy closest, near the cash register.

The Lord of the Dead had changed. He was now a man nearing his prime. Early thirties and built like a wrestler with an excess of brawn around the upper arms and shoulders. Army pants and a short-sleeved tee emphasize his size and strength: his neck—bullish and thick and encircled by a clubbed golden band, matched a pair of thighs easily the size of tree trunks at the other end. The only trace of the effete young man was in a slight petulance around the mouth and the languid cast to those glassy eyes.

Erin stood behind the counter near the coffee machine, her nose practically buried in coffee grinds. Her shoulders were bowed, her face drawn. Her arms cradled her lower abdomen as her hand burrowed into the black barista apron below her waist. Pain radiated from her in sharp, straight bursts while a dank fear spiraled around her like fog.

Angus wanted to draw them from her and take them into himself. To free her. To free them both. Nothing to do with the ghoulish pangs in his gut.

He edged closer still.

Whose soul wore the face of the woman he loved: Erin or Breda?

Impossible to tell without kissing her. Impossible to join her side with the display case of cakes and sandwiches and salads blocking his access.

"I believe," Manann drawled, "I ordered an Americano to go."

"Bite me," she gritted out between clenched teeth.

"Don't be impatient, my dear Lady. All in due course." Stroking the collar of gold at the base of his throat and smiling indulgently, he turned to Angus. "I see you have found, being free of the earth comes at a cost, son of the Dagda. Without a hollow hill of your own, you seem somehow…lacking."

"It's my fault." Erin's voice was tight. "I shouldn't have taken Newgrange from you, Angus."

She sounded like Erin. Nor could Angus detect any trace of Breda's colored lights. But Manann had called her Lady. How could that be unless his sister had moved in?

Unless, somehow, *Erin* was now Lady.

"Where's Breda?" Angus demanded.

"Your sister passed on her mantle and retired from public life. Let me introduce you to our new Lady of Erin." Manann bowed to Erin then straightened with his palm pressed to his chest. "I, of course, remain your Chief." He looked piously upward. "Such a shame poor Breda couldn't revoke me without revoking the hallowed hills which our people require to survive." After a pause, he dropped his dramatic pose and put forth his hand. A tiny plant with a yellow flower like an open mouth grew from his palm as he beckoned with all four fingers. "Come along now, Erin. Don't be shy."

The scent of hay grew stronger, laced with the bitterness of hops.

She raised her head and bared her teeth, then moved in a stuttering walk out from behind the counter to Manann's side. She stopped beyond his reach, her hands scrunching the apron spasmodically, while she made a small dance of coming a little closer than shying away.

Her movements were oddly familiar, but Angus was more concerned by a greater mystery. "If you're the Lady, why are you obeying him?"

"He's been grooming me. Playing teaser stallion, so when you get here—"

"Shall we show him, my Lady?" Manann extended his plant-bearing hand and stroked it along her hair. She halted in her restless to-ing and fro-ing as if welcoming the gesture. No. Surely not. She couldn't want such false intimacy, not after she'd experience the real thing. But then, she thought his own love an enchantment and their time together too brief. How many weeks had His

323

Lordship spent working on her mind?

At first disgust marred her face, but too soon it warred with something else. Something unexpected. The slack mouth and heavy-lidded look of desire. She wanted *him*, Manann, the Lord of the Dead. A man at his peak, a god of harvest and plenty—when appeased.

When a Lady chose her Chief, the consummation happened regardless of time or place. A primal mating where the masculine took and the feminine gave. Exactly what Breda had striven so hard to avoid with Angus. Exactly what would happen between Manann and Erin.

She would Choose him as her Chief because Angus was in no condition to be Chosen. He'd lost too much time while unconscious and immobile. That or she despised what he'd become to get here.

His skin iced and his limbs froze as Manann's hand continued down from her hair to trace over her breasts then down below her belly. It dipped through her clothing, into her flesh, stroking to the left and the right in line with her hips until her expression was a rictus of pleasure/pain.

"Plump as grapes," Manann crooned. "Such a ripe harvest you'll bear me."

Angus frowned. This was not a Choosing. Not yet. Manann's hand passed *through* Erin.

The Lord of the Dead remained in spirit.

The ice inside him melted and boiled and steamed into a roiling rage. "What did he do to you, *mo chroí*?"

"Me?" Manann answered with a laugh. "It is *your* generosity that knows no bounds, *Óenghus Óg*. By sharing your heart, you shared the conditions you must live under and that includes being unable to hide her inner beast."

He smirked at Angus. "I believe the phrase is 'horses for courses', is it not? Stags may rut in the Autumn, but fine young mares mate in the summer months, and, until they are successfully covered, they are in heat every three weeks. Our Lady here requires servicing, and you lack the strength to resist her charms. Become the *leanán sí* you were always meant to be, *Óenghus Óg,* and feed off her ecstasy. Do as I say, and I will let you live, as I let the banshee live, heart-bound but homeless."

"I'm no fairy lover," Angus growled. "I will never kill to sustain my own life."

"So said your banshee and look what love made her do," Manann said with scorching dryness. "I grow tired of your virtue. Enjoyable though it would be to watch you slowly succumb, like so many today I am into instant gratification." His Chief pointed at him as his voice took on the deep and terrible resonance of power. "You may keep your form *Óenghus Óg*, but henceforth you will be unhindered by your excess of conscience."

"You can't make—" But he couldn't finish the sentence.

"I can't? Oh, but I have. It is already done." Manann turned to Erin. "As your Chief, I call on your judgement for this oath breaker, my Lady. Will he live cursed or die free?"

She tossed her head. "You're bluffing. He's the only one who can restore the *Tuatha Dé Danann* to light and life."

"True, but I can give them freedom or flesh, depending on your choice. Let him live and breed, and I will harvest what he sows in your womb to raise a fine crop of fierce avengers, able to bear the sunshine outside the earth for eternity. Break his heart and take his life and I will withdraw my blessing on this building. You hold our many guests in the land beyond time because this is your earth and the seat of your power. Should this no longer be a hallowed hill, you will lose their souls, and I will have perfect hosts for our people to fill to live as changelings."

"You bastard!" She balled her hands by side, her face contorting with hatred. "Thought of everything, haven't you?"

He bowed to her again. And didn't straighten but stayed fixed bent over with his chin up and self-satisfied smirk on his face. Why wasn't he moving?

Angus clicked his fingers in front of his enemy's eyes. No reaction.

"What did you do?" he asked Erin.

Puffing like she'd run a marathon, she strapped her arms across her stomach, and turned with her face lit with triumph. "I can't believe it worked! But I figured out how to put him into *Tír na nÓg* along with everyone else in this building—everyone but us."

He heard the part about *Tír na nÓg* but what his brain locked onto was *everyone but us*.

When he didn't respond, she sobered. "Dear God, Angus, you're skin and bone! You look like a dead man."

"I've been dying to see you, *mo chroí*." The horde nearby chittered, but his attention remained solely on her. She'd trapped the old Chief to Choose a new one.

*Me.*

All he needed was some sexual healing, and he'd be himself. Probably.

"I'm sorry I couldn't visit you in hospital. Shit got real when I became the Lady. As you can see, I haven't got a grip on the job yet." She nibbled her bottom lip. "But I know we need to take Manann out. Then we can change the rules and lift your curse. Once we get you healed. Why aren't you better?"

Her eyes wouldn't let his go. They were black holes, those eyes, if he stared too long, they would suck him in and hold him forever. Yet when he tried to look away, he found his gaze caught by how her hands ran over her hips and down the sides of her thighs with her thumbs pointing inwards to show him where he was required.

The gesture raised more than his blood pressure.

She edged closer, uncharacteristically skittish in his company and the sweet-tart fizz of power he'd tasted at the entrance grew stronger as she neared him. It bubbled through his senses, making him feel giddy and drunk. It was as if the air around her danced with the joy of being close to her and every lungful he drew in spiced his blood further. He wanted to take her in his arms or fall at her feet—or do both together, most likely, given the state of him.

A sobering reminder he wasn't worthy of the Lady while injured.

*Erin. My heart. The Lady.*

"Power becomes you. I can't imagine how you convinced my sister to relinquish her position, but you should consider it your first miracle."

"You nearly dying had a lot to do with it." Her voice cracked. She had warned him not to do anything stupid. Did she think he'd injured himself on purpose?

"I swear it was an accident, Erin."

"Hardly. Caer took you down on purpose. I got there just after. You're alive because I couldn't let you die. I know it's what you wanted, but I just couldn't, Angus.

I…" She caught whatever she was about to say and pulled a face. "I've been trying to feed your heart, but all I've done is create a power sump and attract the local wildlife."

It wasn't all she attracted.

He couldn't help but remember how her mouth under his had been so sweet and willing, how her breasts had fit so well in his hands, how the wet heat between her legs was so delicious. He wanted to span her waist with his hands, slide his hands over her hips and pull her onto him. He wanted those legs wrapped around him as she called his name. He wanted and, this time, he couldn't take.

If he moved, he'd show how maimed he really was. Better to fake he was fine and wait for her to take the initiative.

Next time—once she'd had him—he would have her.

"Caer is gone. I mean she's alive, but she's fully a swan and there's not enough left of who she was for her to remember how to turn back into a girl. She was in so much pain, I gave her what she wanted."

The mix of relief and sorrow which briefly assailed him came as a surprise. He'd thought he had no feelings left for his ancient lover. Greater still, however, was his gratitude and admiration for her ability to choose kindness over revenge. It gave him hope for the people he'd abandoned.

"On behalf of the woman she was, I thank you for the soft end you granted her hard life, my lady."

"Don't."

"My lady?"

"Don't call me that. It's what *he* says."

Angus struggled to remember speech. "I wish I could serve you as your Chief. I wanted to be a god for you, but there is too much of an ordinary man in me else I would have healed sooner."

"I don't want a god. I want you, Angus McCraggan, because I love you."

Her words echoed inside his skull, empty of meaning. How could she love him?

"I want you, too." She came up against his injured left side. His nostrils flared as her scent deepened. More than half in love with him, but, more importantly, entirely in lust. Her desire made his cock rigid. "You can't feel how I feel?"

There was an edge to her tone. An emotion he couldn't place. He shook his head, confused. The pressure in his loins was growing too intense to ignore. She could ease it. He shifted his stance so she couldn't fail to notice his arousal.

"When Marie called to say you were on your way," she continued, "it seemed safest to put everyone here out of it. I didn't expect, though, you'd be—"

"Damaged?"

"I was going to say like Caer." Tentatively she stroked his beard then smoothed back his hair lifted by the crackle of power arcing between them. Her touch sent fireworks popping inside his skull, making it impossible to concentrate. He had no willpower when it came to her. He was no better than a glutton scorning dessert, or a drunkard turning down a free drink. "You're close to losing it, aren't you?"

Losing it? He was lost.

He managed a twitch, which might be taken for a nod.

She straightened his collar in an endearingly possessive gesture then undid his buttons and opened his shirt.

"This is my earth. You share my heart." The heat of her palms burned against his bared chest. "You had me ground through you at Newgrange when I had no earth of my own, to share the difference. Can't you do the same?"

His reply came out rote. "You are my heart and what is mine is yours. But you, Erin, you are the Lady of the Land. Only your Chief can ground through you."

"But I have so much power. What do I do, Angus?"

Cupping his good hand around her cheek, he ran his thumb along the seam of her mouth until her lips parted. Her breasts rose and fell against his sling as her body leaned into his. He pulled her closer, until her aura and her scent mingled with his, salted cranberry and smoking turf, the mix of their energy unbelievably intoxicating. It eviscerated all his aches bar the one in his cock. He squeezed the tight curve of her gorgeous arse and was rewarded with her sighing in his ear. It wasn't enough. He wanted to make her scream his name, aware her pleasure would take him from zero to hero.

"Let me take you and you'll make me a god."

Chapter Twenty-Six

Her Fair Judgement

Angus might have one working arm, but damn, the man knew how to use it. Erin fought back a moan as his fingers stroked between her thighs, the inner tingle becoming a tight, urgent demand. Oh God, she wanted to ride him so, so bad. Anything to ease the explosive pressure building and building and building. It took every ounce of her willpower to deny herself the pleasure, not when her poor over-stimulated ovaries were grenades with the pin pulled.

Manann had made a major mistake having all the eggs in her basket. The volume had clued her in that he wasn't prepared to wait nine months for a litter of changelings. Whatever he said just now about letting his rival living cursed and crazy was a lie. Once Angus delivered his payload, he was fair game.

Stalling hadn't given him enough time to heal. Without Newgrange, she couldn't restore him by grounding. Breaking his already broken heart would kill him, sending her back to square one with his lordship. As if she could deal with more survivor's guilt.

Angus was not only gaunt, his skin had the extreme pallor Hollywood gave consumption victims before they coughed up blood and expired. He also had a beard. Combined with his long hair, it should have made him look more hippy than hipster, but the stark black against his waxen skin highlighted the elegance of his bone structure, while the absence of his intransigent glower gave him the beauty she'd once thought he lacked. He was so close to the glimpse of the man she'd seen in *Tír na nÓg*, but when she looked into those deep blue eyes, there was no clarity, only a barely leashed hunger.

It matched her own.

She undid his belt, then his zipper. Then blinked. "Red plaid boxers?"

"Blame Marie." He almost sounded like his usual, gruffer self, but that Angus would never take her wrist and guide her hand to the pole tenting the cotton and insist, "You're going to come on this."

Erin shivered, unsure if it was with anticipation or foreboding. She stared hard, trying to glimpse the man she had fallen in love with, the one with that particular mix of decisiveness and consideration, passion and restraint.

With that strange, otherworldly ability she saw him differently: as he truly was and he was already gone. A fine pelt of fur spread along his arms. His neck grew to almost the width of his shoulders, covered with a thick ruff of fur stretching down to his navel. His face lengthened and furred until his head was entirely a stag's, complete with a great rack of antlers springing from his temples. The rest of him remained a man. An extremely virile, highly aroused man. The combination was grotesque yet utterly carnal.

Her nipples budded as her breasts weighed suddenly heavy, an inner line plumbed from them straight down to hot wet mess between her legs. Frantic with desire, she nearly climbed on him, then and there.

It was his lack of affection that held her off. The Angus she knew preferred to kiss or talk or laugh while he made love. This was him cursed and uncaring.

*Because of me.*

She fought down the sickened panic rising in her throat. Something had to give. No. *Someone* had to give, and that someone was her. She loved him, but it wasn't enough to be in love. It wasn't even enough to say the words. The first time he'd called her out on her crush. This time, when she yearned to connect with him with every fiber of her being, he hadn't registered her admission. She needed to show him, not that she simply had feelings but how important he'd become to her.

She couldn't Choose the man to rule by her side and she couldn't earth her power through him, but she could bridge the gap between his past and his present by loving all of him, even the parts he didn't love himself.

"There's something I need to give you, Angus."

"You need to give yourself to me."

"Got it in one," she agreed, trying to focus while he nuzzled her neck. Falling to her knees, dropped her lower than his mouth could reach. "It's time I put some skin in this game."

His pelvis thrust. "Skin?"

"I owe you a favor, remember?"

"I don't…" For a heartbeat he seemed anxious, but as she took him in hand, the worry became a keen, feral interest. Skin-to-skin was a good connector, although blood was better. Mouth-to-mouth, she assumed was best since both Angus and Manann had used that approach. The catch was—willpower—or lack, thereof. If he kissed her, she would never resist him. But there was another option. When it came to returning favors, could she double-up?

Leaning forward, she ran her tongue across the salted tip of his erection. He made a growling noise, deep in his throat and jerked his hips for more. She licked again, just to be sure this was a positive, and he fisted a hand in her hair. Definitely a 'go' for her new take on resuscitation.

Taking him into her mouth, she worshipped his cock.

It was lucky, in a sense, the experience was new to him, and he was already lust-drunk or else he might've noticed she wasn't giving him her undivided attention. As she'd once done before, she slipped her hand inside his chest.

There!

The small stone was sharp enough to slice. She gripped it tight. This was where she'd made her mistake earlier. Between snapping him from Newgrange and slipping out of time on the roadside, she knew what *not* to do when it came to mending the broken half of his heart. Both times, fear had owned her. Now, she had no room for fear. If she didn't do this, she lost him and she lost herself. No guarantee this would work, but Angus had agreed she could give herself to him, so she was going to do what he always did and take that literally.

He was hers and she wanted to be his—and his alone. For always.

It was easy, really, to give him everything she had, to pour herself into the stone. Grounding had spread her thin until she'd adapted to the new boundaries of her building. This was more like funneling. Concentrating her energy and love and beaming it like a laser into the chipped off fragment of his broken heart.

*I love you, Angus.*

The stone warmed.

He sucked in a noisy breath through his teeth.

*I'm giving you everything I have and everything I am.*

Inside her own chest, the heart he'd given her went supernova. Instead of shrinking from the light and heat, she embraced it. And she didn't cook. She melted. Her insides took on a sweet, thick liquid flow, as if she'd become caramel-centered. Slowly, steadily, she seeped into his chest to fill the lost half of his heart.

*This is mine.*

*And that makes me yours.*

No barriers. No reserves. She swirled in his blood then flowed through his body to heal and restore. This was far more amazing than surgery. She was a part of him, giving his flesh the power to knit damaged nerves together, plump out the wasted muscle in his arm and leg, and calcify bone. The intimacy of her essence combining with his was incredible.

*By the power vested in me…*

She gave and she gave until he had more than he needed, the excess power back-washing through her and carrying his feelings with it. Oh God, she was making him come. She moaned around his cock, drawing him in deeper and sucking harder as his pleasure became hers.

When he came hard, he took her with him.

Damn, but he'd ruined her. After this, any other man was unthinkable.

She rose to her feet, stumbling as she wiped her mouth. Woah. The room waltzed. With the arm he'd broken, Angus grabbed her wrist to keep her upright. His grip was steady and strong. Healthy skin, hunky beard, blue eyes clear and concerned and mapping her face with an intensity that made her knees soft.

"What did you do, Erin?"

"I married the two halves of your heart together."

"You married me?" His eyebrows shot upward. "But that would bind... *Why* would you bind your life to mine?"

A terrible fear squeezed her heart that she'd done something wrong, the same as at Newgrange. Yet he didn't seem sick so much as amazed. To be fair, no one was more astonished than she was to have accomplished the deed exactly like she'd planned.

"Because I love you, Angus McCraggan. I love you as much as you love me. You share my life now—and my power—because you're the only man I want as my Chief."

He blazed in response. The warm and golden glow poured from his skin until he was made of light. She had his heart and she felt his overwhelming happiness as though it were her own.

"Come here to me, *mo chroí*." He stood with his arms open and his pants below his knees. With a wry smile, he leaned down in a swift and easy motion to snap off his boot-cast, before kicking off along with the rest of his clothes.

Her body was the earth. He was her sun. There was no resisting gravity. She went to him without a second's thought. The remnants of her self-control dissolved as he kissed her forehead with a gentle reverence then held her tight against the wall of his chest. Melting against him, she burrowed into his shoulder, snuffling into his skin because he smelled amazing, not because she was emotional or anything.

Breathing in his scent was a bad move. While she might have tricked her mind by sharing his release, her body wasn't fooled. He'd left her wet and ready, and he was still hard. Her pulse yammered in her ears, demanding she put two and two together. Her fingers scrabbled against his chest.

He adjusted his stance, so his leg slid between hers, preventing her involuntary rubbing against his groin while giving her the firm muscles of his thigh to press against.

A crown was growing around his forehead. Nope. Not a crown. Those were antlers. Little ones, sprouting from between his ears and his temples.

"Why are you still horny?" *Stupid mouth.* "I mean, you're still cursed. *We're* still cursed." The effort of withstanding the animalistic *need* sweeping through her made her tone sharp.

"I must defeat Manann to break the last of his power." Determination was written across his face. "Then our people will swear fealty to me as your Chief and, together, you and I will lead our people to light and flesh."

*People?*

With difficulty, she looked beyond Angus. The staff and tourists were still out cold. Thank heavens! The fact they were there hadn't crossed her mind for a second while she was going down on him.

The *púca,* on the other hand, had broken free of her enchantment: probably while she'd been lost in ecstasy. Looped and knotted, stretched and contorted, they looked like animals shaken loose from the Book of Kells. They wouldn't touch her. As their Lady, she was sacrosanct.

The same could not be said for Angus.

He might be Chief, but his destiny was to die, not to lead. Caer had showed her how this situation was rigged to play out. It was brutal and bloody. Erin held him tighter, ready to shield him from the stings and barbs of the creatures who were going to tear him apart.

Squeezing her eyes shut, she drew on her earth to pin down the *púca*. Not being physical, they were a tough crowd to lock away. She'd almost done it, when something white-hot scythed through her waist below her navel. The pain was incandescent. She sagged in his arms, unable to stand without support, grinding her molars into chalk to prevent herself screaming.

He made a guttural sound, his rage wafting through her as potent as his musk. Stags fought and fornicated in almost equal measure and right now he was no different. Fierce and furious, he looked about ready to slay Manann barehanded.

A pity his hands were full holding her.

Weakened but no longer hurting, she wriggled out of his grasp to slip to the ground and the source of her strength.

Angus stepped in front of her and crouched into a wrestler's stance. Much as appreciated his protective instinct, fat lot of good it would do. Manann was untouchable.

"You have cheated me, my Lady." His lordship held aloft a strange yellow flower to the light. A further handful of the stumpy thick blossoms he cradled against his chest, cupped in the palm where the tiny mistletoe plant he'd used to kiss her sprouted. "Somehow you took his seed and yet these contain *nothing* of your essence, son of the Dagda. I had hoped to count the blessings of

338

your union and now I am left quite bereft."

He buried his face in his hands as though defeated.

*Uh-huh. Yeah, right.*

Sure enough, when he raised his head a bunch of mistletoe berries were glued to his face. Every berry was worth a kiss.

One kiss had been all he needed to steal her will and access her power and enable Breda to take her over. Erin slid her hand to the scar on her temple. The former Lady was still around hiding in the seething swarm of her kin. Breda had only wigged out on screwing her brother in Erin's body. Once the *Tuatha Dé Danann* took Angus down, Erin would die, too, and everything would run as he'd predicted: Breda and Manann co-rulers once more with their people freed of their ancient banishment to stay within the earth and restored to flesh.

Her stomach dropped and kept right on falling. Her guts probably weren't unwinding and spooling out of her belly like a rope, but it sure felt as if they were. Her grip on the *púca*, locked safely away, loosened.

"Kiss me, my Lady," said Manann through a face of budding leaves.

Despite herself, Erin rose to her feet. "You were never going to let us live."

"True. You are an abomination, and he owes me for everything I lost when I took his place as Chief. My arts saved the *Tuatha Dé Danann* from slaughter and, once in their new bodies, I will use them to rule this land as absolutely as I once did my own."

The air above the floor began to shimmer and spin as all the sunlight she'd captured was siphoned into the ground. Unlike the delicious, sensual flow that Angus had created in Newgrange, this hurt. A lot. As if Manann was draining the magic out of her, as well as the building. A deep resonant hum sounded, like overloaded amplifiers about to blow. The vibrations throughout the building became more acute and the mezzanine floor began to buzz with a worrying accompaniment of groaning harmonics. Barreling through the supporting steel columns, the flow was forming a magnetic field that was going to do a lot more than align a few paperclips.

Stealing her earth was creating a vortex.

This was how Manann was going to strip body from soul. He and the *Tuatha Dé Danann* would be at the eye of the storm, safely anchored to her earth through him. Anyone *physical* was going to get the best part of them sucked out, herself and Angus included the moment he severed her connection with the Visitor Center.

As if he had a *right* to take her earth just because he was the Lord of the Hallow Hills.

This was why the new Chief took out the old. She totally got it now.

There were maybe forty or fifty people unaware of their danger, out cold because of her enchantment. They didn't deserve to wake up as someone else.

She staggered against the swirling waves as they undermined the ground beneath her.

*She* was the source. Therefore, *she* controlled the flow.

It was like trying to hold back the tide.

Manann was too strong.

She was losing, like she'd lost her fight against the Boyne.

A strong, warm hand settled on her shoulder. Angus. There was so much she wanted to say to him. To tell him she loved him again. To wish for more time. To try for one last kiss. Oh, how she ached to feel his lips against hers, but kissing him would be fatal. They would forget themselves. Too busy screwing to fight, he would be torn from her forever.

*To have, but not to hold.*

Her only hope was to take Manann out of time again and keep him there while Angus dealt with his kin. To do that, she had to step into the spider's embrace.

The *púca* were almost free. They were slipping from her grasp. There was only one thing she could do to save the sleepers from becoming empty vessels for Manann to stuff with old souls: give the *Tuatha Dé Danann* what they'd always wanted.

With one almighty yank, she pulled free of her husband's hand and faced him. Da had smiled as he released her. She did the same for Angus, willing him to understand this was necessary.

It was the right choice. The only choice.

"I order you to die, *Óenghus Óg.* Be MEAT to your people."

If he failed, she died, too. It was only fair.

Then she stepped into Manann's arms and set her mouth to his.

She knew how this was going to go. Same as before when she'd dissipated across the countryside, spreading as thin and insubstantial as Breda's cloak...

The mantle of the Lady of the Land.

Dammit, she wasn't thinking BIG enough. The Visitor Center was a speck in the scheme of things. If Angus was Chief, there was no need for hollow hills to house the *Tuatha Dé Danann.* What did she need a single earth for anyway, when she could use the whole damn island to support her new Chief?

All she needed to do was go large, just like Breda's cloak, and claim it all.

*Erin is Ireland and I am Erin.*

Chapter Twenty-Seven

Till Time and Times Are Done

Angus had always accepted his elevation to chiefdom would come with a death sentence. He'd even anticipated it might be immediate—no sooner consummated than commanded to die. But he'd always imagined it would be Breda making the call before restoring Manann once more to the chiefdom.

Not Erin.

Not his newly wedded *wife*.

Ash coated his tongue. Ash from the charred remnants of the fierce joy that flared so briefly before the other half of his heart betrayed him with a smile.

How could she smile then go to their mortal enemy?

Why restore him then forsake him? Why make him her Chief then demand his death? Her smile made no sense. Not when she'd tied her life to his and knew she would die, too. Where was his chance to fight? She could feed him her power as Lady, and he could override every binding and curse Manann had placed on them both. On them all.

Stags backed into a corner went into a frenzy and he didn't want to think any further. He lowered his head as the beast within demanded he attack his rival. To ram his budding antlers into his enemy's body, gore under and up through the ribs before trampling his foe into the hard, concrete floor. A mindless death would still be painful, but he'd care less.

Something held him back. A memory that his former Chief had no substance. If he stabbed in with a killing blow, he would pass through the other man and plunge into the heart of his Lady.

*Her heart is mine.*

Yet, his own heart stayed whole as her love burned in his chest hotter than a midsummer bonfire. It made the air seem cold against his skin. Cold enough to make him shiver as though he was growing fevered. Or perhaps that was the words of her decree seeping into his consciousness.

*My name.*

She hadn't called him *Óenghus Óg* to his face since the first day he'd met her at Newgrange. If she was pissed with him, she stuck to McCraggan. Hastily he played back her words, seeking cracks in the blank wall of his future. His father had spoken of his mother as the best kind of partner a man could ask for: a woman who did more than challenge him, a woman who demanded he be more.

What if Erin demanded he be *less*?

For three thousand years he'd been trapped within the earth. Three thousand years of belief, veneration, and ritual. Such a hoarding of time and power, if divided among his kin, would grant each of them a solid lifetime of three-score-and-ten years. Lives they could waste or celebrate or pass on to others the same as everyone else.

Hope straightened his spine and swelled his chest until he thought his heart would burst. *Óenghus Óg* was the sacrifice, not Angus McCraggan. She loved the man, not the god. If only there was some means of separating the two…

Behind his back, he heard scratching and rustling, cawing and baying. He bared his teeth as he turned. Great swooping arcs of wild color swarmed before him. Anything but gray. Anything but dark. Something blue and purple, head ridged like a dragon but with a lion's face, reared and roared. A stork-like bird, with a white head and a red beak, flew by his ear. So many and so far from human. With their numbers, this was not going to be a fair fight.

It was not going to be a fight at all.

*Be meat to your people.*

Meat. To feed his kin. To make his flesh become theirs.

But not as a man. Not this time. Made to be a beast by nature, he'd make himself a beast by form. A stag's size and heft required an enormous quantity of energy. No problem when he could still call on Erin's power. His trembling grew to a full body shudder, then increased to become a fierce head-to-toe shiver.

Shape-shifting was a wild, unpredictable ride. While it required skill, the process was impossible to control. Energy and mass must be made to dance to a tune, but every dance was different, and the song was never the same. Angus loved the thrill, the need to be precisely in the moment, to let go of the familiar and feel his way into a new form.

The heat from his heart spread out from his core, squeezing organs and liquefying bone as he molded a new shape from the old. Ribs, liver and spleen. Antlers he had, but now a head and body to match. Cloven feet. Short mane. Velvet on the tines. Ruddy fur, short for summer. Layering in the details until his body matched the image in his mind. Not just any stag, but a hart—mature and experienced. The Lord of the Forest.

The favored game of the hunt.

Planting all four feet firmly on the ground, Angus stretched forth his long neck and roared.

The *púca* paused. There was a long, unearthly stretch of utter stillness. As one, they drew closer. The intensity of their interest scorched his hide. The rush of a Change over, his new body's instincts kicked in. He sidled a little, swinging his head from side to side, listening to the rapid thudding of his oversized heart. With a body weight over two hundred kilograms, they saw him as a nice, juicy venison steak.

Deep down, he'd always known this was his fate, to be a sacrifice the same as his father, and he'd always been afraid because he knew the truth of his father's courage. It hadn't been there. The Dagda, mighty and brave and wise, had been none of those things when Angus held the dagger to his throat. He'd been afraid and ashamed. Nor had Angus killed him with kindness. Clean and quick was merciful, not kind. Pain had tracked the path of the dagger's edge and he'd cursed the gift of his empathy for laying his father's emotions open for him to read as easily as the blade had laid open his throat.

Experiencing his father's suffering as his own had been unavoidable. Every unendurable moment shared. The Dagda had found it a comfort not to die alone. Angus had hated him for such weakness when he'd expected a noble strength. He hated the pain, hated his duty and their tribe and their customs, and, more than anything, hated himself. His father's last breath should have been taken while wrapped in his son's love, not his hatred.

Now the wheel had turned.

Erin had called for his death. The only way to spare her conscience was to survive. The only way to salve his own was to give himself to those he'd denied. As their lord of love, the leader of the young, he lowered his antlers and offered himself.

*Take what you need to be free.*

A hound-like creature broke free of the pack to circle around him. Angus watched it warily, holding still to get this over with quickly, if not painlessly.

With a belling bark the hound sprang. Teeth pinched through the skin underneath the ruff of mane on his throat and stayed clenched. With a wrench, a strip of his pelt was torn away. An almost pleasant warmth trickled down his neck.

First blood was claimed.

Any moment now the pack would descend en masse, and the frenzy would start. His nerves turned treacherous on him, urging him to bolt while he could. Refusing to fight, refusing to flee. A stag's body wasn't built for such human notions. Willpower kept him still, but terror's visceral hold was nearly as great. His eyes rolled, forward and back; small huffs of panic slid out of his mouth.

*What the hell are they waiting for?*

The hound leaped again, biting into his shoulder and pulling back another flap of skin. Another animal, something that might have been a boar, ran underneath him, slicing into his abdomen with its tusks as it went. A bird of prey—from the shape of its beak if not its over-long neck—launched itself over his antlers. Its claws pierced the soft skin at the back of his skull and lifted another piece of hide off.

He was being flayed alive.

He reared in horror, hooves flailing. Not slow. Not merciful. Not even mindless, the way Caer had attacked him on his motorbike. Each would take their turn and he knew exactly how many strikes there would be. Thirty-seven, one for each minor mound within the Bend of the Boyne.

So much for the hope he might shed his godhood in a whole piece like a reptile molting.

The dog-creature barked. They stopped. The silence that settled was profound, the only external sound within the gallery was the steady drip-splat of his blood onto the concrete. Where the bites were deepest, the ache was dull and throbbing. But the shallow lines of exposed flesh burned like being scalded with salt water. The weight of his antlers seemed impossibly heavy; his head began to droop despite his efforts to keep it held high. His mouth was terribly dry. He was sure he could drink his bodyweight in water and still be thirsty.

Body low, chin flat to the ground, the hound slunk toward him, skirting the weary orbit of his antlers. Angus flinched as it drew nearer, anticipating another chomping.

The hound's tongue lolled out in a doggish smile, long and pink from its blood-rusted muzzle. A gentle warmth suffused through Angus. With a stuttering effort, the dog turned the red of glowing iron before expanding outwards, thick as molten bronze, from a hound-like shape into a sleek red setter with a coat as rich an auburn as Breda's hair.

*Breda?*

Before he could be sure, the rest of the *púca* clambered over each other and down his body to lick at his wounds. It always came down to blood with his people. Blood linked life and power and separated the living from the dead. The stutter of the hound's transformation was replicated by others until his tribe were a roiling, roaring herd of birds and beasts. Why they had not returned as humans was a problem to solve later. His people were returned to flesh.

*My people...*

The twitching anxiety he'd always felt in their presence faded as he let them rub and scrap across his hide with an intimacy he would never have previously imagined, let alone allowed. He collapsed down to his knees, out of both humility and shock, his skin oddly loose and his senses confused. Unsteadily, he kneeled back on his haunches. No. They were his normal, human legs. He raised a limb. It had fingers. The fingers found the rough leather tie which bound a pair of worked antlers to his temples and undid the knot. The skinned deer hide came off with a shrug. He threw off the outfit he'd been interred with. It never hit the ground. Only a cloud of ancient dust hung thick in the air.

*Óenghus Óg* was gone. His past was finally dead.

Elation was too much, relief too soon.

He was not done.

It was time to deliver his people from darkness.

Angus fisted his hands when he saw Manann and Erin locked in a fatal and familiar kiss. There was an odd stillness to them and no sign of breathing on her part, but the energy pulsing between them showed a visible tussle.

The small white berries glued to Manann's face flexed then burst. Thick stems squirmed out, clamping onto his skin which puffed and blistered at each site. Then they grew, wriggling and twisting to weave their way outwards, pairs of thick, oblong leaves multiplying rapidly until tiny twigs curled in and out of his ears, sprouting out from his nose and spread to replace his hair.

Erin's skin became almost translucent and began to blotch with what looked like mold. Her shoulders slumped. The area where her flesh was mottled darkened and withered. Spasmodic jerks shook her body.

Manann was draining her.

Hatred was a deluge, spiking his blood with poison and spurring him to act. He moved to fit himself into Manann's place but the hound who reminded him of Breda leaped in front of him and barked a warning.

Ah, of course. When he'd stood in death's shadow and broken Manann from the last tug-of-war, the backlash of power had gone through Erin, and he'd lost her to his sister. Erin was Lady. If the battle between her and Manann was on the scale Angus suspected, then a backlash this time would kill her. And himself.

Intervening was unwise, but that didn't mean he couldn't put his weight behind his Lady. His heart shared had been a heart divided. Thanks to Erin returning his love, their two hearts were joined as one, stronger together than standing alone. Switching sides, he slid his arms around his wife's waist and pressed his chest to her spine.

There was something between them, spread very thin and very far. A patchwork of warm and cold, wet and dry, peat and loam. His sister's cloak. As a child, it had been his mother's. By the time he could walk, he'd learned every inch.

It had changed, because the land changed. It was changing again.

Slubs and slurs in the fabric were being re-woven as Erin reclaimed the hollowed hills and hallowed ground formerly ruled by the Lord of the Dead. While Manann stole her life, she was stealing his land. She had everything now except Dowth, the root of his power.

"You brave, brilliant woman," Angus breathed.

Her power flowed weak and sluggish. He bolstered her strength with his own until, finally, her heart began to beat, and her ribs rose and fell. About the same time, Manann's eyelids flickered. An involuntary movement, perhaps his first in thousands of years.

"This is my fight now, *mo chroí*," Angus whispered in her ear. "Give him to me."

There was an almighty surge as she pulled on the netting of power she'd woven around the hooks and flanges of the Lord of the Dead's link to Dowth. Brute force would never have worked, but she was cleverer than that. She'd undermined his hold, gone deeper and wider, to leave him isolated and alone. His bond cracking, Manann fell away, tipping like a falling oak. The mistletoe on his face withered and split, dry as straw.

Eyes closed and breathing shallow, Erin sagged against Angus. The power in the land might be near inexhaustible, but it still required mental effort to draw and manage, not to forget the physical strain of claiming her new territory. She had over-extended herself. Badly.

He eased her to the ground, never taking his eyes from his enemy. Manann lurched to his feet, and Angus noted the swell of the man's chest as he took his first true breath in countless lifetimes, watched his Adam's apple bob to swallow and his teeth grind with irritation.

Manann was real and, for the first time, vulnerable.

He also had everything to lose.

A muscle in his jaw twitching, Angus held himself in check rather than strike without thought. With the controlled patience of a hunter, he assessed his opponent. Neither man had weapons, both were unclothed save for the triple-twisted gold torc around Manann's neck, the one which had once belonged to the Dagda. Angus had the advantage of height, Manann the benefit of a body like an ox. The Lord of the Dead could stop his heart at a touch. Relieved of his godhood, Angus was as mortal as any man. And he had Erin to consider, lying near the bloody mess left from his flaying. His Lordship had already shown he was prepared to do the forbidden and harm the Lady.

Manann was going to pay for that sacrilege.

"I have fulfilled my vow," he told his rival.

"Ah, your vow," Manann sneered. "My apologies for not partaking of your tainted offering. While Breda does her penance as a dumb beast, your lady delivered me three stout years in my own form. Not half as many months as your Marie gave for the son she'd always dreamed of, but then I don't intend to squander *my* second coming."

The loaded revelations were meant to hit at two levels: a clip to the intellect and a hook to the gut. But Marie was safe at Newgrange while Breda was here. It was his former Chief's dismissiveness to his own Lady which Angus couldn't fathom. Voiceless, she couldn't revoke her Chief out loud, but nothing could prevent her rejecting the gift of his heart…unless she didn't have it.

An irrelevant point. Breda was no longer Lady.

"You rule no longer."

"Kill me then, *Óenghus Óg*. Repay me for saving your life and your people in the coin you paid your father."

Manann lunged forward, scything hand out. The heavy-set man, unused to having real weight, seemed ponderously slow to Angus who dropped to his knees, and set his palms square into the puddle of gore. Blood singing and hands laden with the last of his former power, he darted forward, deliberately overshooting his opponent.

A deft side-step and a spin had him behind Manann—where he was most exposed. Resisting a punch to the kidneys, Angus wrapped both hands around the torc. The gold sizzled as it absorbed the arcane power from his blood. Here was the tool he needed. With the aid of a knee into the small of the man's back, he wrenched the torc off its owner's neck. With his spine arching like a bow, Manann bellowed his outrage.

The gold was heavy in Angus's hand. His opponent was unbalanced. One swing and he could strike the torc against the soft point under the ear, where jaw and skull met, or he could aim higher and crush the thin bone of a temple. Both killing blows.

Right now, however, the only blood on his hands was his own.

His dream of beginning afresh would die with his former friend and mentor. Without Manann the *Tuatha Dé Danann* would have been eradicated. His people had never wanted to live forever, they just hadn't wanted to die before their time. What example would killing him set the feral, thieving children he was supposed to lead?

He paid for his hesitation when the other man landed him a swift elbow to the solar plexus. Winded, he doubled over, faking a longer recovery to lure his foe closer. His Lordship still thought himself invincible with the confidence and conceit of one whose dominion had never been challenged. His arrogance would be his undoing.

Sure enough, Manann lumbered closer. At the last instant, Angus weaved sideways and kicked his knee out from under him to force the Lord of the Dead to kneel. A step, a twist and a hooking kick from his other leg sent him toppling forward, both hands to the ground in reluctant obeisance. Planting one hand on the dried mane of mistletoe to keep his head down, Angus wedged the torc against Manann's windpipe.

"My name is Angus McCraggan, not *Óenghus Óg*. You are a relic, *Manannán*, son of Lir, an old god in a new world. By rights you are mine to kill. Unless you offer him mercy, *mo chroí*?"

He looked to Erin, who sat amid her menagerie, an arm slung over the red setter. Her eyes very bright, she gave him a weary smile.

"Make the choice you can live with. My power is yours."

Understanding her perfectly, he nodded.

Long years of being worshipped as a god of crops and husbandry had made the sea-faring islander into a settled soul. Travel would be good for him.

Using his bardic skills to add resonance to his voice, Angus drew on the power of the land by his right as Chief and embedded his words into the gold. "I banish you who was once the *Crom Cruach*, Lord of the Dead and of the Hallowed Hills, from this island and forbid you to return to your own for the term of the life you have stolen. You will bear the name Guy O'Leary, and lose all rights to the titles, ranks, and labels you once possessed. From henceforth, you are a lord of no one and nowhere."

When Guy started to protest, Angus angled the torc against his throat harder—forcing the man to silence.

"In reprisal for the dishonor you gave our Lady, I curse you. None will act in your favor, and no one will fall for your arts until you learn to love another more than you love power or life or yourself." Bestowing the bosses on each end of the torc with their new purpose, Angus rammed it back onto Guy's neck. "This torc will ensure you do as I bid and only one who loves you wholeheartedly can remove it. As I have spoken, so shall it be."

Guy raised a shaking hand to the gold, his face bone-white and blank with disbelief. "You can't curse me to love."

"I am Chief of the *Tuatha Dé Danann,* so Chosen by the Lady Erin, and I can make you do what the hell I please."

"Tell him, Breda," Guy implored. "Tell him how you turned my heart to oak rather than take it as your own. Tell him of our deal."

The red setter started forward, her teeth bared in a growl. Angus raised an eyebrow, but his sister communicated as well as his wife.

"Your deal is voided, my curse stands. Now get out of my sight and off my Lady's land."

Guy's legs obeyed before his intellect caught on. He stumbled past Angus, tugging on the torc to no avail as he left the building. Angus didn't bother watching him go. He was already by Erin's side.

"Are you well, *mo chroí?*"

She smiled weakly. "I'm wrecked. Holding death at bay took a lot out of me."

She tipped her head, her gaze sharpening. He knew

that look from his mother and his sister. The look the Lady had to see him as he truly was, paring through who he had been to see the core of who he could be.

"What do you see?" He asked out of politeness, already knowing what she saw. A man, not a god; freed of his curse and blessed with love.

"I see you, Angus. Only you." She blinked but her eyes stayed soft as they made a long, lingering journey down his body and back to his face. "I see a whole lot of you. Much as I appreciate the view, people will be waking soon. Maybe you should put on some clothes."

Until her appraisal, he'd forgotten about attire. Fortunately, his clothes were blood-free. He dressed, forgoing the boxers. They made a useful rag to wipe up the worst of the blood, his kin helped with the rest. At least, those with long tongues did.

Around the three floors of the Visitor Center, the remainder gamboled and raced and flew in a noisy clatter of destruction. They leaped over people stirring from sleep, chased each other under tables and up the bannisters, sniffing and whuffling, and cawing and chirping. Chairs were knocked over and plates of food upset as they enjoyed their unfamiliar physicality.

Like attracting like, they seemed particularly fascinated by the children. The little girl on the stairs was having her hair nibbled on by kid goat while a red squirrel patted her cheek and a hare bounced over and across the child's mother with enviable energy. A toddler in the highchair had a robin, an otter, two magpies and a goldfinch paying it court. As for a baby in the buggy, it was so crowded thick with animals that a heron had spread its wings wide to hold the more curious creatures back.

The Lord of the Dead's responsibilities to them ended, they were left to their own devices. And to Angus and Erin.

"What's your plan?" Erin asked as he drew her in to his side.

"Other than loving you for the rest of my life?"

"Good plan, but I was wondering about all this?" She swept a hand to encompass the chaos. "It'll be headline news and viral over the internet the moment someone grabs a phone."

"I'm not concerned about phones. The energy you trapped in here will have wiped anything electronic, including security cameras. What we need is a plausible excuse for why people were out cold."

"Hm. An electromagnetic pulse doesn't affect people physically. What about a gas leak that needed locking down?"

Angus wasn't sure the Visitor Center used gas for heating, least of all in summer, but it didn't matter. "I can make that work."

Breda came to them then, with her chin tilted up but her tail drooping. Dropping to one knee, he put his hand out. "Can't you change, Bree?"

She shook her head in a doggish negative and looked soulfully at Erin.

"Breda says when she took your curse from you, it inverted. She's stuck as a beast with the mind of a woman for the rest of the summer, maybe longer, she's not sure on how the terms got twisted."

"Breda took the curse?"

"She says it was the only means Manann had of controlling you after I took Newgrange, so he wasn't about to drop it. After her, the rest followed suit so it's possible they'll become human when she does."

"We'll figure it out," Angus promised, taking the liberty of ruffling behind her ears as a gesture of sympathy. Astonishingly, she leaned into his hand in response. "How come you can understand her?"

"We bonded." Erin tapped the scar at her temple. "But it took her finding her outer bitch for me to trust her with my inner one." She dipped an ear to Breda in a listening posture. "Nope, I'm told me marrying you was the clincher. I was never going to be her outerwear once we wed."

Her eyes slid to his and held. The air between them thickened and heated with a world of promises until Breda whined a warning.

"People are stirring," Erin confirmed. "I locked down the building once you arrived, but once His Assholeship sucked the place dry, I couldn't do more than keep those already asleep out of it. We have a couple minutes, at most."

Angus nodded. "Gather our kin, would you, Bree? They can't stay in here once people wake."

She made a huff of agreement and began to weave back and forth across the cafeteria while making short, low barks to round them up before she began to howl by the door.

He didn't need a translator for that one.

"Erin, it's your grandfather."

The old man was in a bad way, sweating and moaning. Angus sank to his knees by his landlord's side. "It's not my gift to heal, but Breda might be able..." he faltered, his throat aching and his chest tight when the hound shook her head. Angus looked at his hands, still red with blood. "Manann never took his share of the years of my imprisonment, maybe I could give—"

"Breda wouldn't let Manann take his cut," Erin wrapped a cool hand around his wrist. "Because his share is yours. Well, *ours*, Angus. When Breda and Manann resurrected you, the life they gave you was only for seven years. It's why they were getting frantic. You said your birthday is Halloween, right? You'd have rutted and died by Manann's terms. Except you'd shared your life with me, and Breda figured that would halve your life expectancy, so she brought the date forward to still give you a month or so to get busy with the ladies."

"Seven years and I was going to die." He almost asked why hadn't he been told, but the answer was obvious: he would have let it run out and done nothing. "And those seven years came from Marie?"

"Manann tricked her into early menopause. She thought she was going to get a baby. She got you." Tenderly, Erin wiped her grandfather's brow. "If you can carry him, I think I've the strength to keep him stable until help arrives."

"The landlines should still work," Angus noted, already lifting Jim. "And Marie is over at Newgrange. Once we have your grandfather sorted, I'll call her and update her on the situation here."

"She was drunk when she shared her story. Don't let on you know."

"Marie was *drunk*?" He could accept everything except that.

There was no time, however, to chat any farther. At the main entrance, he left Jim with her, then returned inside.

The *Tuatha Dé Danann* settled into a wary horde around Breda. Angus went downstairs to the rear exit and threw open the heavy glass doors to the outside.

"Into the light!" he ordered his kin, letting the full resonance of his voice free. The impact of his command rippled through the herd, swaying them back and forth in one body. "And be sure to hide. For now."

The Center cleared of the *Tuatha Dé Danann* in less than five seconds as they spilled into the foliage lining the riverbank.

Angus hurried into the back office and made his call direct to Marie's mobile.

"Thanks be to Jaysus you're there!" she said in greeting. "I was getting worried you wouldn't get in or be able to call."

"How long has it been since we left you?"

"About twenty minutes. I figured you would need ten minutes to get there, another five to walk over bridge, and every minute since has been giving me heart palpitations."

Twenty minutes. Erin had diverted the Visitor Center for at least a couple of hours out of time's flow by his own body clock. Who knew how long she'd spent with Manann in *Tír na nÓg*? There was a good chance she'd need medical attention herself.

"Marie, Jim needs an ambulance. His heart is failing."

"If Emergency Services aren't already there, they're on their way. What about you?"

Angus had suspected that might be the case, given the lack of contact from the Visitor Center. "Don't mind me, I'm grand. Tell anyone who asks, the problem here was a gas leak. It's left people sleepy and disoriented but otherwise unharmed. Do what you can to reassure everyone there it's safe. If the authorities ask, a local man with connections to Dowth was to blame. His tampering might have been meant as a prank, but it could have been lethal. Unfortunately, he fled before we could catch him. I doubt we'll see him again, since he knows I'll have his head if he ever returns."

There was silence on the line.

"I'll spread the word. And Angus?"

"Yes, Marie?"

"I always knew you had a gift for leadership."

"Taking the job nearly killed me, but I'm pleased to say the lady I report to works miracles."

"I'm sure the hospital will be amazed at your recovery," she returned as a dry reminder how recently he'd been an invalid.

Once he was off the phone, the back-office staff peppered him with questions. Out in the foyer, the milling mass of tourists did the same. Freed from the truth, he sold his version of events with bardic fluency and the authority of his chiefdom.

People took him at his word.

Disconcerting when he'd never been viewed as an expert on anything other than Newgrange. He must be mindful in future to use this ability sparingly.

In the carpark, there was chaos. A barrage of lights flashed from Garda squad cars, a couple of ambulances, and a fire truck. Distracted by Erin's absence, he convinced the relevant representatives the emergency was resolved before persuading them to leave.

****

The gray morning clouds having broken, the midday sun was a hot brand across his shoulders when Angus followed his heart to take a stroll along the banks of the Boyne. No jacket needed today, he stretched out his arms to capture the light only to be ambushed by a rush of animals and a mixed flock of birds. He went down in a rumble, unable to wipe the grin off his face. They were here, in the daylight and in the flesh, and if that much was possible after so very many centuries, then the rest would follow.

"Is this a private party or can anyone join?" Erin's voice was husky from fatigue.

He opened his arms to draw in his lady and his heart, but before she snuggled into his embrace, he held her a moment to get a proper look at her as she'd looked at him.

It was Erin and it was not. She was not the woman he had first met, bearing the chameleon armor too brittle for deep emotions. This was a woman who knew her own power and had the courage to love someone more than life. Her eyes, dark and knowing, reflected an equally changed man. One who had regained his honor and who was ready not only to lead but inspire.

"Hey Chief, you just having a moment or is something up?"

At first, he didn't answer. No one had ever called him that so it took a few seconds for his new title to settle. A balloon of wonder rose in his chest, cramping his lungs as he kept it caged within his ribs.

"I'm not used to being this happy."

"I know, right? It's going to take some getting used to. For both of us."

"How does it feel to be the *Bantíarna na hÉireann*?"

"Like I'm home wherever I go." She gave him a half-smile. "You're not alone in being stuck here now."

He snagged a loose strand of her hair and used it to wind her closer. "If you're home wherever you go, then

I am, too."

Her face lit and her smile spread. "You mean I could show you America some time?"

"Once we've the tribe settled." Who knew how long that could take? But he wasn't about to shed his responsibility until then. Not after winning it by combat, sacrifice and blood.

"Maybe after my studies are done then." She understood. Of course, she did. Her trials had been as severe. "In the meantime, we have the summer, and you have a whole island to explore."

"I'd prefer to start our honeymoon by exploring my wife."

Her eyes sparkled with unshed tears. How had he ever thought her eyes dark? There was light deep inside them, like veins of gold beneath the surface.

"Did I tell you already that I love you, Angus McCraggan?"

"My recollection is a little hazy. Tell me again."

"I love you, Angus. You and only you, for always."

"I love you, too, Erin, *mo chroí. Éirinn go brách.* I am yours—as my heart is yours—always and entirely."

He kissed her then. Kissed her with whole-hearted enthusiasm and pure human passion. For a long while they were able to ignore the caterwaul, hiss and bark of jubilant spectators. As their exchanges grew more heated, however, so did the response from their audience.

Squaring his shoulders, he stared out at the assembled mass of his people, wondering what to say to them; how best to introduce them not only back to themselves but to a very different world. They might be little more than animals, but it was up to Erin and him to make sure they became good neighbors to the living. On the plus side, Jim had taught him how old things could be made anew if one was prepared to take the time and effort.

"My name is Angus McCraggan and I am honored to be your chief," he began, the natural resonance of his voice cracking with fierce pride. Rousing speeches were not his thing but, when he chose, he could be an excellent guide.

"Welcome back to the light."

**A word about the author…**

Kat Chant is a bookworm who grew into a history buff. Some years ago, she exchanged beaches for castles to move from Australia to the UK. There, while studying medieval history, she met a lad from Ireland…and fell in love with him and his country.

They now live in the heart of the Emerald Isle and share their passion for the past with their family. When not exploring ancient ruins, Kat is a keen baker and karate-ka.

https://www.katchant.com

## Glossary and Guide to Pronunciation

Irish is the native language of Ireland. In Irish, the language is referred to as *Gaeilge.* (The term Gaelic can refer to Irish people and culture but when used to talk about a language, it usually means the native language spoken in Scotland. This is related to Irish but not the same.)

Irish is thought to be at least 2,500 years old, perhaps older, making it one of the oldest living languages in Europe. When written, it uses eighteen letters of the Latin alphabet—those not used are: j, k, q, v, w, x, y and z. It also adds an accent, called the *fada,* to lengthen vowel sounds. For these reasons, the grammar and phonetics are very different to English, which is a much younger language.

A guide to some digraphs:
- Generally, a 'bh' together makes a 'v' sound.
- 'Ch' is almost always the sound in the Gaelic *loch*. (In Irish, this is spelled *lough,* but pronounced the same.)
- There is no 'th' sound as in *this*, which is why a lot of Irish people will say "tree" instead of "three" or "dat" instead of "that". When it's used in Irish, the 'th' usually indicates a slight pause or an intake of breath.

Some vowels are slipped sideways:
- An 'a' makes more of a short 'o' sound, as in hop. When it has a *fada*, á sounds more like 'aw'.
- An 'e' sounds more like an English 'uh.' With a *fada*, it sounds more like 'ay'.

| IRISH TERM | PRONUNCIATION | MEANING |
|---|---|---|
| Bean sí | Ban-SHEE | Banshee (Literally: woman of the Otherworld / fairy woman) |
| Breda | BREE-da | Goddess of the Hearth, Metalwork and Midwifery. Often conflated with St Brigid. Also spelled *Bríde*. |
| Brú na Bóinne | Broo na Bo-in-yah | Palace of the Boyne / possibly also womb of Bóann, the goddess associated with the River Boyne |
| Caer Ibormeith | Kyr Ih-vur-may | Goddess of Dreams and Prophecy |
| Crom Dubh Crom Cruach Cenn Cruach | Cruhm Dov Cruhm Croo-ach Kenn Croo-ach | Crooked Dark One Crooked or Bloody Mound |

| | | Gory Chief / Lord of Slaughter Put simply, the Lord of the Dead |
|---|---|---|
| Dagda | DOG-duh | The Good God |
| Dubh | dov | Black / dark |
| Dubhadh | Doo-ah | Darkness |
| Éirinn go Brách | AIR-in guh-BRAH | Ireland forever (For Angus: Erin evermore) |
| Go raibh maith agat | GUR uh muh HAG-ut | Thank you. (Literally: May you have goodness.) |
| Leannán Sí | LEN-awn SHEE | Fairy lover / Otherworld lover |
| Manannán Mac Lir | MONon-awn Mac Leer | God of the Sea (The Isle of Man is named for him.) |
| Mo chroí | Muh-KREE | My heart |
| Óenghus Mac Óg | Ungus mac Oge | God of Youth, Love and Summer |
| Púca | pooka | Ghost / shapeshifter |
| Sí an Bhrú | Shee on Vroo | Otherworld palace (Literally: Otherworld |

| | | |
|---|---|---|
| | | residence of the palace) |
| Tá mo chroí istigh ionat | Taw muh-kree ish-tig un-it | My heart is yours. (Literally: My heart is in you.) |
| Tír na nÓg | Teer nuh Noge | Land of Youth/ Land of the Young |
| Tuatha Dé Danann | TOO-uh day DON-onn | People of the earth goddess (Literally: People of the Goddess Dana or Anu) |
| Uisce beatha | ISH-ka BAH-ha | Whiskey (Literally: Water of life.) |